MW01133119

Heartland

Survival in the 1930s

Best wishes! May all your dreams come true,

Ellablanche Salmi

Ellablanche Salmi

2009

iUniverse, Inc.

New York   Bloomington

This is a work of fiction. All of the characters, names, incidents, organizations, and dialogue in this novel are either the products of the author's imagination or are used fictitiously.

iUniverse books may be ordered through booksellers or by contacting:

iUniverse
1663 Liberty Drive
Bloomington, IN 47403
www.iuniverse.com
1-800-Authors (1-800-288-4677)

Because of the dynamic nature of the Internet, any Web addresses or links contained in this book may have changed since publication and may no longer be valid. The views expressed in this work are solely those of the author and do not necessarily reflect the views of the publisher, and the publisher hereby disclaims any responsibility for them.

ISBN: 978-0-595-52929-2 (sc)
ISBN: 978-0-595-62979-4 (ebook)

Printed in the United States of America

iUniverse rev. date: 12/11/2008

HEARTLAND

The short-waisted blue organdy dress floated down over her head, as she smoothed out its wrinkled ruffles. Running her fingers through her hair, then tossing her head from side to side, made her shoulder-length lusterless hair fall over the neckline of the dress. Her breath rose in a mist-like cloud to mix with cold air. The bare skin of her legs became goose-pimpled and bluish in reaction to the freezing winter air.

Under the broken small attic window, heavy dust lay upon old trunks, piles of clothes, boxes, both wooden and paper, Christmas decorations, and stacks of books. Her abandoned clothes lay on the floor in a mound like a body asleep. She shivered and looked at the trunk left open with its rounded hump back tilting back toward the floor, exposing its paisley paper lining. It released a hint of lavender mixed with dust. She wrapped her arms around herself in an attempt to get warm. Beautiful...beautiful? She asked herself.

Gathering up her abandoned clothes, she carried them to the child lying upon an old mattress. She covered him with her clothes, all the while crooning under her breath. The child was white-faced, a heavy bruise appearing across his right forehead, and running down his cheek. His eyes were closed. He was motionless.

My pretty baby, pretty baby, she sang-- pretty baby. And she laid a heavy gray sweater across his still form, covering his cotton shirt and worn blue jeans, with yet another layer. Cold...cold ...are you cold, too, my baby? She asked. The shoelaces of his high-topped shoes were tied in knots to the bottom rung of an old oak chair, as if to keep him from running away.

1

She opened a drawer in the old chest, seeking blankets to cover him even more. In her search, she carelessly threw things about the room -- clothes, newspapers yellow with age, and parts of old books.

Still humming her song under her breath, she looked down at the papers in her hand, and then turned to a small dome-topped trunk. Tipping it over with a look of recognition on her face, she pried at the slatted bottom with a rusted screwdriver found on the floor close by. After three tries, the bottom came loose. Under the bottom was a cloth-covered hinged lid with a leather thong. She pulled on it to open the trunk. Out of the trunk, fell bundles of paper tied up with string. The bundles tumbled across the floor. Bundles of money...

She shivered again, and moved toward the child to stroke his hair and feel his skin, as if to see if he is warm. Then, she reached into the pocket of her sweater she covered him with to remove matches.

Dresses are so pretty, aren't they, little darling? But we are cold, and we need to get warm.

Wooden matches light easily. So do newspapers, and even old bundles of money. Pretty baby...pretty baby...she sang, lying down beside the still child, and covering herself and him with the old gray sweater, leaving her own feet exposed and bare, and the child's feet tied and unmoving.

Pretty baby...pretty baby, she crooned softly into his ear, closing her eyes, and putting her arms around him.

CHAPTER ONE

The dead grass of hot summer flattened underfoot, dust rising up in cloud shadows. The man following her spoke of crops and farmers, his words drifting away in the air as her thoughts ran ahead of him. A square, white schoolhouse opened its doors to the smell of oiled floors. There were blackboards above the wooden desks, which wore the ink-stained wounds of carved initials.

An empty room could be filled with excitement. Could she fill this room with words, with music, with color, or with dreams?

As a small child she had dreamed her dreams sleeplessly, squeezed between two sisters. She had been hot and restless in the middle of a shared bed. As the family grew larger and space became more precious, beds were shared. Sisters either quarreled or giggled, but never were still. Mama always had a silent, unceasing frown, which created a scar-like wrinkle of worry. And Papa -- always one of the worries. Neighbors talked. Mama didn't talk, except to say the Papa was in Canada for his health.

Rozella's dreams had been private things, the only pretty things she could own. She had drawn into them more as the family grew larger, and she created them out of things, which gave her pleasure. In school, she watched her teacher, noticing the colors in her dress, and the sweetness of her perfume and the softness of her voice. Her dreams were soft moments, and the moments she remembered; she would travel into her dreams to become part of the fantasy world she was building for herself.

I'll be there someday...where she is...in a school.... somewhere...I'll lose Mama's accent...and all around me these shouting, noisy children, my family...living all mixed up in closeness...I'll have my own house...I'll sleep alone...I'll read books...have nice clothes.

"The salary, Miss Ehalt, ain't...isn't high, but it's all there is to offer." His voice interrupted her daydreams and her memories. She shook her head and returned to the real world. Some light brown hair escaped from her braid and curled upon her neck from the heat and moisture of her skin. The lace of her blouse was stiff and it scratched against her throat. Rozella ran a finger under the lace to sooth the roughness.

The desk that would be hers was in the corner. As she looked at it, she counted drawers. Imagine having a desk to keep things in. Imagine having **things** to keep. Pencils had been precious things, used until the last inch gave way. She had hidden them from her sisters. Extra pieces of paper from school had been hidden under her mattress. You could only write in secret with the younger children around. Always having paper and pencils was something out of a dream.

"Folks around here ain't wealthy, you know," the man continued, "the board decides for me what I can offer for the job."

"What is the salary?" she asked, ignoring his talk as he walked around the room becoming part of her own dream as she imagined herself talking with children, touching them, and making things happen.

"$500 a year."

"That will do, I guess." She didn't want him to know that she had never taught before. Perhaps he wouldn't read her application too closely. She stood a bit taller, stretching to reach new confidence.

"Good. Miss Sims was getting so crabby. That's the old teacher. New blood will be good. Yes. Changes are good for all of us." His voice had a little of the Scandinavian lilting sound, rolling up and down like the northern seas. "Sims did a fine job, but she had worked many years. She was my teacher, you know? But tired out now. It isn't always easy. Young tyrants, but you must know how they are..."

"I hope they like me."

"How could they help it?" He was blushing, as he became aware of his words. He wasn't accustomed to paying compliments, even indirectly. "You have a nice smile, and..."

Rozella didn't hear him. She was opening drawers and looking at the books, which remained on the shelves. **All this room**. She moved her head from side to side as she looked at the empty room. She would live here if they would let her. Even the closet looked large. Actually, she would like to live here, in solitude, she thought. "Where can I find a place to live?" She asked aloud, "Is there a place where I can board?"

"Well, Miss Sims owned her own place. Her family left it to her. Sold it the month before she went south. Maybe..." He looked through the window to the north thoughtfully. "The Queists have a cottage that has been empty for awhile. Used to use it for hired hands before John came home, that is. Maybe they would rent it."

"Is that possible? It would be nice to have a place to...cook, to have a garden, and ...would you ask?" She turned to look at him now, hoping for his help.

"Look," he pointed. "You can see it from here under that big tree. Just a small place, but you wouldn't need much room. You're not very big..."

She went with him to the window to look across the bare fields. Now stripped of their summer's harvest they lay in wait for the coming winter. There was just a hint of white siding and a part of a window visible beneath a tree. The distortion from the glass made things swim and she grabbed the windowsill, hanging on, as she blinked her eyes to clear her vision.

"I'll ask right now, if you'll promise to stay. We need someone. Do you want the job?"

"I want it very much. Both the cottage and the job," she smiled at him. The first home of my own...and a chance to be alone, she was thinking.

"Let's walk over there, then. No one will care if you look around the place while I talk to Queist. They are peculiar folks at times. Maybe I should go over there by myself first? They never invite folks in, and they keep a couple of dogs next to the house. Never bit anyone that I know of, but sometimes I'd like to have them tied up. Wouldn't want to scare you away."

He closed up the schoolhouse, locking carefully before they crossed the yard again through the dusty grass. Rozella stepped carefully, hating the burrs in the grass, which stuck to her stockings. She stopped to look backward. The school bell was hanging motionless, as if waiting for something, and a shadow of the bell tower fell across the grass before her. A tractor was laboring down the rutted road headed for the fields beyond the school. The man with her waved at the farmer who was bent over the wheel of the tractor. Above the man the blue of the horizon was broken by a flight of geese, heading south, a slowly floating arrow against the sky.

They found the cottage they had looked at set back into the trees, shaded from the sun and away from the road. Rozella walked around it, trying to look into the rooms by leaning close to the glass with a hand over her eyes to erase unwanted reflections. Her companion left her and disappeared into the brush on a trail, which led to the other house, the Queist house.

Either unwanted reflections or faded curtains kept her from seeing into the rooms. Dust lingered on the cottage, hanging in penciled lines from the white siding. Some of it clung to the trees, powdering the leaves over her head. She tried the door, turning the knob guiltily. It didn't move.

This yard was dry, too. The rainless last days of summer had left dust blowing across everything. Withered plants dropped and rotted upon the ground, beginning to dry there in the sun.

She heard the dogs barking, a sharp sound filtering through the woods, and she knew the man (Sorenson, wasn't that his name?) was talking to someone. She was impatient. It was taking too long. Curiosity kept her moving about the exterior of the cottage, as if taking possession of it and its surroundings. She bent over to dig into an abandoned flowerbed, prodding it with a pencil that she took from her purse, trying to see if there were bulbs left beneath the surface. Her hands felt the dirt and the dry earth-dust drifted over her skirt. As the sun reached her in this spot, a sudden circle of warmth surrounded her. Beads of perspiration formed on her forehead.

"Miss Ehalt?"

"Yes?" She jumped up to look directly into the sun. It blinded her.

"How much is this place worth to you?" the voice said. She still couldn't see the man behind the voice. Standing, her vision began to clear and the voice came into focus with her sight. His shoulders were bent and a greasy, sweat-stained cap was pulled down over his uncombed hair. Stubble from yesterday's beard made his face seem unclean. His overalls were missing a brass button, and a large safety pin held one strap. The hands, which hooked themselves over the edges of his pockets, were thick and gnarled. The eyes seemed bound by the weight of his brow and the marks of a deep frown. They were animal-like and darted up and down, appraising and evaluating.

"What it's worth to me and what I can afford to pay may be two different things. But, I would like to rent it. Can you tell me how much you want?" She asked.

"Being as most school marms board in someone's house...this place should be worth more. You see that you could have a garden? That would be worth more." There was a certain unidentified sarcasm in his speech. "How much, Miss Ehalt?" He continued, emphasizing the word "Miss."

"Well, it's too late to plant a garden. Gardening won't happen until spring," she reminded him. "Whatever's fair...if I have it," she looked to Sorenson, who stood just behind the demanding owner. She was pleading for his help, but he avoided her eyes, as if he didn't want to get involved in barter.

Queist smiled then, a one-sided flash of his mouth, which did not light up his eyes. His eyes were still cold. One of his hands reached into a pocket to draw out a large ring of keys, which was as grease-stained as his cap.

"Well, let's go in. We'll talk about it some more inside." He turned the key in the lock and pushed open the door. Its rusty hinges abused the silence. "Go in. Go ahead," he waited impatiently for her to move ahead of him, his hand motioning her to move.

She stepped in hesitantly. It was dark. It smelled musty. She wished Sorenson were ahead of her instead of behind the older man, Queist. The room was shaded because the curtains were pulled shut and the shades were drawn down to the windowsills. Barely furnished, there were still the essentials, a cook stove, table and a couple of chairs. The pump was rusted and damp. It stood beside the kitchen sink. At least, she wouldn't have to carry water from outside the cottage. She walked over to the sink. A few bits of leftover food had rotted and molded. The rooms smelled musty and moldy. The linoleum was worn. Black spots showed through the tarpaper backing on the floor covering.

"How much?" she asked the question this time.

"$25 a month?"

"But, that's half of my salary."

"If you was boarding, you'd pay more than that."

"Maybe, but I'll need other things," she answered, already seeing that she would want to paint and buy some new furniture. He knew that boarding included everything. This didn't.

"Mr. Sorenson," she turned to the other man, "What do you think?"

"Since she will want to fix up the place, it would be improving it, Queist. Couldn't you let her have it cheaper? Your price seems a bit high. After all, it has been empty." Then, he stopped speaking, and resumed his quiet pose. He couldn't push too much. Queist was one of the board members, and if he didn't get his way, he could suggest reasons why Rozella shouldn't be hired, whether true or untrue. The smell of money was upon Queist now, and the idea of renting the cottage. This was the moment for decision.

"$20.00 then, and not a penny less. Of course, I have to have an advance," he said grudgingly, moving toward the door, wanting to be done with the business. Rozella walked into the room. It was empty except for an old chair with torn mohair. It was dusty and the floors were bare. The room beyond that must have been the bedroom. A double door opened into it with no doors hanging there. There was a wide space, and a bed with a lumpy mattress. It had stained ticking with iron marks like rust, and more -- dust. An old painted chest was in the corner, drawer pulls missing. It was painted dark blue, almost black. She could still hear Sorenson bartering for her in the kitchen where the two men remained. "$17.50" Sorenson was saying, " and that's enough. We haven't had anyone else apply who has even been through normal school."

She smiled, knowing then, that she had won. In spite of the dirt and ugliness in the cottage, she already possessed it. Her mind played with ideas of color, furniture, and curtains. The cottage was attractive to her because she could change it. And, she had exactly one twenty-dollar bill in her purse. If Sorenson got the place for $17.50, she would have enough left over to buy food.

Why had she bought the new clothes? They had cost so much. But, if she hadn't bought them, would the job have been hers? Would it? People were judged by clothing. Her vision...her dream still played a part in her mind.

The bartering still continued in the next room. She pulled open the ragged curtains, and tried to open a window. It was stuck shut. Nothing remained to give a hint about who had lived in the cottage before her. Just dust, long undisturbed. There was an old shoe under the bed. Only one shoe. A man's high-topped black shoe with a hole in the sole.

She managed to pull open the heavy drawer of the blue chest. Someone had left a black-covered photo album there; it was on top of a yellowed newspaper dated 1920. The edges of the album were worn as if it had been handled a great deal. Her hands shook a little as she reached for it. She started to open it when the two men entered the room from the kitchen. They stood there in the empty space, in the room she would like to use for a living room. Sorenson was smiling. He had been successful. "You can have it for $17.50," he said.

"In advance," Queist added, with emphasis.

"All right", she answered, stepping toward the bed where she had dropped her purse, as if to reach for the money and conclude the business.

"What do you have there?" asked Queist with an angry tone in his voice.

"Just an album that I found in the drawer."

"Must have belonged to my hired hand." Changing his tone, the old man stepped forward to take it from her. He tucked it under his arm. "I'll throw it away. They never leave us addresses. Always run off." He was holding out his hand, palm up.

Rozella finally understood the gesture. She had been frozen by her interest in the album, and his reaction. The money. His rent money. She hastily pulled it out of her purse and put it into his hand.

~

Arriving back at the hotel, Rozella looked at it carefully for the first time. Its windows left half-open without screens let the flies buzz angrily over an abandoned dinner tray left beside the entrance door. A balcony that extended veranda-like girdled the middle of the building. Dark green window shades were splitting with an overdose of sun and running white veins of pulled-out threads. Voices came from an upstairs window. The smell of frying onions and grease made her feel a little sick.

The clerk had skin that looked like a pale sheet of paper, and he smelled of cigar smoke. He pulled her bags out from under the scratched oak counter. Handing them to her gruffly, he acted as if he was angry to lose the only paying guest.

Sorenson took the bags to the car. Rozella followed silently, wondering what was making the clerk so curt.

Returning through the countryside, their car was the only one on the road. The sun was somewhere beyond the brush-fringed horizon, casting a pale light across the sky. The fall air was turning chilly. Rozella pulled her sweater about her shoulders.

"Put your arms in the sleeves, child," Sorenson had noticed her shiver. It gets cold early now."

Lights were coming on in the farmhouses along the way. Kerosene lights perched in windows as if waiting for the milking to be finished and the chores to be done. Her cottage...she thought. It was dark, and the cottage seemed to draw backward into the woods as she looked at it. They turned up the road and she could see that the door had been closed. Queist must have returned.

He had. After Sorenson reached in his pocket for a match, then lit a lamp he found on the kitchen shelf, the darkness disappeared and she could see the change, $2.50 had been left on the kitchen table and there was a key there also. Rozella picked up the key. It was slippery and smelled of oil. She dropped it, and unthinkingly wiped her hand on her skirt to rid herself of the greasy feel.

Well, Miss Ehalt, I'll be going now. But we'll be over in a bit. The missus and me. I'll bring the contract, and she'll bring you over a bite to eat. Nothing here for you to eat." He shook her hand, then left, his model A backfiring all the way to the main road.

With the sunshine gone, it was cold; the room was no longer inviting. Had her vision of it faded with the sun? She opened one suitcase. Clothes. Notebooks. A few towels. Silly things she had made to keep for her hope chest. They seemed silly now – doilies, lace. No food. No blankets.

But there was the teakettle on the cook stove, and a dipper lying in the sink its chipped enamel rusting. There was a bit of a ragged and dirty curtain in front of the bucket. The dried-up pump resisted her will as if stubborn, but finally yielded water, water to fill the teakettle. Water to wash with. Fortunately, she had brought a bar of soap. That was in her suitcase.

By the time the Sorensons had returned, she had washed and she had changed her clothes. Putting on a soft dress and removing her stockings made her feel more relaxed, but she was now very hungry. It had been a long day, and her head ached from the strain and from her hunger. Tillie Sorenson brought in hot stew and some bread. Her husband carried in a box full of household odds and ends, but it was a womanly thought that had put it all together. In the box were some P & G soap bars, a few rags for cleaning, a kettle, an enameled washbasin and even a roll of toilet paper. As Rozella put that on the table hesitantly, she realized she didn't know if there was a toilet, or where it could be.

"Of course," Tillie answered the unspoken question, "Outside, along the path toward the Queist's. Another path. But, you shouldn't go out at night. Buy a chamber. You know – a pot," she whispered when her husband was in the next room trying to quiet the children, who had found the bed and climbed upon it. They were now jumping up and down enjoying the springs.

Still another box appeared from the back seat of their car and it held food. Jars of canned goods, butter, and a quart of milk. It was enough to feed Rozella for a couple of weeks.

When she tried to thank Mrs. Sorenson, she was shrugged off with, "The Lord provides. He'd expect us to share." Whatever the source, the food looked good. It was good. Rozella was now so tired that she could hardly keep her eyes open. As nice as it was to have people with her, she was eager to go to bed. As soon as they left, she fell across the bare mattress, fully clothed covering herself with the one blanket they had brought to her. She fell immediately asleep.

CHAPTER TWO

When morning came to the chilled rooms, fall frost made the air even cooler. Rozella went out into the yard to collect bits of twigs, leaves, and scraps of wood to start a fire in the potbellied stove standing in the center room. As the flames began to leap up, the isinglass windows in the doors of the stove seemed to cover the warmth as eyelids try to cover private thoughts; but, she could still feel the warmth and she began to feel more like moving about to put water in the teakettle, wash herself, and change clothes.

She scrubbed the kitchen floor with some hot water and the P & G soap, crawling around on her knees on the worn linoleum. The suds cleaned and created fresh smells. The cleaning became a kind of happiness in just being there. After she had washed and scrubbed every floor in the house, she went out to clean the outhouse. The boards were dry from weather, and the place seemed as if it had been cleaned already by the wind sifting through the cracks between the boards. An old catalog lay on the seat, pages brittle from the harsh wind.

As she returned to the cottage, after cleaning the outhouse, she stopped to throw the scrub water out under the trees. She saw a young man coming down the path so intent with his thoughts that he hadn't seen her. He was walking along hurriedly, hands in his pockets, dressed in trousers of dark wool and a white shirt, which was open at the throat. His light brown hair was cut short and his skin was white, almost too white, as if it had not been exposed to the sun. Different, she realized suddenly, because she had come to expect the sun-browned skin of the farmers.

He stopped a moment where the path broke into the clearing around the cottage, as if lost in thought, his hand on his chin. Rozella opened her mouth to call out as she came plunging out of the brush, her scrub pail bouncing against her legs. Her words didn't come out quick enough, and he turned at the noise she made in the woods. Round hazel eyes met hers. He seemed startled, not expecting her to come from that direction, or to be in the woods at all.

"Miss Eh…Eh…alt?" He looked down at a piece of paper in his hand, and then looked up at her. She had appeared in the woods like a faun. Now, soft and beautiful, in his eyes, she was looking up at him in anticipation.

"Yes?"

"My father said to give you this receipt." He felt clumsy, almost forgetting why he was there.

"You must be the son – Queist's son."

"I'm John. Yes."

"Hello. I'm Rose, Rozella, that is." Shadows from the big willows dropped down over his shoulders as he stood in that particular spot and he shivered even though it was midday.

Before he realized it, he was saying, "I wanted to ask something else. You don't have any car. I go into town tomorrow for the family. If you want things, I could bring them. Or, you could ride along." It was an offer he knew that his father and sister would not agree with, but how could this girl exist without some help?

"There still are a lot of things that I need. The Sorensons were very kind to me. They brought over many things, but I just didn't think that I would be keeping house. I didn't prepare for it. There are things like blankets and sheets and towels…"

"You could buy those things in town."

"Yes, but you see – I don't have any money. Just the change your father brought to me. I don't even know when payday will be." It was an embarrassing reality. "Come, let's go in. We don't have to stand out here and talk," she said, inviting him in while walking ahead of him to the cottage. "Some things I could get," she continued, "There is enough food for awhile."

He stood in the doorway, "I'll be going in the morning, about eight."

"Oh, I'm sorry. You don't care to hear about my problems. Come in. You have a receipt, you said?"

"Will you come with me?" He continued talking as he entered the doorway. "If you can, I'll come by and pick you up."

"Yes, of course, I'll come. It may be the only chance I will have to get to town again for awhile."

"Well, I go every week, and you can always go along. Hannah sends me in with eggs to sell."

"Maybe I could telephone my sister and get her to send me a few dollars until payday. I hate to do that. We'll see. I'll think more about what I really must have, and what I can do without." She laughed then, trying to ease the worried expression on his face. It didn't work. The rest of his face was so young, so smooth. It had seemed for just a moment that she had been pressing her worries unto him.

"I'll see you tomorrow, then," he turned and reached for the door, still with a serious look on his face.

"Yes. Okay. Bye." And the screen door slammed behind him.

He was there the next morning, as early as he had promised. The sun was bright, but it seemed harsh upon the frost, which was left from the night. Rozella's breath preceded her into the truck, then steamed against the glass as she said, "Good morning. You are just as early as you said…"

"As I said I would be, I know," he smiled, pleased that she was as young and pretty as he had remembered. After leaving her the day before she had seemed dreamlike to him, and almost imaginary.

Rozella saw that the back of the Ford truck held egg crates and milk cans that bounced with every movement. The truck smelled greasy, just like the old man had smelled when she had rented the cottage from him. The smell reminded her of him. She shivered. Even John now seemed cold and withdrawn, after his welcoming smile. He was silent with a cap pulled down over his eyes and a denim jacket buttoned up to his chin. He pulled at the throttle and choke levers impatiently. Then, the truck jumped.

"Damned thing never runs right. New spark plugs might help."
He cursed at the fogged up windshield, as if alone.

Each bounce of the truck penetrated. Rozella wasn't used to trucks.
The leather seat was cold on her legs. She pulled her legs up, as if she
could avoid touching it, and she turned her list of needs over once
again in her mind. It had seemed to stay there all night long. Each
time she awoke in the dark, the list was there to haunt her.

She couldn't call upon her sister, Ola, for money. Their mother's
illness was too costly. Every cent was needed at home. She had to
make it alone.

Buy one more blanket…a piece of muslin for a sheet, a couple
of small towels. Make do; she told herself. The truck was shaking
everything about, and she had to grab for her purse just before it fell
to the floor. As she leaned over, she noticed the black picture album
Queist had taken from her so abruptly. It was under the seat, sliding
out from under it as the truck vibrated.

"What is that, John?" she asked. "Is that yours? Or, is it the book
your father took from me at the cottage."

"Probably just some junk of father's. He never puts anything away.
You're lucky to have room to sit. But, then you noticed how it was at
the cottage?" He smiled down at her.

"Well, it'll take some cleaning. And you? You're different than
your father? You like things to be neat and clean?"

"Different? Yeh. Too different. Never did like the farm. It seemed
always dirty…one way or another."

"You don't even look like a farmer, actually. Have you always been
here…all the time…since you were a child?" Sorenson had said that
John had replaced a hired man, or more than one, she remembered.

"I've been home about six months. Went to the cities to business
school, but I couldn't get a job after I graduated." He shifted the truck
once more.

" Not many jobs to be had right now. The veterans want their
back pay. People are hungry. I'm lucky to get a job. I know that."

"You are. I tried. Walked the streets. Father…I called him. He
wouldn't send any money. Said I could come home and work. He
talked about keeping his books, but…" He shook his head, as if not
believing himself.

"But, what?" Rozella looked at him.

"When I came home, he had fired his hired man. I knew what I would be doing."

"Maybe you could still keep trying, in town."

"I do, sometimes. It isn't any better here, you know, than in the cities. And father and Hannah, well, they want me here. It suits them."

"Your mother?"

"She's different. But, she's not strong." They turned the corner into the center of town. With the turn Rozella watched the album slide about the floor; again, she was curious about its content. John reached down impatiently, picked it up and threw it behind the seat.

"There. That will lose it for awhile."

Patches of pale brick, soot-rimmed, became storefronts. The truck slowed down, then stopped. Rozella was excited to see the mahogany store door, brass doorplate reflecting the sun. "I'll pick you up here, after I finish my errands," he said abruptly, dropping her off.

Rozella was in no hurry; she walked slowly through the entrance displays, looking around at everything. She wandered through the aisles, touching fabrics dreamily. In her mind, she was fitting things into her house, and she wondered when she would get her first paycheck.

Looking up she was startled by her own image, as it appeared in the plate glass window. For a moment she thought she was seeing someone from out of her past. In the lace-like weaving of reflections: fabrics, colors, and shapes, she saw a slender girl with her hair pulled up at the back of her head. The girl was moving in the mirror of the glass, melting and becoming one with lace and velvet and all soft things. She couldn't believe she was in this world. She stopped to reach up and touch her cheek to assure herself of her own reality. Had she become the person she had dreamed of becoming so long ago? Was it true?

Is this me? She was asking herself. She knew she had very little money to spend, but her presence here was something out of a glorious dream. She was independent, making choices that were hers alone to make, creating a home for herself, looking forward to getting a paycheck every month.

She browsed through the clothes, knowing that she couldn't buy any, but needing to know what they had to show the local women. She walked through the kitchenwares, reading price tags, and deciding in her mind what were the most important things to have in the kitchen.

The clerk showed her the choice of blankets and she looked carefully at each one, even though she knew she would have to buy the cheapest one. Seeing her hesitation, the clerk offered to open a charge account for her if she had a job. "I have a job. I just contracted to teach at the La Cross school, but I don't charge things. It's just something my family never did. Thank you, anyway. I'll make do until I can afford something better."

"Nice to hear," he said as he wrapped the light pink blanket in brown paper and tied it with a piece of string.

"You can carry it by the string," he offered, handing her the package. She gave him a dollar and a quarter for the blanket as he congratulated her on the new job. She found she could afford to buy a one-quart can of paint for the kitchen and a small can of turpentine, as long as she didn't buy an expensive brush.

In the grocery section, she picked out only a couple of things she didn't have. She had to choose carefully in order to keep some money back in case she forgot anything. She would write to Maggie and ask her for a few dollars until payday. If she was lucky, there wouldn't be any need and she could send it all back, but she was so alone here without her family – there was no one she could borrow a dollar from. This kind of planning was new to her. She had shopped for Mama, but never for herself.

There were cases with glass fronts that held cookies and dried fruits. The dried fruits would keep well. Not this time. Wait until payday. Wait – just one yard of cotton for kitchen curtains. Can't wait.

It seemed a matter of minutes and John's truck returned, pulling up to the curb in front of the store. She hurried out to meet him. It would be inconsiderate to keep him waiting when he had been kind enough to take her along to town.

He met her on the sidewalk to help her into the truck with her packages. The step was high. He put his hands on her arm to help her step up. She liked his touch.

"Finished?" She asked.

"Yeh."

"Did you make lots of money?"

"Better ask Hannah," he answered.

"Well, I spent all I could." She did not want to ask about his last statement. Evidently, egg money belonged to Hannah.

"I hope you bought a blanket; if you want to keep warm at night, that's the most important purchase. It snows early here. But, you know that. You grew up in this part of the country, too."

"Yes, I bought a blanket," she laughed at him, as if appreciating his tone. The truck jostled and jumped through the streets. Traffic was heavier now, at noon.

"Oh, damn," John suddenly slapped at the steering wheel.

"What's the matter?"

"I forgot. I forgot to get the flour for Hannah. I'll turn around." He turned abruptly at the first cross street, making a u-turn in the center of the road. The truck leaned, scattering packages. Rozella's purse slid to the floor. She reached down to pick it up, hanging unto the dashboard, prepared for sudden stops. Then she saw it again. The black edge of the album. It came sliding out from under the seat once more. John soon came to a stop in front of a small store. "I'll be right back," he said, as he slammed the door.

"Don't hurry for me," she answered, but it was to a closed door. He didn't hear her. As soon as she saw him disappear into the store, she reached down and pulled out the album.

She was curious why the old man had been so anxious about it. Queist wanted to get rid of it, and John wanted to ignore it. The photos on the first page...who were the people? The house...where was it...it was large...it looked gray and stark, owl-like with eyes of dark windows. Bleak. The next page. Surely, this was a mistake.

There was a truck. A man in front of the truck. A man without a head. The head cut out of the picture neatly, as if it had been gouged out with a razor blade, but the black paper marred where it had been pulled out. The same house in the background. What house? The man. He was young. The truck? It was this truck. The man. Who was the man? What was this? And, there were more pages.

She closed the album without seeing all of the pages. John was coming through the door of the store. Hastily, she put it under the seat, her heart pounding.

CHAPTER THREE

It was the first school day. It began crisp and almost brittle after the frosted night. Rozella had tossed and turned all night nervously, turning over school plans in her mind. The hours she had spent arranging the school during the days prior did not ease her mind. A shared one-room school must reflect the interests of all the age. Although she had studied the names and ages of all her students, trying to picture them in her mind as a group, and then as individuals, she did not really know them. Not yet. A few family names were already familiar to her, and she found that as she thought of these children she was recalling their parents. The children of her mind became miniature tired farmers with young faces, visible recreations of the parents.

She had worn out the pages of all the notebooks she had brought with her from normal school: the plans, the ideas, and the suggestions on how to handle eight classes in one room. From these pages, she had drawn her ideas. But, now, as she waited, she was nervous. Her hands were perspiring, and she paced the floor restlessly.

Multicolored leaves cut from colored paper were pinned above the blackboard in a paper mockery, interspaced with real oak leaves in deep shades of red. She had asked herself about what children look at and never see every day, and she found a list of many things. Creating this list only made her more aware of things, and ideas rushed in upon her. It was like discovering a new world, a world she wanted to share.

From her list of ideas, she had created a bouquet of weeds upon her desk, local weeds that she had dried and arranged in a large gallon jar. Unto the jar she had glued scraps of colorful materials like pieces of patchwork. Her name was written across the top of the blackboard in perfectly formed letters: MISS EHALT, as an example for the students to follow. The lines declaring boundaries for the proper formation of letters were delicate yellow chalk. The date balanced her name on the right side of the board: Tuesday, September 4, 1930.

She had drawn a seating chart on the blackboard, knowing the names and grades of the children. The seating by grade level and alphabet would save confusion on this first day. Get them seated, a voice in her mind nagged, or they will sit near a friend and never settle down.

The first child arrived with a brown sack clutched in one hand, a pencil box in the other. Her face had been scrubbed until it glowed. She was round and pale, her braids pulled back so tightly that her ears seemed out of place. The starched dress she wore bent as if to break when she found her seat, slid into it shyly, and sat stiffly – her eyes wandering around the room, reaching for everything.

Tina came in next, holding the hand of a younger sister. She was fiercely maternal. "This is Betty Lou." She pushed the child toward Rozella. "You saw her when we were at your house, but she's bashful."

"Hello, Betty Lou."

"You don't have her on your roll, I bet. She hasn't been to school before. Can she sit by me? She might cry if you put her somewhere else."

"There's a place for her. See your name up there, Betty Lou? In the front row, right next to me." Rozella smiled at her.

"My father didn't think you would remember," Tina said defiantly. Betty Lou's knuckles were white where she was clinging to her older sister's hand.

"Why don't you sit in your desk and look at this book while Tina finds her class, and her desk?" Rozella handed Betty Lou a book she had taken from the shelf. The little one looked up at Tina with a questioning glance.

"Okay," Tina answered the glance. "You're gonna half-ta let go of me. Might as well be now." she said to Betty Lou, before she flounced away to the rear of the room where the sixth graders were seated.

A group of boys had gathered in the cloakroom, some remaining on the front steps. By pushing, giggling, and punching each other they delayed making their entry.

The quiet ones, the small ones, and the well-behaved ones were in their seats. The model students, and the frightened children, those who were successful, and those who were afraid they would fail. It was time to ring the bell and call them in. The bell-pull was in the supply closet, locked in. She unlocked the closet, checked time on the school clock, and pulled the rope. Three times.

The boys came crashing through the door, sliding across the floor four abreast, tripping each other and falling into the empty desks. Breathless, ruffled, and smothering laughter, they looked up at her as she reached the front of the room. Two of the older girls frowned as if bored with the foolishness, but several smaller children in the front row looked frightened. One little fellow was already crying.

Rozella waited a moment quietly looking at each of them.

"Are you in the right seats?" she asked, as if not noticing the tumultuous entry. They looked at her puzzled.

She pointed at the blackboard and the chart she had drawn there.

The scuffling began all over with more noise and pushing and shoving, and a fight over a desk with two boys sitting in it began. One of the boys fighting was a school board member's child. She could tell by his name. Rozella held her breath, hoping they would resolve the issue themselves. They parted with a grin at each other, and at last it was quiet again. Every desk was filled except two, and they were planned as extra desks.

"Fine," she said to herself.

"Now, we all stand up and pledge allegiance to the flag." They all stood up. The smallest children in the front row not saying anything, but listening, large-eyed, to the older ones as they repeated the memorized words. Some fidgeted. Some held a hand over a spot where the heart was imagined to be. The crying boy couldn't raise his eyes. A trickle of urine ran down his leg and into his shoe.

Oh, dear, where is the mop? thought Rozella.

Then, they were all seated once more and watching her intently. "My name," she said introducing herself "is on the board, MISS EHALT. Can you spell it?"

The day, and the new school year, had begun.

Confusion of names and books filled the morning. Rozella looked at her plans and saw that they were unrealistic. Not enough time for organization. Suddenly it was time for lunch and she had not yet begun to teach. The children burst out through the doors, an explosion of energy released into the schoolyard. She sighed and realized that she was hungry.

Her sandwich was now warm and beginning to dry out, but it seemed inviting. As she began to eat, the shouts in the schoolyard increased to a frenzied pitch, and she dropped the sandwich to run outside. Two boys were fist fighting.

Get em. Get em, Hans. He deserves it. Nail em.

Get up Get up!

Dust flew as their feet scuffled around in the dirt. They fell to the ground, legs tangled, faces red, exerting their combined rage. The cheering sections had divided into groups according to sympathy, family, and emotion.

She plunged into the fracas, grabbing the smallest boy by the collar of his shirt and pulling him to his feet. Losing her control over the fighting and momentarily becoming as angry as they were – gave her the strength to stop the commotion.

"What's it all about?" she demanded.

"I was here first," the smallest boy said accusingly.

Stay out of this. It's between the two of them, Rozella thought, feeling like a referee in a wrestling match. Yet, she said, "If you two must quarrel over the swings, you'll have to decide in advance to take turns, or I'll have to keep all of you off the equipment at lunch time."

She managed to disperse the rest of the children and restrict the two quarreling boys. They could not use the swings at all because they had lost control in their anger, she told them.

As she returned to the classroom, she realized that there were only ten minutes remaining of the lunch period. Her sandwich lay dry and unappetizing where she had dropped it.

Rozella threw it into the wastebasket and sat down, putting her head in her hands and closing her eyes. I didn't think it would be like this. Will I ever be able to organize it? Do I really belong here? She asked herself.

Her hands were shaking. Her head began to ache. It was the dust, she thought. The never-ending dust that filled the yard, that blossomed into clouds every time you stepped out. It laid a film over everything. It was there now, even in the classroom. With the doors open, the dust had floated in and settled over all the clean and bright things she had brought into the room. In a mere half-day it had lost its polish. What had happened to its charm? She had threatened and restricted them. She had used her power to control. She was still shaking when she looked up. Tina was watching her.

"Do you want me to ring the bell for you?" she asked.

"Yes. You will need the key, though."

"I know." She smiled, but it was a self-satisfied smile, almost smug, and she reached for the key. "I know where the key is. I did this last year, you know, and the year before that."

Rozella said nothing. She stood up and walked over to the window as she tried to imagine what would happen when the bell was rung.

Taking her silence for approval, Tina took the key and went into the cloakroom. The door scraped open and Rozella heard the bell. It seemed to toll, and for a moment the scene in the schoolyard was frozen like a picture painted upon glass. Then, it broke from her mind as the screaming and pushing children rushed through the door.

"There you are." Tina replaced the key. "Anything else I can do, just let me know." Her eyes were appraising Rozella. They didn't seem like the eyes of a child; they were the eyes of an old woman. "I'll stay after school and help you clean up." And she disappeared into the back row where her eyes blended with a chain of eyes. All waiting.All watching.

The plans looked foolish and empty to Rozella now, as she looked down at them. Her book was open on her desk. Do I begin with arithmetic, or geography? Do I talk to all, or just to some, in groups?

Another one in the front row wet his pants. And he just came in from lunch period. Why didn't he ask to go to the toilet during lunch, or just go to the toilet by himself? Did she have to go out and ask each one if the toilet was needed?

Her head was pounding, her nose filled with dust. It filled the air, and she couldn't breathe. She picked up the green and black covered reader, and said, "Turn to page three and follow along while I read."

The afternoon passed quickly when she gave in to the confusion and relaxed with the children. The tensions of the first day began to ease with the reading.

Tina waited for her after all of the others had left.

"Where is Betty Lou?" Rozella asked.

"My brother takes her home. I just take her to school. That way I can stay and help you after."

"That's very nice. But why? Don't you like to get out and play with all the others?"

"I like it here. I might be a teacher someday. Father already has some money put away for my schooling. I'm a straight 'A' student, anyway. People say it's natural for me to teach. I can help a lot, you know."

"I can see that. You already have helped me."

"Where do you want these papers now? "She was straightening up chairs and collecting books and papers. "I can grade papers, too. I bet you didn't know that."

"Not much to grade the first day."

"Did you get acquainted with the Markham boys?

"I don't think I have their names related to their faces yet."

"You will."

"That sounds ominous."

"They can be pretty bad. You better be prepared to handle them. If it gets too bad, you can always run and get my father. Usually he is close enough to the school."

"What happens – with them?"

"They didn't do much the last days of school. But that is only because Sims had been here too long…and then, she used to keep a baseball bat under her desk. She used it, too."

"Really?"

"Yes. They are bigger than you are. You might need one. And there is some talk around that they intend to torment you. They think it is funny."

"What strange ideas. Are they always this way? I hope it isn't something that I say, or do."

"Just cause you're new, I'd say." Tina was wiping off the desks. "Father pays me for this," she explained. "It's my job, in a way." She looked up and out the window toward the road. "There are quite a few strange folks around here. You are renting from one of the strangest... my folks say. Old man Queist. There he goes now. Look."

Rozella joined her at the window.

"Look at the horse," Tina said.

The old man was walking along the road behind his horse, holding unto a leather thong lead. The two of them made a silhouette, which moved slowly toward the Queist farm. Headed toward the barn from the fields, Rozella guessed. Then, she saw the horse and realized what Tina meant to tell her. The horse was so thin it was emaciated, its ribs protruding. Next, she saw the raised arm, and the leather thong reaching across the horse's back. The animal jerked its head and tried to push forward, almost lurching.

Tina was watching Rozella look out the window. The child's eyes, which had seemed so old, glittered. "Yeh. They eat horses, too. At least, some people say that." And she turned away from the window.

CHAPTER FOUR

Rozella was painting the day John came over to collect the rent. The turpentine soaked rags stacked on the wooden stepladder were covered with spots of blue enamel, the smell filling the room. She reached up to push back her hair as she heard his knock. Her hair stuck to her fingers. Hurriedly, she made the last step to the floor by skipping a rung of the ladder.

"Hey, watch out," he cried as he saw her tumble, "Don't break a leg."

"I almost forgot I was on a ladder."

"Looks like it's raining blue sky, too, if the drops on your hair mean anything." He was laughing at her.

Looking at her hands, now covered with blue enamel, she laughed, too, "Painting a ceiling is terrible. I never realized how hard it would be. Everything runs or drips. It's a wonder there is any paint left on the ceiling."

"Never would of thought of blue." He looked up, admiring the color. Blue ceiling, white walls. Blue curtains with flowers in white. The place was changing. A certain colorful charm was there now.

Her brown eyes sparkled, knowing that he liked what he saw.

"Say, clean that paint out of your hair," he said, "or you'll have trouble later."

"With turpentine?"

"Rub it with a rag; just a little turpentine on a clean rag. Then, shampoo your hair."

"I better do it right away. I've heard of blue-nosed teachers before, but a blue-haired teacher would be a bit too odd."

"Let me," he began to help her, noticing the shine of her hair in the sunlight. Her hair was a warm brown and inviting to the touch.

"You've come for the rent?"

"Yes, father was busy in the barn. He sent me. Thinks because I went to business college I ought to take care of such things. Too bad he won't let me take care of the money." There was a hint of sarcasm in his voice as he laughed softly.

"Did you ask him about giving me credit for the paint?"

"I did, but he doesn't believe in paint. Says scrubbing ought to be good enough. He said I should bring you some of Hannah's soap! Sorry." An apology was present in his voice.

"Oh, well, it would have been helpful. It did cost me money, but I don't suppose he'd approve of blue ceilings anyway." Rozella tried to joke about it.

John was cleaning the last of the paint out of her hair, trying not to get any of it on his shirt. God, she was lovely, he thought. Her skin was the color of her name. It looked touched by roses. Even in her faded working clothes she looked soft and feminine. And the feel of her hair…it was as silken as it looked.

"Wash it right away, or it won't be dry before tonight. I'll wait." He took his hands away from her with reluctance. I'll go get some water for you."

He picked up a pail and went outside to the rain barrel. Rozella watched him through the window, the clean-shaven face. A hint of fragrance, was it lavender, or rose water? There was an interest stirring in her that she hadn't experienced before. His difference seemed to reflect her difference, a need for cleanliness, and a need for color.

She had seen him only once since they had ridden to town together, and that was just before school started. They had talked about her plans for the cottage, but they had not talked much about John, or John's thoughts, or least of all – her own.

The smile he had seemed special as he handed her the pail of rainwater, excusing himself for being so slow. "There wasn't much water left in the barrel. You know how dry it has been. I had to reach down several times before I could get a bucketful.

She placed the metal bucket directly on the kerosene stove, where the flame hissed and spit steaming bubbles as it touched the water on the pail.

"We could have some tea while we wait?" John asked. He seemed to be quite at home.

"Sure." She put a kettle on the stove and sat across from him at the table, the shiny new oilcloth spanning the space between them.

He looked at her hands instead of into her eyes. Her fingers were long and white, the nails even and neatly filed. No rings. Just a smidgen of blue paint on one finger. A boy's flannel shirt was unbuttoned at her neck. It was a long graceful neck, the kind dancers have, and he found himself thinking. Her waist he knew was not much more than two hands around. Very small. He had thought about it a lot since he first met her.

John watched her pour the tea and cut slices of cake, heavy, brown spice cake with raisins. Her movements pleased him. They ate, both of them self-conscious and quiet. Rozella watching him eat, and John's thoughts running away with him. He wanted to stay. He wanted to be with her. It was pleasant in the kitchen with sun streaming through the windows. Even the smell of turpentine was not unpleasant. The laughter they had shared was good. It was different from home. No one smiled there.

Eyes meeting, they both smiled.

"I think the water in the pail is hot," she began.

"Get your pans. I'll fill them for you," John suggested.

When the pans were full and the soap and towels laid out, she pulled the pins out of her hair and let it fall. Brushing it carefully, she leaned forward, her head to one side, and her hair fell with the movement, loose and shimmering. Then she began to wash it, pouring the soft water over her head with a dipper.

"Let me," John said again, blushing. He had never helped a girl wash her hair before. But, Rozella couldn't see him blush. Her eyes were tightly shut to avoid the soap.

He rubbed the scented soap into her hair and watched the bubbles rise, strong and sweet. Her small back bent over the pans. The shirt pulled up and her bare waist was showing. Smooth skin and very white. His fingers lingered in her hair.

"Gotta get all the turpentine out," he mumbled. Finally relinquishing his enjoyment of the suds and wetness of her hair, he rinsed once, and then rinsed it again.

She searched for towels blindly, keeping her eyes closed to avoid the soap.

"Just a minute. I'll do it," he said, wrapping her head in a towel, then carefully wiping her face, as if she was a child.

"I can dry it," Rozella said, opening her eyes.

"Yes, of course." John blushed again, sitting down suddenly, becoming an observer. He watched her rub her hair with her towel, her head turning to the side as before. There was a sudden aching loneliness in watching her, as if something had been taken from him. He stood up, asking "Did I get it clean enough?"

"Perfectly. At least it feels clean. It doesn't seem to smell of turpentine anymore, I don't think. Although it's hard to tell in this room." She looked up at the wet paint, sniffing and trying to smell it.

"No." He got up from his chair to put his arms around her waist and bent to smell her hair. "It doesn't smell of turpentine. It smells like flowers."

She looked up at him, and still he couldn't let go

He could only pull her closer. His fingers were in the wet hair at the back of her neck and he pulled her face toward him to kiss her. The kiss seemed to cling and to answer his aching. Her body was so tender and delicate; yet, these feelings were new and frightening, and he pulled away with embarrassment.

Rozella picked up the towel and began to dry her hair, turning her face away.

This gave John a moment to control his reactions and prepare to leave with the rent money he had been sent to collect. It gave Rozella a chance to get her breath, as she looked through her purse to get the dollars she had put aside from her paycheck.

Watching him leave, she felt like she had never been kissed before. Thinking about it, she knew that she had not been kissed like that. The furtive kisses of young people at dances and church socials were not like his kiss.

It frightened her, but excited her. Never before had she caught a glimpse of what passion might be like. This was new to her.

CHAPTER FIVE

The school days became easier than they had been, but Rozella still felt all of her mistakes keenly. They were mistakes that she couldn't forget when she left at night: the unsuccessful ideas, the ideas that once seemed exciting but now were dead because they fell on deaf ears. The students wiggled, talked, and evaded her. Every day was a new effort, and every class another attempt to reach them. She thought back to her training and smiled bitterly. It had seemed so easy.

The short days turned into night early now. By the time she left the school it was already dark. She and Tina would lock up together and hurry across the road, the chilled air blowing through their clothes. It brought memories of other winters. They talked about it. Would Rozella go home for Christmas, or would she stay in the cottage? She had not yet decided. It seemed such a big decision that she and Tina turned it over and over – a subject for conversation almost every day.

Tina had become so much a part of Rozella's teaching life that she forgot she was talking to a child, and a student. Tina had maturity. Perhaps it was the minding of smaller children in her family that had turned her into an early adult; but there was the reflection of adult understanding and companionship in Tina's child's eyes. Both of these Rozella needed. There was no one else to talk to.

The women in the area were busy with babies and farm work, often working beside their husbands in the barns, milking cows, shoveling manure, filling hay mows, and waiting for the next baby, or the next chick to hatch. Socializing was not possible for them, even though Rozella might be the same age.

In church on Sunday, Rozella still played the role of teacher. Her presence was expected, and her conversation was anticipated also. She was the source of information about the children. Was Georgie good in school? Had he made up the arithmetic problems? What about Belle and Lucille? Do they still talk all the time?

The pastor asked her to teach Sunday school and seemed offended when she refused. It made her feel guilty. Did all teachers teach on Sunday as well as the rest of the week? She excused herself by saying that it was her first year there and she needed time to prepare her lessons. It was true, but it didn't stop his frown. The frown fleetingly crossed his face. A woman standing close by turned smugly away, but not before her thin smile caught Rozella's eyes. The smile said, *I told you so.*

Nights she would lay and dream about John, when there was no wind and it was not quite dark, shadows would fall across her bed. As the nights grew longer the air became sharper and colder, she left wood in front of the heating stove as if anticipating that he could be there.

As she dreamed, she wrapped a heavy quilt around her, her breath rising in the coldness of the room where the fire had gone out. She could smell the odor of the pine tree in the front yard. Its needles were pungent, and the resinous sap drained from the wood. The smell was lovely and fresh. The smell of new wood-smoke and burning leaves all brought something back, and something was stirring.

Letters came from Ola now, telling about their mother's illness. Mama was confined to bed most of the time, seldom walking except to the mailbox, Ola said. Every day she went to the mailbox by herself. Rozella wrote at least once a week telling her about her school. Mama kept every letter, Ola said, but everyone knew that her greatest hope was to get a letter from Papa. He never wrote unless he was on his way home. It was as if it was the only thing of importance. He shared nothing of his thoughts, or his experiences in the north.

In spite of the letter from Ola, Rozella had not decided to go home for the holidays. Ola wanted her to come. She wanted some relief. Rozella felt selfish, not answering. She didn't want to leave. There was a dream in her, a dream of marriage. There was an unspoken hope that John would ask her to marry him. Christmas would be the time. How could it happen if she was not there? How could he ask her?

Dear Olie, she started her letter, I will try to come.

Ola was alone with Mama. Maggie was still home, but she was bitter and angry with everyone. Her salesman lover had been married. Mrs. Jacobs had aborted her baby. It was discreetly done, and no one was ever sure just how many of those little operations Mrs. Jacobs performed each year in their community. No one had talked about it at home. Not even when there had always been room for another baby, even the unwanted ones. But, there was no room for Maggie's illegitimate baby.

When Mama had first learned of Maggie's pregnancy, she cried for days, pounding on her pillow as if trying to dissolve her Russian wrath. Disgrace. Disgrace. Ola had questioned her through the tears and anger. Disgrace to have children? What about the disgrace of leaving the caring of the children to others? Breed them, then give up and run away -- what difference? Mama had turned the wrath against Ola then, screaming at her. Rozella wondered about both parents. Running away to Canada or running away to illness, what was the difference? Someone else was left with the burden of care.

Rozella wrote Ola in the next letter: I'll be there. I'll try to send money. You are so good. Such a good woman, she kept telling Ola. With every sentence, Rozella felt guilty for being where she was, guilty because of John and because of her dreams.

Just the same, she delayed her trip and Thanksgiving passed.

Sometimes she and John would talk to each other now during the trips to town. It was their embarrassment over their feelings that had kept them from talking. Every minute spent with him was valuable to her.

She had never seen John's sister, or his mother. Sometimes she was tempted to walk up that path to the big house and visit them, but when John was so careful about picking her up and dropping her off, how could she go there? It seemed like a silent injunction, which closed her out.

At times she tried to open up conversation about them with Tina, and then felt guilty for prying in a child's mind to ask for small gossip, in order to learn more about John's family.

But, the children whispered in school regardless of what Rozella asked, and even so, their laughter was edged with fear. Hannah, they called a witch. They said she was out on a broomstick whenever there was a full moon. When she heard that, Rozella remembered the peculiar photos and the headless people in the old photo album.

One day she asked Tina about the Queists, pretending that she didn't know John at all.

"Don't you ride to town with John?" Tina replied to her question.

"Yes, but he doesn't say anything about his sister." Rozella looked away.

"She went to school with my mother."

"Well, John, mother says, was born many years later. Their other children, they say, all died. They were babies for awhile, then they were gone."

"I wonder how come John lived."

"They got a doctor from town."

"What is Hannah really like?" Rozella wondered aloud. "Did you ever see her?"

"Once my brother and I…don't you tell mother! We went there and threw rocks at the house until she came out. We didn't believe that she really was a witch, and we wanted to see for ourselves. Besides, my mother kept telling me that she knew her and she was just sort of… funny you know?"

"What happened?"

"She came out waving something at us and yelling that I f we didn't go away she would get us."

"That's not so bad, is it? Anyone would get mad at rocks."

"No. At least, she wasn't riding a broomstick." Tina said in her own straight-faced humor. "And, she does come to church once in awhile. She just doesn't speak to anyone when she is there."

"Does she look old?"

"Not any older than my mother. But, she dresses in men's overalls and her hair is all pulled back under an old cap. Sometimes you would think she's a man, except in church. When she goes there, she wears a dress. One time, I thought it was her father out in the fields until I saw her face. He's always covered with whiskers, all red and wrinkled."

"Is she a big person?"

"Yeh. She is pretty tall. But then, that was a long time ago when I was a little kid. I wasn't so tall then."

"Ever see the mother?"

"Never. Mother says that she is in a wheelchair. Sick."

It had taken Rozella days getting around to the subject of their conversation. She had wanted it to seem casual and normal. Sometimes people looked at she and John with interest when she went into town with him. After all, they were both young and single. It seemed like it should be acceptable. Rozella reminded herself that she was the schoolteacher, a perfectly acceptable woman to marry. Not all schoolteachers turned out to be old maids, like Sims. Not every one. What was wrong with Rozella?

The days John and Rozella spent in town had become like special dates. Unfortunately, the days didn't come around too often. Queist guarded his miles on the truck. He recorded and added and begrudged every mile that was driven. Rozella felt obliged to offer part of the cost of gasoline. John, embarrassed, accepted it, knowing that his father would be more apt to let him go to town if he saw money.

While driving back and forth to town, Rozella tried to talk to John about his family, but he became still and withdrawn. The first time she spoke about them, he didn't talk to her all the way back to the farm. She felt like an intruder and the fear that she had offended him upset her. That night she cried in the dark, convinced that he would never return. But, he did return, and eventually she learned that it was easier for him to talk about his mother. Still, she felt underhanded when she coaxed him to talk about his mother by bringing up his childhood. But, these things made conversation easier on the trip to town.

His father, like Rozella's father, sounded like a stranger. Her father, gone all the time, had never spoken to her in a personal way. He had leaned on her sometimes when he was drunk, but never talked to her about who she was, what she wanted, or how he felt about her. John's father was always there, yet, so far removed emotionally that John spoke of him as an unknown, an unpredictable but dire facet in his life. There was always the sound of hatred in John's voice when he said, "Father," as if he spit the word out of his mouth like some foul taste.

Thanksgiving passed, along with the dream of sharing her dinner with John. What was left of her dinner was put away long before he came to visit, but he did come. They shared a piece of her pumpkin pie. Later, she stood in the doorway watching him disappear into the shadows of the pathway, her bare feet cold on the linoleum. She felt a disturbing emptiness that none of their laughter had eased. It was hours before she slept. The coldness wrapped itself around her like a boa constrictor.

The next evening, before she had time to retreat into her dreams, she heard a tap on the door, and answered it with surprise. She never had visitors.

It was John, and in the darkness, she couldn't see him blush. He stood there as if frozen in the doorway. The light from the open door made a circle around him like a halo, and she drew in her breath as if she had been running. "Come in. Don't just stand there," she whispered.

"I...I...You're beautiful...I love you," he said, barely audible. She reached out to take his hand and draw him into the cottage.

"John...yes, I love you, too," she answered him before the blindness of his desire moved him. She looked up at him and he pulled her close. His fingers were in her hair at the back of her neck and he pulled her face toward his to kiss her once more. The kiss they had been waiting for, in answer to their combined aching.

He pushed her nightdress aside to touch her breast, and as she felt his hands upon her, her nipples rose with this new desire. The sweet smell of her, the softness of her made him groan. She inhaled sharply and moaned as she breathed in rhythm with him. Their feelings flowed blindly and wildly. He wanted to cry and he thought she was crying. He looked up. Her mouth was open and her breathing was growing deeper and deeper. Her eyes were closed. Then, she moved as if to rest her head upon his chin, but her hands pulled his face deep against the softness of her breasts. When he raised his head again, he could see the tears running down her cheeks. He had not imagined it. Standing up, he picked her up in his arms and carried her to the next room. There on the soft old bed, he laid her down.

Her nightdress had been left behind on the kitchen floor. Her eyes were still closed, but her breathing became slower. He touched her gently, running his fingers up and down her sides, barely touching her. She jerked and reached for him, as if in sleep. The mound of reddish brown softness was now there for him, moist and waiting. She pulled forward again—toward him and moaned, hands reaching in the night's darkness. The urgent throbbing in his groin acknowledged her loveliness. He quickly came to her, his mouth on hers again. She clutched his shoulders, her her hips rising from the bed. She felt his body hot upon her, then touching her, then – into her. And he almost came with the first thrust.

He stopped, waited. She relaxed, opened her eyes.

"Love you," she was whispering as his tongue went into her mouth, and the heavy full part of him pushed to its limit once more. He could feel the wetness that belonged to her, and the intense warmth of her, the tightness was growing and growing, until he could stand no more. His whole being felt torn away from him once more, and drawn into the heart of her, pulsing, and pulsing...

The heat was heavy and oppressive, with clouds rolling and black. Mama had been closed in the bedroom all morning. Maggie came in from the house across the street, her mouth drawn up to a pucker, and her face in a frown.

"Clean up the kitchen," she was pushing Rozella aside angrily. "It's a mess."

"Why isn't Mama up yet?"

"She's not feeling well, that's why. Can't you two keep busy, and keep out of the way?" She crabbed at them, like an old woman. "Get it done and get out of here for awhile. A nurse is coming to look at Mama. Get things done before she comes."

Maggie picked up buckets and went outside for the water, pumping frantically, cursing under her breath. All the bad words she had heard came pouring out of her mouth, but the wind was rising, and the wind blew the words away. Rozella felt the scent of fear on the wind as she watched the leaves of the willow tree fall into the buckets of fresh water that Maggie was pumping. Maggie came slopping water across her bare feet as she carried the two buckets into the kitchen. The door banged behind her and she poured both buckets into the copper clothes boiler on top of the kitchen stove. She shoved some wood into the open hatch, slammed it shut, and started out of the kitchen, stopped, turned and shouted at Rozella. "NOW". Then she disappeared into the bedroom.

Rozella found the greasy dishpan under the sink, filled it with water from the boiler on top of the stove. It was still cold and had leaves floating on top. She dropped the yellow cake of soap into the cold water, and began to put the dishes into the pan, one at a time.

Tonie, with her six-year-old simplicity, spoke from where she was observing all this, the corner in which she dressed and undressed her doll: "Let 'em soak. That's what Mama does." She continued. The rumble of the electrical storm filled the room, and Rozella saw lightening cross the sky. It cracked loudly, and the trees bent suddenly in the wind.

"I don't like storms," Rozella said. "Maggie screamed at me. She never does that." It was as if she was talking to herself, and not expecting Tonie to listen or to answer her. She pushed her wooden box up to the sink, stirred around listlessly in the cold water, found a sour rag lying next to the pan, and started to scrub the crusted dishes. Out through the window she could see the large drops falling on the wooden back porch, making blotches the size of half dollars. The sweet smell of dust mixing with water drifted into the kitchen and mixed itself with the smells of sour dishrag, stale food, and something else...

With the wind sounds came the moaning from the bedroom, from behind the closed door. Tonie went toward the door to listen.

"Get away from there," Rozella whispered coarsely. "She catches you there and she'll take a switch to you. She's really upset today."

"I wanna know what's going on. Why can't I listen? I want to go in there."

"Get away, I said. Come and help me with the dishes."

The rain now came in torrents; the wind that had pushed it out of the clouds had ceased. The rain fell in sheets, the cracking of lightening rose behind the rain and across the darkening sky.

"I'm afraid," Tonie whispered. "Lightening can come anywhere, even through the walls. It'll get me." She dove under the kitchen table retreating from the bedroom door.

The water was now boiling on the kitchen stove. Heat from the fire filled the room, making an intense oven of the kitchen as heat mixed with the stale air of yesterday's late summer heat. Beads of sweat ran down Rozella's childish face.

The front door opened, then slammed. Mrs. Jacobs came through the living room, dropping water behind her, completely drenched from coming through the downpour. She carried a small black bag with her. The two girls in the kitchen only stared at her wide-eyed as she, too, disappeared into the room without a word spoken to them.

"I want Olie," Tonie was crying to herself under the table, "She's nicer to me than you are. Why isn't Olie home?"

"Hush. She won't be back until Monday. She's staying with Mrs. Toth this weekend. Besides, it's not true. You always say that when you don't get your way."

The sniffling continued from under the table.

Maggie came out of the bedroom, ladled the hot water into a pan and carried it toward the closed room. Tonie followed at a careful distance, and stood peering into the room as Maggie opened the door. Tonie whispered to Rozella as the door closed, "Mama is in bed. The woman, that woman, is making the bed or something."

Sweat faded from Rozella's forehead, replacing itself with goose pimples. There was a smell in the room that she couldn't understand, a heavy smell, a barn-smell, ripe and pungent. She breathed deeply as if reaching for answers that were hidden within the smells. The voices were rising in the bedroom. The moans were louder now that the noise of the storm subsided and became a steady rain. She looked out of the kitchen door and saw puddles of water gathering in the garden, lettuce whipped down, laying in the mud, clothes left forgotten on the clothes lines, ripped and hanging half on the ground. A moan became a scream. Then, silence. Then, words, words she couldn't hear.

The woman came out, dipped into the boiling water with another pan, and returned to the bedroom. The words were still there, as if hanging in the air. Rozella drifted over next to the door where Tonia sat, curled up into a ball. She sat down next to her, put her arm around her, suddenly

*soft—saying, "It's all right. It's all right. Don't be afraid. Mama'll be fine."
Still not knowing what would be all right.*

*WORDS...don't want...don't want...not enough...can't... damned
drunk...women always have to do it...do it...the dirty part...men...
animals...mating like pigs rutting...don't care about pain and work...
the pain, oh, the pain...can't have this...I told him...we can't...he didn't
care...he just shoves it in...all stinking and sour...coming home...oh god, it's
tearing me...pain...dirty diapers...GOD...is a man...GOD said I must...
if...must let this happen...oh, stop...let me die...I don't want this baby...*

*Then, there was silence, and the rain stopped. Tonie was sleeping in
Rozella's arms. Out of the silence and the closed room the woman came,
a white bundle wrapped in a linen towel. The bundle was closed. Then,
Maggie came. Maggie was crying. Mrs. Toth left, with her black bag.*

*Maggie noticed Rozella holding Tonie. Quietly, she touched her on the
shoulder, saying, "Go upstairs and find something to do for while." The
anger was all gone now: Rozella knew as she watched Maggie dry her tears.
Tonie stirred and fully awakened.*

"The storm is over," Maggie said, as if in afterthought.

"What about Mama? That was her I heard?" Rozella asked.

"She's okay, sleeping now. She's well now."

*Rozella just waiting for answers, her eyes reaching for answers, not
moving, not offering to leave.*

*Maggie said, "The baby was...dead. It died. There won't be another
baby. There isn't...Mama is okay, I tell you. It's all over..."*

Rozella woke later that night, when she couldn't sleep. She woke
from a forgotten dream, through it crying, "Not me," and John was
gone.

She washed then, and found that there was very little bleeding. It
was over. She searched for invisible scars. There were none. No one
would know that she was different. Was John different? Did men lose
their virginity? Laughing to her image in the mirror, she asked: Where
does it go? The mirrored person seemed no different, its slender legs, its
flat belly. She smoothed her hands down over her stomach. Somewhere
she had read that woman felt things like men. There would be a great
fulfillment, and as orgasm they called it. She had none, she didn't

think...but there had been such a great feeling of need. It made her want to join him, to reach up, but there was nothing more. How could you know? Who could tell you about lovemaking? She didn't want him to stop. But fornication was what they called it in church. The same as adultery. She and John had said that they loved each other, but what did that mean? Did that make it right?

Her mind was restless remembering her feelings, and she felt frightened about what had happened, surprised by her desire, and wondering how he felt. No, the children at school would not know the difference, but she would.

When school started on Monday, Tina noticed how pale Rozella was and asked her if she was sick. Rozella just remained deep in thought, her fears, her memories and feelings all running together.

She had her dream about Christmas, and she hated to leave Ola alone with her duties to their mother. *Dear Olie, I will try to come, she wrote.*

CHAPTER SIX

So, this was home. What once was so familiar seemed now so different. The memories were there, but Rozella was seeing it as if a stranger, sensing new things, recognizing truths that had not appeared before: the buildings were old, a heavy tangle of weeds had crawled over the rooftop and had been left there to die. Frozen and brown, they halted a fine drifting snow piling it up in ruffled peaks.

The bus left Rozella in the middle of the town. Walking down to Wahaset Street, snow beneath her feet, she cataloged the old and the familiar, as if seen with a fresh vision. Her suitcase became heavy and she shifted it from side to side as she walked. Smoke from brick chimneys hung lazily above the rooftops and a halo of heat-melted circles in the snow, was capping the rooftops.

Hesitating for a moment where a shoveled path turned toward the door, Rozella looked up at the house where she had grown up and wondered how it had become so small. It looked crowded in between two other houses, so close that they looked all squeezed together. Her own cottage was smaller than this, but the surroundings left room and space and open fields. It was a place where you could breathe. This house was closed in, leaning to one side, sinking into a soft earth when the river ran high in the spring; it stayed off balance, listing like an old boat. The second story window had been a special window for her. She used to sit there for hours, dreaming of walking down the street and away, but never dreaming of returning.

And this was returning! She stood there a second in anticipation. When the door finally swung open, two squealing bundles of energy ran toward her, grabbing her legs, and she fell laughing to the floor, hugging them both at once. Myrtle and David. The babies.

Ola stood in the kitchen door, a towel wrapped around her waist, waving a soupspoon at the little ones saying, "Sh- h-h--, Mama's asleep," but her smile was welcoming Rozella.

"Where are the others?"

"Joe is out back chopping some wood. Val and Tonie went over to Mrs. Carver's place. They heard that she was ill."

"They beat me home?"

"Yesterday. They came on last night's bus."

"I couldn't get away until today," Rozella blushed.

"Maggie?"

"She'll be here later. And her boss."

"Really? Who is he?"

"Manager of the Singer Store. Real spiffy looking, too. Always wears a suit."

"Is it serious – between them?"

"We hope so. She doesn't say much about her hopes, though. Afraid, maybe."

"Mama? How is she?"

"No better. She doesn't sleep much during the night anymore. Let me put your coat away. So, if she sleeps during the day, it helps. I give her some wine, but you know how she is about alcohol. You have to put it in a medicine bottle before she'll drink it."

"Coffee on? Thank goodness," Rozella helped herself to a cup and sat down beside the kitchen table, suddenly tired. The two children clung to her arms, one on each side.

"Wha' didja bring us?" David asked.

"It's not Christmas yet, "she pretended to look at them sternly.

"Pretty soon it will be, "Myrtle whined and sucked her thumb and observed expectantly, while David coaxed with his eyes.

"Go get my suitcase."

"He dragged the suitcase across the floor, pushing the rag rugs aside, rolling them into balls as if he couldn't lift the suitcase. She opened it to find a bag of horehound candy and give it to him with instructions, "Now make it last. One piece only, and one before bed."

"All right," he said, handing one to Mrytle and putting one in his mouth. Keep it for me, Ola."

Ola took the bag from him and placed it on the shelf above the stove. "He'll forget that promise by tomorrow," she was saying.

"Papa? Any word?"

"No. She sits there everyday watching the street. It's good when you write. It is something to bring her from the mailbox. The girls send money, and whatever else they can. Maggie gives everything – except what she spends on clothes. Most of those she sews. Papa? We haven't had a letter or a bit of money from him for almost a year."

"I suppose I shouldn't say this, but at least he doesn't leave her pregnant when he doesn't come home."

"Well, she couldn't now, I don't think. She's too sick, and too old…"

"Not much stopped it before. Two more little ones since he left for the north. Each time home, another baby."

"Two to feed. One buried."

"Maybe we should count our blessings."

"Maybe, but it's hard to watch her sometimes. As much as she fought with him, she still looks for him."

Just then Joe came in, dumping the wood into the box beside the stove, creating a din. The stove rattled and the wood box lid slammed shut.

"For heaven's sake, be more quiet", scolded Ola, raising her voice, contradicting her own orders to be quiet.

David came in, this time without Myrtle as a shadow, announcing," Mama's awake."

Rozella went into the room where he mother lay. Mama stirred and held out her arms. Embracing her, Rozella noticed that her arms and neck had become very thin. The veins stood out. Mama is becoming smaller and shrinking away…those brown spots on her skin are strange…I don't remember her skin being so yellow…the odor… the body odor… She had to breathe deeply to keep from retching.

"Anything wrong, girl? You look pale." Mama could still speak in that tone of voice, the voice that made Rozella feel upset, or apologetic.

"No. I must have eaten something that didn't agree with me."

"You always did have a bad stomach. When you're born with it, it stays. Rocked and walked you for a whole year. You had colic all the time. Try tea for that stomach. Black tea. Get Ola to make some. She knows how to do it."

"I'll get it. Want some, too?" She knew that her mother liked tea.

"Yes. Make two cups and send those screaming kids outside. Maybe Joe can take them sledding."

"Why does it always have to be me?" Joe muttered, as he heard her from kitchen, "I'm always stuck with those two."

Ola cuffed him on the side of the head, "Who else is there? Go now. Mama wants some peace." He started pulling on his black overshoes, buckles rattling with his anger.

"You dress 'em. It's a pain in the neck getting them ready for anything," he scolded.

The little ones already had their coats and hats on and were jumping up and down as they waited for help, dropping mittens and picking them up periodically. "Here, I'll do it," Rozella said, "give me an arm." Finishing, she pushed the three out the kitchen door.

Ola had carried the steaming black tea to their mother and placed it on a small table beside the daybed where she lay. Mama was there all the time now, never leaving the bed. They had pushed it in front of the window and she could watch people walk by. The sun shone through the window and the sunlight flooded her with intensified heat. At night, she could lie there looking up at the stars, whenever she could persuade Ola to leave the shades up.

Mama's mail was stacked up on the table along side the frosted lamp with the broken shade. The old mahogany table with its carved legs seemed the sturdiest piece in the room. The quilt covering the bed was made of sewn parts of woolen trousers, blacks and browns, and it still smelled of mothballs from its summer storage. Lace curtains on the windows bore more holes than the originals; sun-rotted, they were coming apart here and there. A faded picture of Jesus praying on the Mount hung over her bed.

Rozella breathed deeply, trying to accept the body odor, which came from her mother. A dying liver left its aura. The tea eased her nausea, but she couldn't look at her mother without feeling disturbed, so she tried to look past her and out of the window. There was the fear of seeing the swollen stomach, which raised the covers like an apron on a pregnant woman.

"Mama, you need a haircut."

"I waited for you to come home. I don't like the way Maggie does it. She hurries and cuts it crooked. Ola can't do it at all. I think she has two left hands…right hands, I guess, since she is left handed."

"She's too busy, that's all, Mama. They both are. Maggie works long hours."

"And one left hand is enough to keep me in trouble," Ola interrupted.

"Maggie's not too busy for a man, though", continued Mama with her complaints, "and she…ought to know…" the voice trailed off and her mind seemed to vanish as if into the snow.

"I'll do it. Tomorrow," Rozella said, wanting to change the subject.

"How is your school, Rose? You are so lucky to have a job." Mama seemed to reawaken.

"It's fine, Mama. Just fine."

"But a house all to yourself? All alone? That's a lot of work. I know. And, it costs more, doesn't it?"

"Not really. In the summer I'll be able to have a garden, and maybe can some vegetables."

"Summer? Aren't you coming home in summer? You don't teach in summer."

"I didn't think about it. Not until now. How could I leave the house, and then come back? Queist would want the rent money anyway, or he would rent it to someone else. The kids…Myrtle and David…why not send the kids to me for the summer?"

"And not see them all summer?"

"It would be easier on you, and on Ola. David is old enough to start school. I could start him reading and writing."

"They do get tired of being hushed whenever I sleep. The pain is bad sometimes. I don't like them to see it." She looked away, as if to hide her face.

There were sounds of laughter and chatter, and then two young women came in, shaking snow from their overshoes, and dropping packages on chairs as they took off their winter coats.

"That is the heaviest old hen around." Val shook her hands and removed her mittens.

"Except for those walking around on two feet…and you had the privilege of carrying it," Tonie laughed, " I chose to carry the small package."

"We did it, Mama…but Rozella, you're home! You look so good. Just like a schoolteacher. That's what they always tell me." Tonie couldn't resist sharing the mischief of her undignified self, masquerading as a local schoolmistress. The three of them were all teaching in different farming areas, all three at country schools. They could share ideas now. And they were all home together this once.

Val hugged Rozella. "How did the first year go? Did my notes help?"

"A lot. A lot."

It was getting dark and the small children came in the back door, red-nosed, red-cheeked, scuffling and pushing each other. Myrtle was crying and Ola demanding, "Why didn't you take her to the toilet before you left? Now, she's wet. All through everything."

Joe stomped by them silently and disappeared into the kitchen. Mittens began to sizzle on the oven door, and the smell of wet wool came across the room.

Mama's white hands fidgeted on the sheet, worried the edges, and she looked from one child to the next. Pain lines crossed her forehead. The lines made a frown that really wasn't a frown.

"My mail? Where is my mail? "She asked of everyone, looking around the room.

"Joe brought it in earlier, Mama. Nothing but the coal bill," Ola eased her as she offered a cool liquid. "Here, take this. We'll have dinner soon."

The girls were settling the table in the room, which served as living room, dining room, and hospital room all combined. The table was next to Mama's bed. They were getting out the best dishes and trying to make it seem like a party. They clowned around, pretending to quarrel, like naughty children, over who was doing most of the work. Rozella couldn't help but laugh

"What's so important about who is doing the most work?"

"It's important when you get to do it all, " twelve year old Joe added resentfully, hearing her remark. "I don't think it's so funny at all." His voice went unheeded. The light from table lamps was casting warm circles on the floor and the room seemed cozier as darkness closed in around them.

The hot borscht, which Ola had learned to make from Mama's recipe, was delicious, and so was the bread, which came directly from the oven, still steaming. Ola had learned her housekeeping lessons well.

Rozella ate with a ravenous hunger. The food of home was good. The three women talked "school talk" while they ate, words flying as fast as knives and forks, interspersed with laughter. Ola was silent and seemed withdrawn into her own world of fatigue. So was young Joe, as he drifted away into his youthful dream world. His mind wandered away trying to find the land of his father, a world where there were no women.

The two small children ate messily, and then demanded their candy. Joe took a piece of it too, from the brown bag, acting as if he didn't really like it.

Ola drifted in and out of the kitchen administering to everyone's needs like an old woman. She would attend to her mother, and then appear at the table, almost simultaneously. Out of long practice, she had become adept at service. Rozella noticed that Ola's plate remained almost untouched. She would eat later, after everyone had left the table. Then her dinner would be cold and the bread would be dry.

Rozella could see that Ola was thinner. You could notice it if you looked carefully, but no one seemed to notice Ola. She had become so much of a convenience for all that no one stopped to see what Ola was doing to herself.

Rozella left her chattering sisters and walked over to her mother. "You finished your dinner?" she asked.

"I managed. Ola cuts it up for me. If I turn on my side, I can feed myself."

The shadows now seemed exaggerated and the windows had become opaque and mirror-like. "I'll take your dishes. Don't you need some more light now?" Rozella looked around the room.

"Not just to lay here thinking."

Maggie and Jack arrived just then, suddenly and quietly filling the doorway like extensions of the shadows. Cold air drifted across the floor rushing inward from the winter landscape. The cold air ran icy fingers up and down Rozella's legs and she shivered as the warmth of her body repelled the cold.

"You're home. Good."   Maggie said, hugging her. "Meet my employer, Mr. Byre. You can call him Jack, though. I do."

Jack's handshake was firm and warm. His eyes were bright and full of light. Nice looking, Rozella noticed, and well dressed. Looks like a salesman. Maggie always did like a well-dressed man. Wonder if he knows…about…

Mama stirred, hearing the conversation, and turned toward them waiting for them to come to her.

"Counting stars again, Mama?" Maggie asked.

"Different number every night. I don't know if they change, or if I can't keep track of which ones I already counted."

"Pin a ribbon on the ones you counted," Jack suggested with a grin.

"He's here to make plans for tomorrow's dinner," Maggie said, "but I think the only real plan he wants to make is to eat a lot."

"You bet. I can suggest what you girls should make. Let me get my list out," Jack added.

They were all there now, finding chairs to gather around Mama. They did discuss the dinner for the next day, although there were not many plans to be made. Pies were in the oven already baking while they talked. The hen would be put in the oven to roast the next morning very early. Smells of spices and apples drifted through the room, making everyone hungry in advance.

Finally, sensing their mother's fatigue the children were put to bed and the women went into the kitchen for a game of cards. They played at the kitchen table while Maggie walked Jack down to the corner, taking a very long time to say goodnight. The big room was dark now, and Mama's breathing could be heard in the stillness.

They giggled and teased Maggie when she returned, then finished the game before they all went up to the loft-bedroom that they had shared as children, lighting the way with a flashlight, as the electricity had never been wired into this room which should have been an attic.

Shy, now that they had learned to live apart, they kept to themselves while undressing for bed, turning their backs to each other, and then quietly slipping into bed. Memories of childhood nights came to each of them...the many nights they had crept into the same beds, flannel nightgowns and cold feet snuggled next to each other. Now -- they were afraid to touch each other, and they carefully lay, on the edges of each shared bed.

The flashlight was turned off and the conversation dwindled, and then it finally paused altogether. Remembering other nights...nights of her childhood...nights when...

They buried the baby that had no name without witness or discussion. As a miscarriage, or abortion, it was carried secretly and silently away and disposed of. No funeral parlor, no preacher, no casket, no expense. The times were hard. They told each other little white lies, and asked no questions. Only the children, as they grew up would remember the baby's full term. Wasn't it nine months that Mama carried the child? Wasn't it full term? But the answers came only in dreams, the nightmare stuff that is not recalled in the morning, the stuff of remembering what is eaten when people are near starvation, what is done when they are hungry or homeless. They had buried the baby somewhere, and no one asked why there were no services.

CHAPTER SEVEN

When she awoke it was fully light. Sunlight was breaking now upon the snow and the street below the window had a blue cast. Watercolor blue.

"Must have eaten too much, "she mumbled to anyone who wanted to hear, then blushed when there was no answer. "It gave me nightmares." There it was.

The fear that her mother had given her: Look at Maggie and what happened to her: What happens to women who give themselves too freely...to women who believe in love.

But I love him. I couldn't help but love him. I gave because I wanted to. Wrong? Could it be wrong? They say...women always say...men blame the woman...she is to be blamed for giving in...Eve's sin...the man takes...then resents...to win you must never give in...negate...backward... how reverse...wouldn't it be easier to just love...then, they would still tally up the score in the same old way...according to the standards...women were evil...men were natural...following their natural drives...now, I'll have to go home...to John...home...back to the cottage...wait for John... Maggie...they were hysterical when Maggie...the tears...crying... accusations...demands on Maggie for...the abortion...Maggie let them do it...she was young... with no way out...Mama...the furtive trip...paying for it with months of laundry work...we all put in hours to help...why Maggie's baby and not Mama's ...Mama's born to wedlock...did it have the right to live...not Maggie's baby...Maggie's baby without a father...

immaculate paternity...my father always gone...was that a father?...did I have a right to be born?...the butchering job...Maggie home all bloody and weak...in bed for weeks...still sick...now we know...but never talk about...Maggie now would never have a baby...did Jack know?...has she told him...would she have to tell him?...would he want her if he knew?... what if... I want to go home...home...John...want him near...don't want to care...I'm afraid...

A dark hand was hanging over her, the dark hand of fear. She wanted to leave, to be alone with her love and her fear of that love. The faces around her seemed empty and exaggerated. They interrupted her daydreams.

The day before Christmas activity in the kitchen heightened. Chattering over the stuffing for the hen, which would substitute for the dreamed of goose, the delicacy Mama would have desired, the young women decided whose recipe would be used. Ola's hair was pulled up in a knot on top of her head. A few wisps of hair curled around her ears. A bright red apron Maggie made for her trimmed her tiny waist in a festive note of color. The red was reflected in her cheeks; and, she looked younger than usual and more cheerful.

Sunlight streamed through the kitchen windows, the white glare upon the snow cascading in square window-laced patterns across the floor. The coffeepot boiled incessantly on the iron kitchen stove top, bubbling and dripping down the sides to coat the blue enameled pot with brown coffee foam. The little ones played with pickup sticks in the corner; David fussing because Myrtle couldn't understand games yet. All she wanted to do was to throw the colored sticks down and squeal with delight as they rolled around the floor.

Joe had gone to find a tree. He would find a small one somewhere in the woods, and pull it home behind him on the old wooden sled that was always used to haul wood. Yesterday's baking was neatly arranged on a table covered with white tea towels. It waited undisturbed except for an occasional stolen crumb, a taste.

Mama lay restlessly in her living room bed, turning from side to side, asking questions, then giving orders, which were generally accepted, then ignored.

Small packages appeared mysteriously from hidden corners. Last minute wrapping in red tissue paper, last year's stickers that wouldn't stick, and no string, created strange and awkward packages.

Tonie and Val made a kettle full of popcorn, then sat down on the kitchen floor with thread and needles, showing the children how to make popcorn strings for the tree .The four of them ate popcorn and threaded the billowy white kernels unto the strings alternately.

Rozella found the packages she had brought in the bottom of her bag. Alone in the upstairs loft as she searched for them, she lay down. For just a moment, she thought. The stillness in the room was good. Accustomed to living alone now, the noise and confusion of the household, which used to be home, had been overwhelming. She wanted to be alone with her thoughts, yet feared them. The package beside her on the bed seemed so little, each one a token – the work of her hands.

She heard noises in the kitchen below and knew that Joe was home with the tree.

They would be looking for her soon. Freshening herself by washing, she noticed the color of her skin. It was not good; a pale reflection stared back at her from the mirror, dark eyes almost sunken.

The empty beds behind her in the room suddenly seemed full of ghostly spirits. Where will we all be next year, she asked aloud, and the answer came to her in tears. Brushing them aside, she didn't want to hear more of her own answer. She hurriedly left the attic bedroom, this time to escape her thoughts.

The postman had come and gone. There was no package from Pa. There were only a few cards, the last straggling few. One came from Russia; three had a local postmark. As she left for the mailbox, she could see that the tree was in the living room, puddles of water beginning to form where the warm air melted snow from the frosted branches. Joe looked proud of his choice, and waited for a compliment. "It's nice," she told him, "really the nicest one yet. Where did you find it?"

"Out behind Culpepper's barn. You know, the grove where we used to pick berries."

"Yes. Oh, that's a good spot. They've never minded us poking around in the woods there."

"I'll have it up in a minute. Wait til I get my hammer."

They trimmed it with popcorn streamers. A box of old ornaments appeared from a closet. It had Mama's European crèche figures, a china Jesus, and angels with worn off paint. "Look at Mrytle's teeth marks on baby Jesus," Exclaimed David, eager to start some excitement. A few paper angels with tinsel hangers added to the color, miniature silk flags in strange colors from far lands, cranberry loops...then, the box was empty. The tree was adorned, and heavy fragrant branches filled the corner of the room.

In the afternoon the sun became weaker and the room grew heavier: it seemed to shrink before their eyes as the light faded. Suddenly, quieter, they laid the gifts beneath the tree, as David and Mrytle asked about each one. Whose is it? They had to know which were theirs so they could squeeze and poke and wonder over each one.

Maggie and Jack came in, and then disappeared into the kitchen where they produced a steaming and spicy scented cranberry punch. They brought it in by the tree in heavy mugs to be shared by all. The children turned up their noses at the cups and refused to touch it.

"Ugh," said David.

"It's not alcohol," Maggie insisted, "Just fruit juice."

"Smells like it. Don't wan' any," he replied.

The children begged for a cookie from Ola, and Mama stared bleakly into her empty cup. Rozella, watching her, felt in the sudden silence a fear that seemed to cross her back leaving goose pimples on her skin. Don't say it, she thought, don't say that you thought Pa would be home. I can't bear to hear it. You haven't heard from him since last June, but I don't want to be reminded of it.

Lights were showing now from the houses across the street. Through the window she could see silhouetted against the snow two people walking home, hand in hand. She felt her mind play upon them, imagining them to be going home to their first Christmas together. The touch of his hand would be firm and warm. The girl would be looking up at him, and wondering about the future.

The dinner hour came with its masses of Christmas delicacies; each daughter had prepared a special dish. They opened their gifts by candlelight after dinner was over, slowly savoring each gift and knowing full well the hours of work that had gone into every one. Hand knits, crocheted doilies, Tonie with her small paintings -- miniature scenes done in oil, stuffed rag dolls for the children, preserves of canned wild berries that had been gathered early in the year. This was their usual Christmas, nothing deleted for the Depression. They had always remembered each other this way.

Later, once in bed, the sisters talked until far past midnight, remembering all the crazy things they had done as they grew up, remembering all the dreams of Santa Claus they had shared. "Visions of sugar plums, heck" Val interjected, "I always had visions of oranges."

"When I get rich and move to California, I'll mail you an orange," Tonie said.

"Dream on, you loonies," Maggie interrupted. "No one gets rich."

"What else is there to do but dream?" Val wanted to know.

"You could dream about something other than food, after so large a dinner." Maggie countered.

"One could dream about men, I suppose, but Maggie here – doesn't have to dream anymore. She has one."

"Shut up, little sister," answered Maggie, "Don't you think it's about time?"

"We're happy for you, Maggie," Rozella said, "It is serious then?"

"I hope so," Maggie answered, sort of wanly.

There was a part of Rozella now that was yearning now, and wanting to be back, waiting for John. Even the waiting was better than nothing, the endless nothing. Slowly all of the sisters drifted off to sleep as they had in their childhood years, as the night became a blanket of privacy into which one could retreat.

CHAPTER EIGHT

By Sunday noon when Rozella walked to the bus depot with her sisters, she was very eager to leave. Their excited talking never ceased. Mama had kissed her goodbye, and begged her to come back soon. Even while saying goodbye she was remembering that John had promised to pick her up at the Crenston bus terminal. He had errands in town that had to be done on Sunday, so there was a reason for him to take the truck to town.

Most of the farms were quiet. It was a day of rest. In Biblical style, on the seventh day, they rested. There was church for everyone, and after church, a big dinner, not always the best food, but a lot of it. Normally, all the farmers ate their fill, then spent the afternoon lying around the house. On this Sunday, they had probably all dined on leftover Christmas dinner, but still – by evening, they would do the usual chores, attending to the cows, horses and other creatures just before dark.

Rozella counted telephone poles and fence posts along the bus route. The bus smelled of perspiration, hair oil, and stale lunches. People coughed and rattled newspapers. The man next to her snored, his head falling to one side, his mouth open.

When the bus pulled into the Crenston terminal, she looked eagerly over the people waiting for the bus. She searched for John, but he wasn't there. A couple of old ladies sat with their shopping bags resting at their feet. A farmer, his red and black checkered jacket pulled high around his neck to keep out the cold, waited by the doorway. But, John was not there.

She picked up her bags. Feeling so terribly alone, she almost wished that she had not returned. Rozella started to walk across the vacant lot next to the bus terminal, not knowing, not caring what she was doing. She had not even begun to think about how she would get back to the cottage…five miles out in the country. Her bag was heavy.

Suddenly a hand touched her shoulder and turned her around. "Where do you think you're going, young lady?" John's smile met her surprised look.

"John! I wondered what had happened. Oh, John," she threw her arms around his neck, forgetting all about the fact that they were in the middle of town. People across the street heard her exclamation, and looked up with interest.

She began to cry then, without control. The sobs broke against his neck, and he realized that she was nearly hysterical, and she couldn't stop crying.

"What happened? What's wrong?"

"I've been…I am…I feel terrible. The holiday was lonely without you. I wanted it to be fun, but it wasn't anymore."

"What do you mean?"

"It was depressing. Maggie was happy for the first time in her life, and so were my sisters, but Mama…is just fading away. Life is changing."

She was still crying, but strangers were watching this display of emotion, and he pulled back from her, patting her shoulder, waiting for her to control her tears. She pulled out a handkerchief and tried to wipe her face.

"Well, we'll talk about it on the way home. Those nosey people over there seem to want to hear every word we say. We'd better move along." He took her arm and picked up the bag, turning toward the corner, taking her to the truck, which was parked on the other side of the block.

Just feeling his hand on her arm seemed to quiet her down. Her breathing became easier, and she suddenly felt better. The thoughts could be shared now, and they wouldn't be so sad.

He was whistling an odd melody as he walked her to the truck. "What is that tune?" she wanted to know.

"Dunno. How does it go? Now, the words come back. The song they sang last fall, I guess: we'll eat our wheat and ham and eggs, and let them eat their gold – remember the farmer's holiday?"

"Are prices getting any better?"

"Still burning corn to heat the courthouse, they say."

"It seems impossible and unreal."

"Wood costs more." The casual conversation seemed easier, and it served to prolong the time until they would have to talk seriously. Trying to keep their own worries out of their minds, they continued.

"Any news on the Keller family?" Rozella asked.

"The mortgage people held the auction just as planned, the day after you left. But we thought about it. We all got together and bought back the equipment and gave it back to Keller. Nothing they could do about it. I bought his plow for twenty-five cents. Someone bought his horses. Are they mad!"

"Clever. Will they be able to think of another idea…to exclude the local people from the auctions?"

"I think they have to advertise the auctions, or they aren't legal when it is a mortgage auction."

"Good. Good. It's one way to fight back."

They reached the truck and he helped her into it, throwing the bag in the rear pick up bed. "You okay now?" he asked, looking at her with care. With that look, her tears came again.

"I don't want to talk about it right now. I want to talk about it when we have time together. You still have to be home at the expected time, don't you? There are only so many hours in a trip to town."

"Well, Pa doesn't know exactly how long it might take to locate Lens Hubbard and get the tractor parts. Used parts are cheaper than new. Pa should be glad to get them. And it is…Sunday."

"I know. No doubt he will be glad. But, I want more time to talk than that," her voice trailed off and she began to cry again.

"Don't know why you can't say what's on your mind. Does it take so much time as all that?" John asked.

She didn't answer him. The truck left the edge of town, and she felt free, as they left local eyes behind, to lean against his shoulder, quietly letting the feel of his warmth comfort her.

The gravel roads were covered with ice, which had been packed down by travelers on the way to town. Tire tracks left iced ruts on the surface of the road. The drizzle of an undecided winter had glazed the surface during a sudden thaw.

There was grayness to everything. It extended from the sky into town, and fell over the countryside. More than the color of the sky in 1930, it was on people's faces. The turning of the New Year – 1931 – had to promise better things. There had been a store on the crossroads between the Queist's place and the town. The signs were still up, but the building was boarded up. It had been closed.

"When did they close the store, John?"

"Last week. The Smiths said they had charged as much as they could to people hereabouts. To stay open they charge their own purchases to the major companies. Finally, their credit was cut off. They had to close up. No more groceries could be had."

"Where did they do?"

"To live with some relatives on a farm east of here." He touched the brakes again.

"But farmers have nothing. Pork at two cents a pound, they tell me. The farmers are killing the hogs; the kids in school all talk about that."

"Killing and canning. Hannah puts meat in jars."

"Isn't that dangerous? Won't meat spoil?" Rozella was interested.

"Not if it's done right. Better than throwing it away. We can't feed all the animals."

The turn down Main Street went past a small bar. The men standing out in front leaned on a plate glass window, which was painted green. They were bearded and dirty. One sitting on the curb was puffing on a hand-rolled cigarette, ignoring the cold weather.

"They look half asleep. What are they doing hanging around in the cold?"

"They are not as sleepy as you think, Rozella. They watch to see who brings produce to town to sell. They're angry and determined to keep things out of the market, to drive prices back up again."

"How can they do that?"

"They can stop us from selling. And they do."

The truck came to a stop at the corner stop sign. A burly man seemed to come out of nowhere and jump unto the back of the truck. He jumped in and out – and away, running off before they started.

"What was that all about?" Rozella asked.

"Just what I was telling you. He was checking to see if I had cream cans in the back."

"And if you had?"

"They would take them off the truck and dump them into the street."

"How can this stop hunger?"

"How can anyone stop hunger? They try – the best way they know."

Later, when they returned that way, there were more men in front of the bar as they passed. It was darker now at nearly sundown. Sundown came early this time of year, and sometimes it couldn't be seen as the low clouds hid it from view. The men appeared more agitated, and as they talked to each other they waved their hands. A case of eggs lay overturned in the street, broken and smashed, yellow streaks upon the dirty snow. John just shook his head and drove by them, saying nothing.

"How long can this go on?" she asked him.

"Who knows? People are starving. We don't know what to do. The government will have to do something."

The road was bumpier than before, the ice now crusted and thick from the freezing temperature. Rozella bounced with the motion of the truck. She must write to her mother, but she really couldn't say they were engaged. What could she say? She didn't want her mother to know that she had failed to live up to her promise, the promise that she wouldn't do what Maggie had done. Rozella had promised she would wait for marriage.

A few tools lay on the floorboards. They bobbled with the motion of the truck. Staring down at them, yet not seeing them as her thought moved back and forth in time, Rozella did not notice them until she remembered the photo album that she had pushed back under the seat of the truck, the one she had first seen in the cottage. It made her think of the men who had lived in the cottage before her.

Was it really their album and their pictures? If so, why were they cut out? She reached down, as if to place the tools in a less conspicuous place. Pushing them under the seat, she didn't notice anything under there. The album was gone now, no longer in the spot where she had pushed it in her fright, not wanting John to know she had seen it...and why was she so uncomfortable with it?

"John, who were the men who lived in the cottage – the hired hands?" she asked now.

"Why? Just men, that's all."

"Sometimes I think about them, about who they were, and where they went. Isn't it natural, when you live in a house, share the same bed...I mean, sleep in the same bed they slept in."

"Hired hands are a dime a dozen these days. Men travel through on freight trains. We are lucky if they keep traveling. There is no work here, and not enough food to feed them. If they stay, hiding out in the woods somewhere, they start stealing."

"There were two of them?"

"I think that they changed several times while I was away, Rozella. It wasn't always the same two."

"Who were the last ones?"

"You are full of questions, aren't you? Seems to me that father said that one of them was a lumberjack named Nels, big blonde fellow, Dutch perhaps, or Danish. The other one a small dark man – older. Italian? The Italian wasn't much good. I don't think he had ever worked on a farm before. At least, not if what the folks tell me is true. The cold bothered him, too. He just couldn't take it." John explained.

"Nels stayed on?"

"Yeh, for quite awhile. He seemed to get along with Hannah. That's not easy to do. She is...well, she wants a lot. But then, that was a few years back, too. Hannah was younger. She's older than I am. Fifteen years older. I don't remember much about her when she was young. When I was five, she was twenty. You see?"

"Then, you don't really know for sure that she has always been so demanding, if that's the right word for her?" Rozella pulled her coat around her, as she spoke.

"No, not really. She seems to be that way with everyone, except maybe my father. Then, the roles reverse themselves. He orders her around, and she obeys."

"That photo album—I wonder who it belonged to."

"What album?"

"Don't you remember? I found it the first day I rented the cottage. Oh, that's right, you weren't there. I didn't even know you then. Your father was there. He took it."

"I don't remember it, so I don't know what you are talking about. Did it have any names in it?"

"No, but, I thought..."

"What did you think?"

"Well, it seemed such a peculiar collection."

"If it was...you probably didn't really recognize the people. It must have belonged to Nels. He was there the longest. I don't think the Italian man left anything behind because he traveled like a hobo, everything on his back. A typical rail rider."

"Who was a rail rider?"

"The Italian or the blonde? I meant it must have been the big blonde man's album. Pa used to call him the Svede. I could ask Hannah if she has seen it."

"No. That's not important. It's just my curiosity. I didn't really get a good look at it. It doesn't matter. Funny how your mind stays with things, and how something reminds you of something else."

"Right now, I am reminded that we are almost home, but I'll be back later."

"Promise me you will be."

"That's not hard to promise." He reached over to hug her.

They were now turning down the road that left the main highway, turning at the mailbox on which Rozella had crudely painted: Ehalt. The next one would read: Queist. John's house.

John helped her into the cottage, and then lit the stove so the rooms would warm up, but he didn't stay. He was in a hurry to get home.

As she watched him leave, she could see him turn down the road, which led to the main highway. His headlights were not on. How could he see? Then, she realized he did not want his father to see the truck on this part of the property. He did not dare to let his father know that he had picked up Rozella in town and driven her home. How could he be so afraid, so much a prisoner of someone else? Surely it was an innocent thing – a simple ride home in the late afternoon?

But the costs, the costs were imperative in this time, she told herself, rationalizing the argument in her mind. Anyone else would have done it. It was not an extra trip. There really were parts to be purchased in town, but John had lied. Why? Why did he have to lie to his father? Wasn't he a free man at all? Didn't he work for his father many hours a week? These were such strange ties.

She pulled a chair over near the fire to warm her feet. The heat felt so good. It helped her relax, and she slept, feeling at home and secure in the small place. The preceding days had worn her out. The day and night chattering of her sisters had been exhausting to her. After being away from it for several months, she had learned to enjoy her solitude. There was quietness here in which to think and to do things without constant interruption.

CHAPTER NINE

John opened the door, startling her. She jumped up from her chair, "But you just left."

"If that's the way you feel, I'll leave again," he teased her.

"Oh,no, no. It's just that…I must have slept all this time. It can't be 10 o'clock. Is it?"

"Yes, it is. Almost, that is. I hurried a bit."

"I haven't even put my coat away. Maybe that's why I fell asleep. Wrapping it around my shoulders kept me warm."

"Here, let me take it." He was using it for an excuse to put his arms around her. His hands were on her breasts; he was seeking her nipples with the tips of his fingers.

"John. John, don't you know?"

He was kissing her. "What don't I know?"

"What this could do?"

"What could it do?" He was ignoring her as he talked to her, and coaxing her toward the bedroom with her steps.

"I'll tell you. I meant to tell you."

He began to undress her. The room was cool after having been empty over the holidays. It was not yet warm from the fire in the stove. Her nipples, responding to the cold and his fingers, were already erect. He found them with his mouth, holding them between his lips, first one then the other. Pulling her body closer to him, he had one hand on each of her sides. Then, he didn't have to pull; she was stretching forward toward him, feeling the heat of him through his trousers.

"Yes. Yes. Oh, please," he asked in whispers.

She was opening his trousers. There it was, hard and strong and waiting. The heat of it on her hands further aroused her. She fell back unto the bed and he was on top of her. There was no longer any waiting or hesitating. The frenzy of their desire was there. It would have no restraints put upon it.

It was over quickly, leaving only the knowledge in her mind that there would be another time before the evening was over and he would leave to cross the dark pathway to his house.

"What would you tell me?" he asked, now that the physical drive had subsided for the moment

"I would tell you how afraid I am." And with that statement, she began to cry again." I may be pregnant already."

" Really? Perhaps, you are only afraid."

" But, I remember what happened to Maggie."

"What happened to Maggie?"

"She got pregnant with someone who couldn't marry her. A married man."

"I'm not married, Rozella."

"No, but we aren't married. They made Maggie get an operation, an illegal operation."

"Because she couldn't get married?" John sounded shocked.

"Yes. She was young, and the operation was very dangerous. We all worked to pay for the operation, so she wouldn't be shamed before everyone. She was very sick after it, and doctors say that she can't have any babies now."

"You're afraid it might happen to you? I'm an honest man, Rozella. I would marry you. You shouldn't be afraid. Let's not worry about things that haven't happened yet .Let me plan. Maybe by springtime we can plan to marry, after school is out."

"Yes, because I can't teach after I marry."

"Let me think about things. I do love you," he answered.

And, it became easier to love him, since the words were there now. It was almost an engagement, although she had no ring to show the world. Even if she could...the school board would not allow it.

But, by their next meeting, the fear had not left her. Meeting him at the door, she began to cry again, whispering through the tears, "I'm sure. I'm must be pregnant already."

"Are you sure?" he asked cradling her head in his arms.

"I didn't want to believe it. But I have been feeling queasy in the mornings, and I have sore breasts."

"So soon? So soon? I suppose I should have known that we couldn't get away with it. I hoped that your fear had made you sick, and it was really okay."

"We can't help what we feel." She answered him.

"Why do things have to happen this way? Why can't people plan these things?" he said.

"They always say it is God's will," she defended the world in general.

"I know, but what do we do now?" He asked, as if to himself.

"I know that I can't work when the school board finds out. I'll never work again, and I just started. A single girl, pregnant. I feel just awful. I'm so embarrassed, and I feel so dirty."

"We'll get married. At once. I'll tell the family. They won't like... but I'll tell them. This weekend. Next weekend."

"John, are you sure? You want to do this? You do love me?"

"Of course. I just didn't think about what to do. How can I handle this? I just didn't expect..."

"How can I teach this way? What if I get sick in school?"

"You'll get better. At least, that is what they say.""

"But I can only work a couple of months maybe...what if I begin to show? They find out about these things. You have to bring a certificate from a doctor. They are terrible about pregnancy."

"You might be able to work through until the spring, if you don't show too much. Don't worry. We'll get along. We have this place to live in at least."

"What can we live on if I don't work? What will be our income? We have to have something for food and doctor bills, and rent, maybe."

"I'll think of something. There has to be a job somewhere."

"No jobs right in the country. No jobs really anywhere except the one you have, working for your father...or the one I have, that I wont' have very soon."

"I'll look in town again. I'll ask again. There has to be something."
They cuddled down in the covers, keeping each other warm, both of
them lost to the practical worry of survival. There was no more sexual
excitement that night. They clung to each other like children in their
fear, until it was time for John to leave. Around midnight, he left,
covering her carefully, before he slipped out of the door into darkness
and the cold walk home.

~

He came to her the following Sunday, early in the day. She looked up,
surprised to see him on a Sunday. He was dressed in Sunday formality,
navy blue suit, black polished shoes, a white shirt and black tie.

"I have come to take you to the house for dinner, Rozella. You
should meet the family, and we'll talk about marriage today."

She excused herself to change clothes, brushing back her soft hair,
yet allowing a few ringlets to frame her fine-boned face. She was happy,
almost floating, as if her whole future was contained in this moment.
Her subdued woolen dress fell in folds. Like her mood, it was soft.

Reaching for his hand when she entered her living room, she looked
up at him, but there was stiffness in him and his hand fell away from
her, cool, limp, and strange. He was not the man she had known during
the night hours. John had withdrawn to a mental world of silence that
seemed to possess him. Rozella wanted to believe it was strength, but
it puzzled her. She didn't like to feel unwanted, and she couldn't bear
to tell herself that...so, she reached again for the physical reassurance
of this touch, but again the hand fell away. He was oblivious to her.
As they stood there a cold wind came bursting through the doorframe,
and the sun slipped behind a cloud as they turned toward the pathway
that led to the house on the other side of the trees.

The house wasn't what she imagined it would be when they came
to it, not at all. How could she have lived here separated from it by only
the woods and not known what it would be? What had kept her from
seeing it? It had a worn-away grayness, and slivered bare boards. Years
of rain and snow and sun had stripped it of every vestige of color. It
stood defiantly against the horizon like sun-faded earth. Yet, its shape
created a giant-like ugly protrusion. A wisp of smoke came from the
rear chimney and seemed to link it by a thread to the sky, which now

writhed with clouds that were foretelling another snowfall. Yes, it was the house of the photos!

It stood on top of an abbreviated mound of earth with no decorative bushes or trees to ease the shock of its site. An unpainted water pump looked like a solitary sentry, and became a signpost standing mid-snow-bank between the two of them and the front porch. Two dogs burst forth from the open barn door and came running up the snow-packed path barking, ruffs of fur standing up on their necks. One was a black and white longhaired shepherd mix, the other looked like a cross between a collie and something else. Rozella wasn't usually afraid of dogs, but these two reminded her of their owner, John's father, and she shrunk back.

"Get down. Get back," John had to shout at them, and point at the barn. He lifted the back of his hand as if in a threat; they cowered and pulled back, lingering on the pathway, watching them as they climbed the front steps of loose boards, frozen over by layers of dirty ice and snow.

Rozella felt swallowed up by the silence, which could sometimes be a part of John. She couldn't speak to voice her feelings, or her fears. She was overwhelmed by the house, and the mood that surrounded it. The oval glass in the front door reflected their shadows, which were barely visible and ghost-like, becoming a frosted picture. They stood there for a moment unmoving. John at last took her hand, as if in reaching for reassurance for himself, but before he could reach out to turn the heavy brass doorknob, the door suddenly opened.

A woman stared at them coldly. "Well, John. You're late."

The dogs were standing at watch, growling in their throats. The woman's black eyes greeted them, the look of them matching her tone of voice. Her salt and pepper gray hair braided around a drawn face, was just another reflection of the interior of the house. Her high-necked white blouse was buttoned austerely around her neck, and a mournful black woolen skirt fell down to her ankles. There were worn spots on it, and they had been mended carefully with tiny stitches. Rozella was noticing every thread.

It was John's sister, Hannah, who swung the door open so it slapped against the wall covered with musty yellow-brown paper now faded to colorlessness. John did not choose to answer her statement.

"They're waiting." She pointed to them, her arm crossed space to indicate a room adjoining. She closed the door behind them with a hand that seemed almost claw-like. Rozella looked up at John questioningly.

"It's Hannah," John whispered in answer, as if Hannah were not even there. These were his only words before they followed her toward the room where his parents waited.

Patterned by lace curtains, sunlight fell across the lap of the small women seated in front of the bay window. Her hands were clasped in her lap, upon drab clothes, shadow-like in color. She was pale, so white the skin seemed almost transparent.

The gruff old man standing beside her Rozella recognized from the day she rented the cottage. When they came into the room, he moved toward them restlessly. "You're here," he said, abruptly. "Hannah has dinner ready. We'll eat."

It was then Rozella noticed the woman was sitting in a wheelchair, for Hannah began to push the chair toward the open door. The dining room held a large oak table, now covered with a white cloth. There were platters of chicken on each end of the table. The chicken looked as if it had been boiled because it was colorless. There was a bowl of hot steaming potatoes, dark spots of the eyes still showing, and the flesh yellowed, as if they had been frozen in the fields before picked.

Each person seemed to have a place: the mother was pushed to one end of the table, and the old man sat at the other end of the table. Without a hat, his brow was white as death, the gray hairs rising above his white forehead, and the ruddy skin beginning where his hat had ended.

Hannah took something off of the sideboard and placed it beside her mother's plate. Startled, Rozella realized it was a Bible, a very large one. As John seated her politely, she watched the tiny woman's hands turning the pages of the giant book.

"We have a daily Bible reading, Rozella. We are Christian. I hope you are," his mother said over the pages of the book she was holding.

Rozella nodded her head, unable to speak. She had lived with her mother's quotations and threats, pictures and icons, church...dark and ornate, but there had been no ritual in their daily lives. The omen of the chastising hand had been woven into their household, but they had not practiced reading the "word." John's mother read with a voice clear and imperious, as if gaining strength from the power of the words:

> *Such as sit in darkness in the shadow of death,*
> *being bound in affliction and iron;*
>   *Because they rebelled against the words of*
> *God and contemned the counsel of the*
>   *Most High, therefore he brought down their*
> *heart with labor: they fell down,*
>   *And there was none to help. They cried unto*
> *the Lord in their trouble, and he*
>   *Saved them out of their distresses...*

Now, we'll bow our heads in silent prayer to ask forgiveness for our sins...and God's blessing upon our guest, and this food."

They all sat silently for what seemed to be several minutes. A lump in Rozella's throat felt incredibly large. She couldn't swallow. The contemplation of sin seemed directed at her. It hadn't occurred to her before. Sin and a child...sitting in darkness. Were they all sitting in darkness or were just she and John in darkness? Even the room seemed to grow in darkness as the thought came.

One of the platters of chicken was passed silently. As she put one piece on her plate, her hands were shaking. It looked like skin, like dead skin, awful boiled...baby skin. It was madness to think such things, but her stomach turned and she bit her lip.

"Excuse me," she mumbled as she rushed from the room. Once outside she was fighting the heaving of her empty stomach. Nothing in it but the morning tea, still her body rejected emptiness. The muscles in her stomach clenched and knotted as she bent over. She wiped her perspiration from her forehead, at the same time she was shivering from the winter cold. Then, she walked back toward the house. She noticed as she turned that Queist was standing by the dining room window. He must have watched her as she struggled with her retching. A heavy green shade was pulled half way down to cut out the sun. For a moment it appeared that his head was cut off by the shade. She could only see the arthritic hands, and the dark Sunday suit—that was all.

John met her by the door. "Better now?"

"Yes."

"Can you eat?"

"A little. I was just too nervous."

They returned to the dining room and sat down again on opposite sides of the table. Hannah had kept eating without interruption, but the old man now returned from the window where Rozella had seen him standing. "Don't like chicken?" he asked.

"Yes, but I'm just too nervous today."

"Well, nerves? I always say there's nothing like hard work to cure nerves. Ask Hannah, here. She puts in a good day."

"Rozella puts in her day at school," said John.

"Head work. It's hard on females. Makes 'em nervous. Maybe you ought to get outdoors more." His father answered.

"John tells us that you want to get married," Hannah interrupted.

"Well, uh," Rozella couldn't speak.

"Yes," John said. "You know that."

"It might be possible if John could save up enough to buy a farm, even a small parcel of this one," the old man added.

"How can I save? I don't earn anything."

"A job in town, maybe, after things pick up. If you work there, and here...it could happen, in time." He answered John.

"We want to marry now," John emphasized 'now.'

"You can't without money," Hannah emphasized 'money.'

"Rozella makes some money, "Queist's eyes glinted. "She could save some."

John's face was becoming more and more red with frustration and embarrassment. Rozella just wished that she could faint or die, or slide right under table. The mother looked at her softly, but said nothing; her hands remained folded on the Bible in an almost trance-like way.

No longer self-contained, John blurted, "We are getting married. Now. Not five years from now. No dowry, Pa. Rozella has...she has no money. She has...she's expecting."

"John. Oh, God," wept Rozella, hiding her face. "Did you have to?"

"Sure. Sure," the old man was now vehement. "Might have expected that any single girl who would live alone like that..."

"And what do you mean by that?" John exploded.

"Well, she invites men by staying alone."

"Don't talk about her as if she isn't here. Rozella, Rose…" John reached across the table toward her, as if trying to touch her.

"Why not?" Queist asked, "Everybody else'll talk."

"Yes, added Hannah, "There will be plenty of talk. You can count on that. We won't be able to keep our heads up in church, and what about the neighbors?"

"Never had a disgrace like this in this family," John's mother murmured joining in, but no one was listening to her.

"I don't care what anyone thinks; we'll be married." John declared.

"By the Justice of the Peace, the church won't marry you. Not to a harlot, and according to the church—that is what she is." The father banged his fist on the table.

Rozella now cried openly. This agony had surpassed whatever dignity she had left. What had made her think this would be a happy day? Hannah watched her smugly, finally saying to John. "Take her home, John. Then come back and we'll discuss the arrangements."

Crying blindly all the way back to the cottage, Rozella clung to John's arms. She could not see where she was walking. The humiliation was more than she could have imagined. She didn't know what she had expected, but it wasn't this. Acceptance? Ordinary acceptance? What dream had propelled her into this? There were no possibilities. How could she believe that a job would magically appear for John? And her teaching days were over. Already over.

John didn't talk, his anger and fear contained him, tied him within himself, even more than before. He held her arm, steering her toward her door.

"It'll be all right," she murmured as if assuring herself. "Go ahead. Your family…they want you to come back."

"You sure you can stay alone? I have to go. Get it settled. Once they start, they won't quit."

When he returned to her it was late afternoon and Rozella sat in her chair staring into the blankets of snow, which stretched across the road and into the yard. They were drifts and dark hollows against the wavering horizon. Blankly, she wondered how she had come to this particular moment.

"John?" she asked, when she heard him open the door, wondering silently if he loved her.

"Sure. Who else? It's all settled. It's all right now."

"How? What will we do?"

"We'll get married and live right here."

"My job? You know. I'll have to quit." Rozella reached for him.

"Not right away."

"Will you have work?"

"For my father," he looked away. Something distasteful crossed his face, as it went through his mind. His voice was too soft, too easy on her.

"Doing what?" she asked.

"The same thing, in exchange for rent and food. Later, I can find something else. I'll keep trying. You know that."

"When will we get married?"

"As soon as we can. We'll go to Crenston next week for the papers." He reached down to take her hands and pull her up from her chair.

"The wedding?"

"The Justice of the Peace, I'm afraid. Quickest and easiest. It will cost less, too." He wanted to make it logical, to ease her away from any dreams that she might have held.

"You mean that we really wouldn't be allowed...to marry in the church?"

"It doesn't make any difference. We know how things are with us." He held her close.

"We know. Yes. But, what can I tell my family?" She was tearing up again.

"Just write and tell them we're married. What difference? They don't need to know when or where, do they?"

"I wish I could have met your family differently. You don't know how I hated...to hear it said...would they come here sometime for dinner? I know they don't think much of me, but we could try to get to know each other."

"Maybe. Sometime." He was leading her toward the bedroom.

"Shouldn't we try before the wedding, John? They will be at our wedding, won't they?"

"No, I'm afraid not," he answered her.

"Why? Oh, I shouldn't ask. They are still angry. Ask them here. I'll say how sorry I am," she tugged at his sleeve.

"They won't come, Rozella," he couldn't look at her.

"Why not?"

"I know them. They'll make me...to get the cottage...the work... promise never to bring you...Oh, God. I'll have to do it..."

"What are you saying?"

"They may accept the child after it is born because the child will be a Quiest, they'll say. I even know the quotations, 'the Father forgives the child...' but you are not their child. According to them, you will have to make your own peace. Oh, Rose, forget them. Ignore them. They don't matter, but we matter...we have to survive. There is no other way. Not right now."

"You forget them. Can you?" She sobbed.

"I can't. We have to live."

"It cuts me off from the whole world...at church, in the town. People -- will they care that much? If I can't go to your home, everyone will see. They will all think the same thing. John, we can't let this happen."

"It's only for awhile. I'll find something, some way."

"I never thought about sin with us. Sin seemed to belong to other people, or to the Bible, not to us," she said.

He didn't answer, for he couldn't think of anything to say.

CHAPTER TEN

The truck pulled up in front of the courthouse, and Rozella and John were suddenly confronted with their problems. They clung to each other as they walked up the sidewalk toward the heavy steel doors. They were alone on this day so important to them, and they felt cold and uninvited.

The courthouse doors swung open. They doors had meshed glass inserts, which made it look like an entrance to a prison. Maybe it was, because the local jail was in the rear of the building. The floors were shining with multiple coats of varnish, while the hallways remained dark and musty smelling. Small signs protruded from the doors along the hall, announcing the offices within. They searched for the county clerk's office and found it on the first floor. There was no one in front of them at the counter. Marriages were not many during this season, or during this time of depression. The forms were simple. It didn't take long to fill them out. They paid their fee to the clerk who seemed to ignore them, as if they were applying for a dog's license. Then, they left.

There were directions posted on the wall, which pointed the way to the Justice of the Peace. It was all so business-like. They could have been clearing a title for a car, or buying a hunting license. Rozella felt divided from herself, unfeeling, and observing, as a spectator might. She had never imagined that it would be like this. However, she had never imagined it at all.

The Justice of the Peace was a stout man, who left his false teeth out because they hurt his gums. Gruff in manner, he did the job, as he called it, briefly and abruptly. Before she knew what had happened, they were married. There was a simple gold band on her finger, the ring that had belonged to John's mother. It was not hers. She looked up into John's eyes, searching for some sort of feeling. Someone had to feel something, and she felt numb. This was some sort of strange dream. It couldn't be real.

As the sky became darker, snow began to fall. One by one the lights of the town came on and the buildings began to look warmer with the light.

"Well, we can go get a wedding supper, anyway," John announced. "It will be our celebration." He turned toward the restaurant in the center of town.

"I don't feel married, yet," Rozella said, in a puzzled tone. I thought that I would."

"I don't feel any different myself. Maybe we're not supposed to." John answered, as he opened the door of the truck.

The restaurant was lined with booths on each side of the room, shiny looking leather seats with tables between them. There were not many people in there so early in the evening. The waitress leaned over the counter talking to a man who was drinking coffee as he listened to her complaints.

Rozella and John waited patiently while she concluded her conversation. "Yeh, what'll it be?" she asked, looking them over as if trying to determine if they could spend the price of a meal.

"Could we...what is on your dinner menu?" John asked.

"The full menu?" she wanted to know. "It's fifty cents, you know."

"Do you have any hot beef sandwiches?"

"For a quarter each."

"Okay. Bring us two, with coffee, please." He answered.

"I never...I have never eaten in a restaurant before," Rozella confessed, as she adjusted her coat and scarf in the seat beside her. "It's very expensive. How did you get the money?"

"Hannah gave me a couple of dollars for the occasion. Seems like it ought to be some kind of celebration."

"It is—for me," Rozella smiled.

"For me, too, Mrs. Queist." John answered her smile.

"That sounds so strange to me. I suppose it will for quite awhile. I don't think I will tell the children at school, not until I leave. What do you think?"

"Perhaps it would be better. The bigger ones, the boys, like to tease. They might make it difficult for you."

"How long do you think I can teach, John? You know how they are about pregnancy." She whispered the last word.

"As long as you don't look big, as long as you don't act sick. The kids notice anything yet? You've been sick." John moved the salt and pepper shakers around the table nervously.

The waitress brought the sandwiches, dropping them down on the table, as if they were hot. She also laid the bill down before them, and stood there waiting to be paid. As she left with the coins in her hand, walking toward the cash register, Rozella began to answer.

"Tina has seen me sick, but I told her it was the flu. Lots of people have had the flu."

"That's true. Some of it is the flu, and some of it is from eating food that is rotten. Frozen vegetables. Some have eaten meat that they have tried to keep. Got to keep it frozen, or can it. Most people can't do anything to freeze the meat but throw it up on the roof until spring."

"The Bjornson boy died. Surely, that wasn't what caused it." Rozella looked up from her plate, where she was cutting the sandwich into bite size pieces.

"No one knows for sure. The county coroner doesn't say much about what people die from these days."

They ate their sandwiches, which were thick and hot, and covered with heavy gravy. It was the best meal that Rozella had eaten in several days now. With the early days of her pregnancy and her nerves, she had not eaten much. As they left the restaurant, they saw a scale next to the front door. It had a mirrored front, and a large question mark painted upon the mirror: **Discover your Future** it stated in large letters. John Looked at it, and then at Rozella. "I think we ought to invest a penny on such a special day as this," he said.

"Let's do it. Maybe it will tell us if we will have a boy..." She looked around to see if anyone was listening to the conversation. The waitress and the man were again deep in small talk. It looked like he was making progress because she was leaning over further and smiling.

John put his penny in the machine. "Stand on there, Rose. It will weigh you. You need to know how much you weigh, anyway." She stepped upon the flat square in front of the mirror, seeing herself in the distortion of the glass. A worn coat falling open, a wool dress of coarsely woven maroon threads, and her hands trembling. In spite of herself, she was still shaky. It had been a frightening day, one of unstated needs that kept evading, shifting and losing themselves. There were unspoken things that lay between them. The cardboard fortune plunged out of the machine on a ticket. She took it in her hand and began to read:

This will be your year of happiness, but beware of those close to you who may wish you harm.

"How strange," she handed it to John. "I'm glad it will be our year of happiness. I just hope it won't be the only year of happiness."

Then they left, the door banging shut on them, closing in the warmth of the restaurant. The truck was cold and uninviting as they climbed back into it. Smells of oil and gasoline mingled with the frosted air. John had to crank the truck in order to start the motor. It had turned very cold.

"Right now, I am reminded that we get to spend the whole night together for the first time," he said as he climbed back behind the steering wheel. "Promise you won't wake me up in the middle of the night and send me home."

"That's a promise that I won't have trouble keeping," she smiled, and looked down at the wedding band on her finger.

CHAPTER ELEVEN

The next weeks were filled with many changes, but the happiest changes were those Rozella made in trying to please John. Breakfast for two was much better than breakfast for one, even though it was harder to get out of bed now. His warm presence made her want to dawdle mornings. Since the morning sickness had eased, she wanted to sleep a lot, and there were never enough hours in which to sleep.

The school board had to be notified of the marriage. Rozella had thought of keeping it a secret, but with pregnancy – it was impossible. She would have to tell the board, and it would be necessary to resign, hopefully, not right away.

Nothing was turning out as she expected. Every small thing created a conflict, or turned out differently than she anticipated. Rozella had looked forward to spending long hours with John in the evenings… but he was kept later and later at his father's place. Often it was nine o'clock when he returned to the cottage in the evening and he was more tired than he cared to admit.

"Why so late, John?" she asked one night.

"The chores are endless," he answered, taking off his shoes and warming his feet next to the heating stove. "I keep thinking that I'll be done early. Then, either Hannah or Pa will find something else that has to be done. I don't like staying so late, but…I hate to say anything. I keep hoping they will ease up in time. Maybe it's just that they are upset about my…"

"I don't know why they should be upset. Nothing has really changed."

"Yes. It seems like I'm over there all the time, even more than when I lived there. Maybe it will get better. It has to get better. There isn't even time to get into town and look for work somewhere else," John said in a discouraged tone of voice.

"Don't worry. There's plenty of time to look for other work. I can still work awhile, although the children know about the marriage already. How I dreaded telling them!"

"Why?"

"Because – the biggest boys. They are hard to handle. They make much of a marriage one way or another, with their giggles and stories. With boys it's more like snickering…"

"You won't be there long," John interrupted, "Soon it will be over and you'll be home all day. You can take care of the house and sew."

"It sounds nice, but I really like teaching. I hate to quit, now that I'm learning more about it. I think that I would do better in time because I see things, learn things…you know what I mean?"

"It's like any other job, I suppose. Experience helps."

"How is Hannah these days?" She had been reminded that his family was his job.

"Fine. Why do you ask?"

"The children at school. I hear them talk about her sometimes John, they call her a witch. Some of them, at least. Why do they do that?"

"Who knows why kids do anything? She is cranky. Sometimes she even scares me. Probably it's her unfriendly attitude. My family has always kept to themselves. When people do that, others talk."

"Yes. They talk. I don't hear all the stories, just tidbits. Whenever they realize that I'm listening, they stop talking."

John was falling asleep in the chair. She covered him with an extra blanket. He looked so tired. His work started before light in the morning, taking him away two hours before it was time for school to start. The morning milking, he said. Maybe if he worked hard enough, maybe they would accept the idea of the marriage. Maybe they would get over the anger. Maybe by the time their child was born his family would be friendly, and it would all be forgotten.

His hopes, and her hopes, too, were soon to be dampened. The first Sunday she and John went to church together as man and wife, they were welcomed by most of the congregation as they arrived. But, when Hannah and her father arrived a few seconds after the services began, they sat down on the far right of the church and removed themselves as far as possible from John and Rozella. Throughout the entire service they were stony-faced. After the last hymn was sung, John's family rose and left quickly without speaking to anyone. Their actions made a silent statement.

A few people spoke to John and Rozella as they left the church, but they were careful not to mention that the Queists had been seen that morning. People were embarrassed and didn't know what to say. Rozella felt humiliated. She told herself that she shouldn't have expected friendliness or acceptance, but this display of coldness, as if done to instruct the community made her want to escape.

John became even more embarrassed when he was forced to tell her that he had to leave and go up to the Queist house for dinner after they returned from church. "It's part of the arrangement," he explained.

Her eyes filled with tears. She had known that there was agreement of sorts, but she had not wanted to know what it was. Not knowing left her hopeful. She had not known that she could feel so alone.

"You know that I have to go, Rozella."

"Yes."

"They will give me our share of the food for the week. I promised that I would go each Sunday. My mother…"

"I know. Yes, I know. She reads the Bible. She can't go to church. I wish that I hadn't gone to church. I won't go again. I'm sorry," she started to cry again.

It was the pregnancy, John thought. Later, it would be easier. Getting adjusted was difficult, people said. With a baby coming right away it was worse. She would feel better later. Things wouldn't bother her so much. And, these were just practical matters, things that had to be done in order to survive.

"We don't really need the food, John. We have money."

"We won't have money for long. You'll soon be through working. Might as well take what I have earned. I have put in plenty of hours."

"I suppose. I just hate to see you go."

"I'll be back as soon as possible. Okay?" He left quickly, not wanting to make it difficult for himself. He wanted to be in his home with Rozella. He was tired of the exhausting work during the week. It would have been so good to have one day with her, just one day quietly at home, doing nothing, going for a walk, napping next to a warm stove.

It was a long day for her. The afternoon stretched out endlessly. She felt so abandoned and alone. In the middle of the day, she went for a walk down the road and then, not knowing where to go, she was suddenly afraid that one of the neighbors would see her walking and question where she was going. She felt exposed on the bleak, snow-covered road. So, looking around her to see if anyone was watching, she unlocked the schoolhouse and went in. Sitting there in the unheated schoolroom, at her desk, turning over the papers, she wondered: Who will take this job? Who will sit here next?

She took some colored paper and stencils out of her desk. It would give some purpose to the afternoon. She made pictures to hang up in the room. It was time she changed the decorations. The activity made her feel much better and she left there in a more cheerful mood, returning to the cottage to wait for John.

When he returned after sundown, he was smiling and seemed happy. The basket he carried was full of food. Jars of cream and milk, butter wrapped in waxed paper. Potatoes, carrots and apples and a piece of meat. A half dozen eggs. Queists were careful of how they used eggs. Eggs could be sold. Even if the prices were low, it was a source of income if you could get through the farmer's picket lines, and the eggs were not thrown to the ground and destroyed. The loss of revenue would be unforgivable in the older Queist's eyes. Even if the destruction raised the prices temporarily, the Queists wanted the money now. The basket, Rozella noted, was invitingly full. John's mother had even included bread.

"Did they say that they saw us in church?" she asked. There was still the dim hope that the Queists had been unaware of John and Rozella when they came into the church. There must be some mistake, she had thought.

"No," John found himself lying. He couldn't look at her. He couldn't answer her hope with Hannah's brutal honesty. There was no gentleness in Hannah. She had accosted John.

"You know that we would speak to you if you came alone. You know what we said about your marriage. We meant it. Sooner or later…and most likely sooner, the people around here will know about her pregnancy." Hannah's words were still ringing in his ears.

"I know how you are, Hannah," he had answered. "I know what you said, but Rozella can't believe it. She has been respected since she came here. Now you expect her to accept your kind of treatment?"

"She reaps what she sows, father says. And there is not a better place to get what's coming to her than in church. God can see through her even if other people can't…yet. They will." Hannah was emphatic, and hard.

John couldn't let Rozella know of these bitter words. He found himself wanting to excuse their behavior not for them, but for Rozella. "Forget them," he said to her, kissing her, eager to be with her. The day of rest made her body seem even more appealing to him and he came to her, not wanting to wait until later to make love.

Later in the evening, he told her that his family was going to install a telephone in the cottage. He seemed proud to have one.

"Why? Isn't that expensive?"

"Sometimes they might have to call me. When there is trouble at night, or if they decide to run eggs to town during the night, they can call me. Some people get through at night with their eggs."

"You work so many hours now."

"It might work out better actually. I could come home sooner, if they knew that they could call me back." He was checking the hinges on the front door.

"They could come and get you. It isn't that far."

"It takes time, and anyway, why argue when they will pay for the telephone. It's included in the rent that I pay by working." He swung the door back and forth, after oiling it.

"Of course, it would be good to have one. I was just trying to understand what they are thinking. It's unlike…it's not something everyone has in these times. But, if my mother becomes worse, my sisters could call me. It would be good to have."

"It's just a party line. We probably won't use it for much. Just emergencies."

"The baby, too. When the baby comes, we may need it. But, we haven't even talked about who will help me."

"That's right. We haven't. Let's talk about it. Right now, in bed." He laughed. When he laughed she couldn't think of the worries that went through her mind. Everything seemed better and brighter in his arms. Lonely thoughts disappeared in their closeness. She could close them out. It was a way of becoming quietly accepting. From bewilderment and disbelief, she could move to acceptance by blotting out thoughts. She could come to an almost dream-like trance in which she waited for the baby to be born.

Her body was only showing a small swelling as the child within her grew, and the quietness and dreamlike quality of waiting made her even more attractive to John. There was a translucency about her. She seemed so fragile that he touched her with aching tenderness that only made his desire more strong. His own hands seemed rough and coarse, too much the farm worker's hands, and not tender enough to touch her soft, white skin. She never complained to him. She became almost motherly. The urge to passion often faded from her, becoming enveloped by a need to nurture.

John found himself repeating with her mentally: *after the baby is born...*

CHAPTER TWELVE

Rozella did not go back to church. In her mind was the memory of the avoiding eyes of the parishioners, the feeling of living as an outcast. The family denial of her was too hard on people, too confusing. Everyone was pretending not to know what was happening. It would be easier for John, she told herself, if she didn't go to church. Since he had to go to the Queist home afterward, it would be easier for everyone if he just went to church with them, and she stayed at home. And, it was easier for her to stay at home. The pattern for Sundays was working out, even if it was different than what she had imagined.

After the child is born, it will be different, she dreamed. She dreamed a lot these days.

But, by the time she was three months pregnant, the school board had replaced her and she was at home full time, and the dreams faded.

Occasionally she would try to make a pie, rolling out the crust with an old jelly glass. But, when apples were in the food supply, sugar was not. Planning for cooking was chaotic. The Queist's basket seldom contained sugar and flour both. She asked for flour so she could bake, and then waited for two weeks to get some. John said she had to wait until he bought it in town. The family supply was not adequate.

At times he would come home late to find Rozella sitting on the floor beside a basket of baby things she had made, touching them, holding them in her hands. She had fallen into such a dreamy state that she had forgotten everything. Supper had not been made. Without

John, she rarely ate anything. The pregnancy showed little signs of an increase in her weight. Her face was thinner, the color less bright, and her skin began to look lifeless.

One of those evenings, she looked up at him when he returned saying, "Imagine how tiny the baby will be."

"Did you eat?" he asked.

"No. I forgot. I was busy." She answered.

"Let's get something now." It became a way to get her to eat, pretending that he was hungry.

Another night he found her wandering through the rooms of the cottage in the middle of the night. He had reached for her and found her side of the bed empty. There was the sound of shuffling feet, a slight rattling, and someone tugged at a door. He couldn't see in the darkness for a moment, then suddenly he saw her, the whiteness of her flannel gown a blurred shape against the wall.

"What did you hear?" John asked. "Tell me about it."

"I hear a baby cry. Really. It gets louder and louder."

"Where could that sound come from? Think about it now. There is no one within miles, and the night is very cold. There is nothing but wind. It must be the wind that you hear."

"Yes. Where could the sound come from…the sound."? She repeated, bewildered. "At first I heard it in my sleep; I must have because I kept waiting for someone to pick up the baby, to quiet it, to take care of it."

"It's a dream, only a bad dream," John led her back to bed, tucking her in under the covers, sitting beside her in the dark, stroking her hair as if she was a child. "You imagined it. You think about things too much. Worry, you know?"

"I can't help but think. It's all I have to do. I wish they had let me keep working."

"I know, but you know what the law is like. Some places they wouldn't let you work at all. As soon as they were married some women were let go. There aren't enough jobs. They say the men have to have the jobs to support families."

"A man did take my job." She retorted.

"Yes."

"But, he doesn't have a family. Why did he need my job?"

"He just happened to be available at the right time."

"What was that I heard?" she jumped again.

"The wind…and your dreams."

She seemed better in the morning, but the night's anxiety didn't end. She was drifting, and the baby filled her thoughts. She was endlessly occupied with these thoughts of a life not yet begun. Sometimes she sat and stared for an hour at a time as if her life was all contained within her mind and her body. She didn't want to leave the house anymore.

Her last trip to town had been a bumping and shaking ride. She spent most of her last paycheck on baby clothes, and excused herself from further trips because riding in the truck was too rough.

Winter was appearing along with scattered snow flurries, as the sun withdrew behind the clouds of fall. Days ran together fused by the common denominators of everyday life. Rozella's weeks became marked by letters from home, from Ola. The telephone man came and went, leaving an oak box installed on the living room wall. It rang now sometimes, but it was never for them. Tina came to visit twice, and then stopped coming. Her adoration for Rozella had passed to the new teacher.

Rozella missed Tina, suddenly aware that most of the companionship she had known during her teaching days had been with this young girl, the rest, what little there was, with John. John's working hours grew longer even though the days grew shorter. She read every book in the house, and begged him to bring library books from town. Sometimes she tried to read the Bible now, a childhood copy that belonged to John, but it always filled her with fear and she would put it aside with strange feelings of discomfort. Even the words would not accept her; she found the Bible both confusing and accusing.

She wrote long letters to Ola and then was embarrassed to mail them, so tore them up and put them in the stove to burn, burning up the thoughts and painful feelings she couldn't understand.

The cottage was quiet all hours, only the clock marring such perfect silence, quiet as if waiting for something. As it waited, fall came into the air. The leaves changed colors and the garden foliage faded and drooped. Her body was now swollen, and the child moved and kicked within her. She watched the leaves fall, and saw frost in the mornings. She felt an urgency within her that could not be explained.

The days and weeks grew interminably long. As the clock counted off the minutes, she waited and waited for some voice to break the silence. Often, as John did not return until midnight, she sat sleeping in a chair, still waiting, dreaming before the fire in the stove.

John... the sun is good...it is warm...water...water wrapping me... so nice...so warm...this floating against it...into it...it runs into me... through me...reach to draw it in...it pulses...it grows...swells...I ride... dream of warmth...it holds me...what is the warmth...it is wet...John, my back...there is pain...no...no...not now...keep eyes shut...push it away...push...John...he is gone...John...he won't answer...where is he...at the house...the big house...gone...repairing the roof... wetness ...is this my bed...my sheets...my hands...they are in blood...warm... my hands...the blanket...John...where did the waves go...hurt...hurt my back...it tears...who is pulling me apart...the baby...my God...this is what it is...my legs...it can't be...the baby...pain...voices...voices... come and go...talk about the baby...about a woman... woman...me?... the woman screams...who is she...it is me...the baby lodged...can't pull it...she is unconscious...no, I'm not...I'm here...why can't you hear me...I am shouting to you...my mouth moves...can't you hear...Rozella...who is Rozella...I am...listen to me...I am behind the...who is behind the pelvic bone...it will die...they are saying...don't say it...it's not true... can't you hear me...she may die...who is She...not me...not Rozella...you just won't hear me...I float...like the water...who is crying...a man... surely, it isn't a man, men don't cry...God doesn't weep no matter what happens...something is tearing...the pain...I fall through the cloud...I hear the tearing...my flesh...my body...how can I hear it tear...cold steel...and instruments...a man's voice says you must turn the baby... another man weeps...it can't be...I dream...funny smell...makes me float again...like an angel looking for cloud...someone screamed...me...my mouth...was it open...I was swimming in the sky...God, it hurts...the pain...someone tears me apart...two people have my legs...I see them... they pull and pull...I hear someone...there is crying...sharp, shrill...a baby...my baby...my son, someone said a boy, my son...where am I...help me, please help me to find myself...see...see...I can't see the baby...

The cloud, which floated through her mind, was beginning to clear; she could see shapes forming, dark and shapeless forms were weaving in and out of the cloud above the bed. She blinked her eyes as if to clear them. A black form was walking through the cloud; it held a bundle. The bundle was laid beside her, and she reached out to touch it. The blackness faded back into the cloud, and the bundle remained. Her fingers reached to touch the soft being. They ached with a weakness, as if stretching was too painful. Was it love? Her fingers pained her. The blanket was filled with softness wrapped in flannel, and it was warm like the down on a duck's belly. It moved, so slightly. Her hands were closing to clutch and hold it, her mouth moved in the silent mouthing of the words that ran through her head, but couldn't come out. Her vision cleared and the small pink face of a baby came into focus, the mouth opening and shutting as if trying to make words, as she was doing…Son…little son, you try to talk like I do…and no one hears… it's all right…I hear. I will always hear…her fingers caressed his tiny face. He squirmed in his blanket and began to cry. The cloud floated in again, and it overcame. Her arms were striking out, trying to push it away. She searched for the baby again…he is there…I know it…I held him…give him back…the black figure came through the cloud…then left…and Rozella's arms were empty…why will no one listen? I shout and no one hears…I can't make my mouth move…sleepy…can't stay awake…that smell…I won't sleep…not now…

Mama had put the baby in her arms. "Careful now, don't trip. You're a big enough girl to tend a baby. Put him in the basket. He's asleep." Sun shone across the bed, blue and white squares of quilt playing games with patterns. Mama was smiling, now that the long night had passed. Her brown hair was brushed into a wide braid that hung over her shoulder and down unto one breast. The muslin nightgown was parted where the baby had nuzzled. Before she closed the gown, Rozella saw the large nipple, milk running out of the brown circle, and down across the white expanse of skin. She could smell the warmth, smell the milk, and something else… something tightened in her tummy with a fierce pain, and Rozella looked down at the sleeping baby in her arms, put her smallest finger in his fist, and watched the tiny pink and white fingers curl around her finger.

"Yes, Mama, I can do it," she said.

CHAPTER THIRTEEN

With the smell of coffee boiling, the red geraniums blooming on the windowsill, and the wallpaper patterns of flowers came into focus. Back in the real world, Rozella blinked her eyes and this time did not lose her vision, no cloud came to blind her and cut her off from the world. She could open and close her mouth and found that it followed her commends. Who was that in the kitchen? John? She called, "John?" Her voice was again her own.

"Yes?" A woman's voice answered, and Rozella could hear footsteps.

"Where is John?" Rozella asked her, knowing the answer before Tillie could speak.

"At his father's house…with the baby."

"The baby is all right?"

"Fine, but you are ill. The birth was too difficult. You'll be a long time healing. They are feeding the baby on a formula and he is fine. Hannah is keeping him for you. John looks in on him."

"When will John be back? Will he bring the baby?"

"John will come at night after the chores are done," Tillie answered.

"How long have I been laying here?" Rozella wanted to know.

"You've been drifting. No wonder you don't know. Two, three days now. John comes home late in the day. He'll be here. Just sleep and rest. Now that you can eat again, you'll get stronger faster."

"The baby, Tillie? Will I see him? Doesn't the baby come home at night with John? Couldn't he?"

"Not yet. You can't care for him. You haven't been able to care for yourself. Later…when you are stronger. You haven't even been awake to feed him. Somebody had to take him. Hannah wanted him. She acts like an old hen. The baby is just like John. He is John all over again. Hannah looks so hard that we always thought she wasn't the motherly type, but you ought to see her. She acts soft as butter with that child of yours."

"I haven't even seen him. My son – and I haven't even seen him." Tears were running down her cheeks, and she was embarrassed to be seen that way.

"You have seen him, Rozella; you were too sick to remember. You held him in your arms. Think now what is best for the child. You are too weak to even stand up. .How could you care for him?"

"Couldn't John? I wish…couldn't John bring him home at night?"

"After awhile, when you are stronger. Right now, you will need to sleep all night through to get your strength back. You're not a strong woman, Rozella. Perhaps you will have no more children."

"What did you say? No more?"

"Well," Tillie blushed, as she had not meant to give this bit of news, "the birth was very difficult for you. You have been damaged, and it will take a long time to heal. Pregnancy could be dangerous for you. But don't think about it now. Only worry about getting well. The doctor will explain it to you later. You don't want to be pregnant anymore, at least – not right now. How about breakfast?"

Rozella didn't answer. Her body was responding to the smell of food. It was an honest hunger, and a sign that she was mending. But, her mind was still confused by what had happened. Her baby, living and well, but in Hannah's hands. Hannah didn't approve of Rozella. She had judged her, and counted her guilty. John wasn't guilty, only Rozella. Maybe... Maybe Hannah would be different now: maybe her feelings for the child would change things. Maybe.

"Yes, I would like something to eat, Tillie. Something in the kitchen smells good. And, I smell coffee"

Tillie brought her a tray with hot coffee thick with cream, and biscuits topped with butter. Her morning in Rozella's kitchen had not been wasted. She had been busy baking biscuits with ingredients she had brought from her own home. She had noticed the empty shelves and Rozella's thin frame. She saw there was very little food in the house, certainly not enough for a woman recuperating from childbirth. It's a good thing the doctor put the baby on formula, but it's not good for Rozella, Tillie thought. It means there is no need to keep any food in the house. What will Rozella eat when I don't bring food anymore?

Rozella could not eat as much as Tillie offered. The days of illness and drifting consciousness had left her with an appetite smaller than she imagined. Coffee tasted delicious, and so did hot biscuits, but only one biscuit filled her flat and empty stomach.

"I'll bring you some fruit later, after you have had some time to make room for it," Tillie said, understandingly. She had brought a jar of her canned peaches along and she could open them for Rozella later.

"What time is it? What day is it? I have lost my sense of time, and I feel like a stranger."

"It's Tuesday, Rozella. You have lain there since Sunday night. John found you on the floor after he returned from the evening church services on Sunday. He was a long time getting through to the doctor. By the time he reached the doctor, it was midnight and you had bled considerably. You were badly torn when they brought the baby."

"What do you mean – brought the baby?" she asked Tillie.

"All I means was that the baby had to be pulled out with instruments like big tongs."

"Was the doctor here to do that? Who delivered him, Tillie? Who? Did you? Tillie?"

Silence.

"I suppose it doesn't matter," Rozella spoke as if to herself in subdued tones, but I just wanted to know. There seems to be a memory…some things that I'm trying to remember. I wasn't out all the time. Was I?"

"It was Hannah," Tillie answered her at last.

"Hannah? How could she do it?"

"With instruments they use for calves. They need pulling and turning, too, you know. I know you didn't expect her to be here, but she was the first to come. John ran back to their house. She came, then me. And, my husband. I helped. She did her best…she…"

"I know. She is good with animals." Rozella looked at the wall. "It is all the same. Only sometimes…never mind."

Tillie didn't answer, but her silence was not without understanding. It was a secret knowledge that women share. To talk about these things would seem to verify them; not verbalized perhaps they could be forgotten, as if erased.

"I want to see my baby," Rozella brooded aloud.

Tillie busied herself removing the tray. There was nothing she could say.

Hours passed and Rozella dozed while Tillie worked around the house, scrubbing floors that were already clean, and dusting furniture that had no dust. Rozella woke to notice that the leaves on the trees were gone now. The fresh air that filled the room through a window was full of the smells of fall. Through the window came the sound of the children in the schoolyard, shouting as they played. It was a familiar sound.

"Did you see the quilt square I have started?" Tillie asked. "This is a new one. A pattern I sent away for."

"Where did you get it?" Rozella asked, not really caring.

"*The Workbasket* from Chicago had some new patterns. Couldn't buy new material, so I'm cutting up some dresses that belonged to my mother. I found them put away in an old trunk. They seemed to be good material. What do you think?"

"It looks good," Rozella noted, her mind wandering and remembering the baby things she had made, wondering if all the baby's things had been taken to Hannah. Her stomach turned over. She thought for a moment she would throw up. Nauseous. The cloth Tillie held out for her approval smelled strongly of mothballs. Was that what made her feel nauseous?

"The colors are still bright. The material will do fine, Tillie," she responded. It was true. The colors were still strong. When the mothball smell washed out, the quilt would be like new. We cut and sew, and cut and sew. Material outlasts people, and we cut up other people's memories to sew them into our own. Why am I thinking this way? When will John be home? He will be late. They will work him as long as there is light to see…she slept again, suddenly tired.

The light was on, and Tillie sat in the faded carpet rocker patiently stitching away when Rozella heard the door open and footsteps cross the kitchen floor. The footsteps came toward the doorway, but it seemed an eternity. All of her waking moments had crawled toward this one moment. Why had she needed John so much? Couldn't' she be the typical farmer's wife, stoic and accepting? Why had she needed to turn to the wall again and again, hiding her tears from Tillie, who only pretended not to see?

Once in the middle of that afternoon, Tillie had tried to explain awkwardly that all new mothers feel blue. She had reminisced with Rozella about her own babies, telling how she had cried for days after the last one was born. It had been right in the middle of threshing time, Tillie told her, and she had cried right into the pans of bread dough that she was making for the threshing crew. Her husband was patient and understanding. He had just ignored her and pretended not to see as he waited for her to get over it." It's like having your period, I suppose", she mused, as if to herself, "you are blue for days, and suddenly it's over and you feel like yourself again. There's no point in bothering the men about it. They never really understand."

But, you had your baby, Rozella wanted to say. I don't even have my baby to hold. I feel so alone. You are here, Tillie, her eyes said, but I am so alone, except for you.

So, it was with tears that she greeted John that evening. It seemed like they had been apart for years. He held her closely and she could feel his tears on her neck. She patted him tenderly on the shoulders, knowingly. He wasn't supposed to cry either. She wouldn't tell Tillie, who had retreated into the kitchen, and was packing up her sewing things about to leave for her home where she would work another six hours doing family things that she had left undone.

"The baby, John?" How is he?"

"Fine. He is fine. He eats well, and cries very loud. I see him every time I come into the house for coffee, or lunch."

"What do we call him? I want to call him John."

"It would be too confusing with both of us called John. I don't want him to be called Little John."

"Well, if we name him John Daniel, we could just learn to call him Danny."

"The family wants to call him John, too. It's me. I don't want the confusion. If we don't call him John, I'll agree to name him that way."

"We can still think of him as John. Maybe it will make him like you. I want him to be like you…only more free…to be anything he wants to be," her voice trailed off.

"So, we'll call him Danny, then, from Daniel in the lion's den, and he will be different from me."

"He's bound to be a little different. What does he look like? I remember holding him, but I don't remember the color of his hair. I only remember his red face."

"He has black hair and his eyes look black now. They may change later. Tillie tells me that baby's eye color change during the first six weeks."

"What are they feeding him?" she asked.

"Some sort of canned milk the doctor recommended. We buy it in town."

"But, it must be expensive."

"It has to be."

"I could feed him. I think. Look at my breasts. They are swollen and sore."

"You can't feed him now. You don't have the strength to get up and care for him, to change him, to wash diapers…and he has adjusted to the canned food. He couldn't take your milk now."

"Oh, God. I want him," she cried. Her stomach cramped with knots of pain.

"I know. I know." He patted her gently. "But, we can't help this. You are sick, Rozella.

You don't realize it. You haven't been awake enough to realize how you are really feeling."

"I feel good."

"You haven't tried to stand up. You can't stand up for a week, the doctor says, and then you will have to learn how to stand and to walk. You would faint now, if I tried to put you on your feet. Have you noticed yet the bandages that Tillie changes for you? You are still bleeding, and heavily. It's not an easy thing. You were hurt…damaged by the birth." Changing the subject, he continued, "People ask about you. The families of the children you had in school. Bjornsen and his wife, Bonita. Nickles, what is her name? I tell them that you can't have visitors yet."

"How do they know about me? And the baby?"

"Tillie – coming and going. They know everything that goes on, you know."

"My family? Do they know? I must write to them."

"I wrote. Not much, but a note so they would know that there is a baby. You can write in a few days when you are stronger. There hasn't been an answer yet. Maybe one of your sisters will come and stay for awhile."

"They work. They teach. Mother...is very sick. Dying, I really think. No, they can't come, but they needed to know. I'm glad you wrote."

The door closed after Tillie's quiet departure and they did not notice. He held Rozella closely. It soothed her, warmed her, and she fell asleep again.

Her strength came from within, drawing from nature's regenerative and recuperative powers, and stirring to life her desire to have the baby. She must stand, she must walk, and she must become strong enough to care for him. Her body bloomed, as if in reflection of her hopes.

Tillie forced her to stand on her feet, and then to take steps slowly. Proudly as a child, she would look forward to showing John what new thing she had done during the day. Her family wrote their congratulations, in broadly scrawling letters on coarse lined paper. Ola sent baby clothes, embroidered sacs, and carefully hemmed diapers. Reluctantly, Rozella sent them with

John...to Hannah, so the baby might wear them.

Ola's letters seemed to whimper about the hardships of caring for a sickly mother, as well as her own confinement to the house, and her own depression. The letters only made Rozella feel restless and unhappy and dependent as she remembered that she was tying down Tillie, taking her away from her life with her own family.

"You can't keep doing t his, Tillie. It's too much."

"It won't be long now. You are stronger each day."

"I can do it now. You could only check with me each day. I can try to do the housework. Soon I can have the baby with me. John says he will bring him Sunday to stay, after He goes to his home for Sunday dinner. I…or part of the day…I can try that day."

"Another couple of weeks, maybe." Tillie remained firm.

"Next week, Tillie. I am much stronger."

"You still need to sleep. Every day you nap. You don't seem to realize, Rozella, how much a baby demands of you. Once you have little Danny home with you, there will be no more naps. He won't pay any attention to your need to sleep through the night, either."

"It can't be that bad. I feel so strong."

"What you feel and what you can do are two different things." Tillie continued with her cleaning.

Tillie continued to bring extra food from her home in her basket each day. The added food helped Rozella to fill out and her cheeks became pink again, flushed with her growing health. In the afternoons, they would sew together, carefully ironing pieces of salvaged cottons before cutting them into small pieces. Rozella started her own quilt top and they worked together each day, but usually after an hour Rozella would begin to nod sleepily and her head would fall down upon her shoulder or her chair, and she would be asleep. Tillie watching her would say to herself, *You are not as strong as you think, young lady*, and she would continue to rock quietly as Rozella slept. Tillie stared out the window and wondered how this small family would piece itself together.

Her thoughts seemed to wrap themselves around the gnarled tree standing in the center of the field, the wire fence around it falling loosely to the ground. The wind, the snow, and the rain had worn the old tree, yet it stood in the weeds and matted growth, which were still clinging to its roots. A wagon wheel lay beside it, decadent with cracked and broken-off pieces of wood. Fallen leaves drifted up against it.

She could ask to see the baby herself. Tillie wondered how to help Rozella. It would be perfectly natural thing to do. How could Hannah refuse a neighborly visit, and a gift for the baby? Telling about the baby, and telling Rozella that she had held him would please her. She could bring the story of the baby back to her, telling her how Danny looked and felt in her arms. Tomorrow, Tillie determined, she would stop at the Queist's on the way to the cottage. It had been years since she had crossed the yard of the Queist farm, but for Rozella – she would do it.

The sleeping face of the young woman was so at peace, so naïve, so unsuspecting, with the light brown hair damp upon her neck as the sun shown through the window and became warmer. Rozella smiled and stirred in her sleep, as if hopeful and dreaming. Let her dream. Tillie said to herself. Let her dream. When dreams go…

She could see that the summer sun had browned Rozella's skin, but beneath the sun-colored glow the bones lay close to the surface, not padded by flesh, nor rounded by an extra bit of food. Behind the abject terror of the times was the certainty of simple folks: That they had done wrong, that God had ceased to love them, or that they were stupid and unable to handle their affairs.

As Tillie fought it in her home when her husband's shoulders slumped and fell in defeat, she fought it everywhere. As the only woman brave enough to curse the government, or to blockade a street, she was feared by the neighbors and shunned by the clergy for her toughness. But, the tough side could turn to tenderness, and in her own humility she did not credit herself for intelligence: she only felt the pain and confusion of the young girl she cared for now.

The years of growing up, knowing the countryside, knowing John's family, and John, only made her softer. She knew the rules laid out by the local clergy, but Tillie's head was harder

than her heart, and she followed the rules despite disbelief. Play the game their way or lose, she had decided at age twelve. Don't believe in love or pretty things. Follow the rules and keep the peace. Love is for books and there is not time for romance in the fields, and there is no place for it. She literally chose her "stud" as carefully as a champion breeder. And that was all marriage was to her: safety, propagation, and avoidance of conflict.

Tillie had watched John along with others as she went to school, knowing his sister Hannah from a distance. Somewhere between John and Hannah in age, she had gauged their differences, and decided she was glad not to be a part of their lives, which always seemed slightly twisted and peculiar. Hannah had been a pale quiet thing who mooned over poetry. Her father often came to see her home after school, walking along behind her as if to drive a pet heifer. There were days when Hannah didn't appear in school at all.

And once Tillie heard her in the woods behind the big house with a man…at least, she thought it was Hannah. There was the sound of crying from beyond the trees and a male voice saying, "You can't allow this. You can't…"

Finally, Hannah never returned to school again. People said she was working at home. Her father wanted her there, it was said. No one saw her except at church, where she gradually became a steely black-clad person looking ten years older then she should have looked.

At that time John was a bundle of shyness. He couldn't speak and kept to dark corners, wearing long black stockings, short pants and white shirts; he shrank from everyone, eyes sinking into his head. The heir, they said. He was also whisked away as if under guard as soon as the last Sunday school class was over. The fabric of their lives could not touch Tillie. She chose for herself when she grew up an "heir" whose health and mental depth were always level: no worries, no mysteries. Breeding people was like breeding animals, Tillie decided; and it simplified life.

Yet, here she was in these hard times, surviving her own chaos, standing strong and speaking out. The farmers collective had burned the trestle bridge to keep the grain from market. All night she had trampled through the black weeds with a kerosene can, pretending to walk like a man. No one the wiser, she woke to the morning clothed in the innocence of her family while remembering the blaze, and a blood-red sky. While some people slept, Rozella for instance, in her waking dream, as if unaware of the world, only troubled by her inability to cope with a family that was twisted by nature: John, who wouldn't ever be strong enough to leave home, who would always be dictated to, and controlled by Hannah, such a bitter person, and the peculiar father they both had. The brother and sister could not see beyond themselves, could not see themselves victims of the spell of the times. They were too close to their own emotional pain to know the world and the cruelty of it. They will blame themselves forever, Tillie thought, by blaming others, and what can be done about that?

Tillie, in her thoughtful way, was the bearer of many worries. As special as Rozella had become to her, and as primary as her concern was, she was aware that Rozella had lost touch with the world. The farmer's problems had been overshadowed by the reality of Rozella's own separation from her baby and the conflict with her husband's family. People were losing their land, and land was life to them.

They were becoming desperate in their losses. Rozella, closeted up in the small bungalow, had been sheltered from all of this even while feeling the repercussions and deprivation of the world. She had known the hunger and the poverty in her own way, but it was a personal thing, not a national catastrophe. Crenston was becoming a ghost town, buildings stood vacant how, businesses wiped out. Most farm towns without the support of the farmer's purchasing power were dying. Children were leaving the land for the cities; yet, the cities were dying and rotten. It's always someone else that you hear about, then, suddenly it's there – it's your next-door neighbor.

The Nickles place had gone into foreclosure. Losing the land was bad enough, but the judges wouldn't leave well enough alone; they had laid on a deficiency judgment, and tried to make Nickles pay for what they had taken away from him. It was land that had been in the family for three generations. He had mortgaged it to buy seed, to feed his cattle, and to survive. Now the family land went to the bank, the loan company, and not just the land, money that they didn't have. The children went without shoes, but the mortgage holders sat back and waited for money to come to them. There was no money anymore. The Nickles family would face the judgment court next week. Papers had been served.

Men talked. Farmers gathered on the corners in the town, anger washing their faces. They talked of ways to stop the judge…they talked of murder sometimes. This was a thing called mob violence, and mob anger: Tillie could taste it, while Rozella slept.

CHAPTER FOURTEEN

The morning was cloudy and Tillie walked the fields, crossing to the Queist place as she promised herself to do the day before. It was a road she hadn't looked forward to taking, a path she avoided when crossing to Rozella's cottage. Hannah always had a way of meeting you with barriers that made you feel embarrassed and clumsy, and…the old man was strange. His eyes would dart about restlessly, and he didn't talk much. Even in church, the two Queists separated themselves from the congregation, protecting their privacy with silence.

As she crossed the porch, she heard a baby cry. How could it be that so much time had passed and she had not yet seen the baby she had helped to deliver? Now, she heard him. It was a healthy cry, a wailing that demanded food. As suddenly as it had begun, it stopped. Then silence hung there blanket-like. She stepped impulsively to the window. Through the lace curtains she could see some of the interior of the room. Cautiously, Tillie stepped closer to the glass.

She could see Hannah holding the baby in her arms, and the look she was giving the child was soft. It was the softest look that Tillie had ever seen on Hannah's usually expressionless face. Hannah was holding a bottle to the baby's mouth, and she gently rocked and crooned to the child as she fed it. When Hannah came closer to the glass, Tillie could see much better. The fern in the window blocked out part of the scene, but she was visible to Tillie, in her usual long skirt, which she usually only wore on Sundays. Now, she was walking back and forth with the baby. Turning now, Hannah faced the window and Tillie jumped self-consciously, feeling sure that she had been seen. Then, she relaxed somewhat as she saw the total woman in the room. Danny was nursing eagerly and hungrily, pulling at the bottle. The lace collar of the blouse Hannah wore was pulled down and the whiteness of it…but, no. Tillie rubbed her eyes. It must be the glass. It must be.

She looked again, drawing even closer. The dress was open, Hannah was smiling into the baby's face, and her right hand held the bottle to his mouth, but the bottle was resting on her bare breast. Her dress was open to the waist, and her large breasts were pushing outward and upward, the bottle nestled deeply into an exposed breast. "Here, here, darling," she was saying and her hand pushed the nipple of her breast up tightly against the bottle's nipple. The other breast hung lower, but her breathing was raising its bareness. "My God," Tillie whispered, "My God."

A coarse voice behind her said, "Did you knock?" It was the old man. She had not heard him come up the steps.

"No. No. I thought I heard the baby cry. It…it…I stopped to listen." Her heart was pounding. Her face was red. Had he noticed? Did he know about this?

"Well, come in then," he said, opening the screen door and reaching for the knob. "Hannah is probably feeding him. He is a greedy little sucker." His smile was like a lingering snicker, or did she imagine it?

Tillie wiped her feet on the old rug in front of the door before she entered.

When the front door opened into the parlor, the room was empty. At first Tillie had been afraid to look up; she was embarrassed to see again what she had seen through the front window. She entered the room looking down at the rag carpets in front of the door, avoiding lifting her eyes.

"Hannah…Hannah!" the elder Queist called loudly. Hearing that, Tillie allowed herself to look up.

"I'm here," the answer came, "Putting the baby in his bed. "What is it?"

"You have…we have company," he replied, "Tillie Sorenson."

"Who?"

"Mrs. Sorenson, you know, from the church," as if there were a half-dozen women she must know, all having the same name.

"Coming," a black clad figure appeared in the doorway of the bedroom. Tillie found herself staring at Hannah's dress, trying to see – trying to prove that she had not imagined what her mind had told her. Fully dressed and buttoned up, Hannah didn't show a sign of the unusual sight that Tillie had seen. Hannah's face was now somber and straight. It was the face that Tillie was accustomed to seeing every Sunday morning.

"Did Rozella send you?" she demanded.

"No, I came because I wanted to see how the little one was doing. If I had something to tell Rozella that would cheer her up, it would be nice." Tillie felt just a little vicious with the last remark. Apparently, Hannah didn't care a bit about how Rozella felt about anything.

"He's fine. Just tell her, he is fine."

"Could I see him? I haven't seen him since he was born." Tillie asked.

"He's sleeping, you know. He just had his bottle."

"I won't wake him. I just want to look at him. Can we tiptoe into the room?"

"For a minute," Hannah conceded.

The old man seemed to enjoy the exchange of words between the two women. Looking from one to the other, his head swinging like a rusty pendulum, a peculiar smile played about his mouth. He must know something about her, Tillie thought. How could he not know?

She followed Hannah into the next room, and making good her word, tiptoed every step of the way. The child slept, it was true, healthfully and deeply, evidently not disturbed by what Tillie had witnessed. His mouth was slightly open, and one hand lay upon the flannel towel that had been used as a sheet. That hand was open and relaxed, the other hand clenched into a fist. His mouth moved into a pucker, and then fell open again. Dark brown hair was showing under the edges of a crocheted cap, and he was well covered with a small quilt. His bed was a clothesbasket, and it was setting on the foot of Hannah's bed, in this small room adjacent to the sitting room.

"He sleeps in here where I can hear him," Hannah said gruffly.

"I don't hear him anyway," her father grimaced. "Couldn't stand too much of that when I get up before it's light. Lucky thing that John doesn't have to put up with it yet. He wakes up early, the baby, that is.

Wants to have his bottle right away, she says. Since I sleep upstairs, I never hear him."

"Rozella thinks she can be up and about next week, well enough to take the baby. She is very anxious about him, and lonely, too."

"Couldn't we bring him over to see her?" Tillie pushed her request forward.

Hannah turned away abruptly, talking as if to the wall. "It is so late when John leaves. Too late for the baby, it wouldn't be good for him." She seemed to be fussing and folding diapers, which lay in a heap on the bed next to the basket.

"I could take him. Like this. Like now. In the morning. She is well enough to be left alone now. I could return the child in the afternoon. It would be easier for you."

"No. No. He is used to his schedule. Don't you know anything about babies? They don't eat well when they are disturbed…moved from place to place. After awhile, when he is older. Right now is too soon." Hannah's face was red when she turned back toward Tillie.

There was a strange possessive force here. More than normal for a new aunt and a tiny baby. Hannah had fear in her eyes, and thrust her body between Tillie and the basket where the baby lay sleeping, her shadow falling between them.

A dark thought crept into Tillie's mind as she remembered that Rozella didn't go to church anymore and she had never said why. John, Hannah, and the old man were there every Sunday. Rozella had gone there once: earlier she had gone every Sunday, although she had never said anything about what she believed. Tillie thought it was her schoolteacher mind, or perhaps shyness, as she didn't want to believe that Rozella could be a non-believer. There was something else here, her instincts said. The air was vibrant with feeling, and the picture of Hannah crooning to the baby crossed her mind once more.

"I'll talk to John," Tillie said.

It seemed a long walk across the bedroom floor, then through the empty living room. The fern lay against t he lace curtains and the leather-covered chair; the horsehair rocker was unmoving against the yellow-waxed boards of a bare floor. Tillie thought she could feel the eyes of the two upon her back, but she didn't look backward, she only spoke as if she could see them. "Thank you for letting me see the baby. I'll tell Rozella that he is well."

The door closed behind her. She pulled on the heavy handle twice, as if it would never close. Then, she turned down the steps and toward the pathway that led through the woods toward the cottage. She was retracing the steps that John took every morning approaching his home, returning to Rozella from his father and mother and Hannah. Where was John's mother? She hadn't been there. People had said she was ill, confined to her bed, only occasionally sitting in a chair. She never went to church any more. Who looked after her while Hannah attended the baby? Was she even still alive? Of course, she must be. There had never been a funeral. Silly thought. Tillie shook her head. Where was John? The old man – always there – watching and listening, but not John.

John was out in the fields already. Tillie could see him as she passed an opening in the trees. He was standing there checking the fencing, as if to measuring its straightness. Clouds were hanging heavily, over-ripe with moisture. The black velvet loam was touched with frost and horse droppings. His horses were waiting alongside the fence, their flesh twitching. His cap pushed back showed the winter whiteness of his brow. His face was still sunburned from summer. Not noticing her on the path, suddenly he dropped his cap, looked up at the clouds and hurried forward, as if to beat the clouds and get his work done before the rain.

She couldn't call to him, for what would she say? There were too many questions in her mind. Even if she found the answers, what could she say to him? Tonight when he returned, she would ask if Rozella could have the baby next week. Don't make her wait any longer, she wanted to plead, it would be better if she needed to help Rozella every day after John had gone to work. He wouldn't need to know that Tillie was there helping. She could let him think that Rozella could handle everything by herself. The baby must go to his mother. Hannah had no right. No right. Why couldn't John see that? Why?

Tillie looked back at John and remembered her own mother saying: you never really know people until you live with them. Tillie had known this family all of her life, yet there was much she didn't know.

She had gone to school with John in the same country schoolhouse across the road. They weren't the same age, but she had been there, too. And after she left, there were the stories told by her younger brothers and sisters. They had called John a "Mama's Boy" and they teased him because he wore white shirts to school. Sometimes they would push him down and send him home crying. They were cruel little monsters, but John would always return, only to become more silent and withdrawn. He never spoke unless the teacher called on him; he never volunteered; yet, he always had the answers down on paper. He was trying hard not to be noticed. As Tillie remembered it, maybe he hoped that he could be left alone. He was pale then, as now, white-skinned.

No white shirt now, John, Tillie thought. In the fields you dress like all the farmers. What was it really like for you? They called you "Mama's Boy," but I haven't seen your mother since I was a child. It was a birthday party, the only one at your place. My mother was more excited than me...I remember...a new dress. Maybe that's why I remember your party...no...there was something else. The dress was all ruffles. Mama sewing for days. This was special!

I didn't know then, but Queists must have been rich. At least then. No one had been invited there for a party before. Mama said they had nice things; laces and china, but they never had a Ladies' Aid meeting there, or anything else. No one went there. Was Mama excited to have me go, or just excited to take me there to see the inside of the house? That had been years ago. What did houses and furniture and china mean to me then? I was a child, older than John, but still a child. Tillie tried harder to remember the inside of the house, the day and the party, as she stood silently in the pathway where she was, looking down at her worn black shoes and not seeing them. Her hands were deep in her apron pockets, a frown creasing her forehead, as she began to remember.

John's mother answered her knock on the door. She was walking then. She had worn   some kind of a soft, cream-colored dress. Her face shown with her smile. Tillie was asked to come in. Her ruffled new dress picked at her bare legs. Tillie felt uncomfortable, and too dressed up. The birthday package felt awkward in her hands; she didn't know where to put it. There were some other children there, all the children she had grown up with. Yet, here – they were different.

There was a large cake on the table. Above the white linen tablecloth it looked huge and was colored pink, the color of Tillie's dress. Tillie had never seen a pink cake before and her mouth dropped open as she stared. "You match," John said. She remembered him saying that.

The two of them had looked at the table silently, counting out the silver spoons and forks. Tillie touched one, stroking the heavy ornate handle as she would a cat's back. It was smooth and slippery. It had the feeling of richness. She would have silver when she married, she determined then, not tin spoons as there were at home. She pushed her package at John, saying, "Here."

"I can't open it now," He whispered.

"Why not? It's yours."

"I have to wait until my mother says I can." Then she saw the other packages on the table. He laid hers with the others, and pulled nervously at his tie.

"I wish this was over, " he said.

"Why? Don't you like parties?"

"Never had one before. My mother wanted it."

"I never had one either, but it looks pretty nice. More presents than I ever see at Christmas," she observed.

"My father says parties are for girls, or babies, and then only if you're rich."

"Aren't you rich?" Tillie wanted to know.

"Father says not. He says he works harder than anyone to make a living. That he just can't live up to my mother's…"

"Mother's what?" she wanted to know, for John had interrupted himself in the middle of a sentence.

"I mean…" the voice trailed off as a hand grabbed John's shoulder. Tillie saw him turned around abruptly by his older sister, who said, "John, you should join the games. You, too, Tillie."

And they were pushed into a group playing musical chairs.

It was the last time she spoke to John that day. He was pulled and pushed by Hannah, who kept him always in the center of things. She never left the two of them alone to talk again. There never was another party. And, Tillie couldn't remember ever seeing John's mother walk again.

Her next memory of John's mother was the memory of an immobile person, the same soft smile, but a woman in a wheel chair. People said they never saw her at the farm. Hannah answered the door at all times, and Hannah controlled the household. Hannah did the shopping. Tillie shook her head, reminding herself where she was, and that she was late. Rozella would be waiting for her, this frail girl who seemed so much an outsider, married into such an odd family.

Rozella was left too much alone, Tillie thought, without friends, without family and sometimes…sometimes, Tillie was sure – without food. But, maybe she only imagined these things. There was so much she didn't know, too much she didn't know about the Queists.

When she opened the cottage door at last, the quietness reached out to engulf her. This time she was more aware of it. It was as if closing the door behind her had cut off the entire world. The only sound was the ticking of a blue enameled clock on the kitchen shelf. She knew Rozella was there, so she did not call out, but went into the next doorway.

Unaware, the girl sat in front of a window, her stitchery resting on her lap. There was vulnerability in the softness of the back of her neck where newly grown hair escaped its pins. She was staring through the window without moving. Tillie followed her gaze to see that her eyes were turned to the schoolyard, the world she had left behind.

Deliberately Tillie bumped into a chair and it slid clumsily on the floor, making a scraping sound. It was enough to bring Rozella out of her daydream and back to reality.

"The child looks well, Rozella. Really," she said. "You don't have to worry about him."

"Did you hold him?" Her eyes lit up with her thoughts.

"No. He was asleep, but he looks strong and well. I think I agree with you, though. It's time John brought him home."

"You do?" Rozella seemed surprised.

"Yes, I can help you for awhile. See that you don't overtire yourself. I'll talk to John this afternoon, as soon as he comes in."

"Oh, I know I can do it. Tillie. I'm stronger than you think. You see – the breakfast dishes are done. Look. I cleaned up the kitchen."

"And, you're not tired?"

"No. I don't feel tired. I've been sitting here doing this because there really wasn't anything else to do. If I had the baby here, I would be busier."

"You certainly would," Tillie said. "How often I have wished for moments like these, Rozella. You will never know, I guess. At least, you will never know until you have taken that full burden upon yourself."

"What do you mean — burden?"

"Oh, I don't mean to sound so harsh, or selfish. Maybe that's it – I sound selfish, but mothers don't ever get through until the youngest child is gone. By then, you are old and worn out. It seems like you never get a moment that doesn't have some sort of demand or need in it from husband or child. You never have a moment that is yours alone, as you have had…just now."

"And that's what they mean: a woman's work is never done?"

"Yes, that's what they mean."

"I don't care, Tillie. I want that. When you have your baby and they take it someplace else, it's just not natural. You wouldn't like it; you wouldn't let someone else take your baby, would you?"

"I know, dear, but some days I would give them all away gladly. Still, I wouldn't keep my bargain for long. I do understand that. We create our own…whatever it is."

"We create our own place, Tillie our place in the world. We create our own family. We couldn't become whole women without them."

"Maybe. Maybe. But tell me, now, what do you hear from your own family? Your mother?"

"She's pretty bad. Really. Every time I get a letter from Ola, I hate to open it. I don't want to read about it. It's another reason I have to be strong and get around. I have to go home to see her, at least once more…"

"Are you so sure, I mean so sure that she won't get well?"

"Yes. They told us a couple of years ago there was nothing they could do. Time was all. The doctor said a year perhaps, depending upon her care. It's degenerative. They can't give her new organs. Ola has worked so hard with her, and Mama is still here. It's been almost two years now." The tears were welling up in her eyes as she spoke of it. "She's still here, but I can't get home to see her. I want her to see the baby, and hold him, just once." She turned her head away, not wanting Tillie to see her cry.

"Now, now. Don't think about those things. They are the Lord's will, you know. That's the only way to think about it, or you will go crazy with thinking. I shut such things out of my mind. That's easiest."

"Nothing else to do," Rozella said, "I suppose there is nothing else we can do. There were plenty of babies at our house, Tillie, but they weren't bottle-babies."

Tillie reached for Rozella's hand and pulled her up and out of her chair. Like an old lady, or a child, Tillie thought. And at the same moment Rozella looked up at her and suddenly wondered about Tillie's age. She seemed so old, so motherly, and so matronly. She had left school at the end of the eighth grade, married when she was fourteen, and had a child when she was fifteen, she had told Rozella. Her oldest child was already more than twelve years old. She had experienced it all. Her hair was even turning a little gray already, but it was her walk, her acceptance, her subdued way of taking everything as it came along that spoke of age. Was it wisdom that was born of living?

Aloud, she said, "Teach me, Tillie. I don't know a thing about it. Our family was big enough, heaven knows, but I didn't pay much attention to the younger kids. They were breast-fed babies, and all I ever wanted was to get away from them – the sooner the better. It was Ola who spent more time with baby-sitting. She still does it. I went away to school as soon as I could. Now…now look at me. I need to know about these things. I should have learned a little. Mama tried to get me to help more, but I refused her, as if I wasn't going to have kids."

"We don't learn these things until we need them usually," Tillie answered her, " we learn all about cooking, sewing, and cleaning, but about babies…we learn the hard way. By doing."

They spent most of the day in the kitchen, the most cheerful room in the house. After talking about how to care for babies and their food and clothing, they lunched together on cheese, heavy bread, and coffee.

Tillie insisted that Rozella lie down and take a nap after lunch, while she did the dishes and swept the kitchen floor.

As she cleaned, washed out a few pieces of laundry, she cooked the evening meal, and time passed. Rozella slept deeply with a rosy glow on her cheeks. It hadn't overtired her to be up and about so much. The thought of the baby coming home seemed to give her strength. She thrived on it, Tillie noticed. Yes, it was the best thing that could be done. As she worked, Tillie's memory turned back to the strange scene she had witnessed that morning. At least, she thought she had seen it. Could it be true? She had only seen through the glass. What a strange thing to imagine about someone, when it couldn't be true? But, if it wasn't true, why did she feel such urgency to get the baby home with its mother? It was best, best – that's all, she said to herself. It had been too long away from its mother.

She heard Rozella stirring in the bedroom.

"Get up now. You must be awake. You have slept the afternoon away. If you take some warm water and wash up, you'll be pretty and bright for John when he comes in for supper. Here, I'll pour water out for you. I washed the shirts that needed laundering and hung them on the line. They should be dry by now."

"When are you going to let me do that, Tillie?"

"Just as soon as you learn how to take care of Danny. First things first," Tillie retorted, going out the door to the clothesline that had been strung haphazardly between the woodshed and the house.

John will soon be home, Rozella thought. When can he bring the baby? Tonight? Could he get Danny tonight?

So, John found them in the evening: ash blonde Tillie in her faded cotton dress and brogues which had been resoled and resoled again with black rubber dime store soles, and Rozella, lost in a maternity smock which hung loosely on her too thin body, tugging at the heavy bed. They were trying to move it against the wall.

"What are you trying to do?" he asked them.

"We're moving it to the corner…to make room for the baby's bed."

"What?"

"You don't know?" Rozella answered. Tillie says I'm strong enough to have the baby at home."

"Tillie does?"

"Yes," Tillie interjected, "she is. With some help from me. I thought last week it wouldn't work. Now I can see differently."

"Has she improved so much over Sunday, Tillie? Only one day that you were not here, you know. One day. Can't be much change in a day."

"It seems like that would be true, John. Usually it is. But you can't keep a mother from her baby. Look at her. Just look at her and see. The thought of having him home gives her strength."

"Rozella, is it true? You are so thin, and weak." Without thinking about it, he moved over to help push the bed against the wall.

She looked up at him and there was no denying the radiance of her smile. "John, I know I can do it. Tillie says he is a strong baby. Caring for him can't be that much work. Could we, could you get him tonight? Bring him home, please. I don't want to wait another minute."

"Not now. Not tonight. Tillie must go home now to her family. You'll have no one tonight to help you."

"I have you, John, his father."

"But neither of us knows anything about babies, how to feed them, how to change them. What if he gets sick in the night?"

"We'll learn then. All parents learn sometime."

"Tillie?" He turned to her.

"Yes, John. The time has come for the little one to come home. You must bring him home. Just looking forward to it has strengthened her. You can see that."

"Hannah will miss him. You don't know how much he means to her."

"I know. I could see; but Rozella is the child's mother. Tomorrow – promise you'll do it tomorrow, in the morning, so he can have all day to get used to his home." Tillie could feel her cheeks burn with anger. His hesitation was setting her afire. Why? Didn't he want to be a father? Was he so weak against Hannah's will? Rozella had never shown by word or manner that John wasn't happy to become a father, or ready. Even though Tillie, as all the women, could count out the months of pregnancy very easily. Hannah, with her strangeness, could never give the child what his mother could give him.

It wasn't as if Rozella could go back to the school; society didn't allow that. There were the laws and the courts. Someone had always said that a woman couldn't teach once she became a mother, not unless she became a widow and her children were grown. Some schools wouldn't let a woman marry, or even date a man. When a woman's children were grown and she was widowed, usually it was too late. Then, the school boards would say that she was too old. The school boards were the local people after all, so opinion governed them. In order to stay a teacher, you stayed an "old maid."

Did the Queists want Rozella for a farm hand, to plow fields and cut grain? Did Hannah really love the child? Tillie thought about these things. "I'll be here early, John," she said decisively, as if trying to force him mind into acceptance. "Then you can bring Danny back early. Rozella and I will have the whole day to get adjusted."

She left them to put the evening meal on the table for themselves. Banging pots and pans about in the kitchen eased her anger with the world and its ways. When they had seated themselves at the table, she went home, back to her family where problems seemed simpler.

Rozella's eyes were round and dark and nervous. She twisted her hands together in her lap and stared at her plate. The food grew cold.

"Eat now, little one," John smiled brightly, trying to cheer her, to see her smile again. "What's wrong? Are you nervous? We can wait, you know, if you want to. Tillie doesn't have to have her way about this."

"It's not her way, John. I want him with me."

"Why aren't you smiling then? You looked so happy."

"I'm not sure. Frightened. I feel afraid of something, and I don't know what it is."

"Nonsense. Are you worried about your mother?"

"Yes. But it's not that." She couldn't say herself what had laid the chill across her shoulders, what had made the shadows on the glass rise and distort themselves against the evening light. She shivered and words wouldn't come.

Later, in bed, when he drew her close to him, her body felt cold to his touch, and almost stiff with fear. It only made him desire her more—this tender frailty, the bones he felt beneath her skin, which seemed translucent in the moonlight. The warmth of her had vanished and he struggled to find it, his hands growing more demanding, and his lips heavy on hers. His mouth was all around her breast, but not daring to push or to press. He might still draw milk. As he raised her head, he felt a warm trickle on his lips and saw it run down over the curve of her white breast, still firm with unused milk.

His hands were on her legs, fingers between the silky parts, looking for the lost warmth, some fire beneath this ice. She was dry, as if not knowing her was there. She seemed not to breathe; she was so still. He lay upon her, his weight impressing with his presence. He couldn't think of what to say; he could only feel the bursting heat of his need pressed against her. He couldn't help himself; pressing harder and faster, the tip of him trying to find a way into her, pushing against her naval again, and then. The agony. The pulsing. Then, it was beyond him in its seeking, and spent itself, pulsing and surging into its own wetness, a witness to the silent division of feeling.

She wouldn't face him. Her head was turned away. Tears ran down her cheeks.

"I'm sorry. I'm sorry." It was all he could say.

"Afraid. I'm afraid to be pregnant again. Afraid to have another baby. Afraid you won't want a baby. Don't want our baby. Don't you want him, John?"

"Of course I want him. It's you. You're not strong."

"And Hannah?"

"Hannah loves him."

"I haven't even held him yet, John."

"You will. You will." He tried to ease her, but much later in the night he woke to see her still laying there looking out of the window. The moon cast shadows on her face, making the circles beneath her eyes darker than usual. Her thin hands were clasped now and lay above the quilt, quietly. He couldn't tell if they were at rest or not. He couldn't speak for he didn't know what to say, or how to explain his own feelings…even to himself. So, he remained silent and pretended not to notice that she was still awake.

When her eyes opened the long darkness seemed to flow away into the sunlight of a new day. John had risen early without awakening her. He was gone.

She walked about the house, bare feet feeling the morning coolness of the floor, a thick blanket wrapped around her body. He had left so early, then, to get the baby. Just as he promised.

She was finishing dressing when Tillie appeared in the door, also early because she was anxious. Tillie poured some coffee for the two of them and they sat at the table as if drugged by silence, waiting.

John knew when he left so early that it would not be too early for Hannah. His family was always up before light, as if fearful to miss an hour of working time. Yet, his mind and body hesitated and his steps were slow. The old porch was icy where the frost had melted, and froze again. The dogs, knowing John's scent, stirred from their sleeping place near the front door. He stood there a moment trapped by his own fears. He heard the baby cry, the sound coming from deep within the house. Then, all was still again. Now, the only sound was the stirring noises of the chickens as they moved about the yard. Their low sounds mixed with the wild birdcalls from the woods.

The door opened abruptly and Hannah almost collided with him. "What are you standing there for, John? You frightened me." She had her jacket on and was about to go out to the woodpile. He waited while she picked up some choice pieces of wood, holding the door open for her when she returned.

"Hannah," he began.

"Want coffee? She asked, oblivious to his nervousness. "Pa's already out in the field. Coffee's still warm."

"Hannah, I want to take the baby home to Rozella."

She turned quickly. "Yes. We talked about that before. When she is well."

"Today, Hannah. I promised them today. This morning."

"Who?"

"Tillie and Rozella."

"What does Tillie have to do with this?"

"She says that Rozella is well enough to take him."

"How would she know…she's not a doctor."?

"She's a mother, and she has been with Rozella every day. She knows."

"She may know about Rozella, or think she does, but she knows nothing about the child. She only looked at him, once, for just a moment. Rozella…she doesn't k now a thing about babies. He'll get sick. She won't know what to do."

"Tillie will help her. She'll teach her."

"It's not the same. Bottle babies are different. Tillie raised hers in the normal way. Danny has to have special formulas. The doctor told me, you boil bottles. If it's not right, he'll get colic."

"You can tell me what to do. I can tell them. Or, Hannah you could come with me now. We'll take him home."

"Come with you John? Into the place that she turned into a… John, we, I…the baby is yours, your blood, our blood. He is a Queist. Rozella is not."

"Why not, Hannah? She has our name now."

"She got it by…by…"

"By marriage," he said, and then looked away.

"By pregnancy. You haven't forgotten? A fancy schoolmarm. Too good to work in the fields. Too good to stay home and care for her own mother, her dying mother, by the way. People tell me what goes on. She had to come here, showing off her fine ways, her lace dresses and high heels. All she knows is in books, except when it comes to men, John. She fooled you. Still does, evidently. Someday, you'll know, John. You'll know what kind she really is."

"She's my wife, Hannah, She's the baby's mother. You don't even know her."

"I know her. Better than you do." The bitter words dropped between them heavily, "John, leave him here…where he belongs."

"I can't. She'll never be well without him. She grieves, and how would you know about a mother and her baby? You never leave this place."

"Experience, John. The years give a woman more than books."

"Please get him ready. If I'm to work today, it's time for me to take Danny home to his mother."

"Then promise to bring him with you every Sunday. He should be christened soon, and Mama looks forward to seeing him, too. She doesn't say much, but it makes her happy to be able to see him."

"Every Sunday?"

"As you belong with us, so does your son," she answered, but the plea seemed more for her than for the child's grandmother. John could almost forget Hannah's hatred for Rozella as she said that. She had looked at him with warmth in her eyes. But, he remembered that Rozella hadn't learned how to hate, so how could she be so much the object of such resentment and judgment? What was it that burned in Hannah?

Hannah turned abruptly and went into the next room to pack up the baby's things, roughly tossing them into a box as if she didn't care. "The bottles..." she was saying, describing the boiling and the mixing. John breathed a sigh of relief as he listened absently, looking at his boy now sleeping soundly.

"Come with me, Hannah. You would...you could like her."

"Never. She's a...I'll never cross any road to meet with a woman who..."

"Jesus," John whispered.

"Don't swear. I'll walk part way with you. Carry him, so you won't have to make two trips." She picked up the baby, holding him closely and when she held him, there was a softening of her face once more when the baby's head cushioned itself against her. She wrapped another small quilt about him.

With the box of clothing and bottles and the clothesbasket bed filling his arms, John followed silently. He had not yet held his own son, but John had never seen a man hold a baby except at the altar for christening. Hannah held the child tightly. She walked slowly without speaking and they were swallowed up by the silent world of a country morning

John tried to remember when he and Hannah had last walked this way together. One day, years ago, when he had come down the path returning from school, she came out of the woods, stickers and burrs clinging to her skirt, her cheeks red. She had been picking berries, she said, and seemed breathless. There was a mistiness and a softness about her that day, he remembered. She had walked home with him playfully teasing and laughing. Sometimes she stopped and looked back along the empty path that day, and her eyes would go blank and she would not hear what he was saying. It had all been so long ago, but the sun and the quietness, and the path—brought it all back into his memory.

Now, he only saw her silent back in front of him, firm and solid, as unwavering as her footsteps. There was no hesitation, though he knew she hated giving up the child. The buoyancy of the young Hannah he remembered was like a hazy dream. The light shadows of the barren trees fell across them unseen, unnoticed, as familiar as the walls of an old house…in the way that eyes can wear smooth the scenery as hands wear away a wall. As the woods thinned into the out buildings near the cottage, she stopped in the center of the path.

"This is far enough. You can take him now," she said, but she did not move

John set the box and the basket upon the ground and moved toward her. She stared toward the cottage, which was now visible. Her eyes were dark and she held the child even closer, not seeing John reaching out.

"Hannah, won't you come in with me?"

"No, " she answered hoarsely, turning her head away.

"I'll take him, then." And, he held out his arms.

She laid the baby in his arms. "Careful now, hold his head. He is too small to hold up his head by himself. Keep him covered."

John felt the warmth of the baby's body, and then felt him squirm and resettle himself into his arms. Suddenly he realized he had never held a baby before and this one was his own. Until this moment, Danny had seemed more like Hannah's child. He shook his head, as if to clear this thought, for with it – he had forgotten Rozella, the baby's mother, and the reason for the baby's existence.

"Thank you, Hannah."

Her head was turned away still. She wouldn't answer. He left her there standing stoically on the pathway. Tillie, watching through the window, saw the dark form of this woman against the morning mist, a hawk-like hovering thing among the trees watching John who walked carefully carrying his child home to its mother. Hannah stood there, beyond her self-imposed boundary, as if a chalk line had been drawn before her feet.

Inside the cottage, Rozella didn't see the silent drama that Tillie witnessed. She only knew that John was there, and Danny was with him. She ran to the door, flinging it open. Her face was bright and she was again as John had first seen her – vital and alive.

"Baby. Baby. Little Danny," and she took him from John, holding him high in her arms, and rocking him back and forth, crooning and talking to him in a mother's language, as if the two of them had been conversing for days. "Oh, yes, yes, I missed you so. Did you know you would be coming home to Mama? Are you happy? Mother's happy. She missed you so…" She walked with him, taking him through the rooms as she would a visitor. "See, this is our kitchen, where you and Mama an Daddy will eat, our bedroom…and your bed will be right there, so Mama can hear you in the night." They heard her telling the baby all these things and as John looked at Tillie, he saw the moistness of tears welling up in her eyes as she listened to Rozella.

"Well, I'll go pick up the basket and his things," he said.

"Yes. We'll need them," Tillie answered, wiping her eyes with her apron before she looked back through the window to see the figure on the path turn and disappear.

CHAPTER FIFTEEN

It was noon when the old man pulled himself up to the kitchen table, scraping the chair legs on the floor. He threw his cap down beside the chair and began to help himself from the serving dishes, which had been set before him. John lingered over the washbasin drying his hands, not eager to talk, or to listen; and Hannah busied herself at the kitchen range. Her back was turned as if she could disconnect herself from the scene.

Hannah and John knew their father's habits. He would not speak until his meal was finished. As children they had learned to eat in silence; and, as adults they learned to pull away from him during meals and keep occupied with other things. Only on special days did they actually all sit at the table together and try to carry on a conversation.

"You were late this morning, John. I was half way through the milking when you finally got here. What happened?" he asked, when he finished eating.

"I…we…" John looked at Hannah. Her back was still turned and not a muscle moved. "I took the baby home to its mother."

"Why would you do that? Is she going to die, and she asked to see him?" he answered sarcastically, as he set his cup down.

"No, Pa. She is well, but she wants her baby."

"Humph," he grunted through his teeth. "Just a helpless female, I'd say. You better hope that she stays well, John. And hope she keeps that boy well, too."

"She will."

"We'll see about that. It's not just her baby, you know. He belongs to all of us. He's a part of this place; it will probably be all his someday. He belongs here. Right here."

Hannah refilled the bread plate. "I told him to bring the baby over on Sundays," she said. "He promised. The child will go to church with us, Pa, and will stay with John for Sunday dinner."

"Have you asked about a christening, Hannah?"

"Not yet, but I will. When would you…?"

John looked from one to the other as they talked about his child. He felt like he wasn't there.

"As soon as possible," the old man answered, pouring his coffee into his saucer to cool, "in case he gets sick." He looked over at John, emphasizing this last idea. "He's well now. What's his middle name to be John, or August?"

"Daniel John," John said, "just knowing he had to assert himself, and it had to be something different from what his father suggested.

"Why not John, after his father? Your mother, Hannah, does she know the child has gone to Rozella?"

"Not yet. I'll tell her when I take her lunch up."

"The boy seemed to please her," he commented, as if to himself.

John picked up his dishes, carried them to the sink placing them in the dishpan for Hannah. Then, he walked out, seemingly unnoticed.

"Why did you let him do it?" Queist demanded of Hannah when the door closed behind John.'

"I didn't have a choice, Pa."

"You're too soft. He's a mealy-mouthed Mama's boy. If you had refused…what could he do? Sue us? Hardly."

"It's his baby."

"I won't see the boy raised to become like him – soft and useless. Spoiled. We're doing the child a favor, and don't you forget it, Hannah."

John was in the field when his father returned from his noonday meal. He was trying to appease his father for the loss of working time. Side by side they worked with the hay through the afternoon, not speaking.

Through the following weeks a pattern of existence emerged: weekdays John spent in his usual working routine, while Rozella learned to care for the baby. On the weekend, John would bring home his weekly allotment of food from the Queists and Rozella would put it carefully a way so it would not spoil. Tillie cooked as much as she could while she was there during the day. In this way, evening meals only needed to be heated.

After a couple of weeks with Tillie's help, Rozella wanted to be on her own, even though she missed Tillie's companionship. Without her she also began to notice that she missed the extra food that Tillie used to bring each day. But she couldn't let Tillie keep working for her everyday and be unable to pay her for the work.

They were back to bare essentials. It seemed like so much work in exchange for so little. John's days were so long, and he was increasingly tired when he came home. There were other people who were worse off she reminded herself in her disappointment. At least, they had a house to live in. It would not be foreclosed. She was sure of that much.

How she was sure, she didn't know, except she knew that John's father was shrewd. Rumor said that he was the money behind the mortgage and loan business in Crenshaw, and it was the mortgage and loan business that foreclosed on farms, and sued for deficiency judgments. Tillie had repeated this to Rozella, but only because she became irritated with Rozella's excuses for the small food allowances that were sent to the cottage with John.

No, the roof over their heads would not be foreclosed, as long as John did not displease his father. No matter what rumor said, Rozella knew the Queist's property was free of debt, and she had never heard any evidence of their involvement with the mortgage business. Although it seemed sometimes there was no way to really please John's father, they were more secure than most families.

So, John and the baby went to the Queist's on Sundays. There were no meals to fix on those days, and she could get by with a bit of bread, or oatmeal.

They had their breakfast together on Sunday morning. John would then leave, carrying Danny, along with the extra baby clothes and his bottle. The day would be left free for Rozella. At first, when she was still tired and recuperating, the day without responsibility was welcome.

There was no crying baby to see to, no husband to wait upon, and she could do as she pleased.

She would wash her hair and let it dry while sitting in the sun, just dreaming and dozing: dreaming of sewing or shopping or taking a trip to see her family and bringing her baby to see his other grandmother; dreaming of dinner, of money, of more food in the cupboards. It was so hard to cook with so little food.

Her body had become thinner, and the clothes she wore before her marriage now hung limply in folds exaggerated by her boniness. She often took her dresses in with tucks around the waist. The thick sewn-in tucks left marks on her body when she undressed, reminders that clothes could not be replaced. Since her paychecks were no longer there, there was no money. None at all.

But a certain Sunday came, though, when the stillness of the empty house seemed to emphasize itself, and even her breathing became captive. She could hear it as she could hear her heart, and above the inner intimate sounds of her body, came the steady beat of the clock. When the sun is gone, she told herself...they will come, both John and Danny. They will appear on the pathway, but it will be too dark to see them. I will ask if he had his dinner, and he will say "yes." I will ask about Hannah, and John will mumble empty words. He will say that he is tired, and will lie down on the sofa and fall asleep. I will bathe and dress the baby for bed. Danny will sleep, as I listen again to the clock. Repeating sounds in minutes strung together as beads.

A coldness surrounded her. She shook briefly, and moved away from the window to walk through the cottage, touching things as she walked. Sunlight cast a glitter upon floating dust cascading through the air. She ran her hand across the mahogany dining table as if to assure herself that the dust was not gathering. Her hand left no mar, as she seemed to leave no impression as she moved through the room. The phone rang. She could almost see the vibration of the square oak box mounted on the wall. The rings: one, two, three long, and two short. Not theirs. The silence left an inner ringing that was like ringing ears.

"I wish they would come," she said aloud to stop the sounds in her head. Then, the phone rang again, repeating the code of country rings. Phones up and down the road would be lifted in anticipation of listening to someone's conversation. Rozella hated it; but, today, in the emptiness of the house, she reached out for the receiver, looking about the room as if watched. The black receiver felt smooth and cool to her hand; hesitantly, she put it up to her ear. Just then, it rang again... the repeated code. Somewhere on the other end of the line came the muffled sound of someone saying, "The Sorensons must not be home. No one answers." Then, louder, the same voice: "They ain't home, operator. The old man says he saw them leave for church, but didn't see them come back."

"Thank you," the operator answered, trying to remain distant and businesslike. The line went dead. Rozella stood there for a moment, hanging unto the dead receiver as if wanting it to be alive. She replaced it slowly.

As if echoing her thoughts, the phone rang. Again and again. She didn't count the rings now. She knew it was not for her. Looking about the room, she could see that the cottage had taken on a different look since she came. It was her home now. As the darkness crept up to surround the small place, she carefully lit a milk glass kerosene lamp, which brightened the corners as it burst into flame, and then dwindled to a mellow glow. It was later than it should be, she thought, still refusing to look at the clock and acknowledge the time.

Her reflection in the dark windowpane startled her: a white face above a white blouse and thinness emphasizing her cheekbones. There was the long straight nose, and wisps of hair always falling down in loose strands escaping the pins she used to gather it into a brown bun on top of her head.

She returned to the kitchen to prepare something to eat. There was enough tea left over from breakfast to make another cup, if she added water. The Hoosier cupboard held a small loaf of bread carefully wrapped in a towel and placed on a shelf. She sliced off a piece of bread, spreading it with margarine...white margarine which looked like lard, and tasted like lard. The water for tea warmed quickly over the kerosene flame in the three-burner stove, while wisps of kerosene smoke drifted through the air. Turning her back to the window, the picture of herself she had seen was swallowed up in darkness. She drank her tea and slowly ate the heavy bread.

Trying to keep her mind corralled by blankness, she stared into nothing, unblinkingly, and then, to amuse herself began to watch the shadows playing upon the walls. A sound at the door interrupted her fanciful pattern making. First she heard the outer door, the door to the porch, open as it scraped softly against the door frame, banging against the dry wood structure as its spring pulled it tautly shut. Then, the inner door opened, pushing a sheet of shadow into the room. In the distortion of the lamplight, John's face was white and charcoal outlined and appeared as a circle above the plaid of his jacket. His eyes looked drawn and red. Her mind was quick to be self-critical and told her it surely was her imagination. Before, when he came home, the sound of the opening door had dispelled her fears and loneliness and brought back a certain joy. There had always been a surge of awakening when John returned to her each Sunday evening.

This Sunday it was later than usual, and it was different. Trapped and frozen feelings made this a vignette; both persons unmoving, staring at each other, waiting for speech. Rozella's mouth opened as if to speak, but nothing came out. She felt a response to something unknown. Then, John crumpled before her eyes. Like a picture washing away in the rain, the self-containment broke. Handing her Danny, he groped for the table.

"Mama, Mama…" John cried into the bend of his arm, shaking and trembling with his crying.

Rozella, still in the dream-like pallor of her day, turned toward him. In her response to his need, she came alive, and color rushed into her cheeks. "What is the matter? What has happened? Is your mother sick?"

"Dead. Dead."

"When? How?" she asked.

"Today. Right there." The sobs were choking out the words. "Put Danny to bed. Leave me be. Leave me. The baby, the child needs you." He pushed her away, closing her out of his grief.

She took Danny into the bedroom, as if nothing had happened. Now aware of her strength, she went through routine steps. She sang softly to him, easing the vision of the day that must have swept through his baby mind. What did death do to a baby's mind? Were all of the words and tears seeming senseless and lost to a baby's thought?

As she rocked the baby, in the back of her mind she could see the bent form of John sobbing unto the oil cloth which covered the kitchen table, a clenched fist opening and closing; even now, she could hear him slapping at the table top as if to beat away reality, a reality he didn't want to face.

Returning to him through the empty dining room, carrying the bedroom light, which flickered against the bare walls, the memory of him as he looked when they first met returned to her. He had been everything she ever hoped for; but, this day, she saw him as a broken person, bent over the table in pain, only knowing that something had happened to his mother, the one who understood him, the only one who understood him in his family.

"John," she touched him softly, "John, tell me now. What happened?"

"They killed her. They killed her, Rozella, " he sobbed. "I saw her choke to death before my eyes. And I saw their faces. Father didn't move to help her. Hannah had…" He couldn't talk for a moment. "She carried the soup tureen out. Can you believe that Rose? Can you believe that she carried it out to the kitchen and cleaned off the table before…before they removed…Mama's body. I lifted her myself… carried her to the couch…laid her there, her face…her face…she was blue."

"You can't mean that, John. You're just upset and confused. Your mother was very special for you. They didn't kill her. Think now, and tell me what happened. Why didn't you call me? Why didn't you call me to come and take the baby home, at least. I heard the phone ringing, and then later it rang again. Was that you? Did you call a doctor?"

"No…she died before our eyes…It was all over…too late…we called the minister. That must have been the ringing you heard…it must have been us. He came…could do nothing but pray…what good is praying?" John hit the table again with his fist. "The undertaker will come in the morning. Hannah said – don't call Rozella," John tried to catch his breath. "Hannah said don't call because Rozella has been sick, her nerves are bad since her illness. She will be too upset…I didn't think…it seemed to sound right…everything happening…too much going on...father...father...he always lets Hannah speak... he decided, but Hannah speaks for him...Mama didn't say anything before she died. Mama couldn't say anything...she just choked and choked, pulling at her throat and turning blue. Oh, God, they killed her. I know they did. They have ignored her. They have been so..."

"All right, all right," she was holding his head in her hands caressing him, touching his forehead, pushing back the brown hair, whispering to him, and then rocking him back and forth in her arms. His sobbing ceased. She moved gently so that she would not disturb him. Her body was stiff, in an awkward posture, bending over him in the kitchen chair. Again she could see her reflection in the black face of a window. There were broken lines across her forehead, like thoughts, "John, John," she reached for him again.

Later during the night, she reached for him once more, this time without opening her eyes. But, an empty flatness was all she found on the other side of the bed. Then, the memory of the evening forced her awake. She was alone in the bed, but did not remember going to bed. Her only memory was John's grief. She had finally eased him into sleep and not daring to move him, left him lying where she had persuaded him to rest, in the living room.

Alert now, she jumped out of bed, her nightgown of unbleached muslin wrapped around her in wide, swathing wrinkles. What will happen today? Could she shield them all from a grief in which she would not be allowed a part? How?

The baby would need to be fed. Danny was crying hungrily, and became demanding. She dressed hurriedly, straightening her hair before the triple vision of the frightened face that she saw in her vanity mirror. There was oatmeal to be boiled.

Rozella changed the baby while the water came to a boil. John was still sleeping on the couch, and he woke up slowly, as if still in a dream state. She watched him wrestle with his thoughts, suddenly turn his head away toward the window, then toward the west with a blank look covering his grief.

They ate together in a conspiracy of speechlessness. An acknowledgment of grief would be embarrassing. To close grief out one must not put emotion into words, she guessed.

"What will happen today?" she repeated to herself, but this time aloud, as she cleared off the table.

"They will take her body to town."

"The funeral will be at the church?"

"Yes. I suppose." He seemed to talk into his coffee cup. She couldn't ask him, as she had many times before on so many different occasions. Why would things change with death? How could she ask if she should come with him?

I will ask, she told herself, and just then – he looked up, as if reading her thoughts, and said "I will ask them if you should come with me to the church."

"Thank you," she turned away, a dying spark deep within crying out, why do you thank him? Why? She hated herself for hating him at this moment, yet, could not stop the hating. Every time she said, 'thank you' she hated him, and then felt guilty because hating wasn't humble. To want more for herself was prideful. After hating him, there would come the yearning, hungry times, the long nights when she warmed herself against his back and wanted him to wake up.

These became such lonely feelings: wanting and yearning for his body and her memory of loving – the waiting, waiting hopefully for him to turn, to waken. Lovemaking happened so seldom now, since that first night after the baby was born, when she lay awake all night, recovering from her fear. He had come to her as if fighting himself, as if against his will. She understood, and yet – she chastised herself, praying over her desires, which were so mixed up with fear during the sleepless nights of conflicting wishes.

No matter how many hours of isolation and thinking passed she seemed never able to cleanse herself. There was the dirty part of her she couldn't put aside. Where did it come from? Not at the moment of first lovemaking. That had been a joyous knowledge. Had it been the day when she had gone home from the Queist house in tears? Whose hands had made her evil? Their praying hands, or their clutching hands, which had torn away what she had felt to be a natural joy in giving.

How she had first given herself to John! The first kisses overcome by her own intensity, and her body offered with every part reaching for him. Now, during the long nights, she would lay awake in remembering, hearing him breathe, and she would try not to remember. She had turned him away, and yet, she needed him.

The old lady lay deep within the satin ruffles, her gray skin making the white satin look yellow. Thin strands of hair barely covered her scalp. Pinned on top of the hair was a lace cap, round as a doily. The eyes were sunken, deep holes around the closed eyes. Rozella stood staring down into the casket. A sick smell of over-ripe flowers permeated the air. Music from the organ was heavy and drawing upon the velvet of the drapes. Golden crosses and candles laid patterns of light upon an altar. Father wore black and smelled of whiskey and starch and shoe polish. Mama pulled her away roughly, "Don't lean into...don't. It's not polite."

But why are her eyes sinking into her head?" she wanted to know.

"Never mind. I'll tell you later." They trailed out of the room and into the sunlight outside, the other children beside her. "Why?" Rozella persisted, her child's curious fingers probing her own eyes.

"Stop that!" her mother shook her.

Papa was walking ahead of them down the street, eager to get away from the funeral atmosphere. Rozella remembered Grandmother Troast, remembered that she used to give her stale cookies whenever she passed by Granma Troast's house. Rozella's eyes hurt where she had poked her fingers into them. Mama was talking about the body, saying the wages of sin were death. "What does that mean?" Rozella wanted to know.

"That the body wears out, every day we wear out, wear down, with the weight of all our wrong doing: sin. Eventually, we are nothing but a shell of what we were – and it is time to die."

"Grandma Troast...she was a sinner? What did she do? She always gave me cookies, and she used to go to church every Sunday, until she got sick and couldn't get out of bed."

"Every man and every woman is a sinner," continued Mama in her lecture. "In the end, we all shrivel up and die. The more we sin, the faster we die." Her eyes followed Papa, glaring at him as he disappeared down the street.

Rozella lifted her feet carefully, slowly, one at a time looking at the bottoms of her shoes. Weighed down by sin, they seemed frightfully heavy. She felt heavy. Her eyes hurt more now. Mama didn't look weighed down by sin, but Mama prayed a lot and never missed church. Maybe Mama would live longer. Maybe Grandma Troast hadn't prayed.

Papa disappeared around the corner leading to the center of town. Mama had a deep frown on her face. She flipped her skirts as she turned up the sidewalk leading to their house, jerked open the front door, sighing heavily. Rozella dragged her feet on the steps, not wanting to go indoors.

"Come in and change before you go out," Mama demanded. Ola and Tonie were following her. Rozella thought she might as well. They would soon be going out to play, and there would be no more time to talk...about sin or anything else.

The aftermath of the Queist death was even more solitude. The family closed in as if not expecting, or wanting, outsiders to share in their grief. The church people went to the Queist house bringing food and trying to bring comfort. Even when they didn't feel welcome, they felt curiosity. Rozella asked about them. John told her who came and what happened.

After it all was over, she walked to the cemetery one evening with John. They stood there looking at the grave. There were wreathes made of dried flowers, which had been carefully saved from the summer. Little paper flowers, carefully formed and wired together. Some holly branches with red berries.

Crossing the graveyard that evening, she stumbled over a dry root poking out from under the frozen soil. Could she take the baby to see her own mother before her mother died? The cost of travel was high, but the reminder of death made her aware that her own family had not yet seen the baby. John might understand those feelings at this moment.

When she asked him if she could go home once more, he promised he would ask Hannah if the money could be spared.

She dreaded the answer, fearing Hannah's reprisal for taking the baby away from her. But, John bartered well over the following days and agreed to run the blockade into town and sell some of Hannah's eggs for her. Rozella was able to pack again, this time packing her baby's things along with her own.

Home had not changed much. The snow was there again, but it left the old house looking less than pretty, and less than fresh. Smoke from the fireplaces had singed it with black. Something about fresh snow usually made every scene Christmas card perfect. Ice and snow covered weathered paint and hid ragged lawn. But now, you could see the worn and brown lawn, filling in between the snow with dead weeds.

Mama was still bedridden and Ola more sullen, as she felt more trapped. She was tired of the long months of playing nurse, and had become resentful and depressed. Joe was gone, and it seemed impossible that it was really true. Even when they had first written about his disappearance, it hadn't seemed real to Rozella. Now she was confronted with this reality, and found that she expected him to come in the door any minute even now. The family could only guess at why he had left, remembering, even when they didn't want to remember, his resentment of the younger children, and remembered his dream of finding a job. They all kept hoping to hear from him, or to see him return.

There were many missing people now traveling the rails, living out of cans and eating begged-for food as they slept in the "jungles" along the railroad tracks. Newspapers told of many "lost" boys who traveled that way, runaways who were running away to escape, but never escaping. No one could escape what was happening to them.

Mama was clinging to life. Her heart was keeping her body alive, even when all the other organs wanted to die. She was happy to see the baby, her first grandchild. "I'm so glad that I lived to see him."

"Oh, Ma, you'll live to see many more," she answered.

"But, you...you are too thin, girl. Don't you eat?"

"Yes, it's just having the baby. I haven't gained any weight back."

"Most women have the opposite problem." Her mother insisted, not believing her.

"I wish I had it," laughed Ola. "Too many potatoes, too many pancakes. People are beginning to say that I look corn fed, but it's not corn."

Home wasn't the same without Joe, Val, and Tonie. The house seemed empty. The young ones were there after school, but days were subdued by the illness in the house and the nursing the two women shared. Mama slept often and while she did, they visited. Rozella found herself yearning to be back in her own home, and left on a Monday, deliberately waiting past Sunday. It would be one Sunday she could share with her son.

Arriving in Crenston at the bus depot, she expected John to be there in the pickup. Surely his father would let him off long enough to pick her up. There were always errands to do in town that would make it practical, since Queist had to have a reason for everything. Maybe he was trying to run eggs through to market again and had been held up.

Rozella thought how nice it would be to have money of one's own. Chickens, could she raise chickens? Hannah had turkeys, too. That's more money.

A woman came up to her, holding out a piece of paper. "Are you Rozella? Rozella Queist?"

"Yes," she answered, puzzled.

"I'm Joan. I'm a new neighbor of yours. This is a note from your husband. Not really necessary, but I thought you might not know if John was coming. I mean, you might feel uncomfortable going with a stranger."

"You're taking me home?"

"Yes. I was going to town. We were buying some feed at your father-in-law's. John mentioned going to get you. So, I said that I would bring you home. I hope you don't mind." She seemed embarrassed.

"No, that's fine. I'm surprised, that's all," Rozella answered.

Was it the freckles or the casual speech, or the smile that captivated Rozella? She would never know, but this woman seemed immediately familiar, like someone from her own family. Joan picked up Rozella's bag and carried it toward the truck. She was striding along like a teen-aged boy, dressed in jeans and a plaid jacket. Her hair was stuffed under a fuzzy red cap, falling out, spilling into her shirt collar, red straggling hair, making her look like a misplaced Annie Oakley. People couldn't help but stare. Women looked at her, then turned away.

Apparently she didn't care about the staring, or was completely unaware of how she looked. Rozella envied her the freedom of movement she had in jeans as she carried the baby; his bag containing his diapers and bottles was clumsy. She tried to watch where she was walking, but still turned one of the heels on her dress shoes, and stumbled. Awkwardly hurrying along, she tried to keep up with Joan.

"I've been looking forward to meeting you, honestly. I'm glad I happened to be there this morning when you needed a ride. Now we can get acquainted without all the others around to butt in," Joan said.

"How long have you been here?" Rozella asked.

"A couple of months, but we've been so busy that we have just begun to get out and meet people. We've spent most of our time moving furniture, and signing papers."

"Where did you come from? What city?"

"From a lot of places. Connecticut most recently. My husband, Girard, is French. I mean, from France originally. I met him there. Me, I'm just American."

"Any children yet?"

"No, but we're busy enough getting the farm in shape. Girard works in town; I try to keep up at home".

"Work? How lucky. John wanted work, but couldn't find it."

"Tell him not to feel bad. We transferred here: Central Home and Farm Mortgage. His first place was Albany, New York. Now here – but, we asked for it. We wanted a small town where we could buy a farm. It's a dull, low paying job, but better than none. If we're lucky, someday he won't need it anymore." She tossed the bag in the back of the pick up. "Climb aboard. Hey how about lunch? You look as if you could use it."

"I really can't…"

"My treat. I know a place that's cheap. The truck drivers all eat there. Com'on, no one will know when the bus came in, or how long we were at getting home. Your John won't be home until dark, anyway. Right?"

"I suppose. Yes, that's right."

"So, I thought. His old man probably doesn't unlock his ball and chain a bit too early."

Rozella laughed. She couldn't help it. It was funny. Put that way, what wasn't funny became funny, even though it was true. Considering her laughter as acceptance, Joan stopped at a small place on the edge of town.

The clapboard exterior was painted a dull green and there were no windows. On a Coca Cola sign hanging over the door was lettered: Sam's Place. A bell jangled as the door closed. The counter was lined with sullen looking men bent over coffee mugs and cigarettes. Donuts seemed to be a specialty. There was a glass case beside the cash register; it was filled with donuts, round and greasy, but still hot, the warmth creating beads of moisture under the glass. The large man leaving had a grease-stained bag in his hand, and a toothpick in his mouth. Rozella held the baby closer; she could see no woman patrons, although there were two waitresses who seemed right at home with the men.

Joan found a booth on the sidewall where the wooden seats were tall and stiff, but there was room enough to lay Danny down. He slept now, oblivious to the noise and the changed atmosphere.

"What'll it be?" the waitress asked, wiping a stained rag across the tabletop.

"Hamburger and coffee," Joan ordered, "and you?" she asked Rozella.

"The same please."

"Tell me about yourself," Joan demanded as soon as the waitress left them. "I met Tillie. She is the only person in town who knows you, I find."

"What can I tell you? I was a school teacher for while, until John and I were married."

"You still are a person. Tillie says you have a lot of artistic talent. You made your little house a very pretty place. I could use some help finishing ours. It's a real dungeon, and I have no talent for putting things together to look right."

"You mean, like colors of paint??

"Could I come and see what you've done to your cottage?"

"Sure. I'd like to have company."

"Tillie says that you're alone a lot."

"No more than most women, I don't think."

"Well, if you don't go out any, to church, or to town, or to clubs, you don't meet anyone. I'm sort of an atheist myself, and Girard – he an excommunicated Catholic, which amounts to the same thing. At least, in our house it does." She smiled.

Rozella looked curious. "I've never met an atheist before. Aren't you afraid?"

"Of what?"

"That God will strike you dead, or something?"

"How could I be afraid of him when I don't believe he exists?" she laughed again.

Rozella blushed, feeling embarrassed.

"No, I was an atheist long before I met Girard. Good thing. He was married when we met, but couldn't get a divorce. Some law in Europe, Italy, where we were at the time. We lived together a year. We finally got married last spring, but it didn't change things."

Rozella looked around the room to see if anyone had heard this. "Folks around here are very church-bound, Joan. Don't talk about it except to those close to you. People wouldn't understand. And – they can be very unkind."

"Oh, dear. I hope I'm not offending you. Gee, I just took it for granted we were going to be good friends."

"It's all right, really. I want to know how other people live. I'd like to be a friend. I just want you to know how they are here. They don't even know the word – atheist."

"Really?"

"They are tied to their Bibles, Joan. It's like God is the landlord in this part of the country. I've never been anywhere else, but I've read a bit."

"It's different in other places, believe me."

"Maybe, but unless you've seen it, it all seems unreal. This is the only reality right now, and God is a large part of it. I always feel like I'm being watched."

"The eye of God, perhaps? How awful?"

The baby was stirring now, so Rozella found a bottle and asked the waitress if it could be warmed for him. While they waited for the bottle, the hamburgers arrived, thick and hot, on home made buns, a slice of onion on the side.

"Not hard to tell that they grow onions in this valley," Joan said. "When we first came here, I swear, Girard and I came to expect them to put onions on apple pie. Haven't you noticed? Onions come with everything."

"No, I didn't grow up here, but my mother was just as bad, I guess. She put onions in everything. The old timers say it's good for your blood."

"Maybe, but not so good for your breath, or the digestion. However, I like 'em." And she popped a piece of raw onion into her sandwich.

Danny was crying now, and a couple of men at the counter turned around to look at them. He took his bottle the waitress had brought and sucked on it greedily. Rozella's lunch lay before her, growing cold while he drank, and his bottle grousing put him back to sleep. Then, she ate. The grease had congealed on the hamburger and the coffee was lukewarm. She ate half the hamburger, and sipped on the coffee.

"Enough?" Joan asked, "Aren't you hungry? I eat like a thresher, they tell me, and stay skinny. Maybe it's because I never sit still. But you, you don't eat enough. That's why you're so thin."

"Can't seem to get back to it. I was hungry when I was pregnant. Now, I don't care about food anymore. Maybe it's too soon."

Too soon, she had said. Something in her tone was familiar to Joan. She turned her head to one side, listening carefully. Who was it this girl reminded her of? The prominent face bones showing, dark eyes like a doe's. Full of fright and ready to run. Of coarse – she was a mirror of Joan's younger self, the girl she had been before she left for Europe. Suddenly. All the months of therapy passed before her eyes, and she wanted to grab Rozella and shake her and ask: Who are you? Do you really know?

But, Rozella wouldn't understand. She was what others created, Joan could see, what others wanted, and not anything of her real self. It would be interesting to find out who she was, and a challenge to help her find out. Joan remembered how she had learned to ask more of life. She also remembered what asking more had done to her life...

The glass case that held the donuts was dirty and scratched. A radio crackled away in the back of the counter where the waitress stood, wiping glasses with a grimy towel, her eyes gone blank as she listened carefully to "Ma Perkins", the Oxydol story. Customers, accustomed to her habits, waited for the station break to ask for more coffee.

Joan paid the check and they left, a brass bell on a strong bounced against the door announcing their departure in the same tone as it had heralded their arrival. Joan had a pickup to drive, but it was new, newer than any of the cars or trucks parked outside.

"Our first purchase," she explained apologetically, "You can't be a farmer without a truck." The suitcases were still in the back with the boxes of groceries, and tools. No one would touch anything left in an open truck, Rozella knew, but Joan said it was a new idea to her: everything safe.

Danny stirred in his blanket, wiggled. She looked at him, adjusted his clothing, and said,

"He can eat when we get home. He just guzzled up a half bottle of milk while we were getting our lunch."

"Do you have formula?"

"Enough for today. It's just canned milk, with Karo syrup."

"Is there milk at home? I won't be getting back here until next week. If you want to stop…"

"No. We get our food allotment from John's family."

"Really? That's nice. Is it part of an agreement, like tenant farming?"

"Sort of. We get our rent and food. That's more than most people have today," she said, as if defending the arrangement.

"That's true," Joan agreed, and it was – but how she would hate living on such a dole. "Well, I can see that I need to learn a whole lot about babies. I never liked babies much. We don't plan to have any," she added.

"Sometimes they aren't planned. My mother sure had a lot of us and none of us were planned. I wonder what I would do if I could choose."

"More people than you would guess would choose not to have them, especially now."

"Even if you choose to not have them, things -- well, they sort of come with God's will, or fate."

"Mostly. At least, people leave it that way. We are more fortunate. Girard had children by his first marriage, but because he didn't want any more, he had himself fixed."

"What do you mean 'fixed'?"

"An operation. In Europe they will do an operation on a man. It makes it impossible for him to have babies."

"Doesn't that make it impossible for him to..."

"No," Joan laughed, "Not in the least. It doesn't change a thing. Only you don't get babies."

"I never heard of such a thing," Rozella looked puzzled.

The frost had left the trees bare and pumpkins lay rotting in the fields where they had been left since fall. A year had passed so quickly.

"The year has gone by so fast," Rozella said, voicing her thoughts.

"You are remembering something?" Joan wanted to know.

"My first trip down this road with John," she smiled. "The year has passed too quickly, and yet I feel like it was a long time ago. Why such a conflict?"

"If you ever find the answer to that question, let me know. It gives me a headache trying to understand it."

Snow was drifting along the roadsides, and swirls of it dusted the wheels of the truck. Joan turned right by the mailbox and drove up the road toward the cottage, coming to an abrupt stop by the front door. She jumped out of the truck and had the bags in her hands before Rozella could get out of the cab. Holding the baby had kept her from moving very quickly, but she was embarrassed to have another woman carry her bags. The cottage was open, so there was no need for keys.

The kitchen door opened to a sour smell from warm air closed up and unused. There were dishrags lying on the counter and on the table. No one had been here, certainly not often, because nothing looked disturbed. Rozella checked the cupboard. There were a few cans of condensed milk, some jam, a hard crust of bread, and a couple of jars of fruit. Nothing else.

"John will be home soon?" Joan questioned, seeing the same things that Rozella saw.

"Oh, yes. And, he'll bring a basket of food. He probably isn't even staying here, the way it looks. So, there wasn't any need to keep any food here. He'll be here later."

"Okay, but I'll be back. There's a lot more I want to talk about. It's been awhile since I had a woman to talk to, you know. Farming is a lonely business, I find. How some women can stand being cooped up with just a husband for months at a time, I'll never know."

"Some women do better than others," Rozella answered, remembering.

The women sat around the kitchen table, coffee cups in front of them on the shining oilcloth. A plate was covered with warm yellow cake, frosting-less, steam rising from it. They were talking while the coffee cooled. A bag of multi-colored yarn lay on the floor next to Mrs. Trune, who was knitting busily. Grandma Kosinski had pieces of cotton lying on the table and was drawing penciled lines around a cardboard pattern. Making blocks for a new quilt.

It was Saturday morning and Rozella had been asked to do up the morning dishes. The pans and bowls from the cake were on the drain board along with the sticky egg plates and a greasy bacon pan from breakfast. Baking usually done on Saturday morning had been interrupted by the ladies' visit.

Val and Tonie had left already, taking Myrtle with them, pulling her behind them in an old red wagon. David slept quietly in his bed. Rozella had been washing her hair, dawdling in the upstairs bedroom, when the company came. Caught at home! Caught at home, kitchen duty became hers. She felt sorry for herself, and pouted, slipping the dish rag around listlessly in the cold water, not caring, wanting to be outside with the others.

Grandma Kosinski was asking, "How is Crystal these days?" Rozella could remember Crystal and her funny husband who always used to drink beer and sing songs in French. They were songs he remembered from the big war. Mademoiselle from Armentiers – tears? Sometimes he would hold her on his lap when he sang. He was such a good-humored fellow. They had a china cabinet full of small collector's things: tiny hearts, flags from France, Kewpie dolls, satin bows, mementoes. The house always had the blinds drawn and was dark all day long and into the night. Crystal's funny husband who sang was a relative, a cousin to Papa and he had been in the country years longer. Crystal was another kind of person. She was usually the talk of the town, and especially this group.

"Sick again," Mama answered. "She has been in bed for weeks. I don't know how George puts up with it, taking care of the house by himself and working, too at the post office."

"*Seems to me she imagines a lot of things, plays sick, wouldn't you say? She's in bed too much to be real,*" *Mrs. Trune was interjecting.*

"*Humph,*" *snorted Grandma in her sharp way,* "*Its just that that's the place where she is most at home.*"

"*I still feel really sad about that. George was such a good fellow to have married a common…just because she said she was pregnant. And, he believed her!*" *Mama added.*

"*Well, she got her just dues, anyways. No babies for her now. They cut her insides out. Too bad they didn't sew her up while they were at it,*" *Mrs. Trune commented.*

"*That's pretty bad, but you know what they say about the wrath of God. It doesn't pay. You always reap the rewards as they tell us,*" *Mama said, as if remembering last Sunday's sermon.*

"*She's not done reaping,*" *Grandma nodded,* "*There's a lot more to go. Did you hear what was going on with the Keller couple?*"

"*No, tell us.*"

"*They have been friends with George and Crystal for quite some time, playing cards and drinking beer every Saturday night.*"

"*I know that,*" *Mrs. Trune was eager to have her get on with the story, and she moved forward on her chair as she listened.*

"*Well, Jane Terkel had some dishes of Crystal's to return and dropped over unexpectedly one Saturday night. They told her to come in, at least, she thought so, she said. When she went in the living room – you know how dark it always is in there day and night? Crystal was sitting on Keller's lap with a beer glass in one hand and her other hand…*" *she gestured silently.*

"*Where was George?*"

"*Sorry. I didn't mean to disillusion you about George, but he was pretty wound up in Mrs. Keller on the couch. It looked like there had been some heavy stuff going on, or more.*"

"*Poor George. He must have been terribly drunk.*"

"*Whatever is was, it was the worst Jane had ever seen. We thought that kind of swapping was big city stuff; you only read about it in the papers – and not very often.*"

"*She'll have more sickness, then. She's still a whore and hasn't changed. She lost that baby, if she ever was pregnant, now she'll never have another. If she keeps this up, this stuff…her illnesses will never stop, until she…*"

"*Dies?*"

"Sometimes death is too easy. It will be a long drawn out one."

"Don't you believe that we sometimes get our hell on earth?" Grandma Kolinski asked.

"Quite often. I always look back over what I have been doing or thinking to see what it is I'm being punished for. I just know that time I lost my purse and all my earnings for the week; it was because I had cursed at my children. God gets to you if you don't correct yourself."

"True. True. Every time. Sometimes we don't see it right away. But if you look back, like you say, you can always find the heart of the matter. It's good that you are Christian enough to be aware. That's how we learn."

"Working our way to heaven?"

Rozella, hearing this, began to wash dishes faster. Was it a sin to not want to do something for your mother? Uncle George always seemed so much fun. And, Crystal was nice to the kids. There were always cookies for them and photograph albums to look at. Otherwise, it was pretty boring at their house. Who were the Kellers? And what was that all about? Just the usual Saturday morning chatting. Not much interesting.

It was all about adult things.

CHAPTER SIXTEEN

Some moments become confused and forgotten, and transitions come into being without thought. Rozella had already reached a transition when she could say to Joan: *People wouldn't understand.*

Isolation was an embarrassment Rozella couldn't face; she knew only an undefined discomfort that she found herself expressing with defensiveness. Neighbors could have been forgiving, but the total coldness of John's family was more than she wanted to think about. It was easier not to appear in public when his family was there. It was easier to stay at home. There really was no place that she could go to without transportation: a walk down the road, a visit to the woods, a talk with a neighbor. How far down the road? Anyplace was too far.

Talking to Joan was easy. And, Joan came to her in the weeks that followed their meeting, for she was free with a truck to drive and no children to tie her down. Joan only had the chores to do around their farm. Since she worked quickly and easily, it took her no time at all.

Time was what Rozella had most of these days. Joan was a good listener, a person who listened and accepted. Perhaps, the first such a person that Rozella had ever met; she was not critical, or agitated. Only sometimes she changed the conversation to other things.

When Joan talked, it was to reminisce about her life in Europe, the years when Girard and she had spent working out their problems. Their lives had not been without ups and downs. She talked about Girard's ex-wife, and talked about her early love life with Girard. It always turned out to be funny, although the incidents could not have been funny at the time they occurred.

"We were so in love," she began one day. "The more we saw of each other, the more we

wanted to see each other.. We were greedy for a word or a touch. For weeks he would wake in the middle of the night, unable to sleep, he told me, and get up quietly, slip out of bed and walk across town just to walk by my window."

"Stupid me. I slept so soundly, not thinking that men can be romantic. He had to tell me one day. Then, once he had told me, I couldn't sleep, and I would sit by my window all night waiting for him to walk by." She laughed.

"For several days this went on. We were exhausted from lack of sleep. Girard would fall   asleep while he was at work. His wife was beginning to wonder about the tired look he had. I began to expect him at 2AM, and my little clock on the bureau would strike the house just before he turned the corner."

"What a wonderful story," Rozella said, "it's just like a book."

"So far…but novelists don't tell you all the facts, dear. I decided to surprise him and slip down to the street in my nightgown just before he made the turn in the road. It was a warm summer's night, but dark. My gown was long, white cotton, and full. There never had been anyone around at that hour, but if someone looked, it wouldn't look too bad. The darkness would hide me. I was only careful to be very quiet in my bare feet so I wouldn't wake up the concierge, who was a dirty, old lady and always checking up on me."

"Did it work?" Rozella asked.

"Oh, yes, it worked, all right, " Joan laughed again, "I caught him as he turned the corner, seeing his face looking up to my window, as if hoping to see me. He was startled. It took a minute for him to realize I wasn't in the window." Joan was silent for a moment, remembering it. Then, she continued: "He kissed me, of course, and my body under the cotton was…well, only too willing…"

"What happened?"

"Need you ask? Before we knew what we were doing, we were leaning up against the front porch, or was he sitting? No matter, we were making love right there."

"In the street?"

"Yes, and it was absolutely wonderful. I recommend it for all lovers at least once, preferably – once a week."

"Did anyone come?"

"Rozella, you are so naïve. I'd answer that facetiously, but you wouldn't understand. Yes. We heard this voice, a woman's voice calling: Girard. My heart was in my throat. He pushed me down. I crouched behind the stone steps. He brushed off his trousers. The voice came nearer. "Girard," the woman called.

"Did she see you?"

"No, but I thought she would surely hear me breathe."

"What did Girard do?"

"What could he do, but invite her to walk with him, as if it was the most normal thing in the world to be doing."

"And, you?"

"After they left, I crept back to bed, but I lay there in the dark the rest of the night, shivering and hating her."

Joan was like a creature from another world to Rozella, out of a book, or a movie. She couldn't be of the same material as the people Rozella had lived with. All the gossip she had heard had been somber and sad, the just return for the sin, and the judgment. Joan was funny and happy with a sense of joyous celebration of life. Rozella felt guilty enjoying listing to her stories. One wasn't supposed to like things like that, but how could she think of Joan as sinful? It was impossible.

Evenings Rozella would go over the conversations again and again as she lay unable to sleep, staring out of the window, feeling restless, listening to John's heavy breathing as he slept, and waiting for the baby to wake up for a 2 o'clock bottle.

As time passed their husbands grew to know each other by listening to the woman-talk carried from house to house, and by getting together to play cards on Friday nights. Girard taught them how to play whist, and it became a weekly ritual. John was often quiet on those nights, concentrating on the card game while the other three chattered as fast as they played their cards. The yellow light of a kerosene lamp circled the table as the darkness became more intense. Danny slept soundlessly, secure in his own bed. Sometimes they played until he awoke for his bottle in the middle of the night. Then, Girard and Joan left sleepily to drive home.

As Rozella began to feel more at ease with Girard, she began to ask him questions about his home. His eyes would light up with pleasure as he talked of the places he loved. Joan would enjoy seeing the sparkle and remembered asking the same questions, only she had been there, and he could take her to the places she asked about. This time, with Rozella, he was telling stories, not showing her the way, or sharing an experience as he had with Joan. He was now creating a make-believe world for Rozella.

She liked it, just as she liked being called "Rose." He had started to call her Rose, insisting that when she laughed she was like a pink rose. Talking over her head, Joan and Girard decided on her name, just as if she didn't have a name already. It was true about laughter; she did laugh now, and she wondered if she ever had laughed before. Perhaps, her cheeks turned pink when she laughed. She didn't know.

John kept his silence. Silence was the center of his life. He didn't care for foreign lands, or foreign customs. Experimentation in living was beyond his daily care. The business of survival was serious to him. Rozella knew it was the life he led, for everything at the Queist house was either too serious, or tragic. But, she didn't want it to be that way anymore; she was tired of being afflicted by depression, and tired of worry, and of lifelessness.

Girard's charm was in his eyes and voice, Rozella decided. Of course, he had both mirth and gentleness, but the exterior-self was dominated by the warmth and glow in his eyes. When she learned his first name, she was startled. She had understood it was Girard because Joan called him that. Everyone did. But, Girard was his last name, the one he and Joan shared. Antoine was his first name, so it was understandable why they called him Girard. This man could never be a Tony.

The farm that Girard and Joan were rebuilding was blossoming. Rozella often spent afternoons helping Joan paper and paint, cut curtains, and refinish old furniture that had been left in the barn. The living room was now soft with a pale lemon light, golden oak furniture, and a burnished hardwood floor, which gleamed under colored rag rugs. Green and white chintz drapes trimmed the windows in spring. There were delicate scents from the incense that Joan loved, just a hint of cinnamon and spice. It was hard to leave this warm, sunny house and go home to an empty house and wait for John.

When Girard came home some afternoons while Rose lingered on, he looked like a different person. He was dressed in a gray suit, and carried a newspaper. Joan would meet him at the door, grab his paper, ruff up his hair, and say: "Get out of the ugly outfit while I go pour us some wine."

He would wink at Rose, and then go in to the bedroom to put on his Farmer Jeans, as he called them.

"All right now, ladies?" he would prance around the room barefoot.

"No, you forgot your shoes," Joan would scold.

Rozella would then excuse herself and get ready to leave.

"I'll drive you home," Girard suggested often.

"No, I'll walk. I need the exercise."

Bundling Danny up warmly, she would close the door quietly behind her. Walking past the pickup truck she noticed the bag of groceries still in the cab. There was no hardship here. In the midst poverty, there was still food and all the necessities. The farm buildings were bright with fresh paint and the yard was kept clean. She knew Girard's intent – to ride out the depression by working and owning his farm free and clear after it all was over. "But, you can't let it break you, make you give up. You have to keep on with it, care for it, as if you were successful. You keep working for tomorrow, or you'll never make it, he had told her.

"Yes, that's true," she had agreed with him but wondered how you could keep going when it wasn't yours. There was nothing of yours to work for, and you survived daily because you had to, or die.

Danny tried to crawl now, and tried to pull himself up. When she got home she put him on a blanket on the floor, and surrounded it with chairs. She lit the lamp before going to the wood box for firewood.

What did Girard do in town? The mortgage and loan business, she answered her own question. He was quiet about it, sometimes too quiet. He and Joan would stop talking when Rozella was there. The business must control the foreclosures around the county, at least some of them. He handled the paperwork, but didn't talk about it because it involved the people who lived all around them. Maybe that was why they hired a man from the east coast – Girard. It was easier for a stranger to do the work. Becoming friends with them could have been a risk – except the Queists had no mortgage.

And what did John do? Hard labor in the fields and barns. Was it necessary for all those long hours? It seemed to be after 9PM every night now when he came home. There had been a time when she turned away from him at night. Time had passed, and now things were different. She was still frightened of sexual relations, but her body was healed and much stronger. There were times when she wanted him close to her so badly, and all there was – was the snoring body of a tired man.

She looked at herself in the mirror, ran her hands over her breasts, watching the nipples rise under her fingers, and she wanted to touch herself more, and was so embarrassed for wanting to do it that she was almost relieved when the baby rolled off his blanket and began to cry. Danny needed her now. He distracted her from what she was about to do. The nights were much too long now, and there was no softness between John and her. Something was dying between them. Perhaps it was something that had never lived, she began to think as the memories dimmed.

The mail in the morning brought news from Ola. Their father had died in Canada. The family had just received a letter telling of his death from pneumonia, so far up in the Arctic Circle they had not been able to bury him. The ground was frozen and covered with snow. How did Mama take it? Terribly, Ola said in the letter. The mourning went on for days. She threatened suicide daily, even when she was at death's door already. How long could this woman live? And how strange her passionate attachment was for a husband who didn't live with her anymore, or didn't bother to send money to help her survive. Still, in her own stubborn way, she grieved steadily and lost herself in fatigue from her grief, and in prayer.

So, father was gone. No more would Mama wait for the mailman, and the letter that never came. How could Mama stop herself from waiting for letters? You couldn't tell her to stop waiting for letters any more than you could tell her to stop grieving.

Rozella felt nothing. She was puzzled by her feelings. There was not a bit of grief in her for this man. Yet, she remembered the things that he built.

A cutter rounded the corner with bells dancing to the horse's movements. The man's laughter trailed behind him like the snow, as if it laid runner, silver and sleek. Rozella saw the ornate Russian scrollwork on the side of the cutter and knew the dainty iron patterns on the runners with her eyes shut: her father's signature was his style. All that was left of his artistry now driven by the local bootlegger. It paid the debts, but they walked through the snow. Rozella couldn't look at her mother.

As if reading her thoughts, Mama said, "What good would it be without a horse? We couldn't even keep a horse." They avoided each other's eyes.

"Tomorrow is Christmas Day," she reminded her mother, "do you work tomorrow?"

"At the Ronstad's, for their yearly family dinner."

"You cook or serve?" Rozella asked, as she tightened her scarf.

"I cook. Sylvia serves. She's their full time maid."

"How much will they pay you, Ma?"

"Enough. Enough. Don't worry. Little ladies shouldn't worry so much," Mama patted Rozella on the back gently. They stepped over the cutter's trail, both careful not to break the silver threads it had left behind. The sound of bells thinned, and then vanished into the cold air.

Rozella, however, remembered the drunken nights, and the quarrels that he had with her mother, also. So, she could not cry over this death.

She felt more like crying over Ola, who nursed the sick woman, and was at the mercy of Mama's needs. Ola was tired to the point of complete exhaustion. More than physical fatigue, it was the emotional stress that drained her. How much longer would it be? Mama had outlasted all of her own predictions.

She could promise no trip home this year for the holidays. John apologized that there was no money from Hannah. He knew that Rozella's mother was so ill that she could not live much longer, but his family said that there was no money. They were suffering the same difficulties that everyone else was having, they told him.

Rozella wrote letters weekly so Ola wouldn't feel so alone, but she still felt as if she wasn't doing anything. John helped her put together a Christmas package for her family. There had been no word about her missing brother Joe. The family didn't speak of him anymore. Not talking about it was denying his possible death. They continued to hope that he was alive somewhere.

It was the first Christmas for Rozella and John, and it was difficult to believe that they had a son now. Their first Christmas together and they would share it with their child.

Joan and Girard asked them to come over early on the day before Christmas. They would have a late breakfast or lunch together. Rozella didn't want to think about Christmas Day or ask about it. She was trying to ignore what might happen, hoping that it, too, would go away and things would be normal. As every Sunday, John would be commanded to go home…with the child. This could be expected. She knew it, yet couldn't ask him about it. She didn't want to hear the answer. Girard and Joan seemed too cheerful, as if play-acting to cover up for what seemed to them an unusual and twisted arrangement.

Entering their house, Rozella felt the burden of both families upon her, the illness of her own mother, and the heavy requirements of John's family; she envied these two people, who were her best friends, their freedom. They had no families left. But, how could one wish not to have a family? Is there no balance, she thought? Do you either have them possessing you, or have no family at all? She shrugged her shoulders, as if commenting to herself: there is no solution, and went into the kitchen to Joan.

Joan looked spunky as usual; only this day she had tied a red ribbon around her hair, pulling it behind her ears. It was a touch of holiday spirit. A spring of holly was lodged behind her ear.

"I'd make it mistletoe, but it wouldn't do me any good. With Girard, I don't need it, with John, he wouldn't notice it."

One thing about Joan, she didn't care if she ever dressed up, so she had her usual blue jeans on and a shirt. It helped Rozella feel comfortable, for she had nothing new or different to wear for special occasions. She had mended, cleaned and pressed the clothes she had worn when she taught school. They were still fine, but not very gay in color – beiges, browns, and navy blues. She had lost so much weight after the baby was born, that there was no problem in size adjustments, except for the tucks around the waist. She was even smaller now.

They brought the hot breads, eggs, and sausages out to the living room where there was a table beside the tree. Joan wanted to eat next to the Christmas tree, she said, so it would seem more like a holiday. The food looked like the greatest feast in the world, coffee that smelled wonderful, with cream that was thick and cold from sitting out on the rear porch in the frosted air. The table was set with red napkins beside the plates and a bouquet of holly in the center of the table.

"Wait a minute. Just a minute," Girard announced, "On this special occasion we must have wine with our breakfast."

"Wine?" Rozella looked astounded.

"Yes, it's a holiday," Joan insisted. "We always have a red wine at Christmas."

He poured the thick red wine in the long stemmed goblets. It, too, was cold. Together they lifted their glasses as Girard proposed: "To a happy Christmas and all the year."

Rozella had never drunk wine before. It was difficult for her to know what to expect, but it was a sweet berry wine, of the Jewish kind, and not distasteful. She looked up in surprise. "I didn't know that wine tasted like this."

"There are all kinds of wine, Rose. Obviously, you're not a veteran wine drinker. This kind would usually go with desserts because it's sweet. Not bad, is it?"

The next swallow went down easily for Rozella. Breakfast was delicious with sweet rolls and candied fruit breads, and the wine made her feel warm inside. She looked at John and smiled.

"Your cheeks are red, " he noticed.

"Are they? They feel red."

"Yes, the rose is really rosy today," Girard laughed.

"And that's not all bad," Joan added.

It seemed like a good thing. She felt rosy on the inside. The wind blew around the house, sometimes lifting snow, hard and crystalline, and tossing it against the window like sand; but, in the warmth of the house the fire was glowing and there was a feeling of closeness.

The smell of evergreen was heavy and the softness of the furniture was about her like a cocoon. It held her, and made her feel secure. They were laughing about some eccentric neighbor, as Girard told about her buying habits, an old lady who walked daily to the store and always wanted to buy just one slice of bread. Even John was laughing. The baby stirred in his sleep and Rozella got up to feed him, then to change him and move him into a bedroom where he would not wake up so easily. He quickly went to sleep with a few bounces of the springs of the bed. Rozella covered him gently with a blanket.

These were moments that she wanted to make last forever. She and John had agreed to spend the night here rather than walk home in the cold wind later on, or have Girard or Joan drive them home. This was a new experience. They had never stayed anywhere together but in the cottage. Joan made up the bed in her spare bedroom for them. The room had just been painted in a delicious pink and she had draped the windows in unbleached muslin, which was trimmed in pink and white checked ribbons. Rag rugs were on the floors. Rozella walked about the bedroom admiring Joan's work. All so perfect, but the colors chosen had been her own choices. Joan had enjoyed sharing this project with her, asking her to help, then asking them over for the holiday so they could stay and share it. She had said it was a favor to her. After all, how could she use a guest room if she had no guests, she explained.

Going back into the room filled with laughter, Rozella thought it was too bad there were no children here other than Danny. Children made Christmas so much more cheerful. Was that why Girard and Joan did not want to be alone? Perhaps. But, Rozella knew that the evening at home with John and Danny would have been a quiet evening, not like this. And, in the morning…

"And could I have another glass of wine?" She asked, intent on forgetting.

"There is no limit today," Girard responded, "unless you drink it all. And since you both are beginners, I don't think you'll succeed." He poured her glass full again. The taste was oddly different on her tongue, but wine was a complete strangeness to her. She and her family had been raised with Mama's definition of alcohol as a dangerous thing with the threat of her father held over their heads, and the cost. For most people, it was too costly to drink. But, it was nice to be forgetful, and let the warm wine flow into her veins to drive everything cold out. She could only smile now: everything seemed so perfect.

After breakfast which lingered on until two in the afternoon, the women cleared off the table, while Girard and John went out to see about the animals and make sure there would be enough feed for them in the barn. Then, Rozella and Joan began to prepare the turkey for dressing. They put it into the oven after giggling over sewing it up, the fat and slippery body sliding around on the table. Joan held it firm while Rozella pushed the excess of stuffing into the cavity and sewed it shut with embroidery thread. It seemed too funny, as if the creature was objecting to colored threads and loss of dignity.

"I've never seen such a resentful beast," Joan exclaimed, "You'd think he'd be honored to be the center of attraction tomorrow… tonight. That's right, we're not going to wait for tomorrow, we're going to eat him tonight."

"Don't say that word," Rose cautioned, "He jumps right out of your hand every time."

"Wouldn't you?"

"Maybe. Maybe not."

"Should we have some more wine?" Joan looked for the bottle.

"But – I'm sure that I'm drunk already."

"How would you know? You've probably never been…"

"Sure. Maybe I'm not." Rozella grinned from ear to ear.

"How do you feel?"

"Good."

"What's good?"

"Not a thought. Not a thought about tomorrow, or any other day."

"What happens tomorrow?" Joan asked her.

"You know."

"Rose, don't you ever say anything?" Joan set the wine bottle down with a thud.

"About what?"

"You're not that drunk. You haven't had that much wine. You feel good because you are not choosing to think."

"About what?" Rose repeated.

"About John, and his devotion or whatever you choose to call it. Don't you ever get mad, just plain angry and scream and holler?"

"I don't know what he would do. I've never done such a thing in my life. I...my mother...always screamed so much. Something in me doesn't want to be that way."

"There's nothing wrong with anger, Rose."

"Yes, there is. It's a sin. Isn't it a sin? Anger hurts people."

"I don't believe in sin. But even you...your books and church. Does it say anywhere that you would go to hell if you got angry?"

"I don't remember. I just hated my mother's anger, her rage. It never did anything but make my father drink more. Nothing was resolved."

"So, you solve things by not doing anything, by not saying anything, by just accepting everything?"

"No...no, but I can't. It's just not part of me. Angry scenes frighten me." Rozella went to check on Danny.

"Sorry. I won't bother you more. This is a holiday and meant to be a happy one. We'll go on as if I hadn't asked. We'll make some pies next. A pumpkin and an apple, how would that be? It makes me hungry all over again thinking about it."

"While the pies are baking we can play cards, right?"

"Good idea, Rose. I think the conversation in the barn is running a bit thin anyway. At least, I would think so. The men will be glad to have something to do."

"John isn't much of a talker, I guess. He's pretty quiet."

"Better today than usual."

"It's the wine again. Basically, he doesn't talk much around our house. We may have the quietest house in the world."

"That I can believe. I couldn't stand it. I like noise, conversation – even if it is noise. Anything, anything, but silence."

The men returned from the barn, tugging at the door to close it in the wind. They wanted coffee. The cards were brought out and spread on the table, which was still damp from washing up the baking mess. John was asking about the mortgages foreclosed in the county, and apparently Girard was avoiding the answers. He didn't want to discuss those who were about to go into foreclosure. He really couldn't, Joan had explained to Rozella. It would mean he could lose his job for talking about confidential things. People who knew him always wanted to ask.

He couldn't answer them.

Rozella excused herself to attend to Danny again. The time had passed so quickly that now he was crying from the bedroom. She picked him up and carried him into the kitchen where Girard was aimlessly shuffling the cards as they waited for her.

She put Danny over her lap, patting him on the back as she waited for the cards to be dealt. He had grown so much, and she now felt his weight on her knees as she began to sober up from the wine that they had shared over "brunch," as Joan called it.

The smell of the turkey in the oven was heavy in the room. There was a gray sky and it looked like a storm was brewing as it began to get dark already. Too early for sunset, the dark clouds were snow clouds, and the wind continued to whistle through the barren trees around the house. Everything seemed far away, removed. Rozella shivered, feeling suddenly isolated, and not knowing why, not wanting to ask herself about it.

Their card game continued through the late afternoon. The two women were playing against the men and feeling powerful when they were able to win a game. They laughed over it. At five o'clock Danny would no longer be still, and Rozella had to feed him once more. She interrupted the game to give him his evening meal, change his clothes and put him down at 10, then he would sleep the night through. He was a good baby, and there was no more night crying. No more getting up with him at two AM. The worst part was over, she thought. The worst of what, was her second thought. There were other things. The Sundays and holidays – alone.

Coming back into the room after leaving Danny in the bedroom once more, she looked at John as he talked to Girard. He seemed a stranger. The soft brown hair fell over his brow. He was asking about grain prices. His brows knitted together over his blue eyes. His skin was pale, such pale skin. His hands were worried into a tangle of activity that couldn't be still. His shirt was worn around the collar and his black pants shining from too much pressing; the old wool was worn through in places. It had been so long since she had touched him, really touched him. Could she even remember how the fine hair felt, the down on the nape of his neck where the hair had not yet been cut?

She watched Girard, and his hardness. Not really hardness, but there was a firmness to him; she noticed the brown skin, even in winter, from the sun. The summer sun had not yet left him. His brown eyes and dark hair were a contrast from the pale complexion of John, who only turned red in the summer sun.

John seemed on edge, as if he were about ready to spring. "Why can't they trade grain for land payments?" he wanted to know.

"I don't know, except that the loan companies won't accept it," Girard answered him.

"Who owns…" was his next question.

Girard looked relieved when Joan said, "Enough. We're back to the game. We get one more chance to beat you fellows. There'll be no dinner unless we have our chance."

"Shouldn't we wager something?" Girard wanted to know.

"I wager that if we lose, we'll set the table and do the dishes," John offered.

"You're on." Joan accepted.

And the women did win the match. Good to their word, the men set the table for the dinner, while Joan and Rozella rested with their feet up on the small oak table, pretending that they were waiting for servants to present the holiday meal. With dinner came wine again. This time Girard uncorked a bottle of chilled white wine from Germany. With it they toasted the day…Blessed Christmas, hopes and wishes to be fulfilled. It was now night and their faces were reflected against the black glass of the windows. Rozella looked down into her wine glass searching for her own reflection there in the almost amber wine, but there was nothing there. She could see her face in the window, but not in the wine. Why? She suddenly felt so cold; she didn't know why. It was as if she searched for an image of herself and had found none… was she nothing?

The meal was delicious: turkey and dressing, pickled beets, hot rolls and more wine. The women were glad to leave the dishes for the men and go to the front room with their coffee and dessert. The tree was filling the corners of the room, drooping from the heat of the wood fire. There were packages under it, in colored paper. They traded their gifts and opened them. Rozella's handwork, towels for Joan's bathroom, embroidered guest towels, tiny and impractical but exactly the sort of thing that she would like. Gifts from Joan and Girard – two warm sweaters, one for each of them, followed by another one for Danny. "It's too much," Rozella protested.

"No, it was all on sale, and I bought it ages ago. Besides, we only give when we can. Next year there may be nothing from us. We're new at this."

"Yes," Girard interrupted her, "We haven't farmed before. By next year we may be over at your place begging for food, or a place to stay."

"I doubt it. I think you're going to be very successful," John said, "But, thank you anyway. We needed these. You knew we did."

Slowly the candle burned down, leaving its fragrance of baywood in the room. The four of them sleepy, they turned to bed wishing each other a happy holiday.

A feeling of strangeness persisted as Rozella climbed into the bed with John. She wore her best nightgown. John wore his underwear. Used to the cold, they dressed as warmly as possible for night, but this was a down comforter, continental style. It was warm in ways that could never be compared to wool quilts. Nice. Rozella reached for John's hand. It lay limp against the top of the quilt. He was asleep already. The whiteness of the snow seemed to cast a reflection through the window and unto his skin. He was even whiter than she remembered him, and entirely too silent. She turned in the bed and heard it squeak loudly in the dark room, the springs moving under her. Danny sighed in his sleep. She lay there, counting her heartbeats, waiting for sleep to come.

It was nearly dawn when the baby woke up for his first bottle. The early light made it possible to move through the room. John lay on one side, turned toward the window, softly snoring. The room was cold. Danny squirmed in his covers, kicking at them, making baby-talking noises. He was bound up warmly to avoid the cold night air. Rozella found him soaked through to his outer clothing. She lifted him from the makeshift bed they had made upon a large overstuffed chair, cuddled him under her neck where he nuzzled his mouth, little fingers grasping and reaching for her. She carried him into the kitchen, murmuring to him all the while. Adding another piece of wood to the dwindling fire in the kitchen stove she put the bottle in a pan of water to warm.

No one else was stirring in the house. The late night bedtime left Joan and Girard asleep. The smell of the tree filled the room, as the stove began to warm the air. In front of the open grate, where the fire warmed the air, she changed Danny.

Last night's coffee was still in the pot. Rozella moved it over the stove to warm it up, pulled her nightgown around her, feeling the cold air swirling up around her bare body from the floor. When the bottle was warm, she held Danny in her arms and watched him drink eagerly. His warm bottle felt good against her cool skin. Christmas morning, little one, this is our first Christmas together, she thought, watching him. She put the bottle down, pouring herself a cup of warmed coffee and sat sipping it in the quietness of the nearly morning hour. The only sounds were the sighing of her baby as he lay on her lap, the snapping of the wood burning heatedly in the iron stove, and the rooftop creaking with the weight of heavy snow. Coffee gone, she rose to look out of the window. The sun was warming up the horizon with a hint of yellow and pink trees without foliage were silhouetted against the pale sky. Frost had painted the edges of the windowpanes in white and furry designs. She breathed upon the glass as she had when she was a child and watched the clouds of steam form magic worlds.

Trying not to think, she occupied herself by looking out and wondering about the weather. Would he take the child away on this day? She knew he would, but wanted to delay it by not thinking of it, put it aside, stay in the kitchen and wish that no one would wake up. In the end, she knew she must take the baby to the bedroom. Lay him down. Maybe he'll sleep now, in the middle of the bed between us .The warmth of our bodies will keep him asleep until ten. She put Danny into the center of their bed, working carefully to place him under the covers without disturbing John. She slipped in beside the baby and lay still, careful not to move. But, she couldn't relax. Pulling the baby to her, when she felt safe, and sure that she had not awakened John, she cuddled the little body into the curve of her arm. The pillow felt good against her cheek Things floated and moved in her mind, then drifted away, as she slept.

She woke up startled, then sat up, not knowing where she was. The room was light, and John was dressing. He stood in front of the dresser pulling on his wool trousers. His white shirt was already buttoned and his tie carefully in place. She stared at him sleepily, not comprehending what was happening.

"Would you change the baby?" he asked.

She didn't answer.

"And, put his bottles together with some extra diapers?" he continued, as if she had answered him.

She rubbed her eyes, and became suddenly aware. "You're not … going to go?"

"You knew I would have to go," he answered, without looking at her. "You never said anything before. You knew how they felt. I can't change things. I want to change things, but I can't do anything. Don't you know?"

"But, we never talk about it. It seems that you never try to talk about it. Does it have to be forever? I can't stand it to be this way forever. He's my child."

"Now, Rozella, you've just had too big a night of it. We're not used to wine and late hours. Calm down."

"It's not that. This is my first Christmas with my baby. And you. It's our first Christmas. It doesn't make any sense."

"It is an obligation to my family. They demand it. I know it isn't very nice for you, but you'll be here with Joan. You can stay here all day if you want. It's much nicer here than over there, believe me. I don't want to spend the day over there."

"Then – don't go."

"I must."

"I can't stand it this day," and she was coming toward him from across the room, then pulling at his shirt, then trying to shake him. "Please, please…just this once."

He picked up the child. "Where are his clothes? The diapers?"

"I won't let you take him. I hate them! They are monsters, wicked…"

"Don't talk that way. You don't know what it does. It's …I can't… we never talked."

"They want me to die. They wanted me to die when he was born. Somewhere in my thoughts, I knew they wanted it. If I died, it would leave you and the baby, and them. THEM. All together. The way you really want it. Is that it? The way you really want it?"

"No. For God's sake. It's not the way I really want it. I want all kinds of things. What good does it do to want them? I have thought and thought. Before I ever met you, I tried to get away. There's no way, not any way out."

He was bending over, leaning against the frosted windowpane, clutching at his mid-section, as if something hurt. Out of her pain, she became silent, and walked over to him, watching his back. Her bare feet on the cold floor made no noise. The thin gown drifted around her flimsily. There was a stifled sound, and his shoulders shook.

"What?" She whispered, aware of his shaking. "What have I done to you?"

"Nothing. Nothing," he answered. And she knew that he was crying, and she remembered that her father had cried before he left. In her own voice she had heard the echo of her mother's voice. Rozella shivered.

"Go then. I didn't know this was so important to you. I hoped that I was important, but the baby…I can't believe this is happening." She picked up the child and laid him in John's arms. John's eyes were red and his mouth set in a solid line.

"His blanket and other things are in the kitchen. Go – before Joan gets up," and she turned her back to him, sitting down on the bed averting her eyes, not wanting to see what he was doing.

The door closed behind him. Then, there was the sound of his gathering the baby clothes, putting on his own rubbers and coat. Another door closed, and the house was silent again. With the silence came her own sobs, and she tried to stifle them in the pillow. The bed was cold now, and it felt like no one had ever slept there, like it had always been cold.

The sun was now bright upon the snow. She didn't look up to watch the shadowed figure of a darkly clothed man, carrying a baby wrapped in a warm blanket down the road, as he stepped carefully to keep his balance. It was Christmas Day now, and Rozella hid herself in the bed, not wanting to get up.

CHAPTER SEVENTEEN

*I*t was dark so soon. Rozella didn't want it to be dark. There was a sense of urgency in the room. Since four o'clock Mama had been busy in the kitchen, baking. But, as Mama moved from kitchen stove to cupboard there was an absentmindedness about her, her glances out the window, and her movements toward the door. It was Saturday and payday. The girls played on the floor, wrapping up dolls in old towels, pretending the game of dressing babies. No one felt the strange something that Rozella felt, or did they? Rozella didn't know. No one spoke about feelings. Her stomach was knotted in a kind of pain. It wasn't hunger. It was a sickness that she had felt before. On Saturday night…this had happened before. Mama stopped her pacing and was now standing looking out the window, absentmindedly wiping her hands on the tea towel she held. Not talking. Not walking. Then, she began again the walking back and forth. At times she would wander into the dark living room, and Rozella could see her there, again watching through the window. Rozella hugged her dolls tighter and pushed her sister. "Look out, you're ruining my doll's…I mean…my baby's bed," Toni grumbled. The cardboard box slipped from the chair where she had put it. Rozella wanted to push, to hurt, to make some noise that would make the feelings go away. Why wasn't Papa home? Didn't he come these Saturdays at this time? It was payday. The day he brought home candy for the girls, and Mama was happy. Sometimes happy. Not always. There were other days, when the darkness fell and he didn't come. The supper was warmed over and over, and bread became dry upon the table, going from hot oven to dry and cold as it lay for hours. Was it late, too late for Papa? Should she *feel the pain in her stomach? It was seven o'clock the little hand was on the seven. The tall clock chimed seven times from the hall. The brass singing of the chime left ringing sounds in the room. Rozella could feel the ringing dancing through her head after the clock had stopped. Mama looked at it as if it was an enemy, and her frown deepened*

There was a noise on the steps and the girls jumped up. It's Papa, they shouted. Mama didn't move. Rozella rushed past her to the door. It was Papa opening the door, fumbling with the doorknob. He had a package in his hand a brown bag. Candy, candy. Toni grabbed the bag. Now, you share it – he was saying, one piece for everyone. Val was tugging at the bag, trying to take it away. "I'm older Let me." Mama still did not move her stance in front of the old clock. Papa looked at her, his cheeks flushed red in the light and the warm air. Rozella could smell the smell on him, the sweet and heavy smell that was almost always there except when he woke up in the morning. It wasn't like the smell of candy. Her stomach began to hurt. Mama moved toward him. "It's payday. I might have expected that you would be late. No matter what you promised."

"Things happened at the shop, Dora, I couldn't get away sooner."

"Things always happen, don't they?" Mama was saying.

"No just sometimes." He went toward the coat rack with his heavy jacket, stumbled and leaned against the wall.

"Sometimes? You never change." She said this in a low key, which was almost like an animal cry, Rozella thought. Then, she remembered that when Mama became really angry her voice would sink to a whisper, as if she couldn't bear to say the things that she wanted to say. Then, she did whisper, but the girls heard her. "Where is the money?" In answer, Papa reached in his pocket and brought out a hand with two small bills.

"This is it. Not much for this week."

"Not much after, after the bar and the liquor," she said coldly. "Now, what do we live on this week?"

"We live the way we have always lived, with happiness…don't we, girls?" He was trying to hide behind them with his speech, wanting to make Mama know that they were there. Rozella wanted to hide him, to silence Mama, to put aside the words she didn't want to hear…or understand.

"We don't live with happiness when we are hungry. Who pays the rent? Who buys the food? You don't think of anyone but yourself."

"Dora, that's not true. Look, here what I have brought for the girls." He pulled a tissue paper out of his shirt pocket. Held it out for their inspection. Rozella moved forward, then stopped, reminded of Mama who was looking on in anger. Mama's hands were tight, knotted into fists. Val went to Papa, took the tissue, unwrapped it. Toni was looking over her shoulder, jumping excitedly. "Silver spoons," she gasped.

"Yes, One for each of you," he said, weaving on his feet, swaying in the darkness of the front room, a puddle of melted snow now gathering around his feet because he had not removed his overshoes.

"Silver spoons?" Mama repeated. "Silver?" The words were torn from her mouth. "How did you?" she was asking, as she reached to take it from Val's hand, the shining ornate-ness of the tiny spoon gleamed in Mama's hand. "It is sterling. Six spoons? You spent your wages on six silver spoons?"

Rozella's stomach knotted again as the voice rose, and she backed up against the wall, feeling the fuzzy softness of the wallpaper against her hands. She didn't want to hear this. Her hand went over her ears. The other girls were sitting on the floor examining the spoons, quarreling over which one could be theirs. Rozella could only see Mama moving toward him; she felt the tears in her stomach as if she was crying inside. Mama was crying, but she was raising her fists and hitting him, pounding him about the head. "You can't do this, you drunk," she was crying. Papa grabbed her wrists and held her. It took all of his strength, as the drink didn't help him. Mama wavered, loosened her hands and struck again. "You don't have any brains," she shouted.

"They were a good buy. The jewelry salesman from the American Wholesale Company was in. He said he would sell me the samples...worth more...worth twice as much."

"What good does it do to be worth more, when we have no money. We have no money to buy things like that when there isn't enough to live on. You do anything anybody tells you, but me...you listen to any man, but not to your wife, who only wants you to do what is right."

Rozella held her hands over her ears. She was still hearing the words. "I can't stand your anger," he was saying, "anything but your anger."

"Then, why do you keep doing these foolish things?" she wanted to know. "We are poor. Candy is enough. Sometimes it is too much. Why do you do this? I can't live this way." Mama was crying now, and Papa was

sitting down on the floor. Rozella's sisters were still quarreling. Val had taken one of the silver spoons and was biting on it, making tooth marks on it. Was she marking it so Papa couldn't take it back to the store, as had happened before to mysterious and beautiful gifts, or was Val biting it to mark it as hers? Rozella didn't care. She slipped away, down the hallway to the stairs, then up the stairwell with the angry words following her. Rozella was sick. She must go to bed; she didn't want a spoon. Rozella's stomach hurt.

Girard was returning from the barn. The yellow light against the gray aura of trees, which were frozen into masses of shade, was a backdrop to crusts of snow. The sheep were wandering pointedly, an essence of time whispering to an inner animal-ear on this Christmas morning, a trail of small hooves cleaving the snow, making their marks. He could hear them speaking their own language.

Joan had not been awake when he went out to the barn to do the milking. He had hoped everyone would be asleep. He needed a quiet time to himself. There were times when he needed that quiet time to determine where he was. The land, this land, was so strange to him, its habits, and its people. Joan was not strange, but all Girard's surroundings were different than those he was used to. He had not been a farmer before. This land wanted to swallow him up. The spaces were too vast. A man felt like there was nothing to hang unto, no place to go; it was living on the edge of nowhere…that was it, nowhere that felt like the edge of the world. Yet, he had chosen it.

No one in this land was close to him, but Joan. The difference in the people kept him at a distance. Sometimes he was afraid to speak in his normal way; when he couldn't express his thoughts and feelings, he became silent, as such, he became a silent reflection of the others. He had talked to John now for quite some time, but John was like the others. He never said anything that was personal. All talk was kept to facts, the hard facts of living. There was no joy or laughter in John, or hope. He was like a dead man walking around in life. There were times when Girard wanted to shake him and find out if he was real, or hit him hard enough to knock the insides out of him and find out if there was anything on the inside. Rozella, too, and the queer in-laws. Always passive, Rose, always passive. She just accepted her life as if it was the most common way to live...her subservience, the insult of neglect and avoidance, and she slept with the man who aided the in-laws in cruelty.

Girard wanted to shake her, too. Sometimes he wanted to shout at her. At moments, he could see laughter and – her mind would come alive and she would talk to Joan and to him, excited about some book or play that she wanted to read, or had dreamed of seeing. These were remnants of what was leftover from the days before marriage, the baby, and John, he guessed. She was rosy like her name when she laughed, bell-like.

If she didn't stop this life she was leading, she would become like John, living death. Her acquiescence tied her into a dull being. He hated it. Joan and he talked about it at times, puzzled over the family, the inscrutable and peculiar family who dominated the lives of their friends. If Rose only would do something, become angry, hit back, or scream...

He kicked off the snow on the mud-scraper, which was filled with crusts of ice that built up round and shining with the daily ritual of added snow. His door opened to a silent house. Joan was not up yet. Then, he heard sounds from the front bedroom. Rozella.

He didn't want to enter and intrude. Was John in there? There was not a voice, only muffled choking sounds and the creaking of a stirring body upon the bed. He opened the door slowly. She lay across the bed, face burrowed in a pillow, her brown hair falling over her thin shoulders, the bones of her back standing out beneath the cotton gown. She did not hear him.

"Rose?"

"Yes?" She moved, but did not try to get up.

"He did go?"

"Yes."

"Did you try to stop him?" Girard asked.

"Yes."

"I don't understand. Is his family really that bad?" Girard leaned over her.

"He thinks so. Oh, yes, maybe they are, maybe I shouldn't want him to stay with me. Maybe it isn't possible, but every Sunday? I thought that would be enough."

"Common, Rozella, get up and come out into the kitchen. We'll make some fresh coffee and talk. You need to talk. You never say anything about this. Talking does help, sometimes."

He touched her shoulder gently, trying to turn her toward him. Then, she did turn on her side, raising her face toward him as she moved to get up. She was so pale, so tired looking. He didn't want to look at her, and he moved away. It wasn't that he didn't care; it was that he couldn't bear to see it. It hurt him that she was living this way. It seemed such an empty and fruitless life. What did she really have to look forward to each day, or each week? He hated it, hated the people who were doing this, wanted to strike out against them, or leave and go away again to someplace where there was some normal life. But, leaving would do nothing to change things for her, leaving would only abandon her to this.

Joan and he could do something. They could do more. Just being with her through the empty hours was not enough. Could they give her some strength, change her from silence and acceptance to rebellion? If they did, what would the rebellion do to her? There must be caution, so they didn't hurt her more than life had already hurt her. It was pity he felt that moment, reaching for her hand and helping her up. The frailty of her struck him as he held her thin hand in his and felt his own swallow it up. There seemed no flesh on her bones; the skin was not far from the bone. He would be afraid to handle her. She felt like she would break. Like thin crystal the patterns of her escaped him, but there remained a sound in the back of his mind that rung like the clear sound of crystal: knowing how to touch it was the answer to all fine things.

This moment he wanted to dress her like a child, to wash her abused face, to brush her hair, and put a muslin dress over her head. But, he couldn't, so he left her to the bedroom and went out into the kitchen to make coffee for them.

Joan was up now, and she looked up at him as he came out of the bedroom shared by John and Rose, "I wondered where you were. Weren't you outside?"

"I was, but I heard her when I came in. John did leave with Danny, as we guessed he would."

"That explains it. How awful for her. How is she? Can you talk to her? Is she listening?"

"One question at a time, please. I don't know how she is, but I do know that she tried to stop him. I don't know how…just that she did at last – say something."

"Good. That's the first step." Joan said, as she put the coffee pot down.

"I can't believe he wouldn't listen. What is it with these people?"

"When they say someone is strange around here, they mean it with great reserve: it's no exaggeration."

"There's a lot that we don't know about John's family."

"That's what I mean."

"Hush, she may come in." He sat down at the kitchen table, resting his head on his hands. Joan continued to put breakfast on the table as the teakettle whistled merrily. She was wearing a skirt, with a white blouse, a bright apron over it. Girard smiled looking at her. So unlike her – the apron, it was a private joke. How often they had talked about it during the days they had planned to live in the country. She would wear aprons, she had said. Now, she wore them on special occasions to remind him. They didn't talk of it, but they both remembered the way things had been, and the dreams they had shared.

Rozella came in, now dressed, her hair combed, still looking pale and hesitant. From the school of no emotion, Girard thought. She doesn't know what she's carrying around inside. All she knows is that she feels sick. She doesn't recognize the sickness, but blames herself. Blames herself for everything.

"Have some coffee," Joan put a cup on the table for her. "It will help wake you up."

Silence. She sat down in front of the cup. Girard looked at her over his woven fingers.

"Tell us about them," he said, softly.

"I don't know much about them. I haven't seen them more than six times."

"But, you have heard some rumors, seen some things. Other people talk. How did you get into this place?"

"Place?" Rozella looked up, confused.

"Position. I mean, how did you get to know them, and John?"

"Renting the cottage from John's father."

"What is he like? I've never seen him, except at a distance. Even in their own yard, he keeps to himself, and walks off when you come about. When we buy feed from them, it's John we talk to."

"The old man looks at you funny, sounds angry, accusing…but I never know what he is accusing me of doing."

"Has he really laid down all the rules that you seem to be following?" Joan asked, as if she couldn't believe it all.

"The rules, as you call them, were pretty plain the day we told them we wanted to get married. I'm sure that they made them even clearer when I wasn't around. We were to get the use of the house, and something to eat in exchange for John's labor."

"That's not exactly tenant farming: it's more like slave labor."

"I would think so, but what can we do? There is no place for John to go. No work. Anywhere."

"Don't the women have anything to say about things? What about his mother, his sister:" Joan wanted to know.

"His mother is dead now. I only saw her once, the day we went to talk about marriage. She was very religious. They didn't like me because…"

"Why?"

"Rozella began to cry.

"I didn't mean to make you cry. I thought we were friends, or we wouldn't talk this way to you. We really don't know why."

"Because I had the baby. Because I was pregnant before we were married."

"You're condemned? For that? My God," Girard said in a whisper. "That's your only crime?"

"To them, it's a big thing. To me, it's a big thing. We were raised to think that way. I thought I could make it right; John thought we were going to make it right. We felt all right about it."

"That's all that counts, Rose," Joan said, softly.

"But," Rozella continued, "the days I spent in labor…they tell me days…I didn't know until afterward, when I was too sick to care for the baby and Tillie came…I spent four days in and out of labor, or out of my head. Then, they took the baby to Hannah."

"Hannah?"

"Yes, his sister."

"I thought that she was so unfriendly."

"She is…I mean she is to everyone, but she does like Danny." Rozella picked up her cup.

"Why didn't it work out as you hoped? Why isn't everything all right? You did marry. You did want the baby. You and John were happy with the arrangement."

"They couldn't bear the shame. They blamed me for everything. They didn't want me around, but they do want the child because it's John's child. That's all right. If I didn't love him, I'd hate him."

"John?"

"Yes, but only because our life is not normal. It's the baby they want. They don't want me. And they will do anything to arrange things into their own pattern."

"How can you go on this way? Can't you say something?" Girard asked.

"I did. This morning. I did. I have never said anything before, but I just couldn't face this holiday…this long day, not living like other people. Always alone. Every Sunday the aloneness. Did you know that we lived that way even before we were married? I would wait for him to come to me; he wouldn't come until night, when everyone was asleep. It's horrible," she cried again.

Joan leaned over Rozella, putting her arms around her shoulders, "I know you haven't thought of this, but perhaps you should – do you really want to live this way the rest of your life?"

"I haven't thought. I haven't let myself think, but there's no place to go. Nothing that I can do. There is Danny, and I must make my peace. For Danny, I must live, must accept."

"And you, Rose" Girard asked, "You? Is there to be nothing for you in this life?"

"We get what…we are intended to get. Or, my mother used to tell me, we get what we deserve."

"My God, that's a mortal condemnation!" Girard slammed his fist down on the table, got up and left the room abruptly.

"Don't pay attention to him, Rose, he just cares a lot. He's soft for people that he likes," Joan said "It's okay for now. I can't think of anything that we can do to make you feel better, but we'll try.

You've cried enough for one day. Especially this day. Let's get busy. Do something." She reached down to wipe the tears off Rozella's cheeks.

"What?"

"Let's start by going for a long walk in the snow. There's nothing like tiring yourself out wading through snow when you don't want to face a problem. Just the snow will keep you busy for awhile."

"They put on their coats, mufflers, and boots. It was nearly noon and the sun was high. Girard was nowhere to be seen. He had made his comment in parting and gone off somewhere to be alone. The old sheep dog that had refused to leave the farm when Joan and Girard bought it came running up to them when they stepped out into the cold. He sniffed at their heels, looked up and wagged his tail as if accepting them, giving them the right to walk on his property.

The snow was crisp, and crunched under their boots, sometimes slippery – sometimes rough where frozen after a sudden thaw. Their shadows played along with them, falling so close behind that they were barely to be seen. Breath rose in frost-like steam, and they walked silently. Which direction should they go: Toward the church in the east, or toward the west of their house where the Queist house stood back from the road. Without asking each other, they turned to the west.

Walking toward the house they had spoken of, neither woman said a word. As if silently acquiescing, instinctively knowing where their steps were leading them, they also knew that they could do nothing but look, stand there in the snow and look at the house so snugly packed into the snow.

Rozella felt like she was a spectator in her own life. In that house… where the smoke slowly rose against the sky, were her husband and her child. The Queist family was with them. They must have already had their mid-day dinner, what was happening now? As exile in her own life, she thought, with a great sense of unreality. She could draw a picture of this, or write a story about this, but she couldn't feel it, or live it, except for the pain. Joan was holding her arm, pulling her along. How long had they stood there, she wondered?

"Let's go now," Joan was insisting. "It's time for our dinner. Girard will wonder where we have gone off to…"

"Does he worry?" Rozella asked, making small talk.

"Sometimes. Although, he is used to me, and my eccentric behavior. We know each other so well, and agreed to give each other freedom. We didn't think it could be love, unless we were willing to let each other be free."

"Maybe…maybe that's what I'm doing. I don't seem to be able to stop what's happening. Maybe I have to do this." Rozella pondered aloud.

"I don't think it's the same thing," Joan answered, smiling to herself. "It's not what we were thinking. Yours is not a giving of freedom, it's a taking of hurt in an unnatural way. Forgive me if that makes you feel worse. It's just what I'm thinking."

"No, you don't hurt me. You make me think, you and Girard. Sometimes I don't like it, but, it seems that my mind moves whenever you are around. Most of the time, in happy ways."

"Good. At least, I hope that's good," Joan answered.

Their dinner was late in the day. It was different than the night before when the four of them had been so close and happy together. It was difficult to be excited over preparing it. Nothing tasted good to Rozella. The turkey tasted like cardboard and the potatoes stuck in her throat. She pushed her food around on her place, and tried to be smiling about it. Girard was sullen. Back from the barnyard where he had spent most of Christmas afternoon chopping wood, he still wouldn't talk. For him, this was unusual. Rozella felt he was on the verge of saying something, and found herself waiting in anticipation; yet, nothing was said. She and Joan filled in the blank and empty spaces with conversation that was also blank and empty

After dinner, and when the dishes were done and put away, Girard and Joan helped her gather things together, her nightgown, the few extra baby things, the baby bottles, and Christmas gifts, into a bundle. They packed up a box full of leftover food: turkey, pie and extras for her to take home with her. By the time they reached the cottage it was dark. She hated the coldness of the house. She knew how cold it would be. Knew it would smell of emptiness. She didn't want to go in, but she didn't want to stay at Joan's and Girard's. John would be home. His home. And with Danny.

Very soon then, things would be brighter. When the lamps were lit, the fire burning, things would be better. She could tell him about the day, and ask him about his day. She could hold Danny, change him, and put him to bed in his own bed. It would be better, she thought as she opened the door to the cold cottage.

The smell was there: the smell of cold and stale smoke from wood fires. Their voices were trying to break the silence and the gloom of Christmas night in an empty house. "We'll put the packages down right here. Are you sure you have everything you need? If not, we can go back to the house..."

"It's fine. There's nothing else I need. I'll be fine. He'll be home soon. There are things in the house, you know. And he will bring a basket from their house. He always does. Our weekly rations," she laughed nervously.

Joan kissed her goodbye and Girard gave her a hug. They left, the door swinging shut and leaving her alone in the kitchen. She wandered through the house, picking up things and putting them down, senselessly. Then, aware of herself, she forced herself to unpack the box, put the food away, and put the clothes away. All was in place before John came in.

She reached for Danny eagerly. He squirmed in John's arms as if uncomfortable. She took him, removed his wraps, and cap, talking to him, talking to him about his day, his Christmas, asking him what Santa brought him.

John sat down, as if relieved to be shed of a burden.

"He's been fussy as can be today," he said.

"Nonsense. He's just telling you that he missed me."

"I wish. I tried everything I could think of. So did Hannah."

Rozella touched Danny's rosy cheeks, red from the cold. Ran her fingers over his lips, soft, soft as velvet, she thought, like his hair, fuzzy and fine. Everything about him was soft. Her womb still would knot up inside when she touched him like this. Something inside of her hurt and reached and wouldn't be still. Everything was all right. He was home, and in her arms.

Girard sat in the chair before the fire, leaning forward watching flames play against the isinglass in the stove door. He was twisting an empty cup between his hands, and string into space without moving. Joan had already dressed for bed and came out of their bedroom to stand watching him. The hair on the back of his neck had grown long and curled over his flannel shirt collar. She could sense the softness of his hair as she looked at him. His moving hands, turning the cup around and around, were saying something. She stepped toward him to rest her hand upon his back. "You're angry. I feel it."

"Yeh."

"Just everything in general, or something more specific?"

"I'm finding it difficult to believe what I'm seeing...and yes, you are right. I'm damned angry. The old man Rose describes...who rations out life to them...do you know?"

"I don't know anything about him. What do you know?"

"Just what I see. He owns quite a few mortgages here abouts."

"What do you mean?"

"I shouldn't be talking about it, even to you. It's business, and supposed to be confidential. Queist has been buying up foreclosures... not all of them, but as many as he can. One of the banks is handling tenant farming placement for him. It's not a lot..."

"Not a lot? Why not his own son and Rose? Why does he keep them on at his place? Why the rationing of food and money?"

"That's the way he gets his money, I suppose. He's frugal to the point of insanity. It has to be the craziest thing I've heard."

"Then, he and Hannah – they really have money?"

"Money on paper, at least. Maybe it's not as much as one would think. After all, who can sell a mortgage these days for more than a pittance? Of course, that's why he buys them. Maybe it's all just one huge gamble."

"No wonder you're upset."

"Upset is putting it mildly. I'm so mad I could go choke the old bastard."

"What are you going to do?"

"Nothing. How can I tell Rose something that would only hurt her? It wouldn't change things."

"John could say something, demand something different."

"Could he? He could be refused, too."

"And Rose...goes on feeling that she is to blame. To blame for what?"

"Joan, it's painful…I…come here." He put his arms around her waist, found a place to rest his head. "I don't like it. I don't like it, but I do like her. You know what I mean? She is so soft and vulnerable. I like her and yet, I want to shake her to make her come alive. She won't let herself object. No one gave her permission."

"Maybe we'll have to give her permission, darling. Maybe it's up to us. We'll think of something."

"Can't we find out more about the Queists? Someone must know about them. What is Hannah really like? What makes them the way they are?"

"We may never know the answers to all those questions, but we could get Rose to start asking a few questions. She might find out from John. I can ask Tillie, or some of the others around here."

"If we know, what do we know? That doesn't make sense…I mean…"

"I know what you mean: if we hear gossip, what do we really know? We've been through all that."

"Yeh. We have. Well burned, too."

"Come on hon, let's go to bed now. We'll talk in the morning. I want to have you near me. It feels too lonely."

Joan breathed deeply, pulled at her navy blue jacket, threw it over the chair beside Rozella's kitchen table. Her boy's shirt hung loosely over her flat chest. "I'm so angry, Rose, so angry. Wait a minute, I'll explain. Let me catch my breath. You're right if you think I'm babbling, but that's not new. You haven't seen any newspapers. You don't have a radio. Damn it, Rose. They're killing all the pigs."

"You're right, I don't understand you. Whose pigs? And who are 'they'?"

"Because the price of corn and pork is so low," Joan sat down on top of the coat, which had slipped into the chair as she moved. "They have burned the corn. Someone in Washington decided that corn and pork go together. They think if they reduce the quantity on the market, they will raise the prices."

"But, there are so many hungry people."

"Exactly, that's why it's madness. People are starving and we kill off the meat supply. The peaches rotted in California, fell from the trees last fall, rotten. All this happens while people starve. Rose, they are going to slaughter six million pigs and turn them into fertilizer. How long has it been since you had a pork roast on your table?"

"Not since I was home. We get a bit of salt pork each week. That's all. My mother used to have pork roast once in awhile. I haven't had a pork roast since I've been here."

"Don't you ever ask what's happening to it? The rest of the pig, I mean? If you only get salt pork, where is the rest?"

"I…I…"

"Oh, I'm sorry. You don't ask anything about what goes on over there. You're the tenant. Only the tenants never get paid, not in money, not in land. God, Oh, God, I've done it again. I have no right."

"We do eat. We're better off than some." Rozella's voice was soft, but defensive.

"Yes, some. But, couldn't it be better than this?"

"We have a child. What can I do? What else can we do?"

"I didn't mean that you should leave. I just got excited and angry with what is going on, about what is happening. The old man…"

"I don't want to hear any more," Rose turned away. "I can't help what he does."

Joan was pacing around the room. "I promised myself I wouldn't do these things, no matter what. Girard and I will get through this. We had some money, the money my grandmother left me. All that was left that I didn't spend. I was a stupid kid and played a lot. I didn't care about what was going on around the world, and I never even thought about my future. We have no kids, so we don't have them to worry about.

Everyone is so damned righteous in this part of the country. What is this *never getting angry business*? Don't ask questions. Accept. What will you inherit in this world?

What kind of a world do you want for your child? A world where they turn food into garbage and plow it under rather than feed the hungry? Their own people are starving and no one notices. Jesus. Girard and I talk about becoming self-sustaining. It's something from the past, your mother's generation, not ours."

Rose was overwhelmed by her tirade, "In a way...but, town people must garden and work also," she answered. "They have similar problems even though they aren't self-sustaining."

"Does John ever talk about going away?"

"Not anymore. He doesn't talk much about anything. He's quiet and becomes quieter all the time. He is accepting what he can't change. That's all."

"Or waiting. Waiting for the old people to die off," Joan responded.

"Joan!" Rozella stood up, shocked.

"Well, it's logical. Come to grips with what he is doing. Waiting for the old man to die."

"But there is Hannah. Think about it. She's not that old."

"If you knew what is in John's head, you'd know what he imagines will happen to Hannah. Maybe he thinks Hannah will be more helpful than her father."

"I think she hates me, but with John, it's different."

"You don't want to talk about it, I know. Another of those things you don't want to talk about, or is it – think about it? It won't go away because you won't talk about it."

Rozella poured them some more coffee. "But, you started talking about pigs and Washington. It's not the Queist's fault what the rest of the world does."

"True, but they have their own form of madness."

"Times are hard. You just said so. You just described how bad they are. There is no hope to be found in this world. That means there is no place for people like us. So, we cling to this place. It's all we have. At least, we're not being turned off the land."

"I can't believe this. I'm living in some kind of a nightmare, and wondering why I came to a God-forsaken place like this. Why didn't Girard and I stay – anywhere, but here?" Joan shook her head sadly.

"Are things better somewhere else, then? Really?" Rozella asked.

"No. Not really," Joan admitted, "It's happening all over the world. It's like an angry disease. It always seems more real when it's close to you. But, where else are they throwing away food? I can't think of another place in the world. And...I wanted to come home. America was home to me. I had some kind of a crazy dream.

"You're getting your dream, aren't you?"

"Only in acres. Everything else is distorted. I didn't mean to frighten you this morning. I just had to talk to someone about this. Now, I want to know more about Hannah. Just because I'm a curious person, and because I have never met her. Because you are my friend, I want you to know that I'm going to ask some questions of people who knew her earlier, before you came here. If you don't want to know, then tell me and I won't share it with you."

"Joan, you have shouted so much that you woke up Danny. You and your excitement over things."

"It's not excitement, it's more like anger. I'm really going to ask questions, Rose. Listen to me. I want you to know, so you can know more about what your life is, if you want to know…"

"Just a minute, I'll pick Danny up," she answered, rising to go to the child. "I'm almost afraid of what I'll find out, but at the same time I don't have the vaguest idea of what could be different. They – the Queists – are just not very accepting."

"That's damned polite of you. I'm going to start one of those sewing circles, or whatever you call 'em. Can't stand that sort of thing, but I can listen. If the conversation gets interesting enough…don't you want to know whose pictures those were…the ones you found when you first came here? You could do me a favor, and I know you won't think of it as a favor, but couldn't you ask John a few questions? Have you ever asked John about the pictures? Rose, we ARE friends, aren't we? You don't keep things from me that you know? Things that you don't want to talk about?"

"No. I mean, yes, I do tell you what I know. I never had a chance to know the Queists. I didn't live here before I taught here. All I know is that there is a sort of general fear of the old man Queist, and of Hannah, but I don't know why. The Queists aren't going to 'do' things to people. What could they do? It's like being afraid of the boogieman. People imagine things because they don't know. They like to guess."

"Is that the way you see me, Rose, imagining things?"

"No, not really," she blushed.

"And you know, Rose, if you don't find them fearsome people, why do you stay here, confined to your own house almost, following their rules, their boundaries? You don't have to answer that, but let me find out what I can."

"I can't let you, or not let you do anything."

"You can tell me if the idea hurts you." Joan touched her hand.

"It doesn't hurt, unless what you find out hurts, and how could what you find out hurt anymore than – I don't' know what you could find."

Then, tell me what is happening in your life. Never mind. I can see."

CHAPTER EIGHTEEN

Greater love hath no friend; Joan quoted to herself entering the pale yellow house from a side door. The oval beveled glass in the door was a reflected pool of light, gossamer webs of color shining through it. Worn glass, like a masque of oil on water, was glistening. The hallway floor was waxed to extreme gloss and the rugs were slipping beneath her feet. She slowed her steps, as she was about to fall. Her dress shoes had smooth leather soles, and Joan was not used to them, or to the dress she was wearing, soft and smoky blue. She looked as different as she felt in her 'sacrificial garments' as she had mockingly described them to Girard.

She held a small bag of embroidery cotton, which she had purchased from the dime store in Crenshaw; she had needles in all sizes.

The ladies were gathered in the front room. (Called 'front room' here, she thought. Why is it always called 'front room' even when it is on the side of the house? Maybe it could be in the back of a house, too. No. It is never on the back of a house, or it would be…don't let your sense of humor out here, she reminded herself).

Hello How are you? Aren't you new to our group? The round lady in a splashy orange print dress was speaking.

Yes. I'm interested in doing some needlework. But, I don't know much about it. I hope someone will show me how.

Show me, please. *Yes, show me. If I ever get the thread untangled. Last time I tried this, I threw it out. I had so many knots, and Girard laughed – he said I had better talents, I didn't have to know how to do those things.*

We have a lot of experts here. Always eager to teach someone new. Aren't they? Grandma Schultz has been doing needlepoint for fifty years now.

My God, fifty years of those tiny stitches would make me blind.

Yes, I always did want to learn how to do needlepoint, but this time I brought some embroidery thread.

Oh, for goodness sake, Joan, that is you! I haven't seen you for ages. Don't you remember me? Tillie?

One person. One person's voice was coming through to her now, and the party began to focus.

"It's been awhile, but I do remember."

"Tillie, the one who took care of Rose when the baby came." She was saying. "Why didn't you bring Rozella along?"

"I might do that some day, if I can get her away from the house. She likes to stay with Danny. Doesn't take him out much, and won't leave him."

"She could leave him with John's family. John would take him over to Hannah."

"Yes. I never thought of reminding her." *But, she has to part with him every weekend, and she wouldn't do that during the week. I can understand it, Joan thought. Once a week, wasn't that enough?* "I'm really awkward at this sort of thing, Tillie. I'm better with a hammer and nails, and painting walls."

"A lot of us are, but don't let it scare you. Besides, the goodies they serve with coffee are worth the effort."

"Even needle holes in the ends of my fingers?"

"It may seem silly to you, but when we do a quilt together, the quilting part is really beautiful. We are proud of our work. Did you ever see the Shaker quilting in the east?"

"I missed a lot of things. Some things I didn't take an interest in when I was younger. No one around me did such work. But I can learn something new now, can't I?"

"Sure you can."

The fern in the window was green, bright with the latticework of the sun, Joan noticed. Red geraniums. Cobwebs tying the geranium leaves together. *(Who are they? All these women? Sitting around the room. Fat legs, clothes in dark silk, hanging heavy over the edges of worn shoes. A red ball of yard beside those shoes. A skirt stretched tightly across the space that marks the heaviness of the legs that cannot rest close together anymore. Fingers knotted with arthritis.)* Mrs. Clover? Glad to meet you. Disconnected words floated through the room. A skinny black and white cat grabbed a basket on the floor with its claws. He pulled himself against the weight of the basket. Go away. Don't kitty. You don't belong in here, said a reddish blonde with a child's face shining above her child's body, which blossomed with the tight belly of pregnancy.

Two women bent over a pattern on a mahogany table, arguing, braided buns on the back of their necks like matched sets of corded balls. Doilies everywhere, on the edges of every chair, covering arms and back and the tables. Yet, they made more doilies.

The whole world – covered in doilies, stretched end to end in thread. Where would it go? Across the Atlantic and back. Tied together, their world is tied together with needles, and knotted. Careful not to pull. If you unravel their world…

And, this is Mrs. Alexander. She just joined us last month. She bakes the best graham bread with raisins. Did you bring some today?

Heavens, no. Who wants to eat bread in the afternoon?

Yours, I would eat any time…

That man. He never will keep his hands…keep telling him that the piece my mother gave us must last until the children get it. He doesn't care. And who has money these days? No one.

How can I stand this conversation all day? I'd rather be at home, home alone.

Pretend. Oh, God, just pretend, when you get a chance, ask a few questions. Be subtle if you ever were, Joan. Now, be subtle. Keep calm. Don't get riled. Don't start anything you don't want to get involved in.

And they said the Clemen's place would go on the block next week. Who said? Well, my husband said. *Always the husband saying, never the wife saying. Why?* No dairy money. No milk money. The mortgage. Let's not talk about it. Ladies. Stay with happier things. Isn't this the Sunshine circle? *Oh, Jesus. The Sunshine Circle! I think I'll be sick.*

Thank you. I'd love some coffee. Then someone can show me which needle to use…Ramsey's kids have measles. That means they'll all have 'em. When did your kids last see their kids? Only every day in school. What can you do? Now, I'll be stuck at home nursing the whole family through some sort of siege again. Just now got them all in school, and I'll get them all back at home. That last one is a real brat, too. The youngest always is, isn't it so? At least, that's what everyone says.

Speak for yourself. I still believe in a strong hand. Maybe it's good. My parents weren't too easy on me. But a person gets tired after the years spent on all of them. After awhile you just don't have any fight anymore. Let 'em go. Let 'em grow, you mean? Can't stop 'em from growing. *Jesus…my finger is bleeding all over this ugly piece of cotton. Bloodstains. What's the formula for bloodstains? How do you get them out? Look what I've done.*

Joan put her finger in her mouth, and then wondered if she should do that. *To Hell with it. It hurts.* Cold water. Put it in cold water. Right now. Not the finger. The cotton. Take it out in the kitchen and Elvie will help you put it in a bit of water.

Not hard to find cold water this time of year. It is hard to find water that isn't frozen. You're so damned funny. Is this the way it's going to be the next hundred years? I can't take the humor. Put it in here. Let it soak for a bit, then wash it with a little soap. It will come right out. Don't look so disappointed. We all do it, no matter how many years we have worked on this sort of thing. You're Joan Girard? It took me a long time to figure out what your last name was. People always call your husband…

"I know, by his last name. I don't even want to talk about his first name. We both hate it. Agreed to forget it long ago."

"We haven't seen much of you. What do you do with yourself?" Elvie asked her.

"Try to do a lot around the farm. Girard works in town. That leaves work for me, taking care of the animals. I spend some time with Rozella Queist. She's good company."

Words were focusing again. Elvie continued: "Rozella? She was a teacher here, wasn't she? For a short time?"

"Until the baby came."

"Queist? It's the same family?"

"She married John."

"It's the same family."

What family? What do you mean by family? You don't say what about the family. Why can't you finish what you're thinking? Don't you know her? Is it like she never existed? "Did you know John?" Joan asked aloud.

"I didn't know him. We must not be the same age. Usually it's the people who go to school together who know more about each other. You end up keeping in touch, marrying each other's brothers... perish the thought. I can't imagine marrying some of my best friend's brothers."

"Who did you marry?"

"You don't know him. I married a fellow from the next town – the county seat, Hamden. Not our county. The next one."

So I gathered, another world traveler. "How did you get so lucky?"

"I worked there awhile. In the department store." Elvie checked the bloodstains.

"And, and brought new blood to the area."

"You'd call it that, I suppose," and for some reason, she blushed. Tillie came in at that moment. *Rescue me. Rescue me from this. I can't stand it another minute.*

"I'll be back in a couple of minutes and take care of that," Joan told Elvie. "Lead me to the cookies, Tillie. I'm starved. I've had no breakfast, or lunch."

"Why? Silly girl, and you look like you were about to jump through the window. Yes, let's get something to munch on and go over and sit in the corner before you explode."

"How do you know me so well?"

"I hear things...about your red-headed temper, and conversations. That's okay. I like it. We could use a little life around here. I get tired of the same old talk all the time, too. I feel like I'm repeating everything my mother said to my Grandmother before her."

"Want to know the truth, Tillie? I really came here today for the gossip. I always understood that these groups were full of wonderful, juicy gossip, and all I hear is these funny little stories about husband's dirty feet, shoes – that is, and the current epidemics. I'd like to hear something really different."

"Not much in the way of exciting tales around here, I'm afraid. The last scandal was the year we fired the minister."

"Fired the minister?"

"Because he liked boys." Tillie grinned.

"Oh, fine. I like boys, too, and men. You mean – in this place?"

"It happens here. At least, they thought it had happened here."

"Everything seems to hang together by the threads of who one went to school with. We're such close friends with John and Rozella. I'd like to know more about his family. He just doesn't talk much, and Rozella doesn't know much about his family either," Joan said.

"I can understand why you want to know about them. I went to school with John, and I remember Hannah. I didn't know Rozella before she came here. All I know about her I learned while taking care of her when Danny was born. If you are born here, everybody knows everything...

How is Rozella's mother? As I remember, her mother was very ill, and not expected to live?"

Joan reached for her coffee cup, "She's still alive, and living longer than anyone expected. There are still two kids at home, watching her die a day at a time."

"They've lived with it so long. They don't notice it happening. It seems normal to them to see her in bed. You don't know kids very well, do you?"

"That's true. And don't want to. Kids are all right, when they're someone else's. I don't mean that I don't like them." Joan sipped on her coffee.

"I know that, but don't say it around here."

The mother image. Yes, the mother image. We must keep it sacred. "No, I won't," she said aloud.

Tillie smiled. "You're a good person, Joan. You are just different."

"Tell me more."

"About being a good person?"

"No, about John's family."

"What do you want to know?" Tillie answered, sitting down.

"Everything...and anything. And, why isn't Hannah here? Everyone else is here."

"Not really. It just seems like everyone else. You're exaggerating."

"A trait I am noted for." *Yes, Girard, she thought, you always tell me that I exaggerate. Where are you today? I wish you were here to talk to. This is a zoo.*

"Hannah never goes to these meetings. She goes to church. – only."

"What about her mother? She's gone now, but didn't she ever go to the circle meetings?"

"She did long ago, years ago, I suppose. I don't remember. I'm not that old, Joan. I just look that way."

"You don't look that way...I just thought you would have heard. That ancient Mrs. Somebody or other who has been doing needlepoint for fifty years should know about anyone."

"She thinks she does, but she's either forgetful or imaginative." Tillie explained.

"Why didn't Hannah go?"

"I don't know. She started staying home from school when she was sixteen. Actually, quite a few girls stay home from school earlier than that. Some are married before sixteen. None of that is unusual. Hannah just never married, or never became active in these groups. We always thought she was too busy to get out, especially once her mother became so crippled up that she couldn't walk. And I can't remember that, either. It seems that it was before Hannah quit school."

"So, you don't really know Hannah?" Joan asked.

"No."

Your eyes are the brightest blue I've ever seen. If I were going to like girls, I'd pick someone with eyes like yours, Joan thought. An explosion of blue in her head. "This coffee is cold. Does anybody know her?" Joan asked, pulling the blue eyes out of her mind.

"I don't think...I can't think..."

"It's all right. I didn't mean to press you. Have there always been the same people living on that farm?"

"*Always* is a long time," Tillie smiled. "To me it means *since I can remember*, and that's true: as long as I can remember they have lived there."

"Was the old man ever young? He must have been. Do you remember anything about him earlier? Or Hannah? Who lived in the cottage? Surely it hasn't been empty all these years, until Rose..."

"They used it for hired hands, long ago – was it before the war?" And the focus of Tillie's voice brought Joan to reality. The war? "How many hired hands? Where did they go?" she asked Tillie.

"Kids don't pay attention, really," Tillie answered her, "and, I was a kid then. There were two men who lived there. First one left, then later, the other. The last one stayed a year. I never saw him except when walking near the field where the men were working. He was sort of blonde, I remember. From the old country. Could he have been an immigrant worker?"

"I don't know," Joan answered, as if she was expected to know. "How old was he, would you guess?"

"He looked old to me, but you must remember my age. I thought my parents looked old, too. Things change, the older you get."

"Did he look as old as John…like his thirties?"

"Younger. Younger. And he looked as if he hadn't done that kind of work so long. You know how men get weathered when they work outside a lot? Why are you asking about things that happened so long ago?" Tillie wanted to know.

"Just curious. Curious about the family, and Hannah. I keep thinking that there must be more to her than what we see. She couldn't have lived that way, all closed up in a house like a prisoner. Something must have made her tick, something must have…how could she let herself be used by that old man – if that is what happened?"

"The same way he uses his son," Tillie replied, turning away. "I haven't been able to figure it out either, except to notice that there have been families like that around here before – children tied to their parents until death."

"Then, you do think about it too?"

"I have thought about it. And I get nowhere."

"If you don't mind, think about it some more. And come to visit with me when you can. You'll remember more when you try. I'll never be able to fit into this place if I can't understand the people who live here."

"You have me," Tillie laughed. "I'm easy."

"Easy as an open book." The blue eyes flashed with her laughter. Don't let them go, she told herself. "I'll see you next week?" Joan answered, as if she was asking permission.

"Sure. I'm always home, when I'm not hanging around places like this." Tillie wove herself into the mixture of ladies now coming out into the kitchen and became absorbed in their conversations.

So, he said…and the snow was so deep last winter that the school closed down for three days…what did you do for curtains on those windows…the heifer died last week…I'm so tired of being pregnant… who asks if a woman wants to be pregnant…if the men had to carry…

Joan brought the stories she collected to Rose. After she had sorted out the intelligible from the unintelligible and the "hardly-likely," there wasn't much to be heard. Most of the women had the picture of Hannah just as she now appeared to them, as if her image had been the same since she was a child. Only a few remembered the family in its earlier years. Bits and pieces of information came only from the old and forgetful. The farm had come from the mother's side. The husband had married into the farm. The wife had been an only surviving child, and inherited the land at the turn of the century when a few Indians still roamed through the area, lost and misplaced, and refusing to live on the reservations established.

Hannah's father came to the area from New York, after he emigrated from Norway. He had spoken little English when he came. He had worked on the farm, later marrying the daughter, to the surprise of the surrounding countryside. She was a daughter left too long, a daughter too old to marry. Her parents had allowed the marriage. They needed a surrogate son to carry on the farming, and to manage the place. And he was eager to do that.

Eager in many ways, people said. Most felt it was a marriage for money: the crass to the refined, the immigrant to the older woman who held the land. Regardless of the reason, the two produced two children by this unromantic marriage. First Hannah, then John. A long span between the two children made the community speculate about the relationship. They imagined that the older woman could not bear children easily because of her frailty, or age, or they imagined that her husband did not feel attracted to her. The more children a woman could bear, the more pride she felt in her sexual attraction those days.

Or was it an excuse to multiply when there was no secure way to avoid multiplying? Either way, no one knew the truth.

Caught up in the stories that she shared with Joan, even Rozella dared to ask John about Hannah. "Tell me about her," she asked, "I don't understand why she never married."

"People don't have to get married, you know. Not everyone does," he answered, avoiding her question and causing her some embarrassment over their own marriage. Had he not wanted her?

"But most women do. And she couldn't have been that unattractive. She's your sister. She makes herself look ugly now. She isn't that old, or that ugly. It's what she does to herself – or doesn't do." She poured him some more breakfast coffee.

"No. Hannah wasn't always that way, I must admit," he answered.

"Well, how was she? What did she look like when she was a girl?"

"Look like? It's hard to describe your own sister. As a kid you don't think about it much. She had brown hair."

"I know. She still does."

"What was she like? She read a lot. She really liked books. Now she never touches them at all. That is strange. And I never thought about it."

"When did she stop reading?"

"After...it must have been after she quit school." John was finishing breakfast.

"Someone said that she quit at sixteen. Did she really want to quit?"

"I thought so. I thought that everyone would want to quit. I did. But Pa wouldn't let me. So, I guessed that she wanted to quit, too." John answered.

"She wouldn't have chosen to quit if she really liked books and things like that,"

Rozella turned to look at him from the cupboard where she was putting dishes away.

"No. But thinking back that far is difficult. You can't really understand what happened – and your own point of view changes as you grow older."

"That's true, but you can remember some of what happened and have some understanding. I only want to understand her. Maybe..."

"Father made her quit. He refused to let her go anymore. He kept her at home. He always used to walk her home. I remember that. And never me. Never me." He said that as if jealous of her. "I walked alone."

"Why did he walk her home? Didn't you ever wonder? Other fathers didn't do that."

"He didn't want the boys bothering her, that's all. One time they teased and chased her. He said he wouldn't tolerate that; he would see that nobody bothered her again."

"What did he mean by that?" Rozella sat down at the table again.

"I suppose they were at the silly age when they wanted to experiment with girls and kissing, and maybe more…and she was…"

"She was very pretty, wasn't' she, John?" Rozella wanted to know.

"Yes. My father used to love her hair when it fell down across her back. How he used t o look at her hair. The only time I can remember that he ever looked softly at anything. Sometimes he would touch her hair. And he seemed angry about every young man that tried to speak to her."

"Couldn't anyone speak to her? Wasn't she allowed to go anywhere?

"She always went to church, but that was with the family. We all went."

"Dressed up in your best?"

"Of course. Hannah wearing dresses. Pa used to see that she had dresses in colors like the spring: pastels with ruffles." He smiled remembering how she looked; "Now she wears black, and things that are old and worn. I'd guess that she digs them out of old trunks up in our attic."

"Does he make her dress that way, or does she choose to do it?"

"I don't know. I always guessed that it was money. The terrible lack of money that everyone seems to have. And they talk about money, as if there never is any to spend."

"What did she do with herself the days there wasn't any church or school? Did she always work the way she does now, in the fields, in the gardens, in the house?"

"No. My mother did some work, when I was small, but mostly we had help in those days. There was always a woman living in the house who did most of the work. It's been since Hannah quit school that she has been doing all the work," John remembered.

"Before that?"

"She read. I said that. Sometimes she tried to paint. Some watercolors. I seem to remember that she framed one or two of them. They may be still hanging up in the house. They must be. Nothing has changed." John was getting up now and preparing to leave the house. It was harder to keep him talking.

"What did she paint?" Rozella persisted.

"Flowers. That's right. She used to go walk in the woods and paint flowers. That's what the pictures were…are."

"And?"

"She walked…yes. I remember finding her on the path that leads down here, to this cottage. And I remember that she used to talk to Nels."

"At last. There was a man here, and he had a name."

"I didn't say that."

"But, you did say you had seen her with him, John. Just now."

"Well, talking, what is that? We talk to a lot of people every day whenever they come around, at least."

"The pictures that I saw so long ago, the photos that your father took from me, were pictures of your house; I remembered when I saw the house the first time. And the truck, it was your father's truck, the one you drive to the market now." Rozella got up to follow him to the door.

"You must be mistaken. I don't remember anyone taking photos. We didn't even have a camera. It's too expensive for Pa, and he mistrusts anything like that."

"But, I did see the pictures, and he said they were left behind by a hired hand…Nels. Nels could have taken the pictures, put them in an album and left them behind."

"Yes, he could have. I don't know that he had a camera, and I didn't ever see the pictures, but he could have taken them."

"Then, you see that I didn't imagine it, they were real photos in a black album. Pictures of real people, the people right here?"

"I know you didn't make it up. I believe you, it's just that I didn't know about this, or even think about it." John opened the door.

"John, I'm not usually so nosey. You know that. I never ask questions of people, but this – the pictures. You won't believe this…"

"Believe what?"

"The pictures had the heads cut off."

"What do you mean 'had the heads cut off'?" He turned in the doorway.

"The heads of the people had been cut out of the pictures."

"That is strange. Are you sure they just hadn't been torn, or ripped out of the book?"

"No. They were neatly cut in round circles, leaving everything but the heads of the people."

"That I can't understand."

"Neither do I. That's why I'm asking. The puzzle never leaves my mind."

"All right – Hannah and Nels. Can we assume that it was what you want to believe, some kind of first love, any kind of love?"

"That's what I would assume. There isn't a word of anything about Hannah and anyone else from anybody."

"And, you've been asking?" He looked at her with anger, suddenly becoming defensive.

"Joan has been asking. I'm sorry. She means well; she wants to help. She hasn't been clumsy; she's too smart. Hannah and Nels – think now."

"Yes. It would fit. Hannah spent a lot of time painting in the woods. She spent a lot of time writing. I never read what she wrote, but I heard Pa once – at night – he was reading something to her out loud, and yelling at her. He burned it, whatever it was. She cried. I remember that. She went into her room and didn't come out. I couldn't get her to talk to me. It was after…"

"After that she didn't go back to school?"

"That's right," and John sighed, as if it pained him, "after that she never went back to school. After that, she went to work in the fields with the men, wearing overalls, working with a pitchfork in the sun. After that, I never saw her wear a pretty dress again, and she kept her hair braided up."

"And Nels?"

"He left. No one said anything. He was gone. One day I passed the cottage and he wasn't there anymore. I asked about him at home and Pa wouldn't say. He acted as if everyone knew."

"What about Hannah?"

"She didn't say anything. Didn't speak at all."

"Your father?"

"Finally he said that Nels had left because he had another job, when I kept asking."

"And no one saw Nels leave?"

"Only father. He is the one who told me what happened."

"But, you don't know that he left – really?" She was holding unto his sleeve now.

"Well, he wasn't there, he had to have left"

"Yes, but who cut the pictures? Would Nels?"

"Nels could have taken them along with him," John was wondering with her now. "Wouldn't he have taken them along? If they were his pictures?"

"Maybe he forgot them."

"If what you are thinking is true, he wouldn't have forgotten. If the pictures were of him and of Hannah -- he wouldn't have forgotten them, unless they had some kind of a quarrel." Rozella and John had now reversed roles, and the questions were coming from John.

"All I can think of is she used to write, and she used to paint, and then – Nels was gone. No one spoke to him before he left, except Pa. After that she never left the farm to go to school again; she never left at all without father. I want to see the pictures," John said.

"So do I, but we don't have them. They were in the cottage. Your father took them from me. Then, I saw them in the truck when we were in town together the first time. I looked at them again. It was the same album, but I put it back under the seat because I thought you knew they were there. I didn't want to ask." Rozella didn't have to hold unto his sleeve anymore.

"I didn't know they were there. I'd never seen them. You know that now."

"Maybe they're still around someplace."

"I doubt it. Pa must have put them into the truck, but would he keep them? It seems logical that he would throw them away, regardless of what they meant."

"Well, I think his interest is peculiar."

"Don't let your imagination carry you away. He is hard, and cold, and merciless, but not crazy. There are other people around here like him. I'm not the only one who has a 'hard' father or a sister like Hannah. Most of us have had the same sort of life. What was your father like?

Rose? Do you remember?"

"Sorry. I do remember. He was quite different, but the memories are not sweet. He was a drunk, a lovable drunk, but a drunk just the same. Oh, John, I'm so sorry. I didn't mean to hurt you." She looked down, feeling sorry for him.

"It's not that. I try not to think about things like this. It's so hard to live here day by day...so hard to put all dreams away and force yourself to face reality...and this is reality...Thinking about mystery and unfairness only makes the living more difficult. It won't make anything any easier." John kissed her on the forehead.

"But you will keep thinking about this, remembering what you can, and maybe you will see the album again, and we'll be able to see who was in the pictures, and you will really believe me."

"I do believe you, Rose; it's not that."

"I know. It's just that you don't want to believe me."

"Yes, I'm afraid that's true," he answered.

CHAPTER NINETEEN

In March a county farm bureau office was set up. Out of its staff of city workers were those who gathered the farm wives together to teach them how to make underwear out of flour sacks, or children's shirts or pants out of gunnysacks. The countrywomen laughed at them, remembering that they had learned how to do these things long ago. It was no new thing to them. They could have taught the bureau workers a thing or two, they whispered to each other behind closed doors. But they went to classes anyway to pass the time during the days of cold weather, which were long in both hours and poverty.

Rozella measured out the days, watching the child grow. Now he pulled himself up and tried to walk around the furniture, crawling at times between chairs and bureaus. He slept less, and moved about more.

With spring came the green gentleness of new air. As if coming out of a strange and far away land, it crossed the fields softly as a woman's touch. It was on a spring day when Rozella was outside digging in the cold ground trying to make a flowerbed that the message came. The phone was ringing shrilly, breaking the day with the unusual sound of a bell, sharp and insistent. Ignoring the rings she waited long to answer the phone. It was not often their call on the line.

This time it was Ola telling her to come home, her mother was really dying now.

It wasn't easy preparing to go home. There was the difficulty of getting the Queists to accept the fact that the emergency trip was real;

she did need to have bus money. There was no problem with leaving Danny with Hannah. The only problem was within her – she didn't want to leave him behind. He was becoming much too attached to the Queist home and the plentiful supply of sweets given to him while visiting there.

At the end of her journey home the next day, Rozella found sickness hanging in the air like stale smoke. Ola looking like a walking skeleton threw her arms around Rozella, sobbing bitterly.

"Don't feel so bad," Rozella told her, "You've done everything that you could do."

"It's not that," she sobbed, "I'm so tired, and I always feel like I've failed. I cry sometimes without knowing why."

"She makes you feel that way."

"It's so easy to say when you're not with her. When you are, it starts all over again. I couldn't keep her well. I couldn't make her well."

"It's not your fault – her illness." Rozella put her bag down, and closed the door.

"I know it, but she makes you think…makes you wonder…about aging and the wages of sin. The wages of sin are death, but how did she sin?"

"That's not what the Bible meant."

"I feel like her death is my sin. You wait…you wait, and see what happens."

"You're too emotional, Ola, because you're too tired."

"I know. I'm always the weeper." She blew her nose.

"If you didn't cry, I'd think you were sick," Rozella smiled. But the smile faded quickly when she entered the darkened room where her mother lay. Thick with the smell of Lysol and decaying flesh, the room made her shudder. Ola had done her best to prepare Rozella, but it was not enough.

The woman who lay on the bed did not resemble her mother. She had shrunken into a wizened elf, eyes sunken, and skin yellow. Her hands lay upon her worn Bible, and her gold-rimmed glasses had slid down her beak-like nose, now bony and thin. Behind the glasses her eyes were closed. She was breathing shallowly, but regularly, Rozella stood frozen, watching her.

"That you, Ola?" the sharp voice cried, and Rozella jumped, not expecting her voice to be so strong.

"No. It's me. Rozella."

"You came. I knew it. You were always a good girl. You would come to your mother on her deathbed. Not all the others will come. Not Joe."

"Joe doesn't know how sick you are. We don't know where he is, so we couldn't tell him to come." Rozella sat down beside the bed.

"I told him over and over, he had a duty to me, a sick woman. I've been a sick woman for years."

"Yes. We know, mother." She reached out to hold her hand.

"The doctor said years ago that I couldn't live long."

"Yes."

"But, I've outlived him. I've been too sick to take care of my family, but I've outlived him...the doctor...and my husband."

"We're grown up, Ma. We can do things ourselves."

"Not all of you. Not the younger ones, but I've always been sick. Even when you were a child. It's a wonder that you survived to be born."

"And I did...and grew up, just the same."

"Because you're a good child. But, there is so much evil. You have no idea..."

"Of course I do, Mama. I'm a grown woman, with a child."

"The young girls, even girls from the church. They let men... I can't talk about it. It's a sin. I know it is. Still they get married in the church, just as if they were..."

"Yes, Mama. I understand."

"I'm glad you and Ola are good girls. No sins like...God can't punish you, remember – it pays. Look at you."

"How's that?"

"You have a nice husband who doesn't drink. A beautiful son. Your husband goes to church every Sunday and does what's right for his parents. Your husband John is a real blessing."

"I suppose so."

"You're lucky. A blessed woman. If I had only had a man who didn't drink. I often told your father – go to church. Go to church or suffer the consequences."

"And, he did suffer the consequences, didn't he?" Rozella finished for her.

"He did. He did. In the north, he reaped his reward. They couldn't even bury him." She began to cry. "The ground was frozen."

"It's all over now, Mama. Don't cry."

"Yes. It is all over. You'll see. How fast it goes. And this is the end now. I'm only 55. Where is Ola?"

"Sleeping, Mama. Sleeping. She's very tired."

"How do you think I feel? Doesn't anybody care?" Mama twisted in her bed.

"We care, or we wouldn't be here."

"Like Joe isn't here. Yes." She closed her eyes and was silent at last.

Day after day the visits remained the same. Ola and Rozella taking turns. Then, the other sisters came home, and they helped share the time beside her bed. Whenever Mama was left alone she would cry out, as if they were cutting her off from life. She would cling to each person who came into the room with her voice and her eyes. Her hands became bonier and hard, the skin loose on her fingers, which now looked like claws.

Between conversations her thoughts would drift in and out to memories and Bible stories. Sometimes the two would blend, and it was difficult to tell where the story and the memory separated. She could no longer read and demanded to be read to by the sisters, but she wouldn't listen. Maggie tried, then Val, then Tonie. The shifts became shorter but more difficult and she became more trying.

Rozella emptied the catheter bag, and the urine was laden with pus. The stench made her gag. She controlled herself as she heard her mother talking softly, as if in her sleep: "You were my best child. A virtuous woman. Maggie…Maggie dirtied herself."

"But, Jesus forgives, Mama." Rozella reminded her, in her mother's own words.

"The Old Testament came first. We live by Moses' law," her mother spoke louder, or we regret it."

Rozella's throat hurt; she felt the lump she was trying to swallow. Days and days of this. The hours in the middle of the night were worse than the day hours. Then, the accusations became magnified in the dark. With praise her mother condemned her. With condemnation of the unchaste, Rozella felt pain, and the lump grew bigger. We… them…we…and she knew that she and her mother were on different sides of the earth, or was it heaven and earth?

Where was love? What was love? Was there nothing anymore but good and bad? When had there been love in their home? Rozella could remember fear and accusation, and guilt, and the miserable lump that she couldn't swallow.

Her mother's voice saying, "and on her forehead was a name written MOTHER OF HARLOTS, and I saw the woman, drunken with the blood of the saints..."

Who were the saints? And who was she? It was spring. Did anything die in the spring? Wasn't it a time for rebirth? Maybe it was the passing into another place, another dimension. She wished that she knew. Wished that she could stop hurting, and stop her mother's voice.

The days passed, and the weeks. When her mother passed to her permanent sleep all the children were there, but Joe, who was not to be found anywhere. Perhaps, he too was dead, and left to lie on a strange and isolated railroad track in some backwoods town in another part of the land.

After the funeral, Rozella left immediately. She was eager to get away. The voice in her ears wouldn't stop night or day. Mama's words could not be shut from her mind.

When Girard picked her up at the bus station in town to drive her home, she knew that she needed John and she was anxious to see him. The weeks apart had been difficult, with she and the sisters fighting death and knowing that they would lose. During the long hours of the night alone beside her mother, she had clung to her need for John, and dreamed dreams of closeness. Talking to him, touching him in her dreams she wanted to try to make him talk to her, to hold her. The months of coldness and the sleepless nights escaped her mind, forgotten now and replaced by what she hoped for.

"What is happening at home?" Girard interrupted her thoughts, and reached for her hand.

"Ola will keep the house. It isn't much, but it's paid for. And she earned it, staying there all those years since Papa left."

"The children?" He turned onto the county road, leaving town.

"You mean David and Mrytle?"

"Yes."

"They'll go with Maggie. And Joe is gone. For good, I guess. It does no good to keep hoping to find him. You remember how many times we tried to trace him? Maggie will fill the emptiness of her life with the younger children – Mama's children."

"How do you mean? I mean, she's still single, or did she marry Jack?"

"Didn't Joan tell you? I assume that she tells you everything, and you hear me too."

"Joan is a good friend, as well as being my wife. She doesn't repeat things casually. You have to tell me what you want me to know."

"I'll try to remember that. They fixed her. I mean, Maggie."

"How's that?"

"She was pregnant by a man who didn't want her. My parents arranged an abortion. Nothing was discussed openly; we were not supposed to know what was going on. But, I took care of her when they brought her home sick. She cried a lot, and talked a lot."

"Abortion? Isn't that illegal here? Or, whatever they did?"

"I know. It is."

"The local doctor?"

"He's not above taking money. We didn't have any money, but my father built him a beautiful cutter."

"That can be worth a lot of money."

"My father was a craftsman in Europe." She answered him, as she looked out the window at the passing fields.

"So, Ola is alone now. What will she do?"

"Work. Now she will go to work as a seamstress, or cigar maker in Crenston."

"Marry?" He questioned.

"If she can find someone. She's considered almost too old now."

The truck slowed down as they turned off the county road. Her hand felt cold and alone as Girard took the steering wheel in both hands. The lights in the cottage made it seem larger than it was. John was waiting for her. As she reached to open the door of the truck, she felt Girard's hand on her shoulder. "Rose?"

"Yes?"

"Sleep well. Things will be brighter in the morning." He smiled and kissed her on the forehead. She jumped out of the truck. Girard carried her bag toward the house where John waited in the doorway, his pale face somber in the shadows, Danny in his arms.

Had it been so long, then, since she had watched him leave Joan and Girard's house on Christmas morning taking her child with him—since she had asked him, begged him to stay with her just that once, on that holiday? She had cried herself to sleep on Christmas night and he had ignored her. The months had been filled with the working, the wondering, and the loneliness. Watching the child grow as they watched the fields bloom and grow, they had come to watch in a mutual silence.

Joan had continued an underground search for information. Through the months Rozella had listened to the gossip Joan gathered, trying not to listen, then becoming caught up in finding excuses for John, and excuses for his family. Hannah, who was she? What was she? Rozella's only knowledge was what Joan had brought to her. This same Hannah had been caring for Danny while she had been gone.

The young Hannah. The young hired man. It was only reasonable. They had found each other. Perhaps on one spring night just like this one. Hannah had once written poetry, John had remembered. That must have been the papers her father was reading to her and destroying. An old school teacher had told someone that Hannah wrote poetry the last year she was in school.

But it was strange poetry the teacher had said. She was calling it strange because it was too deep, she thought, for a child of sixteen. The poems of love and darkness, and loss, a mixture of Bronte and Byron, like stormy weather blended with death. No one had ever seen the poetry since the day the schoolteacher had discovered Hannah's notebook left in the schoolroom. The next day she had returned it to Hannah, and said nothing. The teacher had later suggested that Hannah write more creatively in class, but Hannah blushed, and said nothing and wrote nothing – beyond what she had to write.

Hannah had turned pale, as the days of school had passed that last year, as the people remembered, and the watchful eye of her father became more intense. Everyone who had been around remembered that he came earlier every day to walk her home, meeting her on the road. Then, finally she came no more. The school received a letter stating that she had terminated and was needed at home. There were no laws to keep her there. It was not uncommon. The father was law in the home.

Poetry from Hannah? Hannah, the dark and the mysterious, the hard, the rough looking woman, with red, cracked hands from days of cold water scrubbing. Hannah. Had she a lover at sixteen? Hannah? What had happened to the poet in Hannah: Was it in John? Rozella had never seen it, or heard it. Could there be some core of emotion that Rozella had never touched, or seen?

John handed Rozella the baby, who squealed with delight and wiggled in her arms. As they went into the cottage, the headlights of Girard's truck cast a yellow glow across the dark road, which took him away. She watched him go, a peculiar sense of loss touching her in the darkness.

"It's over?" he asked.

"Yes. At last. The waiting was worse than the death. It was almost…"

"A relief."

"Death is never a relief except to those who die, and I'm not sure of that. Mother was frightened to the last breath. It was as if she didn't expect to be forgiven for anything. And, she didn't really have anything to forgive." Rozella was putting her clothes away.

"No," he answered, as if he knew.

"How have you been?" She wanted to know.

"Fine. Hannah's been taking care of Danny every day and enjoying it. He gets around quickly now. He'll walk soon I think. Maybe he'll walk before his first birthday."

"Then, we'll have to tie him to a bedpost, he's so active. He'll be all over the place." She tickled Danny, who was lying on the bed and watching her. He laughed his baby laugh. Gleefully. Still he was baby enough to have wet diapers, and again she began to take care of him, changing his clothes, getting him ready for bed.

"Hannah does like him, doesn't she?" Rozella reaffirmed.

"She never wants to part with him." John's eyes were shining with pride.

"She always seemed to want him for her own, and yet…couldn't she realize that I'm his mother? He is half mine. He is part me. At least, I think he is. He is growing so fast. Maybe he will not be me at all. He looks more like you."

"So they say," answered John.

"They, meaning your family?"

"Well, yes."

"Couldn't we try…couldn't we ask them to let us be a whole family, a complete family?" She was begging with her eyes.

"You don't want it, Rozella, not really. You remember how it was. You know how they are. The two of them. I do ask, I really do. Sometimes. Then, nothing comes of it, except to make me angry. The anger…"

"Hurts?"

"It's not a very good feeling. I just don't like fighting. Asking seems to lead to argument, then shouting, and bad things get said."

"I don't want that," she agreed. "It would only make me feel worse. And then Danny, he would hear, and feel it."

"Put him to bed, and let's talk for awhile by ourselves. The moon is bright tonight, and it seems earlier than it is."

"You won't fall asleep tonight?" She asked.

"I don't want to sleep tonight."

She put the child in his bed, and covered him with a light blanket. The night was warmer than usual, and with windows left open the curtains blew gently. Turning from the baby bed, she blew out the wick of the kerosene lamp. The smell of kerosene smoke rose and floated in the air.

John was behind her. His hands upon her waist. "Like it was a long time ago, Rose. Remember?"

He didn't often call her Rose. It was a soft sound that she liked, and heard more often from Girard, or from Joan. The fear in her that had haunted her since the child was born, rose within her, her legs tightened, the muscles in her thighs stiffened. But, John's touch was warm on her skin. It was as if she could feel it through her clothes, and she didn't want to be afraid anymore. She didn't want the nightmare anymore, she wanted to lay in the dark close to John and never sleep any more.

Death was an ugly word, and an ugly thought. She wanted to force it out of her head, wash it out of her body. She turned to him in the moonlight and he held her close. He was alive and she was alive. It was all that mattered.

Yet, after they parted into their separate worlds, leaving love behind them, she lay awake thinking:

And there had been Maggie and her tears, and Maggie and her long black hair. Rozella brushing it in the afternoon sun, raven black with blue threads. The tears hadn't stopped. Rozella, not knowing what to say, kept trying to talk of girlish things, and Maggie would not listen. Maggie was bleeding. Maggie...She helped her change the bloody linens, turning her over in bed, sleeping by her side, listening to her cry in the dark...I won't see him...I never will see him...he didn't want me...I thought that he would want me...I didn't know...I don't care about what they say... couldn't he have wanted me...I'm not too young...caring for Mama's babies all these years, since I was ten, watching over all of them...can't have my own, now...I was old enough...love...Rozella...never love...it hurts too much...Maggie at sixteen, crying until the pillow was wet...Maggie not laughing...Maggie never laughing again...

CHAPTER TWENTY

Hannah picked up a grasshopper from the windowsill, the third one she had found in the house. She opened the window, its frame heavily painted in white and sticking from the overflow of hardened paint, threw the grasshopper outside, wondering why she didn't step on it and kill it; then knowing that she didn't want to clean up the mess from a brown-stained green mass of long-legged insect. How often she had watched the grasshoppers on the leaves of the garden plants, driving them off with sticks, seeing them rise in small clouds from the earth. There were more and more of them. The chickens picked at them and grew fat eating them.

The heat of June had welcomed July like a long lost lover. Days and nights blended into one continuous stretch of heat—dry and dusty. Not a cloud. No rain. There had been no rain since spring.

She closed the window, turned to the room, which was hers, seeing the starkness of it, the bare bed she had stripped to change the sheets, the single bed with the hard mattress, and the whiteness of it in the summer sun. She stopped to touch the one picture hanging on the wall, the only touch of color in the room, a delicate painting of wild moccasins in pale oranges and yellows against faded greenery, the whites turning yellow from the passing years. She touched the frame, running her fingers around it thoughtfully. It was the last of her paintings.

There was a part of her she was trying to remember, the feel of the brush, the smell of the paint, the soft ground where she had sat in the woods, the mossy earth under the trees, the place where he had found her. When she went again, intending to paint, she never painted. He had always been there, waiting.

Then, there was the poetry. In between, she would write the poetry of it, the song of it, the story of her feelings woven like colors of paint, making new words, all the words she could think of and put together to recreate…and Papa telling her she couldn't go back to school…Papa telling her she couldn't…Papa always with her…no more afternoons in the woods…never alone again…never alone out of the house…the dirty overalls…the empty windows…looking out of the empty windows at night…wishing, sometimes praying…loneliness, and never alone…Mama not caring…Mama saying that she didn't believe in love…Papa throwing the paints away…Papa burning the poetry…reading the poems, loudly and laughing at her…tearing them in two, burning them, burning the words that said she was real…never seeing him again…Papa saying that he was gone…that he had just gone…she had been promised…he had said…that he would be there…when she could come…he would take her away…and she couldn't get away…Papa locking her in at night…taking the key away…his steps going down the stairs…and looking out the empty window again and again…the day when she had run away from the field crew when Papa wasn't there to watch…running through the woods, her breath catching the sun burning through the trees, past the spot where she had painted those flowers…paint dry and the flowers dead…running and running and looking back…knowing that she would find him…if not in the fields, he would be there – waiting for her…she had escaped…(her fingers touched the painting again, then took it down from the wall)… the cottage was empty…there was nothing there…everything was gone… going through the rooms, tearing open the drawers…opening up the cupboards…nothing…no clothes…no notes…no message…nothing…but the drawer…in it the pictures, photos he had taken, all pasted into a black covered book…in the drawer that always stuck shut…she had the pictures of him…the round face with the blonde hair…the hands holding a rake… were these all she had left of him…where had he gone?…Papa said he just left for another job…that wasn't what he had promised…where was he… her pictures, next to him, the two of them, on a happy day when the Italian man had…what was his name…he had asked him to take their picture together…he wanted to send it to his parents…they had laughed at the

Italian man when he took their picture with his black box of a camera...
why had he left her...there was no such thing as love, Mama had said...
you couldn't believe any man, Mama had said...Hannah reached into
her pocket that morning and pulled out the knife that she had been using
to cut twine in the fields...I must cut them carefully, every head from
the pictures...don't want to remember...don't want to remember how we
were...what we looked like in the dream... two months of the house as a
prison closing in...two months of not being able to get here to see him...he
had forgotten and didn't care...cut...cut...cut...the tears coming all the
while...not seeing the pictures she cut...the pictures in her hands, or the
flowering moccasins of a summer long ago.

Hannah took the picture she had painted so long ago with her as she went down the steps to the kitchen. In the silence of the empty kitchen, with no one to see her, she bent to put the last of her watercolor paintings into the garbage can, digging into the soft wetness of summer cornhusks, and burying it...*let it rot...with everything else.*

As if the sun went under a cloud, there was sudden darkness. The rain, at last, she sighed, relieved to be shed of memory, walking to the doorway. But there was no cloud in the sky, just the blue, clear and endless sky. The darkness was a moving mass closing in – grasshoppers, covering the garden, the fences, the trees, stripping the trees, the paint on the fence posts, crawling over what was left of the grass. There was a buzzing, humming sound whirling through the air.

She heard her father roaring orders to the men in the fields at work, the whip of hoes, shovels, and pitch forks, yet – nothing stopped them, and the ground was a mass of crawling greenness. The sky was shut out, and became black. She felt them hitting her arms as she stood in the doorway, mesmerized by the black cloud of their existence, seeing their destruction; tearing them from her bare arms, she sat down in the doorway and threw up. There was nothing left to fight anymore. They had it all, the insects, the grasshoppers; all that had been left after the drought they were eating. There would be nothing left now.

It was the sound of the wings, the whispering sounds, moving across the road that stopped Rozella and made her look, the thought, the wondering curious fear shaking her before they hit her on the face and arms, passing her to the clothes line where she had just hung the wash a couple of hours ago. Now still, the clothes hung without moving, shells of people, hanging in rows. The grasshoppers hit them, clung, and the strange whispering continued. They were eating the clothes. She woke herself from the surprise of what she was seeing, rushed to the clothes line, beating them off, some falling, only to be replaced by more from the indomitable cloud of insects. Yet, she kept beating and beating at them, and then she was crying. What is happening? What is happening to us? Are we to be eaten by insects? She could see the holes in the shirts with worn collars eaten around the edges by the green monsters. When she finally stopped beating at them, knowing that the effort was not doing any good, she looked to the garden along side the house, and saw it was bare. Nothing left but a mass of crawling, undulating invasion. A nightmare.

They hit Joan's truck as she drove down the road toward home, and the windshield became a blackened storm. She hit the brakes suddenly, and swerved to the side of the road before she stopped. A dust storm. No. Something worse. Watching them from inside the hot, closed truck cab, she saw them crawling helplessly over the window, trying to eat the paint off the truck. Jesus. What kind of curse is this? She asked aloud.

In the town, and in the country the battle continued uselessly. The dry summer had worn down the people. Hopes were bleak. Promises of tomorrow had grown weaker, dwindling to the nonexistent. Now – an attack came, as if from the bowels of the earth, without forewarning. Only the rooted vegetables were safe within the ground, and they were weak and spindly and underdeveloped because of the dryness. The creek was bone dry, and the wavering insect hoard floundered in the base, a muddy hole, drying there in masses of writhing fatigue. The onslaught continued until the sun went down, blazing red and angry on the horizon, and nothing was left but despair and fear rising from every household. Their harvest was over.

Rozella stared blankly at what was left of their garden.

The first winter Papa was gone, the potatoes had frozen in the ground. A too early frost had caught them underdeveloped and still green, not ripe enough to dig. Frozen potatoes rot quickly. Strange soup from the mush, glutinous potatoes, watery without milk. Rozella had eaten the soup quickly, burning her tongue, tasting the salt only. They had all eaten it for dinner, but it lay thin and slimy in the bottom of her stomach, and she ran out behind the house to throw it all up, not wanting to have her mother see that she couldn't hold it down.

Mama had worked as a maid, taking day work, taking in laundry. Sick with that last pregnancy, she had not been able to work every day. The girls had worked over the laundry, scrubbing shirts by hand in gray galvanized tubs, working little lather from the P and G soap, their hands turning red, sore spots where the skin wore through from the harsh edges of the scrub boards. Lessons went undone, and they fell into sleep at night, exhausted.

It took more money, when vegetables had to come from the store. Neighbors shared. Families that Mama worked for let her take home the leftovers. She stewed them. Sometimes the bits and pieces of plate scrapings made the evening soup thick and tasty, and they didn't mind. They forgot. Telling themselves that the boiling made it clean. But there were the miserable and frugal people who didn't want to see a crumb of anything leave their houses, and those women with their cruel and bitter mouths, who stopped Mama from taking the leavings after their family had been fed, and when they stopped her – they told her not to come back again. As if they wanted to punish her because her husband was not home and taking care of his family. God helps those who help themselves…they muttered as Mama closed their doors behind her leave-taking. Shaking their heads in righteousness, they remembered that her husband had been a drunk, and they punished the family, as if they were punishing the drunk. But, none of this could be talked of at home. Mama grew more and more silent in those days, and the wailing and anger that she had used against Papa until he had left – ceased. There was nothing more to say. There was only the hurt left in her eyes, that she couldn't provide enough for them.

One by one the children took jobs that could be done, anything offered – shoveling sidewalks in the winter, raking leaves in the summer, washing windows and changing screen windows in the spring, doing housework, washing walls, or running groceries from the store. They brought home *their dimes and quarters, dumping them into a glass jar in the kitchen. From the jar, Mama took the change to buy what she needed to buy, and the meals became better through the seasons. Mama worked less, the children worked more. Mama worked at home, and took fewer jobs as a daily maid. She withdrew into herself, and complained often of a pain in her stomach that wouldn't go away, stirring baking soda into water and sipping it frequently throughout the day. A constant state of indigestion plagued her. Her anger with Papa grew less intense, but her anger with the people around her grew stronger, and she didn't want to talk with people anymore. She took no more joy in church going, staying home to read her Bible, and avoiding the neighbors.*

The year of the frozen potatoes Rozella could not forget. The sight of a green potato still made her gag. There had been boiled potatoes, potato soup, potatoes with bread, potatoes with onion, all stringing and yellow... day after day.

Like the year of the frozen potatoes, the gardens were gone now. There were those who said the unfortunate invasion of insects would help to stabilize the economy. The absence of garden produce, and the ruin of the remains of the summer crops would drive prices up and there would be more money coming into the marketplace. The eternal optimists didn't ask where the money would come from. No one had any backlog of money to use to buy from their less fortunate neighbors the few crumbs of produce that remained

The rationalizing began all over again. Some in the city gave in to welfare, but there was no welfare in Crenshaw: the final note of embarrassment for the townspeople, the passing out of boxes of apples, the carrying home the boxes so obviously marked "government." until now. Now, there was the hurt with the shame of it – for these people had looked at welfare as charity, and had lived all their lives without charity.

They found one farmer in the south, down by the river, his head shot off with the shotgun he had used for deer hunting for thirty years, the barrel clotted with dried blood. His wife cried, but no more than she had been crying for the past two months in her fear. She buried him, silent at last, speechless against the atrocity of an unknown force. The children looked to her, and she grew strong like a man, brown in the fall sun, cutting out stumps and sawing wood, making ready for the coming winter.

More mortgages were foreclosed, and the cold winds began to blow across the empty plains. In the city, the men gathered to read the newspapers, sharing the headlines, shaking their heads and wondering what would happen next.

Girard came home every night from his job quiet and his face growing more and more deeply lined, his thoughts etched into his face. He always knew which farm would go up next, but couldn't say.

The baskets that came from the Queist's house each week grew thinner and thinner. There were no questions to ask. It was always the same. They had all suffered the same calamity. What could be said? The flour sometimes had weevils in it, and Rozella sifted it several times before she made the biscuits or bread. Sometimes they were sick from the twisted vegetables and the wrinkled apples, which had been left in the cellar from the year before. It was better than none they told themselves, but the days were often spent in nursing stomach upsets, and diarrhea.

Hannah gave Danny cod liver oil, which kept him from getting rickets and becoming anemic, but she doled it out when he came to visit. It was another excuse to have him there more often. John and the baby, now trying to walk and to talk, spent more time at the house with Hannah and Queist. It would be easier to feed them, if they ate up there, John had told her. Reasonable, yet the basket grew thinner, and portions almost nonexistent. And Rozella could not eat the withered vegetables without getting sick. She grew thinner, took in her skirts around the waist some more, and her face was more pale with the circles under her eyes becoming darker.

Girard and Joan came often, always bringing something to eat with them, excusing themselves as easily as they could, that it was leftover food that the two of them couldn't eat. Sometimes they would have to prepare it for her and force her to eat, and John would be gone – always the excuse that there was work to be done on the farm buildings. She didn't have any fight in her, any strength with which to revolt. No matter what Girard and Joan tried to say, she was listless. It was as if the fire had all gone out, the fire that had been just starting to grow within her, and they wondered what was going on in her mind.

"I learned about Hannah," she said to them one day as they shared their lunch.

"What did you learn?" Joan wanted to know, eager to hear.

"Not a lot, only what John and I could guess, or pick out of his memory. There was someone living in this cottage, a man named Nels. He left."

"Where did he go? And what did he have to do with Hannah?" Joan was putting more food on Rozella's plate, hoping she would eat more.

"John's father said he left to take another job. But it was after that, or before that, I'm not sure which, that Hannah never went back to school. We think the pictures that I found in that album were of Nels, and maybe of her, but we don't know who cut them up so strangely."

"The old man, or Hannah? Who would be so full of hate and resentment to take it out on a simple photo? And where did he go? Couldn't you find out anything?" Joan asked.

"John said his father only said that he had left. No one else had any answers. One day he was there, the next day gone, and Hannah was confined to the house for a long time."

"Has John been able to ask any questions of Hannah, or his father?"

"No."

"Why not?" Girard joined in the questioning.

"He has turned quiet about it, as if he resented my asking. He doesn't answer me. My imagination is too much, he says, and won't talk about it."

"And when will he be home?"

"Not until late."

"Don't you ever get angry, ever?"

"I miss the baby – and he's growing up. It seems like it happens daily."

"Rozella, you're not answering me."

Girard left, going outside to walk about in the yard as they talked, as if he, too, did not want to talk about it.

"I can't believe it about Hannah, " Joan continued.

"Neither could I, but I couldn't understand the pictures either, and all the secrecy. There is a lot more to know." They collected the dirty dishes to put them into the kitchen sink.

"And wouldn't I like to know it," Joan twinkled.

"They're a secretive family. They don't talk about things… anything."

"Not even you and John?" Joan asked, "Doesn't John talk to you about himself?"

"He did once. At first. Now, he's silent. It's as if he's joined them – become one of them, whatever they are. Since the baby came, they've drawn him into this. Whatever it is. He doesn't speak a word about things, not a complaint. Not even an explanation, or an excuse."

"I don't know how you stand it," Joan's almost dropped the dishes she was carrying. And her voice cracked like the sound of broken dishes.

"We have a home. We're not waiting for the foreclosure auction. We're not starving."

"Don't be so sure. Look at yourself in the mirror."

"I don't want to – do I look that bad?"

"It isn't bad – or beautiful. You're too thin. Do you know how thin? And the circles under your eyes grow larger and darker every week." Joan put her hands on Rozella's waist and turned her around in emphasis.

"I didn't know. I'm just tired."

"Tired of what? Oh, I know – too many questions. Yet, it seems like we've said all this before. Or have I just said it in my mind"

Girard returned, glancing at his watch as he entered. He stopped behind Rozella, putting one hand on each of her shoulders. "Yes," he said, "It's dark already. I don't like leaving you here alone, Rose. You okay?"

"Sure," she answered, turning to look at him, his hands trailed off of her shoulders and the warm touch seemed to linger.

"Is there anything I can do around here before we go?" he wanted to know.

"No. You already filled the wood box," she smiled up at him.

"We'll be back."

"I know," she seemed to whisper it.

They left behind too much quietness and it closed around her to blend with the waiting. There was always the waiting, wrapped with hope, some kind of a crazy hope that the excitement of having a voice, another body; two bodies in the cottage would ease the dark. Darkness spread through so many of her hours these days. There were days that seemed all dark. Were they really? Or was it her mind?"

The clock had stopped, she noticed. The gold key lay hidden behind the glass door underneath the pendulum. She picked it up, feeling the coldness in her hand. She wound the clock, and the spring tightened under the turning key. She pulled the hands slowly around to their proper hour and minute, or what she guessed it to be, a quarter past nine. Each hour passing beneath the black hand sounded its peculiar tone: one, two…one, two…three…one, two, three, four…

There were the dishes, the cups and saucers, the teapot she could busy herself with. Heat the water, add the soap to the pan, wash the dishes and take up time, slowly and methodically wiping them and putting them away, thinking about what she could make for her dinner, opening cupboards, closing them, not caring, not seeing. She didn't like the feeling of the talk she had with Joan and Girard; it left something behind, a sort of hurt disappointment that she couldn't identify. She was trying not to think about.

Then, she did stop to look in the mirror. The lights were not bright, yet she could see the purple circles under her eyes, the skirt that hung around her waist. Her hands were bony and veins showed. She held them out before her shakily, and was forced to examine them. The wedding ring was loose now. Sometimes it slipped off in the dishwater. She would wrap some string around the band, she thought. The worn straps of her bra, mended over and over, were showing through the thin blouse of white cotton.

She hesitantly felt her breasts. They were almost flat now with her thinness. Perhaps she didn't need a bra anymore, but she would need a slip to cover her nipples. She pulled the blouse off over her head to feel the difference. Her nipples were taut, but her breasts lay flat beneath the worn material. A feeling went through her that reached some inner part of her when she touched her breasts and she remembered suddenly Girard's hands on her shoulders. They had been warm.

She shivered, then, and lay her cheek against the coldness of the mirror, sighing. The bra lay on the floor beside her. As she stood there, the door opened and John and Danny came in. She hurriedly put her blouse back on.

Danny was crying and his nose was running. Too tired, she thought, too long a day for a baby. "Give him to me," she said, "I'll put him to bed. Wait – he feels hot."

"Maybe he has a little cold. My father's been sick with a cold for a week or so. It's not like him. He doesn't usually get sick. Everyone else does, not him." John replied. "Rozella, it might be that the day will come when we'll need to live in the old home, all together."

"But, that would mean me, too, wouldn't it? It would have to mean me, wouldn't it?"

"It would mean an end to this separation. We'd lose our privacy, but gain space, and time to spend together. You wouldn't have to be alone so much," John was taking off his boots as he spoke.

"Living in the same house with Hannah couldn't be called an improvement over being alone, John. Besides, she still may not talk to me."

"Even if she didn't – I'd be there. We'd have lunch, and dinner together. You would eat more. The house is big. We would have our own rooms." He walked over to her in his stocking feet.

"What would happen to this place? She looked around.

"They would rent it out, maybe, or it would set empty until spring. We won't need field hands for the winter season."

"What makes you think they'd do this, and have us live there?"

"Hannah has been asking questions lately. Maybe because father has been sick, so sick he can't help her with anything. That leaves her alone with all the work. With Hannah and I working together outside, the kitchen and house could be yours. It's so much bigger and nicer. You would be much more comfortable." He was enthusiastic.

"And – it would save money for Hannah and your father. One less phone, less heating, no need to send food over here, and you – twenty four hours a day: It's a sudden shock," Rozella continued, "I had waited and wanted to be with my child all this time, to have him with me all the time, and not lose him every Sunday. It's almost frightening. I want it, but I'm afraid, as if something fearful is locked into this."

"How could there be? It's just you and me talking about it. Nothing has been asked, or even offered – yet."

"Your father? How about him?"

"He's sick, in bed. He's very quiet right now."

"That doesn't mean he always will be."

"I know, but we can deal with it when it happens. Besides, if it works well, how can he object, especially if it saves money?" John said, almost sarcastically.

Danny was clinging to her neck with both hands, sniffling into her dress.

"Go ahead, put him to bed. He's tired, and we're only talking about what might be, not what is." John said, touching Danny on the shoulder.

It was late now, far too late for a baby to be up, she thought as she put Danny to bed. That would be an advantage to living with them, regular meals for us. But, facing them every day? How would that be?

Happiness followed by hurt, excitement, hope, and pain like a roller coaster ride ran through her. To be with Danny all the time, to be part of the family, share Sunday dinner, go to church, and no longer spend Sundays alone – this was all she had hoped for.

If it came about, it would be fulfillment, reaching a normal life. But there was sadness in her, a pain so deep that it bound her, made her feel breathless. She had no awareness of the depression that gripped her, except for the pain it was leaving behind. A goal achieved, perhaps, then why the pain? She couldn't know; she could only feel it.

Rozella put Danny to bed, pulling a soft blanket over him, watching his face peaceful in sleep, no longer busy with the things little boys are busy learning. Returning to John, she asked, "Do you think this will happen? Really happen, or do we imagine it?"

"Sometimes life changes things for us," John answered, "We'll see."

CHAPTER TWENTY-ONE

The curve of Hannah's back spelled weariness against the black of the polished stove and it became difficult to observe as part of her outlined form. Drops of water sizzled, and then steam away, falling from her wet hands. She quickly wiped her hands on her apron and pulled the blue enameled pot closer to her. The smell of smoke was lingering in the room from a freshly started wood fire. Thin shadows marked the walls with thread of their own design. The coffee boiled, then boiled over and brown foam cascaded from the enameled pot.

John bent over to pull off his rubbers, which were worn and cracked at the heels; they clung to his shoes. He tugged at them impatiently. The mud, which covered the bottoms, came off in his hands and dropped to the floor. He tossed the rubbers aside, and kicked at the crumbs of mud, as if sweeping them away with his foot; this mud came from the early rain which fell in light sprinkles hesitantly, as if waiting for the frost, hoping to turn into snow.

"Pa didn't come down?" He asked.

"Not today," she answered. "He's still sleeping."

"That's not like him."

"No, but it's this cold he has. It settled in his chest, and he just can't get his strength back. You just haven't noticed how long he's been sick."

"How could I not notice; I'm here every morning of my life?" John picked up a heavy white mug from the table and went toward the stove for his coffee.

"How would I know how you could not notice? Oh, God, why do we answer each other with questions all of the time?"

"I have been here. That's all I'm trying to say."

"Resentfully and absently, both. Your mind is somewhere else. Not here." She wiped down the sides of the boiled over coffee pot with a damp rag.

"I wish it were along with my body, and that the two could get together."

"I know that, John. I know you well. At least, I used to – before…"

"Before Rozella?"

"Yes, before you married someone who doesn't think farming is good enough."

"Rozella has never said that. She's never even hinted at it."

"She didn't have to say it." Hannah carried the hot coffee pot over to the table.

"But, you didn't give her a chance to say anything."

"It wouldn't make any difference."

"Let's not talk about t his, not now, Hannah. It doesn't change things. What about Pa? What's the matter with him? A cold shouldn't carry on this way."

"I can't think of anything to do. He just sleeps more. Maybe it's fever. But he gets crabbier. When he is awake, he hollers more."

John knocked on the door of his father's bedroom. It was a habit left over from childhood, one he didn't think about. Both he and Hannah had been trained to knock on the bedroom door. There was no response. The dark wood confronted him as if it was a seal of silence.

He opened the door. The high footboard of the bed shielded his father; but he could hear the breathing, which was deep, almost gasping. The silences between the breaths were long. John fell into the rhythm of it without thinking. "Father?"

A stubble of gray beard shadowed the sunken jaw, his belly moved with labored breathing, and extended. An arm dangled to the floor, his fingers scraping the rug. His head fell to one side. John jumped at the movement. A trail of spittle ran from the corner of his father's mouth. "Father?" he repeated, afraid to touch him.

"Umph." The breathing rhythm stopped, then started again. The dangling arm swung as if unconsciously trying to reach for the center of the bed.

John turned to the door, calling out, "Hannah." He called again, loudly. "There is something wrong here." The old man's body lurched and seemed to respond to the voice. His mouth opened, worked around the spittle, then his head rolled and there was a long shattering groping struggle to breathe followed by a gargling sound. Then, there was silence.

Hannah was there in a moment. Transfixed, they watched the utter stillness of his body.

Without touching him, they knew; yet, they couldn't believe that he was dead. John was holding his breath as he waited for his father's next breath. It never came.

"He's dead, Hannah." John said softly, as if to make it easier on her.

"I can't believe it."

"The bastard, the old…" then John murmured, as if to himself.

"What did you say?"

"Oh, Hannah, are you still pretending?"

"Pretending what?"

"That he didn't ruin your life and everyone else's life – everyone who ever came near him, or let him take control."

"He's your father! How can you say that? It's blasphemy. You were taught better."

"What about your life, the life you once hoped to have?"

"Don't talk about things like that…not here, not now."

"Well, what became of Nels? Or, don't you want to let yourself think at all?" John countered, as he pulled the quilt up over his father's face.

"I won't talk to you like this, before a death bed."

"Where did Nels go, Hannah? Did you ever ask?"

"I don't even know who you mean…who?"

"The man you used to meet, the man father hired, the one who lived in the cottage, the one you loved. Yes, damn it, loved, Hannah. You did love him, or did father persuade you it was something else?"

"Stop it. You never had an evil mouth before. That evil woman you live with, and her friends are changing everything about you. You don't know what you're talking about anymore." she covered her face with her apron, using it for a shield.

"That's not true," John shook his head.

"You imagine things, then. There never was anyone for me."

"Oh, yes, there was. You don't want to remember. I used to follow you to the cottage. I was very small, but not too young to know. And don't blame this on Rozella; I haven't even told her this"

"What could you know? There wasn't anything to know."

"I know that Pa followed you, too. Maybe he didn't tell you that, but I know what he accused you of doing there. You're no virgin, Hannah. In spite of what you pretend, what we all pretended. I heard you cry after Nels disappeared. I knew you were locked up in your room for a long time. How could I help but notice these things. I lived here." John was emphatic, unusual for him.

"You lie," she insisted, turning away, trying to leave the room.

"Oh, you pray a lot," John followed her, putting his hand on her shoulder. "Tell me, Hannah does it make you believe it didn't happen? Is that what they mean when they say: Jesus wash away my sin? Did Jesus wash yours away? Yours and his, the hired hand?"

"We've had no hired hand."

"No, not since that one left. Pa couldn't risk his daughter having sex with the help. He wouldn't want to lose his cheap labor." John spit the words out.

"Don't say that. What about you? You risked taking up with Rozella.."

"Pa was greedy for money. Rozella's rent money bought him. For $17.50 per month, and my slavery – he thought he was safe."

"Safe from what?" she asked.

"Safe from losing his free labor."

"You're his heir. You'll inherit this place. All sons stay on the old place to outlive their parents, to care for them. Look around you. That's how it done."

"I look. I see. Yes, I see, but I see things changing, and I'm not sure everyone wants it the way it had always been. No, I know that I don't want it that way anymore."

"I can see that you don't want it. Your life is a – sour pail of milk, curdled with bitterness. Like a spoiled child, you want all of your dreams to come true."

"Not all, Hannah, just one or two."

"You see? You're crying, even now you can't be a man. You cry because you can't have your way, not because Pa's dead and lies there unable to speak. You're stuck here, like I am, with nowhere to go."

"And you never cry? You never feel. You're not a woman anymore. Were you ever a woman? What did Pa make of you?"

John and Hannah buried the old man the following week, as silently as they had lived with him, and without tears. Danny stood between them, wearing a shadowy suit cut out of hand-me-down wool suiting and smelling of mothballs. He looked dark and somber as a page in a Victorian book. Hannah was holding the child's hand. Rozella, who dared to go to the funeral now, stood back, mingling with the congregation and the neighbors, yet not seeming part of it all.

The ceremony over, people stared at her and jostled her. She was not familiar to them anymore; she had been too long removed from the family and the church. Joan and Girard were beside her. It was Girard who reached for her, understanding the tears were for herself and her long penance. Had she served her time, and now would she be allowed to appear publicly, he asked himself? But, the neighbors saw Girard hold her hand, and the cold wall of silence remained, separating her from them in the same old way.

The walk home seemed long in the coldness of the fall day. Barren ground was not yet snow-covered, but the cold was penetrating, as if to tear at the inside of you. The three friends watched the silent elder family turn into their own roadway leading up to the old house: John, and Hannah, with Danny between them. The child never looked back at his mother, and Rozella observed, as a stranger, the cleavage of the two roads leading to the two houses. Her stomach knotted, as if in afterbirth.

Joan turned to her as they approached the cottage, saying, "Girard will stay with you awhile. I don't want you to be here alone now, and there are things to do at home."

"You're sure?" Girard asked her.

"Of course," she smiled at him and kissed him lightly on the cheek.

When the door closed, he reached for Rozella's coat to help her take it off. She stood as if unthinking and confused, unable to move, in the center of the room.

"Rozella?"

She did not answer.

"Rose," he spoke louder, then raised her chin with his hand, forcing her to look at him. Then the tears came again and he gathered her close to him to hold her while she cried. She couldn't speak.

"The crying isn't for John's father," he reminded her. "You know that, don't you?"

"I don't know anything."

"It isn't for John."

"I don't know," she whispered through the tears.

"It isn't for your son. Or is it?"

She only sobbed, softer now, as she was calming down.

"Rozella, Rose…" and as she lifted her face, he kissed her lips. It was a kiss that didn't stop; it couldn't stop. It wandered and questioned, it demanded, it suggested, it endeared. As his hand were on her breasts and uncovering them, the auras were pink and full and the nipples extended." She was trying to speak, to call out -- "Joan, but Joan…"

"But, she knows," he murmured. "She knows, Rozella. We have no secrets. It's all right."

His mouth was covering the nipple he held; she breathed sharply, feeling her inner being contract, expand, and reach. There was a pulsing, yearning for life within her, and she pushed forward, leaning into his mouth. His hand, reaching for her wetness, caressed her. Her legs parted; hesitantly, but no longer fearfully; she relaxed into his waiting hand and palm, the wetness and the pulsing of her heart carrying her beyond thought.

She inhaled deeply.

"It's not over, not yet," he said, and picked her up, carrying her to the bedroom. Removing her clothes quickly, he leaned over her while her body still stirred with the throbbing. Her eyes were closed with embarrassment, turning her head away, as she shook all over.

"Not yet, Rose, my love," He parted her legs and buried his mouth between the warm, soft lips of her, and began to drain her gently, and evenly, probing and pulling her buttocks until she came, and came... without ceasing. Only then, did he mount her and plunge himself deeply into the heat of her to find his own immediate finish.

Then, as they lay together, just as if they had always lain just so, and never again would part, he kissed her gently, the ear lobes, the pink nipples, and touched her hair and brows, stroking her again and again.

"She couldn't have known – this." She said at last. "I didn't know."

"Oh, yes, she did. There is no guilt, Rose. Joan has given us to each other. She is generous woman. Unique. Not like any other."

"That is too much. I can't face her. I'm so..."

"I wouldn't have...if...I love her, too, you know."

Then, what is this?"

"It is surely sex. And good sex, " he smiled, "but it is more than that, Rose. Don't you feel it's more?"

"Yes, I want it to be."

"Then, don't pick it apart. Just take it," and he kissed her again. The hungry part of him again demanding, wanting in, he filled her, pushed her, and filled her again, his fingers reaching to lift himself as he pressed against her. Her breasts were hurting as they thrust against the bone of his chest. He bit her throat, and her clitoris responded to him.

The motion, the breathing and the smell of their bodies joined as one, brought her back to him: "I want you. I want you again, now." She was saying as she grabbed his buttocks, squeezing hard with both hands, and he came with an explosive force that brought her with him. It was as if they never wanted it to end, and couldn't stop it. The waves of it carried them both, and she knew now – *in one crying moment* – that she had never felt this before. Life had carried her past the first kiss, to another first experience. One she had never dreamed of, since she had never experienced it.

Moving into the old house came about so slowly that it seemed unreal. The transition was more like becoming absorbed into a way of life. Not much had changed, but the location.

On the first night there after the funeral, they brought only their clothes for the night and an extra change for the morning. Rozella found the bedroom large with windows facing both the road, which ran in front of the farm, and the side toward the woods and the cottage. The room they were to share was stuffy, with the smell of a closed up space. She opened the windows, which were stuck shut with paint, by prying them open with a kitchen knife. The fresh sharp fall air blew in and the unbleached muslin curtains floated softly in the evening breeze. Turning back the heavy quilt, she fluffed up the pillows and opened the drawer of the nightstand, and dresser. They were made of heavy oak, and all empty. The closet was fairly large, and the glass knob with a brass plate including a keyhole, turned with no difficulty. There was nothing to hang things on but black metal hooks placed around the edges of the closet, but there was room for a trunk on the floor, or a cedar chest for clothes.

Danny followed her around the bed and into the closet, toddling and touching and mumbling in his baby language. She took him into the next room which was smaller, to show him his bed. To her surprise, he showed her his bed. Rozella hadn't remembered the many times he had been in this house since his birth. This room was truly his, and she was the newcomer.

There was an old iron baby crib in the corner. It had been painted white. "Beh, Beh…" he pointed to his bed. A chest of drawers without a mirror held some extra clothes for Danny. How odd, she was thinking, as she looked into the top drawer – clothes that Danny has worn that I've never seen. There were diapers, and undershirts, and a couple of nighties. A faded teddy bear sat on the crib pillow, as if waiting for company. "Danny's beh," he added, the little finger pointing, while Rozella smiled at his inability to say all of his words clearly.

"We'll put you to bed, now Danny," she answered him as she picked him up to take him downstairs to wash up. There was a warm water reservoir on the side of the kitchen stove and it still held some water warm enough for bathing. Using a dipper, she filled an enameled basin, and sitting Danny on the edge of the drain board, she washed him and dried him a bit at a time, putting on his nightclothes quickly so he wouldn't get cold. He was so pink and sweet, smelling of soap. With his hair combed nicely to one side, he looked like a miniature man – like John.

"Night – night, now," she whispered into his ear as she carried him toward the stairs.

"Umph, umph," he pushed himself with leverage against her body, trying to convey that there was something missing.

"Your bottle? Yes, oh, yes. How could I forget – you want to take one to bed with you." The brown paper bag she had packed was still on the kitchen floor. She reached into it to remove the bottle. There was milk in a large crock in the pantry. It was room temperature, so she filled his bottle, not taking time to warm it. Danny grabbed it eagerly, and calmed down as he sucked on the nipple, even though he was not getting anything out of it.

"You'll sleep well now, with both bottle and bear," she said to him as she carried him up the stairs. Once put into his bed, he started sucking on the bottle and clenching his bear with his free hand. His eyes were already closing.

Rozella left him to return and pick up the paper bags she had carried with her from the cottage. The house was totally quiet. Hannah and John were out in the barn doing the milking and cleaning up for the night. She had the house to herself.

The space felt wonderful. She found herself stretching out her arms as if to pull in all the space, or breathing deeper to inhale the abundance of air about her. She washed quietly in the kitchen, using a washcloth to wash under her nightie, which discreetly covered her bare body.

Slipping up the stairs with bare feet, she felt the clean air coming through the bedroom window, and she could hear the soft breathing of Danny as she passed his bedroom door. All is well, she thought, as she turned down the covers and climbed into the bed. The light was on in the barn, so they were still working, but she was tired out and longed to sleep.

Her mind drifted, free at last to think of things, which were hers alone. Private thoughts. The lovemaking of Girard, and the warmth of him flooded her as she fell into a dream and then, to a deeper dreamless sleep.

It seemed like it was the middle of the night when she felt John's body next to hers. Perhaps, she had slept past the hour when he had come to bed, but the warmth next to her felt good, and she sleepily reached out to touch his shoulder and turn toward him.

In the morning, he awoke before dawn, and reminded her that they would need her help in the kitchen. She felt unsure of herself in the strange house, but was eager to cook and clean it, as if it was hers. After dressing, she went downstairs. Hannah already had coffee boiling on the large stove, but she could help with the rest of breakfast. "What will you have for breakfast?" Rozella asked, "I'll be glad to make it."

"There's a lot of milk because there is a crock full from yesterday's milking. We could have pancakes. There are eggs in the pantry, too," Hannah answered her as if they had always been together in this kitchen. Not wanting to break the spell, Rozella responded by going into the pantry and finding the bowl and spoon, flour and baking soda. She whipped up pancakes, easily, as her mother often had done at home. Pancakes were a common denominator for their family. There was a heavy iron flat pan on the stove when she came out with her batter. Hannah had put it there to warm up.

Hannah was dressed in men's overalls, and wearing heavy men's work shoes. Being large boned and tall she could wear these things, but it made her look like a man. Rozella put some butter on the grill, and dropped batter by the spoonfuls unto it. John came down from upstairs holding Danny in his arms.

"We smell breakfast," he said, speaking for both of them.

"I didn't know that Danny liked pancakes, " Rozella answered.

Hannah answered, "He really is crazy about pancakes. They're soft and sweet, so he's been eating them since he was six months old. A favorite thing with him."

Rose continued turning pancakes and put them unto the plates, which were waiting on the table. Hannah was cutting up one for Danny, and John was feeding him. It felt good, so far. The food was hot and wholesome. The smell of coffee was enticing. The warmth from the kitchen stove made it seem cheerful in the kitchen. Even though it was still dark outside in the fall morning, it was comfortable here. It was more like home, as she used to know it, except that the three of them – John, Hannah, and Danny – were repeating a familiar action, and she was the stranger, not quite yet part of a family.

By the time she could sit down to eat, John and Hannah had left for the barn and she and Danny were alone at the table. As she had found upstairs, Danny had his place here in the kitchen. He sat in an oak high chair. She looked at him in wonder. He had been here before, and she had not.

The water was now hot for dishwashing. She had put the teakettle on before she sat down to eat. It was daylight and she could turn off the kerosene lamp on the table as she washed dishes and put them away. Danny needed to be cleaned up. He was wet because he couldn't sleep through the night without wetting himself. She cleaned him up and dressed him for the day, putting him down to wander around the kitchen and play as she began to familiarize herself with where things were put, and what was there to cook with.

The food supply in the pantry looked abundant. There seemed to be no relationship between the baskets of food, which had diminished during the past months and the contents of this pantry. There were no rich and expensive things here, but there was plenty of flour, milk and eggs. There was lard in a large crock. She had noticed that the table scraps, mostly Danny's leavings, were taken out to the barn to feed the dogs when Hannah and John left. Nothing was wasted. The chickens, or the dogs ate everything that they didn't eat.

When she explored the cellar, she found a storage room for vegetables, fruit, potatoes, and canned goods. There was an accumulation of glass jars with Kerr lids. Many, obviously, had been canned before the preceding summer. She could read dates written on the lids. So the oldest could be used first, she told herself. Just like Mama used to do. Green beans in quart jars, corn, cut from the cobs, carrots, pickles, apple sauce, glasses of jelly and preserves which had been made from wild berries, probably, and quart jars of peaches and apricots packed in juices. There was a plentiful supply not described by most of the people in the area. Most of the farmers had already eaten up their backlog of canned produce. Their families were large and ate a lot. This family had been small, and they didn't share anything, so they had a store of food.

Rozella didn't want to think about the meaning of what she saw. She only wanted to think that it meant she could cook good meals now, and they would all be stronger and able to work better. Now, she could plan on what to make for meals and Hannah wouldn't have to be in the kitchen at all.

Later in the day, she returned to the cottage to pack up some more of their things in flour sack and move them into the Queist house. Danny played out in his yard, as he knew it in his world, digging in the yard with a kitchen spoon, as she packed carefully, choosing carefully what she could carry and what they would need the most.

She looked up at the sound of a truck coming down the driveway to see Girard's truck. He was coming to see her, not knowing yet that they were moving into the bigger house to live with Hannah. Her heart jumped and her body became alert, as if every part of her was mindful of his presence. She stood up from her packing and waited for him to approach. He stopped to talk to Danny, and looking up, saw her standing in the doorway.

A surge of longing went through her. And he blushed as he reached out to touch her cheek.. The palm of his hand brushed softly against her face, lingering there. It took all of her self-control not to throw herself into his arms. But there was Danny, right there beside them looking innocently up at them.

"I know," Girard whispered, "I know." More loudly, he asked, "What are you doing today, Rose?"

"Packing. Packing up some things to take them to the Queist's house. We stayed there last night, and it looks like it will be permanent. There are some clothes and personal things that I need to take."

"We wondered. Joan tried to call, but the phone had been disconnected."

"I didn't know Hannah had done that yet. It was part of the idea that we could live more cheaply in one house. We really don't need a phone now. She...you...will have to call us at the Queist number when you want to reach us."

"How are things going so far? Hannah?" He asked.

"She has been quiet, and doesn't speak any more than she has to. I'm trying to guess, mostly, what is wanted of me. Doing the housework, and cooking seems to be my job."

"You've become the housekeeper and John has become the hired hand, I'd guess," Girard pondered.

"Well, that's what tenant farmers do – usually," Rozella answered.

"That's true," he said, "but you are family."

"That doesn't make any difference, really, Girard. I know that you care about all of us, but work is work. If we eat better, and can be all together most of the time, then we are better off than a lot of people right now."

"You're right, Rose. It's selfish of me in a way," he blushed again, "Joan and I want to have you to ourselves. We have enjoyed your company, and spent more time with you than with John, if only because you were here – alone."

"Please come up to the Queist house. Tell Joan to come," she answered, looking down at her feet. Somehow, she couldn't say Joan's name and look at him at the same time. It was as if they had to be separated in her mind, and she needed to divide her feelings for them into two parts.

"I'll tell her," Girard answered, "But let me help you. I can put these things into the truck, and drive you up there. You won't have to walk. Maybe there is something you would like to move that you can't carry?" He followed her into the cottage; walking through the rooms with her to look for the items she would need the most. The door closed behind them and he was reaching for her, putting his arm around her and pulling her to him with her back against his groin. The surge of need was compelling. The power was still there, and her body was singing in response to him.

"We can't," she breathed into his hands, kissing the palm of one hand, while his other hand ran up and down her body, as it pulled her close.

"I know, but we will. Come tomorrow, but plan to put Danny down for his nap after he has his lunch. I'll be here," he whispered into her ear.

"I will. I will," she responded, then – trying to think, she pulled away from him to point out the gramophone in the corner. "I would like to take that. I bought it when I first started teaching. We used it in the school."

"Of course, " he answered, "wrap it in a blanket so it won't get damaged in the truck." And they worked together to pack up the few things she wanted to take that day. Gathering up Danny and locking the cottage door, they left together in the truck.

CHAPTER TWENTY-TWO

The gramophone in its heavy oak case sat in the corner of the formal living room gathering dust through the busy days that followed. Rozella dusted it when she went through the seldom-used room, then shook the lace curtains which also became dusty. There were the fall tasks to be done. Without much harvest left, there was little produce to preserve, but there were remaining vegetables left in the cellar, which needed to be cooked and canned before they rotted into unusable form.

Some apples became applesauce. Carrots could be peeled and put into jars after the growth of sprouts was cut off. Potatoes, if caught before becoming mushy, could be cut up and mixed with onions and a bit of soup meat. Then, the results cold be put into jars for the winter. Her days were kept busy between the routine cleaning, the canning, looking after Danny, and meeting their regular meal schedules. In contrast to the sparse household she had left behind her, it now seemed that her days revolved around the processing of food – food that she hadn't known existed. It hadn't been important to her before, as she had not felt hungry. Now, it seemed like a job in a restaurant or a cannery at times.

Hannah in her reserve became a source of wonder, as Rozella speculated on how she had managed to do all this work, and still help in the barn and with the crops. She asked her one morning at breakfast, "How could you do all this work, Hannah? I seem to be busy all day long without leaving the house."

"I didn't do as much in the house, I guess, or not as much in the yard. Pa worked outside all of the time, seven days a week. Maybe I did less of both? Maybe."

"Well, after the snow comes, it must get quieter. Not much to do then, but watch it pile up," Rozella countered.

"Then, we start shoveling," John interjected." "Do we have everything we need from the cottage?" he turned toward Rozella.

"I'll keep on carrying it, a little at a time," Rozella answered, looking away as she thought about her meetings with Girard, and wondering if anyone noticed that he helped her carry things over to the Queist house in his truck.

John and Hannah at times stayed up at night talking long past the time she put Danny to bed. At times she would go downstairs and try to join them, but their conversations usually were over papers and figures, which were laid out on the kitchen table. When she sat down beside them, they didn't notice her, or involve her in the discussion. Deeds, mortgages and mail received. Rozella took the mail out of the mailbox daily, but left it unopened on the kitchen table, except for a rare letter from one of her sisters.

At times the brother and sister would seem to argue over the paperwork, and Hannah could be very strong about her opinion. Her voice would rise, and Rozella could hear her say, "But, Pa would have…"

John's answer usually was, "Give it another month," or "Give it another couple of weeks."

Finance had not been a great part of her life, in the sense that when there was no money, there was none to worry about controlling. It had only been a struggle for survival, keeping the will to get enough money together to pay the rent, or to buy food to feed the family. The Ehalt family had been much larger. There were more mouths to feed than there were in this collective household. But, that was the past, she reminded herself; today, there was food and space. She couldn't see what bothered Girard and Joan about their arrangement.

One afternoon when with Girard, she asked him about it. "Why does it seem like a bad living arrangement?"

"Because it's John's home. To him, it seems like he has never left home. We haven't seen him at all since you moved out of the cottage. In fact, we haven't seen him or talked to him since his father's funeral.

You may be eating better. Danny is cared for – by you – on Sundays," he continued. "Hannah has lost some of her control over Danny because she has to work outside. With you there on the weekends, you have your child back. Your life seems more normal…" Girard pondered, as if trying to respond to her question.

"Is that so bad?" Rozella wanted to know.

"It's so hard to pinpoint what bothers me, us…really. Your circumstances are better, but your marriage has a sense of unreality about it. But, maybe I'm only excusing myself," Girard answered.

"But, if I think about my marriage, then I have to think about us, and think about what we are doing to your marriage – to my marriage – and I only get confused and afraid. My marriage can't be anything more now. For me, it can't. I can't be two persons. Even if John was different, I couldn't go backward now. Before, I didn't know what it would be like with a man. Now – I love you, but I can't separate things like you and Joan do. I'm just a country girl. I don't know if I'll ever be different."

"Sweet little one," he brushed back her hair, which had fallen into her eyes, "I know. It's true; I'm more than a little mixed up myself, no matter what I say. Being sophisticated is easier to talk about than to live with. I have no right to judge your marriage. It's just that my feelings about you demand more for you within your marriage. And that's not because I don't like John. I do like him. At least, I did. Now, I'm not sure that I know him anymore."

"What do you mean – don't know him?" Rozella wanted to know.

"How can I even be sure what I mean? What I think I mean is that I used to think he was too soft, too weak, and let his father and sister dominate him. I excused him because the times are hard, and there is no place to go for many people.

At least, you and John had a home of sorts. But, then – I saw the way you lived, in hunger and need, not only for the necessities, but also in need of affection, and care. People even have that in the midst of poverty, I told myself. Now, since the old man died, he has no time at all for friendship, or for you, even though you are closer to him now by living under the same roof and sharing the same table for meals.

Who is John, now, I ask myself – and Joan. We talk about this in our concern. What was left to John and Hannah? Rozella, don't you ever think to ask about a will? Was there any money? If so, was it left to Hannah, and to John, or only to Hannah? If John did get any of it in his own right, the two of you would be free to live somewhere else. You could get away before you become locked into this arrangement."

"Lots of families live together, Girard" She answered him, as they packed up dishes in the cottage. "Not only here, all over the world. Don't tell me that people didn't live together where you grew up. We all came from the old country. Mostly our ways come from the old country ways, and those are yours: So, how are we so different?"

"Not much different to appearances, but there's something that I can't put my finger on, or express with words. Something not quite right. It's not healthy. It's the smell of money." He shook his head, as he lifted a box.

"Money? In this world – who has any?"

"Just my question," Girard answered, "What happened to what Queist owned when he died? Did it all go to Hannah, or half to John? What did he really own? No one seems to ever hear about his owing anybody anything, and everyone else is either in debt, or they have lost all they owned. We know that he never wanted to spend a penny, and we know he always was there to collect every cent due him and then some – but we don't know much more than that. What do you know, Rose?"

"I know that he paid for everything with cash. He kept cash somewhere, I guess. I have no idea where. I never went to the house, so I had no opportunity to see what happened. When John sold eggs and milk in town, he must have carried the money home to his father, or Hannah, but I never asked what he did with it. I didn't think about it. As I said, in my family we never had any so I didn't learn how to think about handling it."

"Whatever he did with it, Hannah must know. She was with him all the time. Wherever it is, and however it is handled, it must have passed on to her." They took their packed boxes out to his truck.

"Sometimes she sends John to the bank when he goes to town, I noticed recently." Rozella answered him.

"Does she ask him for anything in particular?" Girard asked.

"Not when I'm around, but I'll try to listen more carefully and find out," she promised. "They handle their business together in the evenings, when I've gone to bed."

"Will you ask John to come over on Saturday night and we can all have supper together? We can play cards afterwards."

"It will be so hard. I haven't seen Joan since…what can I say or do?"

"You must come. You can't just stay here and never go anywhere. If you do, it will become just like the cottage was for you – a virtual prison. And, I will blame myself for making your life worse than it was. Besides, nothing has changed. You'll see. Joan is still your friend."

"Only because she doesn't see me as I see me."

"Sometimes we are kind to those we love by not telling them what might hurt them," he answered.

"It may be kindness, but it isn't honesty. I'm not sure that I can do this…go on with our friendship as if nothing has happened between you and me."

"Promise that you will be your own same – self. Don't bring up any painful topics. Let our instincts guide us until we have a better sense of what the future will be. Please, Rose. Trust me."

And she went along with his pleas not knowing what to do or think, and trying not to think. They went to the Girard's place on Saturday night. With Hannah's permission, Rozella had baked a yellow loaf cake in a large pan, leaving half of it in the Queist house, and taking half of it along.

"What have we here?" Joan smiled, taking the cake. "A rare treat, as I don't bake. I'm much better at putting up storm windows." She couldn't help but remember that there had been a time when Rozella would not have had an extra egg, or a cup of sugar to use in a cake. Perhaps the new "arrangement" of family living was an improvement, after all. And, Joan could see that Rose had put on a pound or two. It wasn't easy to see, but her face was a little fuller, and her color a little brighter. She was not so wan as before.

Of course, there was also the time that Girard spent with Rose talking or so he said.

Those were the hours that Joan didn't want to know about. He was the same dear person she had loved for so long. Nothing was missing from their marriage that she noticed. At least, it continued the same as before. A long time ago, when they first met Rozella and John, they had talked about the differences in their morality, the general sense of it, how Rozella was raised and about John's family background. The community was different in thought, if not in deed, than anyplace either of them had known on the continent. It was a type of Calvinism at its extreme – all the stern moral ethic, without the concept of predestination, or even much sense of God's will. Could God's will create such living in total sterility of emotion?

Yes, Rose looked much better. John looked good, too, but he was more withdrawn. His thinking seemed removed from them, as if he had worries that kept him busy. Girard, Joan noticed, looked warmly at Rose, more so than ever before. She had asked him to befriend her and get her to talking as well as thinking about her life. She had told him that he needed to help Rose become aware that she had a right to life, but she couldn't become aware until she knew what she really wanted to have in this life.

"That's a big order," Girard had said in response to her request. Joan had hoped it was the right thing to do. Meddling in other people's lives could have alarming repercussions, it was said. But, she had never felt the need so much before. This young woman, her friend, had seemed so isolated from the world that it pained her to see it. Rozella's life had been abnormal by their standards. Now, Joan would find out if it had changed since the move into a shared household.

"Did you hear about the lynching in Iowa?" Girard asked John. "I mean the attempted lynching. They failed."

"No. I didn't. Where did you get the news?"

"From our radio. A group of farmers got together in the heat of their anger about the bank foreclosures, kidnapped the local judge, who they say had signed the order to foreclose, and tied him up to a very large tree."

"I can see their anger. It's the same around here. It's surprising it hasn't happened here," John answered.

"The judge got away with his life, but I don't know how his heart's going to be after that scare. The sheriff got there in time, and managed to free him by shooting in the air. Just like the old west." Girard was dealing out the cards.

"It's terrible, not funny at all, " Joan said. "The Reconstruction Finance people have only helped out the big financial institutions, while completely ignoring the small farmers. Maybe the judge was helping the finance company out. Somebody had to get their attention."

"How's your place, John"?" Girard asked. "With all the loan foreclosures, I trust your father left the place in good shape. I never heard about him owing anyone any money."

"Near as I can tell," John answered, as they looked at their cards. "He doesn't owe anything to anybody. That's the way he wanted it. Many times we wished he hadn't been so careful with money when we were kids, but now – with all the trouble over money – we can't help but be glad he was that way."

"You mean, nothing owing? Not even taxes?"

"Nothing. It took me awhile to get Hannah to let me see all the papers. She had them hidden away in her closet, and acted like I was still a little kid who couldn't be trusted. But everything is clear. He didn't teach Hannah much about record keeping, but he taught her to be as stingy as he was."

Rozella was more generous about Hannah. "We don't go without, John. There is plenty of food for all of us. Hannah doesn't tell us we can't have anything."

"That because you haven't asked for anything, yet. Wait until Danny needs shoes."

"Well, maybe she'll become softer when she looks into his innocent baby eyes," Joan added.

"Sure hope so," John finished. "But, that's enough about business, who dealt? As if I didn't know."

The card game continued until almost midnight. By that time John was half asleep and could no longer concentrate. Rozella was tired also. She was up as early as anyone else in the household, and though her work wasn't so physical as fieldwork, she was sleepy, too. Girard gave them a ride home since it was late and quite cold out.

There was frost in the air, and the truck windshield steamed up from their breath. Rose could feel the presence of Girard more than she ever had. It was difficult to be squeezed in between the two men when the physical response to one was so powerful. Her thoughts she kept to herself, letting the two men talk around her. It was easier. The drive was short, and she felt almost relieved when they were dropped off in front of the dark old house.

But just before she went to sleep, she asked sleepily of John, "Hannah doesn't use a bank? I never wondered where you put the egg money and milk money, John. You bring it home in cash?"

John answered something, but his words were muffled in the pillow and she didn't hear. It was too late and they both fell asleep right away.

Later on that Sunday when Rozella and John were able to talk as they dressed for church, she asked John what he had learned about his father's finances. "I hadn't been curious before, but now I wonder, especially when those around us are having such a hard time of it. The Raymond's place is up for foreclosure next week. Living in the cottage, the bad times seemed closer, as if I could feel what the neighbors were feeling. Here, it's like I'm insulated. As long as I don't leave here, it doesn't exist."

John was not quick to answer her. "I've had a lot of words with Hannah, Rozella. She hasn't wanted to share information with me. I felt that I should be told since it was my training, my background, to work on record keeping. As a man, I felt I should be in control of the money on the farm. How can I know if it is being handled with any sense, if I don't know what is being done?" John continued to tie his tie in a knot.

"I would have thought that your father would have been talking to you all this time. Training you, in a way."

"It was Hannah who was close to him, and she was the one he trusted, and now it is Hannah guarding what they had put together as if telling me would be disloyal to him. Apparently, it was only Hannah he wanted to share things with."

"Always – since she quit school?"

"Yes. My mother never took any part in business of any kind."

"What is -- was going on, John?"

"The Countryside Building and Loan would offer second trust deeds to Pa when the properties were foreclosed on, the first time, I learned. According to Hannah, he would make a deal to take part of the acreage when the place was foreclosed – the second time, that is."

"Meaning that he expected that the loan he made to the farmer would not hold until times picked up. He did this knowing that they would lose the place in the end?"

"Well, it has been almost a sure thing. Hardly even a gamble that he would get good farm land for $5 an acre, or even less. The president of the Building and Loan Company knows. Sometimes I think that Girard suspects."

"How was the money handled? Check for payments. Some were made, weren't they? It wasn't just an instant failure."

"Oh, yes. I knew about the checks. They were sent for a month or two, sometimes longer when the refinancing was good enough to help out a little. Pa or Hannah used to give me the checks to cash in town when I went in to buy supplies."

"Cash? And you brought back cash? Wasn't that a lot of money to leave about the house?"

"Banks were failing, Rose. Or they had failed. It didn't seem unreasonable to hear Pa say that he didn't trust the banks. He wanted only cash. He hoarded it away, saying that money was better invested somewhere else."

They left for church when Hannah called them downstairs. She was waiting at the foot of the stairs. Danny was already dressed. He looked like a model for a catalog in his long stockings, high-topped shoes and short pants. His hair was combed carefully and his face glowed after being scrubbed clean.

After the first few visits to church, it was no longer a surprise to see Rozella and Danny together with John and Hannah. The church community had accepted the change. No one spoke of it openly, but they knew that the Queist family was living together now in the old house. The cottage remained empty. Hannah had let it be known that it was for rent, but this time of year there were few, if any, field hands or tenant farmers left unplaced. The population decreased when the snows came. Some farm homes had been abandoned, and left empty.

Then, too, people were leaving the land, and there was no need for housing.

Sunday dinner was now Rozella's chore, and since she had learned her mother's way of cooking, the meals were different now than they used to be. She remembered the boiled chicken from her only visit there, that most painful dinner experience when the Queist family was still all together and she was the intruder.

She was browning a pork roast in the heavy iron skillet on the back of the kitchen range. Hannah had removed her Sunday-best clothes, and gone out to take care of her chickens. Pork was not their usual diet, Rozella knew. Unlike most of the farmers in the area, they had not kept pigs; but with the groups of farmers killing pigs to avoid marketing them, those who didn't have any pork traded for what they had. Sometimes farm equipment not being used, or extra hay, or even furniture came into the trading scene. There was more bartering for goods than ever before.

Pork was a basic food for the German-Russians of Rozella's community, so she was well trained in all the ways to cook it. She had learned to make sauerkraut, with potatoes, and dumplings, but sauerkraut didn't go well with Scandinavians. She never did understand why they didn't like it when they ate pickled herring and other awful stuff, like salted fish and dry bread. So, she added potatoes, carrots, and onions.

"Umm, that smells good," said John, as he walked through the kitchen with the milk cans, putting them in the pantry where they would set until the cream rose to the top of the can. After that she would ladle the cream into quart jars, and over it. This would leave the skim milk to be used for baking, or for drinking. After growing up in the city, Rose never had learned to drink the watery milk, but she had been taught by John and Hannah already that cream could be sold. Therefore, you didn't drink whole milk. She could almost look at the cans and watch money rise to the top.

Money. The cash that Queist had kept at home. If the homestead was paid for, they had only taxes to pay, supplies to buy, and animals to feed. Did it amount to a lot? Wouldn't it add up over time? Rozella had never managed money other than what she had earned for a very brief time when she taught, but she did know her math. She could add and subtract, and she could guess at what was received as well as what supplies cost. It was a puzzle to solve, like a mathematical puzzle. And, where would one keep the cash? There was no safe in the house that she knew of. Where could it be hidden?

That's it. Hide it in the most unlikely place. Be illogical. That's what she would do. Since she had never had to hide anything before, except pencils and paper from her sisters at home, she had found it hard to think of how to hide money.

An illogical place could be most anywhere. She wondered if John had thought this through, or if he already knew where the money was kept and didn't choose to tell her. Hannah kept her silence, of course.

Silence may have been normal in this household, but it was not normal in Rozella's childhood home. There – everything had been vocalized, where voices were going as long as the family was awake. Sometimes high pitched voices, in argument, or emotion, and always Mama's voice could be heard, strident or complaining or even crying, until the day she died. In this house, silence was common, but Rozella felt Hannah's silence most of all She had hoped for acceptance, but there seemed to be no way to break through Hannah's shell. When she addressed a question to Hannah, she got an answer; but it was brief and to the point. Hannah never returned an opening for conversation, and she even remained quiet with John. Neither of them talked at the dinner table.

Rozella talked with Danny in his baby language as she helped him eat. Sometimes he was fed before they ate, and without his presence, nothing was said at all. John would get up from the table, and as if excusing himself say, "Well, back to work." Then, he would leave. Hannah would follow shortly after. Only she would say nothing before leaving.

It was mid-afternoon before their Sunday dinner was complete, and being Sunday, they ate in the dining room. This was the only day of the week that they set the table with the "good" dishes and silver. The rest of the time, they ate in the kitchen. She could see that John hesitated by the big family Bible that his mother used to read from before they said grace. Then, he sat down at the head of the table, and mumbled briefly. "Come o Lord Jesus, be Thou our guest; whatever Thou givest us be blessed."

And Rozella sighed with relief that she didn't have to listen to some pointed Bible verse reading. Danny banged his spoon on his high chair tray, and dinner proceeded. It was as quiet as the supper hour with no conversation offered by either Hannah or John. Hannah didn't even make an excuse as to why she couldn't help in the kitchen. Maybe it was like the Girards had suggested, Rozella thought, she was to serve as their housekeeper, or maid. That must be how Hannah now justified her presence in the house

"John," Rozella asked, "Has anyone been interested in renting the cottage?"

"No. No interest at all. There aren't any new people this time of year. It will be spring before there are any extra hands working on the farms."

"What will you do with the cottage, then?"

"Leave it empty. Use it to store some extra equipment that we don't use during the winter."

"Some of the furniture is still there. We didn't need it here."

Hannah ignored the conversation, getting up and leaving the table to go upstairs to her room.

"That's all right. It can stay there. It belongs to the cottage anyway. As long as you have what you need here – clothes, bedding, maybe some cooking things. If hired hands move into it in the spring, they'll need furniture. You can even leave pots and pans over there if you want. My mother had plenty of cooking things here."

"Well, I didn't have a lot of things of my own, but I did have favorites. I have taken those, just because I'm more comfortable using them."

"Just get whatever you need before the heavy snow comes. It would be difficult carrying things when the snow is deep."

"Whatever happened to the Nelsons?" She asked as she picked up Danny to clean him up for his afternoon nap.

"They left. They weren't in church, so I guess they're gone already. People say that they went to her family in Ohio. They had to have a place to live. They're probably living as we are, helping out at home."

"They lost everything?"

"Everything went to the bank. It was sold at auction. The money went to the bank holding the loan." He put on his jacket to leave. "Got some cleaning up to do in the barn," he said as he went out the door.

She carried Danny up the stairs and laid him down on his bed to change his clothes. Pulling off his grown up looking Sunday clothes, she put a long flannel sleeper on him over his undershirt and diaper. He could not yet be trusted to take a long nap, or to sleep through the night without a diaper. She pulled down the window shade, and gave him a kiss. He was sleepy enough not to object to his naptime, and his old teddy bear was clutched in his arm.

CHAPTER TWENTY-THREE

She heard voices in the kitchen. Awakening from a deep sleep, Rozella could not hear the voices of John and Hannah very clearly, but she became aware that an argument was going on.

"...and, I heard that he underwrote second trust deeds for several farms around here. That all seemed to be a good thing. When you gave me the checks to take to town and cash them, I never thought anything of it. Pa always liked to keep cash. He hated banks."

"So, what's wrong with taking acreage for the money?" Hannah's voice intruded.

"It doesn't seem like anything is wrong with this except when these people are neighbors, and you see them driven off the land, land that was their land for years... When, it becomes your land, yours and Pa's... it just doesn't feel right."

"You're forgetting that it's yours, too. You are a member of the family"

"Not so I could notice. You have control. None of the decisions were given to me to make. No one asked me. No one gave me a chance to work with any of the problems."

"But, it has made money." Hannah raised her voice. "Both money and land will be yours when I die."

"Hannah, I'd rather have nothing than wait for you to die to get it! How can anyone look forward to getting money and all the necessities of life when someone must die for that to happen? Wouldn't it be better to stay poor?"

"Some of us have no choice. We have to do it that way."

"You're right, Hannah…I'm sorry. For women, it is that way. There never has been a way to get an inheritance except by waiting and obeying and hoping. Even then, you could never be sure it wouldn't go to the sons. It usually did."

"This time, Pa gave me the control." A drawer slammed shut.

"A most unusual event."

"I paid for it," was her answer.

"Yes, Hannah, you did pay for it. When Pa kept you locked up and wouldn't let you go, you did pay, and you have kept on paying all these years. You destroyed your life."

"That depends on how you look at things. I can't say that your life is so great. Pa didn't think so either. Look at your choice of a wife, for instance. She's not a farm worker. She doesn't even know how to care for farm animals. She has never worked in a field, or milked a cow."

"That doesn't make her of no value. Just because you quit school and she went on to finish and to teach doesn't make her valueless." Rozella could hear John's chair scrape the floor as he got up.

"Not so. No. But she is practically valueless to us. She can't help outside. She should have stayed in her hometown where she belonged, or went to another city."

"You wouldn't have chosen anyone for me. No one would have been right for you and Pa. No matter how I had met a woman, or married one, you would have objected."

"That's not true. We would have liked to help choose one, for your own good. You were always impractical. Pa felt you needed guidance."

"And, you both hid money and lied to me about our finances. Even when you knew that I went to school to learn how to take care of money, and keep books and records."

"When you show people you have money, you are subject to all kinds of begging, in these times especially. If we had given to everyone and spent freely whatever we had, Pa would not have had any money to buy second trust deeds, and the property would have gone into foreclosure long before it finally did go there. We may look cruel to you, but we gave them what some might call – borrowed time."

"Borrowed time, at a very high profit to you. Am I right?"

"Pa taught me, it's not a profit until the property is sold. Until that time, every piece of property is a liability. You pay taxes. Unless it is rented, you don't get any money back."

"You do if you plant and harvest a crop."

"In these days? No one can sell anything. There's a surplus of everything possible. The government tells us to stop producing. The only way we know of to make our living is to produce; yet nothing can be sold. There are no markets in the world to turn to. People kill the pigs they once sold to Chicago, and give the meat away, or burn. It. The government is beginning to pay people for destroying food. It's insane. Don't tell me you can make money from land? I haven't seen any."

"What is that you and Pa kept buried, then? What is in that cache you have hidden away:"

"What do you mean?"

"If Pa bought all the trust deeds that I think he bought, he must have put quite a lot of cash aside."

"Chicken, egg, and milk money – that's all I've seen." She answered.

"Well, you didn't give us much to eat when we lived in the cottage. Now that we're here, it's harder to keep us from eating, isn't it?"

"We always gave what we had. Some weeks there was more than others."

"Most weeks, damn it!" he shouted at her. Standing up, his chair pushing back.

"But, you don't have the right to know about the amount of money we made on things. Pa didn't say so in his will. You have no rights at all until I'm dead."

"I should have some right because you can be so damned tight with money that you cut off your nose to spite your face. For several months now, I've asked to buy a tractor before the spring plowing begins. Everything I have read and heard tells me that work goes so much faster and better with the new machinery. Why use the old plow horses? They are so old now, they'll die in their tracks one day and I'll have to pull the plow myself."

"New fangled stuff. You have to buy gasoline for tractors and that means you have to store gasoline in tanks around the farm. It's dangerous."

"Other people do it."

"Who?"

"Well, the Girards, for instance."

"They have some crazy European ideas, not only about farming, about everything including morals."

"What gives you that idea?"

"Well, you don't see them in church for one thing. For another, Joan has talked a little to some of the women. She's been attending the circle meetings lately, who knows why, and asking a lot of questions. People ask her questions, too. Her ideas are pretty fancy."

"About what?"

"About marriage and men and women. She does things that only men do, goes places that only men go to, and dresses like a farm hand."

"Who are you to say? You haven't worn a dress except to church for years."

"But, I don't go anywhere. I just stay here and work. No one sees me."

"Does that make the difference – if you are seen? That's like the old argument that if the thief isn't caught, there has been no crime. Whatever you can get away with is okay. Is that it? Somehow that doesn't sound like you at all."

This was more conversation than Rozella had heard out of John in months, and she was wishing that she wasn't hearing it. Once she had awakened and heard the raised voices, she had gone to the head of the stairs and the voices carried clearly up to her. John was showing more passion than she had heard before. He had said nothing about asking for a tractor, and nothing about Hannah's refusal. He had said nothing to her about the terms of the will.

The old man, then, had left everything in Hannah's hands, and had tried to bind them, she and John and even Danny to this woman. She had to share his white slavery with him. Hannah wouldn't let go.

There had been more to this than the fact Rozella had been pregnant with John's baby when they had married. There was the issue that everything and everybody presented a threat to a locked-in world. The property must not pass on to anyone else: it must grow; they must acquire more. That had to be the reason Queist kept buying trust deeds on speculation. That also had to be the reason Danny held their attention. When John passed on from this world – everything went to Danny. They had been counting on Danny to perpetuate their own world.

Hannah would have no children. The old man had warped her life, leaving her without even any consideration of that possibility.

There must be money, but where could it be? Rozella didn't want to know, and yet she thought that John ought to know. And what was this strange sort of arrangement in a world where men usually led the way – a woman was in control of everything! Apparently, Hannah had learned a lot about the financial arrangements made by her father, so she knew what he had been doing, and knew enough to continue doing it. She also knew how much cash he had stashed away over the years of penuriousness. She had to know that.

Hadn't the old man trusted John at all? Was that why he had taught Hannah everything, and at the same time kept all the facts from John?

Mama's boy. Where had she heard that? Mama's boy. Was that what he was called in town? He had cried so much when she died. He had said some things then that sounded strange, but Rozella had not fully understood them. He was an outsider in his own family even then.

Now with his father dead, and them sharing the house with Hannah, it was not only she who was the outsider – it was John. John was being used. He was being used as a worker, while Hannah kept all the power and the money. Didn't John know this? Couldn't he see? These were some of the questions that the Girards had tried to ask, and she and John had not understood their questions.

The next time Girard came to visit them it was on the weekend. He had not been spending any time doing fieldwork for his company, so he had not been able to get time off during the week. John was talking to him in the yard, and Girard's truck idled in the drive. The air was crisp and freezing, and the breath of the men clouded the air as they spoke with each other. As Rozella came out of the kitchen door to approach them, Girard looked up; his eyes warm with the light of his caring. Not a word was exchanged between them, but the look repeated his feelings. The feelings were still there, and still strong. It showed. He was telling John that Joan had not been over because she had become involved with a political action group in town and spent several hours there each day. "What is she doing?" John was asking.

"Writing mostly, or gathering information to use when writing."

"What is she writing?" John was leaning on the truck's open window.

"Some articles to be used in pamphlets, and some she hopes to publish back east…in order to help people understand how the farm population is struggling to survive. Maybe if more people who aren't farmers understood, they wouldn't wonder why we are losing our farms, and why we are burning produce in some areas."

"I wish her luck. City people just don't understand. They only know that they have less work, and no money. The price of things in the store is not the same as the price we get. They just resent what we're trying to do, without realizing that the man in between, the hidden man usually, is the one who makes the most money."

"Today, it seems to be all the money," Girard answered. "The hidden men, as you call them, are always the winners."

He looked toward Rozella, acknowledging her presence, "Have you finished your moving? It looks like we'll have more snow. The temperature drops every night now, I notice."

"I think I have everything," she blushed, hoping that John wouldn't notice in the frosted air, "I'll check to see if I have forgotten anything important. Most of the furniture will stay right there because we don't need it. Next spring it will be there for the hired hands."

"Yeh," John looked around the sky, "After last year's drought, I have the feeling we'll have a lot of snow and a late spring. It will make up for the lost crops, if we can keep the new ones until fall without any other disasters."

"Newspapers say that Devils Lake is forty feet lower than usual after last summer," Girard offered, remembering the drought.

"It will recover. It always does, usually with a vengeance." John answered. "I have hoped to buy a tractor in the spring, if Hannah and I can get through the winter with any money left. My point of view is that it will pay for itself by reducing the number of hired hands and harvest workers needed in the fall."

"That's a good idea, John. It's still progressive for around here, but that's only because no one in the area has seen proof of the results. It's a new idea. People are used to horses, and most of them can't handle repairing their cars and trucks, let alone a tractor. The mechanics scare them," Girard responded. "Well, I best be getting back home. I promised Joan that I would stop by and ask Rose know why she hadn't seen anything of her for a while. Let me know if there is anything I can help with." He waved as he put the pickup in gear and pulled out of the drive.

Hannah was cleaning out the chicken coop, making room for the winter weather when the chickens would be closed up. She had the old kerosene heater out in the yard and was cleaning it; if they were to keep the chickens alive and laying eggs through the winter, it would need to be working and they would need a supply of kerosene. If they could keep kerosene in barrels, why couldn't they keep gasoline, Rozella asked herself, remembering Hannah's reasoning about storing gasoline for a tractor.

"John, we still have a large can of kerosene at the cottage," she offered, "If Girard can help me haul it back here, and we'll have it to heat the chicken coop. There are days when I can take care of the chickens and it will be less work for Hannah."

"That's true," he agreed. "Although there won't be that much for any of us to do this winter, except keep from freezing."

"How do you mean? Don't we have enough wood or fuel for the house?"

"There is quite a wood pile in back of the barn, but this is the time we should be adding to it, in case we really have more snow than usual. Some of the men folks should get together and go cut wood. When we share the tools and trucks it's faster and easier."

"That's what the coop is for. Ask them, and get going before it does snow," she suggested, wondering at herself as she offered advice. It hadn't been long ago that she was not a farmer's wife and knew nothing of the business of farming. Now, she had caught herself talking like she had always belonged to the land.

CHAPTER TWENTY-FOUR

When the voices in the night recurred, Rozella wondered if she always heard them, and if they repeated themselves every night. She couldn't stay awake late enough to find out. John had become a chronic insomniac since their move. His involvement with Hannah and their combined duties seemed to be the source of his sleeplessness. He had always like lots of strong coffee, but now he drank a couple of cups after dinner. Hannah shared these with him, but Hannah, Rozella noticed, also went upstairs to her bedroom after their noonday meal, and slept for an hour, sometimes two hours, before she returned to her outside work.

For Rozella, these dark hours of the night were not inviting. If she drank coffee, she would stay awake much of the night. If she slept, it would be a fitful sleep with nightmares as she tossed and turned. In the morning, she would be tired and not have any energy. The mornings with Danny required her attention, and breakfast came before dawn. She had no desire to stay up late; the sooner she could fall asleep the better she liked it. If it were her choice, she would go to sleep when Danny went to bed, right after supper, as soon as she finished the dishes and washed up for bedtime.

"…for grazing reserves at $10.00 per acres," Hannah's voice was saying.

"Let me see the letter," John answered. "This is from the federal government?" he paused. He must have been reading it over.

"Of course. The federal government is the one taking the action. They haven't been able to persuade the farmers to take the land out of cultivation themselves, so they propose to buy up all the excess land and hold it, so it won't be seeded next spring."

"What happens to the farmers?" John wanted to know.

"It has already happened to them," Hannah replied. "Their farms have been foreclosed. Some of them left for the Boulder Dam area where they could count on irrigation in a drought. Some went home to their parents to live and work, or to other relatives in the eastern states, but you know who they are. If you don't, you haven't been listening to rumors as these things happen. Most people hear about it when the farm is foreclosed."

"The land that Pa got, that's what you mean? To sell it to the federal government, rather than hold it.?"

"The price is almost double."

"Why do you ask me? Since you don't allow me to control any of the money or the land?" John asked angrily. "You'll do whatever you wish. I wanted to plant it in the spring, to buy a tractor and get by with only one hired hand during the harvest, maybe."

"You don't know for sure how that will work out," Hannah interrupted his anger. "If there still is a surplus of agriculture products in the spring, you won't be able to sell what you grow on the land. You'll end up destroying it and most probably getting nothing. If I sell the land to the federal government, and that's what they hope will happen, they can be sure there won't be a surplus. They are only trying to do what they couldn't get the people to do for themselves – raise prices by reducing production."

"How do you hold your head up in the community when you know whose land you're holding is beyond my understanding," John's voice was raised. "Doesn't it bother you how you make your money?"

"It doesn't bother me that I'm not your dependent and namby-pamby sister who sits in the house all day waiting for you to provide for me. Like your precious wife, I might add. And what kind of provider would you make, anyway? You have been dependent upon Pa and me since you were a baby."

"Only because you force me to be dependent."

"You have yet to get a good job, in spite of what Pa spent on your education," Hannah answered spitefully.

"I know it wasn't fair to you, Hannah, but that's how things are. Men get the education. Women are even asked to stay at home and not work. The whole county is running almost twenty five percent unemployed. Women have been asked to stay out of the workforce since the war; it's not a new thing."

"I didn't want it this way, John" her voice was softer, an unusual tone for Hannah.

"And I asked you about how Pa made you what you are. You won't ever answer me. You are still avoiding my question."

"What good are answers? What is – is the truth, and it's what we have to live with. We can't change the past." She turned away from him.

"I have trouble with changing the *now*," John answered her. The sound of dishes, and cups going into the dishpan to wait for the morning clean up could be heard. Rozella returned to her bed, as she expected that John would soon be up, and she would be embarrassed to have him know that she heard the arguments between Hannah and him.

City life and country life were tied together, but with invisible strings. The small town life that Rozella had led was only a reflection of the city or a buffer between the bigger cities and the farmland. Letters came from her sisters, and the changes brought about by the times was evident, as well as the changes brought about by their growing older, and separating into their own families.

Maggie and her husband had moved into the city, taking a small studio apartment there. She was working as a seamstress for a large department store, and he was still with the Singer Company; but worried about his job daily. Sometimes he was sent out as a traveling salesman in an attempt to sell machines to the new, small businesses, which were beginning to sprout up in various towns.

In desperation, people with no jobs and no possibility for getting jobs mortgaged their homes and bought on franchises a small beauty shop, small hardware store, and sometimes what might be called a shop for tailoring or alterations. The empty buildings left behind by failed businesses in that way were filled up, the rent was minimal, and some money flowed into the franchise company's hands.

But where, Rozella had asked Girard when they talked together, would the money and the business come from to keep the new businesses going when the old ones had failed? Yes, he told her, her thinking was sound. It was a way for some people to make money out of the depression, and another way to take from those who were losing everything. The money and land seemed to be changing hands – a different kind of exchange than that which had occurred after the Civil War. There was a new kind of carpetbagger at work: the franchise dealer.

"And where did the franchise dealer come from?" she asked him.

No one could tell her.

There was speculation: from the numbers rackets in the cities, from the bootleggers, from the building and loan company managers, perhaps putting a little company money into speculation, maybe even from the federal or state governments. The farm people didn't know, and neither did the people who purchased the franchises. All they knew was they were purchasing hope. The cycle was continuing; however, and the bankruptcies began to roll over again after about a year. Wait and see, the cautious people said, wait and see; the wise said. They were holding their cash, keeping it at home. We don't trust anyone was the message the public received.

Ola wrote to say that she had married a handsome young man who had been lucky enough to get a job with the local post office. He knew the man who was the postmaster and that had helped him. Civil service employment guaranteed them some money to live on. Ola was so in love with him, her letters almost shouted of her feelings. And she was so deserving, Rozella thought, writing back that they should come to visit whenever they could come. How she would love to be with Ola again! All the years of their shared childhood came flooding back to her as she wrote.

The rattling door was threatened by wind, but no one lifted head or eyes. Pastor Johnneson was in prayer and Sunday morning sun, filtered by glass, graced unanimously bowed heads. His voice droned on with incantations in German, supplications in English, but the rattling noise at the door became louder. No longer a "wind noise," it was followed by a voice bellowing through the heavy doors: Rose, come open this damned door. I have come to church, kirken.

A fist banged against the door. Prayers were forgotten. Heads now turned. Two men rose to their feet, but before they could move, two girls rushed to the door. Dressed in starched gingham and white islet, shining brown braids swinging behind them, faces red with embarrassment, they pushed the door open a crack and tried to push away a short, black-bearded man. Father, how could you? Hush, get away. Get back from the door. We'll take you home.

The deeper voice rumbled interruptions, and the door closed. The two men watching from the aisle stepped forward as if to help, but the pastor held up his hand: They know to take care of him, he said. And the rituals resumed, as if uninterrupted.

Outside the two girls half-carried the man down the street. H is dark trousers were held up by thick suspenders. His shoes were dragging heavily. The girls carried him as if practiced, and they were, but never before had he taken his drunkenness to church. Mama had told him so many times to go to the church for forgiveness. Rozella was remembering the quarrels as she felt the rough wool of his shirtsleeves against her arms, the shirt that was heavy with the whiskey-sour stench.. There were always the words between Mama and Papa: Go to church. Pray for help...Not a Lutheran. Don't belong...

Rozella slipped the bottle out of his pocket. A few drops of amber liquid sloshed in the bottom, gleaming now in the morning sun. She threw it angrily into the gutter. There was a sick lump in her throat, just knowing he had drunk up all of his earnings for the week. There would be little food at home this week. His muttering became unintelligible by the time they reached the house. The front door was open. Mama stood there, only a shadow behind a black screen, a short woman, whose white apron and severely pulled-back hair made her seem taller.

I'm sick. Going to be sick. He pulled away, throwing off the girls' hands, reeling a bit as he lost their support.

Sick, yes sick. You deserve to be sick. She stepped out from behind the screen as she opened the door for them.

O, no. He moaned, and bent over to vomit in the flowerbed.

You're a pig. A rotten pig, and God will take vengeance.

O, no. No sin. Even a priest drinks.
She glared at him in answer: PIG.
There were tears running down his cheeks now: Dora, Dora, forgive me. I'll never do this again. I'll never let you see me like this again. Dora, never...again. Dora, please...

And he never did let her see him that way again, Rozella remembered. He had gone to the Hudson Bay area to find work, and was never really part of their lives again, except in the mind of their mother. They had lived on with the chronic fears of their mother about her health and her dying. Now Mama was gone.

It would be a pleasure to know Ola without the burden they had shared over the years. What would she be like now?

Ola had kept the two youngest children with her. Her young husband was a generous soul, because that meant two extra mouths to feed on a very small salary. Ola intended to sell women's silk hosiery by going door to door, she said in her letter. She had seen an ad in the newspaper. Rozella wondered if it was another operation like the franchises, or if it was a real job.

Someone had heard of Joe, Ola had written. Maggie had talked with someone who had a brother in a CCC camp in the next state. He had mentioned meeting Joe. But, none of Maggie's letters had been answered. They hadn't been sent back, so she assumed they were received, but Joe had chosen not to write. His bitterness was so extreme; it had never faded. At least, he was still alive. Rozella had worried about him so often.

Her own world had changed so much that she felt far away from her family. It was almost like reading some kind of story in a magazine, reading about what was happening to all of them. She longed to see what David and Mrytle looked like. They must have grown a lot. It was good that they had been able to stay with Ola. In that way, their lives had not changed as much as hers had changed. She remembered her intention to take them to stay with her for summers, but that was before Mama died, and before she and John had moved in with Hannah. So much had happened since her last visit with Ola.

Val's letter said she had a new job, but it wasn't another country school like Rozella's had been, but a city grade school in Denver. She didn't like teaching; but she had met a young southern man who was also teaching there, and he fascinated her. They had fallen in love and were discussing marriage. She wrote excitedly about what she would do when she married – have a child the first thing.

Rozella remembered that she hadn't had a chance to decide for herself; she might have waited until things were better. She certainly would have waited until John really showed that he wanted her. There was always the lingering doubt that he would not have married her, if he hadn't felt that he had to. The letter made her think of how it might have been. Would John have found a job in another city? Would he have managed to get some land of his own? Somehow, she didn't think that his heart was in farming; it had only become something that he must do in order to survive. Did he ever regret that he had come home at all – and met her?

John and the neighbor men took a week to go north and cut wood. This left Hannah and Rozella alone together, and she had even more time to think. Nothing changed, and they went through the daily routine as if he was still there. Since Hannah didn't talk to her unless it was absolutely necessary, quietness filled the house more than usual. Just Danny broke the silence with his talking. He was becoming more fluent as he and Rozella practiced his new words daily.

As he grew more active, he slept less; and it became more difficult for Girard and Rose to spend any private moments together. They could meet, and talk, if they were lucky enough to find a reason to go to the cottage on the same afternoon, but Danny would be there. She couldn't bring herself to ask if she could leave him with John or Hannah. They were always so busy with their chores; and, there was the matter of her guilt. She felt exposed, like a raw nerve, when she thought of asking.

As winter came on, it would be harder to find reasons to get away, and it gripped her with fear whenever she thought about it. Life without Girard seemed too empty now. Joan had not been around for a very long time; since her involvement in working and writing, she hadn't been socializing with anyone other that the people she was working with in Crenshaw. Danny and his baby talk did little to fill Rozella's need for some kind of companionship.

John and Hannah only became more and more involved nightly in their endless discussions about the land and the finances. Rozella waited on them at the supper table when they ate, listened to them talk, and felt invisible

Alone at night in bed, she hardly dared to remember what it had been like to make love with Girard. She refused to let herself count the days, and then the weeks between lovemaking. Now that her body had learned about fulfillment, the long days that separated them led her into dreams that she couldn't remember in the morning, but they were dreams that awakened her with the throbbing of a sleeping orgasm. Why hadn't this happened with John? Why had he always been the one to be satisfied, and she the one to be left – unfinished?

She had waited for him in those early days of before marriage, and even all the days left alone in the cottage; but, it seemed now, in looking backward, the waiting in their early days was a physical yearning for fulfillment that had never been achieved. Now, in the lonely hours of sleep, her body took itself to completion, as if it had found the way by itself.

The days were filled with household tasks, none of which were easy except for the cooking that she enjoyed. Wash days were dreaded days with the lifting of heavy pails of heated water, pouring it into the old gasoline wash machine, then waiting for the stink of the gas fumes, and the noise. Cold water to rinse with, and heavy dirty overalls left by Hannah and John made the job harder. Her clothes and Danny's clothes seemed clean in comparison to theirs. The long climb up the basement stairs with a wicker basket, and hanging the heavy wet clothing on the line in the air which was now so cold made the hours drag, heavy as the basket of wet clothes, The freezing air left the clothes stiff on the line, and they didn't dry for a day and a half. Sometimes she then took them down to find they were still too damp to iron, but she ironed them anyway, and hung them on hangers to dry. Or, she hung them in the basement on a clothesline strung across the room.

The heavier the tasks the more she became aware of John's inability to get any control of the family finances. Didn't he realize that Hannah would have a difficult time without the two of them? Hannah couldn't possible do all of the work herself.

She asked John about that one night, and he said, "I asked Hannah one time when we were talking. You know what she said? She said that she would get along very well. There were plenty of people out of work, and most of them would be glad to have a place to live and something to eat. And – they wouldn't complain. The money would be all hers, then, because I'd be leaving everything behind me, according to Pa's will."

"No place to go, and no money to get there, is that it?" Rozella asked. "I get the picture."

On a morning soon after that conversation they awoke to a ground cover of pure white, not unusual to any of them, but new snow always seemed like something out of the ordinary. It was a newness of white, so clean that it seemed like it had drifted down from another world, a world where there was no unclean poverty, or hatred, or quarrels over money.

Danny looked out the window with Rose, going "Ooh, Ah, look." She showed him his winter mittens and overshoes, promising to take him out to play after breakfast dishes were done. It made her think of making things that she could put away for Christmas. There were some old clothes upstairs in the attic, some left from John's mother, and some from his father. Stored away in mothballs, they smelled, but couldn't they be made into quilt tops or lap robes, or even sewn into pants and coats for Danny? She could use them, if Hannah and John would let her.

In the afternoon, she went into the attic to go through the trunks and boxes. There were some old sweaters that were not being worn. Hannah and John had taken some from up here, she knew, but there were several left. They had no buttons, or had holes in them, but she could unravel them and wind the yarn into balls as she had seen her mother do. Her mother had often rewound old discarded sweaters and knitted new ones. Some had been given to Mama by other households and were in wrong sizes, but she could make them into 'new' ones for her children. Rose could do that, too. She could knit caps, mittens, and maybe even a sweater or two. It would be great for Christmas gifts.

She asked that night over supper, and they didn't seem to mind if she took some of them. John said he couldn't remember anything particular that was stored up there. "I have everything I want from the trunks, don't you, Hannah?" he asked.

"Yeh, I think so Just don't cut up any suits until you show me which ones. Wool is hard to sew by hand, too, remember that. Your fingers could get sore handling some of that old coarse stuff, and if you let it lay around the house with our new and better clothing, you could bring moths into the closets."

"That's true; don't mix the two. Keep what you work on separate from the closets and chests with our clothes," John added.

Rozella couldn't imagine how she would have mixed up the two but she had learned that Hannah always had an objection to everything, and usually John would agree with it. The only reason she could think of was that he didn't want his own requests to be overshadowed by smaller minor things that Rose might want. Her ideas were unimportant in comparison to what he wanted to do with the farm and the land. He thought.

The two of them still argued at night. Rozella hoped it wasn't every night, and that the nights she slept through were quiet enough for her to sleep all night because they were not arguing for a change. As she lay there in bed listening, or stood in the dark at the head of the stairs, she wondered where Hannah would hide the money she must have. The things she said were contradictory. She would deny having any money to John, then threaten to cut him off, according to the terms of Pa's will, which no one had ever seen – except Hannah.

There were so many places on the farm to hide things, yet, so few where someone else wouldn't get into it by accident. And what would John do if he ever found it? Would he be strong enough to leave? So far, Rozella hadn't heard anything that made her feel sure that he would either leave or take the money.

With the snow gathering daily, and building up along the roadways, John had to shovel a pathway from the house to the main road or the truck to get through. Then, he put the tire chains on the truck and the sound of the chains against the hardened snow made a slapping noise. She thought that winter would ease the work around the yard, but there was almost constant shoveling to do. There was the milking to do twice a day; there were the chickens to tend to, or the hay to be pushed down into the barn with the cattle. Nights came early, darkness falling before suppertime. The fire in the kitchen stove was banked for the night, and they huddled around in the kitchen, wearing their sweaters and warm socks, keeping warm. Bedtime preparation meant putting hot water into water bottles to put into their beds. There was no heat upstairs, and frosted breath clouded the darkness in the bedroom. The warmth of John's body felt good, and Rozella often brought Danny into their bed with them, using three bodies to warm the bed. "Like puppies," she would say, "We cuddle up like puppies to keep warm."

"Puppies?" Danny would ask. "Puppies? Now I lay me…"

"Down to sleep," John finished for him.

"If I should die," Rozella said, then fearing what she had said, she lay there silently in the dark unable to finish the prayer.

"For I wake," Danny added, fearlessly.

"I pray thee, Lord, " John added, "My soul to take."

My soul to take. Take where…the darkness folded Rose into her own world of fear and separation.

Papa…Papa…she tried to shake him with her small hands griping his shoulder. He lay on the kitchen floor next to the door. She tried to lift him, her six-year-old scrawny arms hurting with the effort. His arms fell back on the floor, limp and heavy. The house was dark. Mama was working over the weekend, and the girls had been left to take care of the house, and the family.

We waited all day, Papa, she talked to him, as if her were listening. Maggie cooked the supper and still you did not come. Papa, she shook him again, and then tugged on his shirt collar, shaking with cold and fright. Maybe he's dead. Dead people look this way. Maybe I should wake up sister. Maggie…Maggie…She called up the stairwell. No one answered.

She started up the stairs, slowly and carefully so she wouldn't trip on her nightgown, the nightgown which once was Toni's and was still too big for her. Nothing ever was so dark. She couldn't see. She could only feel. If she let go of the walls to pick up her nightgown and keep it from tangling with her feet, she would lose her balance and fall. If she fell – who would know that Papa lay dead on the kitchen floor?

Maggie…Maggie…she now was crying, tears running down her cheeks as she slowly climbed the stairs to the bedroom where the sisters were sleeping. Finally, in childish frustration and anger, she screamed, MAGGIE, and the sound of her terrorized voice woke the older sister.

Whatever is wrong? Where are you? Rozella? Is that you? Maggie had checked the beds and found it was she on the stairs. She came running, holding out her arms. Rozella could feel the arms around her as she found the last two steps. Whatever is wrong? Maggie repeated.

It's Papa, Rozella cried. He's dead. Down there, sobbing she pointed to the stairway.

No. No. Maggie rocked her. He can't be dead. Maybe asleep. Now go to the bedroom and crawl into bed with Val. Maggie will go down and take care of him. He'll be okay. Don't cry.

Val was sitting up in bed waiting for her. She held back the covers for Rozella. Get in here, crybaby. You have more imagination than anyone in the family.

He's on the floor, Val. He won't wake up; Rozella wiped her nose with the back of her hand.

He's just sleeping. Now shut up and go to sleep. Maggie will get him up. Val turned her back to her, and pulled the covers up to her ears, muttering to herself…or she'll just let him sleep there until morning. That's what Ma does when he's drunk.

What? Sleep on the floor? Rozella wanted to know. Is he really sleeping? Not dead? Her body shook, not only from the cold night air; but also from the fright. She had thought it was her fault that he was dead. She hadn't been able to wake up her sisters. Papa was dead, and it was Rozella's fault. He wasn't dead? And she drifted off to a restless sleep, her tear-stained face buried in a pillow.

CHAPTER TWENTY-FIVE

Rozella woke to a snowbound world. The ground was white and clean, with only a few rabbit tracks to mar the surface. It was cold and crisp outside, but bright and sunny. Inside it was cold as could be. The fire smoldered, catching the new kindling she placed upon the embers, but the water in the bucket was frozen. She put the metal bucket on the kitchen stove, and waited for it to melt enough water to drain off for breakfast. John was already on his way out the kitchen door toward the barn with a shovel in his hands. Danny was toddling about the kitchen floor, dragging his blanket along behind him and sucking his thumb. "For shame. I haven't seen you do that in a long time," she scolded him. Then, she regretted it, knowing that the cold made him feel need for warmth and comfort. She picked him up to get him off the floor. "Sit here." She cuddled him into his blanket in the biggest chair and pulled it next to the kitchen stove. "It will be warm in a minute."

Hannah was still upstairs. Rozella had a frightened feeling left over from her nightmare of the night before. Without even remembering it clearly, her throat tightened as it had when she had found her father on the floor.

Hannah still upstairs? Still asleep? Anyone still asleep made her feel as if they were dead. She looked at the stairs, waiting for a sound. She might hope...but she didn't want it to happen, not really.

The stove was warming up the room, and the coffee began to boil. Oatmeal boiled in the pan, and things seemed more like the real world again, the difference between warmth and cold equaled life.

Hannah came down the stairs dressed in a winter woolen sweater and warm boots. She had her usual taciturn look and furrowed brow, as if thinking. Think about what? She never said. She merely Poured herself a cup of coffee and got a bowl for her oatmeal, sitting down to eat and patting Danny on the head, as if to say that he was the only member of the family present.

She left her empty dishes on the table when she left, as she always did, walking away without acknowledging Rozella's presence. Rozella picked up the dishes and put them into the dishpan before she set a place at the table for John. At least, she would have him to herself this morning.

She poured his coffee, and ladled some oatmeal into Danny's bowl. Then, she cut off a slice of bread and put it on the iron range top, watching it as it toasted on the surface. She was tired of oatmeal, and she never felt very hungry in the mornings. John stomped off the snow on his feet at the door, then slipped out of his boots, leaving them to melt off the snow and drip water on the kitchen floor beside the door. She had put some old towels there for him to put his boots on. At least, they would absorb the water.

"It is really COLD out there," he complained, rubbing his hands together.

"And I had wanted so much to go into town today. There was a circle meeting this afternoon and I haven't been to one in a long time. I was hoping that Tillie would take me with her," she said.

"Well, you have a phone. You can call."

"I do, but she doesn't. They had theirs removed to save money. Maybe Girard, or Joan will pick me up. Maybe Joan. I'll call them later, after breakfast, if you could manage without me?" She felt shaky inside even thinking what she was thinking, recognizing the need to get away, to get to Girard, if even for minutes.

"I'm usually home all day, in the yard, that is. Sure don't want to go anywhere today. Just the thought of shoveling all the way to the main road gives me a backache; but, it has to be done," John answered.

"I just thought – if you and Hannah weren't too busy, if I go into the meeting, you might keep Danny here. That way, he can have his nap as usual. At those meetings the kids play so hard. They all have germs this time of year and he ends up with a cold, or worse."

"I'll ask Hannah if she would feed him lunch and put him down for a nap. She probably will. If she's in the house today, she hasn't anything else to do, except paperwork. He can play outside awhile and help me shovel – pretend, that is. But let me know for sure. Just don't wander off without telling us."

"When did I ever do that?"

"Well, not yet. I just wanted to be sure."

She was so shaky when she called Girard that she could hardly hold the phone. Never having done this before, she felt embarrassed and shy to the point of hardly being able to talk. "Is Joan there?" she asked.

"No." His voice sounded so good to her. He didn't sound angry because she had called. It had been so long now since she had been alone with him. She ached to see him. "But I am," he continued.

She didn't know how to answer him. John was there at the kitchen door still dressing for the outdoors, and he could hear every word. "I hoped she might not be working today, and would go to the circle meeting with me this afternoon."

"That's all right. I'm going into town late today because I have a meeting tonight that will keep me working late. I'll pick you up and take you there. Joan won't be around today; she's working all day."

"No. You don't have to take me. I can get Tillie, if she's going. It's just that I can't get a message to her. She has no phone. You could stop there and tell her."

"I'll be there to pick you up," she could hear him insisting. The sound of his voice was like a knot of familiarity inside of her. Her body reacted to him even this far away. He was adamant now, "I need to drop off some tools I borrowed from John anyway," he added, as if to give her an excuse.

She was still shaking after she hung up the phone.

John waited at the kitchen door, the cold air blowing in through the opening. Well?" he was asking.

"Girard was coming by anyway," he said.

"He's going to take you then? Good. Will someone bring you home? Then it is settled. I'll tell Hannah to help me with Danny," he continued as he closed the door behind him.

She was glad to be left alone, but feeling like jelly on the inside. This was the first time she had reached out to Girard. Knowing she would see him, but not knowing if they could be together for any more than the time it would take to drive to town left her breathless and anxious.

Everything was happening slowly now. Danny played with his breakfast, not eating. She busied herself cleaning off the table and heating more water for dishes. She knew if she let Danny get down from his high chair, he would want something to eat in less than an hour, but she had no heart with which to scold. Letting him down, he went off to search for something to play with. The overshoes in the corner attracted him and he began to move them into the center of the kitchen, sometimes pushing them one at a time like wagons without wheels.

Rozella dried the dishes slowly, as she looked out the kitchen window. The sun was shining so brightly on the snow that it had a glaring whiteness, and the shadows of the trees were breaking across the snow banks of shoveled snow that John was making along the roadside. He had a heavy piece of wood bolted unto a metal frame, which was attached to the bumper of this truck. It plowed a pathway through to the mailbox and highway. It worked quite well when the snow wasn't too deep.

She wondered what she would wear that afternoon. It wasn't often that she even thought about clothes anymore. Hannah was always dressed in working clothes, except for Sundays. John wore his one suit on Sunday also. Rozella made do, as they said, with the clothes she had bought for her first job, and the few housedresses she had left. She and her sisters had always sewn their own clothes. That was what had helped Maggie get a job and earn a living – the ability to sew.

How had they learned to sew? First one sister teaching the next sister, and on down the line, they learned from each other. At one time Ola had worked in the local dry goods store. Rozella remembered that Ola brought home paper patterns, and she and Val had poured over the directions as they tried to sew. Mama had bought a treadle machine from one of the houses where she did housework when they bought a new model. She exchanged her wages for the sewing machine.

Maggie was the first and the fastest to learn how to run it. Val and Ola were right behind her in acquiring skill. They all liked pretty dresses, and buying the cotton fabric and trim at the store provided new dresses. Rozella liked pretty things, too, but she liked to hand sew things, and sometimes became so involved sewing pieces of fabric together that she didn't need a machine to sew with. Before she knew it – the dress was done, and it was all intricately stitched together with tiny little stitches. Mama used to look at her sewing and marvel, saying that it looked just like machine stitching. Ola had spent the first money she ever earned on cotton goods to make a dress, and ribbon with which to trim the dress...Together the sisters had selected the white brocade that they used to make Mama's burial dress. Rozella had kept the scraps.

Today she would wear a winter dress. It was too cold for cotton. She picked out a dark woolen skirt from her closet, and a light cotton blouse with long sleeves. There was also a heavy sweater she had left from teaching days. The schoolhouse had often been cold. She still wore the sweater a lot, but she would need to wear it beneath her coat today. Heating was not to be counted on these days. Most people were careful with coal and wood. They banked their fires at night, letting the houses turn cold, and warming them up in the morning. Some houses were not very warm in the daytime. People only used enough heat to keep from freezing.

She laid out the clothes on the bed she shared with John, and then went downstairs to check on Danny. He was content, but as she expected – begged for something to eat as soon as he saw her. He could say "cookie," the one word that Hannah had taught him. Rose wanted to say 'Thanks, but no thanks' under her breath as she thought about all the days she had been left alone, and all the days there was no sugar with which to bake a cookie of any kind for Danny to have when they had lived by themselves. Those were the days that Hannah could give Danny cookies when she played with him on those long Sunday afternoons, the afternoons when Rozella had waited for hours alone.

Rozella handed him a cookie. Now, there were cookies. She had not been able to overcome her fear of need, and she made them with very little sugar, and skimped on the lard, but there were raisins in them and Danny liked raisins.

Starting the mid-day meal didn't use up enough time. She was eager to be off and on her own. It had been so long since she had been out of this quiet house where there was no conversation with adults. Only a few words with John, nothing with Hannah, and no company but Danny. She had never been anywhere without Danny since he was born. There had been many long Sunday afternoons alone in the cottage, but she had been confined there by circumstances. No one knew she was there alone, except the Queists. There was no place to walk to other than into the woods.

After Hannah and John came in to eat, and she had fed Danny, she felt relieved, but at the same time her pulse was pounding in her throat. She cleaned off the table hurriedly, taking Danny upstairs to change his clothes so he could take a nap. After laying him down on the bed, she took off her cotton dress and put on her skirt and blouse. Danny watched her as she brushed her hair, dreamily looking at herself in the oval mirror above the dresser.

She heard a truck on the drive, and then men's voices. "Danny stay there," she said, and hurried down the stairs to see that Girard's truck was there and he was talking to John. They came in together, stomping off the fresh snow. "Danny is upstairs, John, but he isn't asleep yet," she offered. "He probably won't take his nap now; he'll be too curious about who is here. I'll go up and get him."

"No need to," Girard looked up to the top of the stairwell, "Look who's there."

Rose moved quickly to get him before he fell down the stairs; even as she did so, she was worrying that Hannah and John would forget how tender a little guy can be. What if they forgot and let him fall down the stairs? What if they forgot he was home with them? He was such a well of curiosity, always wanting to know things, always examining things.

She handed him to John, saying, "I'll get my coat now since I don't want to keep you waiting." Then, she returned up the stairs to get her coat and warm scarf to cover her head. Her overshoes were still downstairs, but in the center of the kitchen where Danny had been playing trucks with all the overshoes.

"I sure thank you for loaning me that bit, John. The new one was a long time getting here from the catalog order," Girard was saying to John as they left him holding Danny.

Rozella's heart felt like it was a lump in her throat. She felt like she had never felt when she was a young girl. So many young girls she had gone to school with had talked of feeling this way, and she had not known what they meant – the excitement, the fear, and the hope. With John, it hadn't been that way. It had been good, but it had just happened. This took your breath away, like a long slide when you didn't know if you would fall and hurt yourself at the end, or find a soft snow bank to land upon. Not knowing, was that it? There had been plenty of "not knowing" with John, too.

Not knowing, she was silent as they drove away from the house. By the time they reached the main highway, he had reached over to hold her hand. "Could we?" he began.

"Yes?" she wanted to know if t hey were going to try.

"Would he see us if we went to the cottage?"

"Not if he doesn't go there for some reason."

"Do you have the key? Did you think to take it?"

"I did." She blushed, knowing that as she answered she was telling him that she had hoped for some time to be alone together. "We can't stay long though, if I'm to go to the meeting. And I have to go, because I don't know how I would explain not going."

"I know," Girard answered her softly. She wondered if he felt the same thrust of yearning she was feeling; his voice was so low it was almost a whisper. The key was in the bottom of her purse. It was just a rusty old key and didn't look like anything important, yet it was very important that she have it...

They opened the lock, and the cottage door swung open, creaking on its hinges, cold and stiff from the freezing weather. Their breath clouded around them in the open doorway. Girard closed it behind them, taking her in his arms as if he couldn't wait. Together they moved toward the bed, which had been left in the room without a blanket or a pillow. The striped ticking of the mattress, lay bare and cold in the unheated cottage. There, they found themselves and the coldness disappeared as they came together quickly, searching for the fulfillment of combined needs.

It was over too soon. Far too soon for Rozella. All those empty hours, the quiet moments without conversation, without warmth. The empty hours needed filling. They couldn't be filled backwards into time, which had passed. For her to feel complete there would need to be hours and hours of equal measure in the warmth of their embrace. And who could manage that? For even now, she knew that she must say it was time to leave. They had just come together, and it was time to leave. They had not even had time to talk to each other.

"Where is the meeting today?" Girard asked as he turned his truck toward town.

"At Bergstrom's," Rozella answered. Hearing herself exhale, she realized that she had been holding her breath since they locked the cottage door. The fear of being observed, or caught, had filled her throat. It was as if holding her breath could make her invisible.

She was late for the meeting. She knew it; but someone had to be late, didn't they? She asked herself. They couldn't all arrive at the same time.

"I'll be back at four to pick you up – or Joan will," he said as he reached across her to open the truck door on her side.

"Oh, good, thank you," she picked up her purse, closed the door, then realized that she had left her needlework bag, and opened the door again. By that time, her cheeks were red, from embarrassment and the cold. His smile stopped her and she wanted to cry because her nervousness had erased the joy of the past hour together. "Bye," she waved.

It was better that she was late. With all the woman already there, she wasn't so visible. She hurriedly put her coat away and mingled with the group as if she had been there for quite awhile.

There was a buffet spread on the dining room table. Prepared this time by the hostess, Melvina Bergstrom and a couple of helpers. Thank goodness she hadn't needed to carry a dish with her, Rozella thought, she probably would have dropped it in a snow bank. She toyed with her food, sipped her coffee, and moved about the room restlessly, with the feeling that she really wasn't there.

Tillie welcomed her. "You don't know how good it is to get away without the kids," Tillie was saying, "At last, they're all in school."

"Now you won't be called out by the baby sitters," Rozella smiled, and they both stopped to listen to childish voices coming from the upstairs where a couple of young women had barricaded the stairs to keep little ones from tumbling down. They took turns this year in managing what amounted to a portable nursery: improved safety measures, collected cast off toys, extra blankets, pillows, and diapers. It would be her turn soon, Rozella remembered and how would Hannah and John handle that?

She watched Florence Nielsen and Lucy Cassilov as they unraveled man's sweaters. Sitting in the corner, they pulled and wound, rolling the old yarn from the sweaters into balls. The sweaters were in a big box several other women had collected from old clothes left stored in household attics, like theirs. The sweaters smelled of mothballs, but had few holes. Before they left that day, the balls of yarn would be taken home by other women who would begin to knit "new" sweaters. Usually they would be knitting in children's sizes, even though the colors of hand-me-down men's sweaters were usually black, navy blue, or gray.

At a large table in the dining room Grandmother Truhn and Victoria Kuhse were laying out the freshly pressed pieces of cotton that were being ironed in the kitchen. There were patterns lying about and pins. Someone would pin and cut out blouses and skirts from the pieces of old house dresses. Sometimes they turned the fabric inside out to get a brighter color. Where would this clothing go? Rozella asked another lady. People losing their farms to the banks didn't stay. Those who did stay moved in with other related families.

Some of it was put into what the circle called "welfare" storage. It was kept in boxes at the church parsonage. From there it could be distributed to those in need. Some of it was shipped to missionaries in the field, and they could be anywhere in the world.

Rozella joined the women in the kitchen who were ripping open the seams in the housedresses. It was good fortune to get the dresses that belonged to heavy-set women; they had more yardage. It was interesting to see how the materials were worn. Some were worn in the back from sitting down, and some were worn in the front where the stomach rubbed against the kitchen cupboards and counters.

The treasury reports and missionary goal statements had been held before the lunch, so she had missed hearing them, and had to ask where the next meeting would be held. It was four o'clock, she noticed by the kitchen clock, and her heart was beating too hard as she waited in anticipation of her ride home.

By eight minutes after she wondered if she had been forgotten, or there was some sort of problem with the truck. Then, she heard someone call her into the living room. Joan was waiting by the front door. Rozella's heart felt like a drum in her chest as she searched Joan's eyes. Was there anything wrong? Could she guess – about today? But, Joan smiled her usual smile, saying that she had been leaving her office when Girard dropped by to ask if she would pick up Rose. He had a late meeting with his board of directors. That's right, he had said that. That was why he was home late enough to take her to town. She had held a secret fantasy that she would get to see him again that day. It wasn't to be.

"Just a minute. I'll get my coat," she answered Joan's explanation. Going up the stairway to pick up her coat and purse, she had the strangest feeling. It was painful. She felt hurt and disappointed that Girard wasn't there. There had been so much joy in their meeting that day, but now she felt so lonely, even more lonely than she had felt before. Joan had been such a good friend to pick her up and take her home, but what was Rozella? What was she doing to Joan? She smoothed the back of her skirt, as if it were wrinkled. Underneath, her body felt warm and swollen from lovemaking. It seemed that anyone could see right through her clothes. She glanced at her cheeks in the mirror; they were highlighted in red, the remains of a blush that came from within.

As they left the house, a couple of women watched the two of them going down the steps together. They exhanged a few words in a whispered tone. Neither Joan or Rozella noticed. Rozella was engrossed in wondering how John and Hannah had managed with Danny, and worrying about what they would say when she returned. She felt so uncomfortable about it. This was really the first time she had allowed herself the freedom of doing something away from the house.

Joan wore her boots over the blue jeans that she preferred to wear. Her hair had been cut short, and a cocky navy blue knitted cap sat on the top of her short hair. She looked like a boy – no make up, a few wrinkles on her weathered face, but her face was a happy one. She had smile wrinkles at the corners of her eyes, a lively, interesting look.

In contrast, Rozella felt so much older with her pale skin, and woolen coat and matronly overshoes. She may have been dressed like all the other women, but she felt like Joan was the only one really alive. What made her feel that way? Rozella had never known anyone like her before. Joan didn't act like anyone in the countryside, and didn't look like anyone in Rozella's family. Yet, it was Rozella's softness and femininity, maybe, which Girard yearned for. Thinking about that didn't make her feel any better. She still felt old and tired and plain as they rode home together in the dark winter afternoon.

There was light in her kitchen, which left a square block of yellowing white against the dark shadows of early evening. Joan had talked about her work most of the way home. She didn't talk about her marriage, or what she and Girard planned to do together in the future. It had been a subtle change, Rozella noticed. When the two women had first met they had talked a lot about love, marriage, and dreams. There was a joyous bubble about Joan then. She didn't seem sad to Rozella now, but she seemed very involved, or distracted, almost as if she lived in another world and only traveled into this one for a brief moment to do a favor or run an errand. Her mind was somewhere else. So, Rozella didn't feel self-conscious when Joan dropped her off, she felt unnoticed, as if her friend had really been talking to herself all the way home.

Things were different in the kitchen. When she opened the door, all the old fear rushed in with her as if riding on the cold wind. Hannah was standing over the stove sullenly, with deep furrows between her eyebrows. Danny's face was a mess. His nose must have been running and he was wiping it with the back of his hand, like little boys do, his nose and cheeks were sticky and dirty. John was pouring some coffee that looked so heavy and black that it must have been left over from breakfast. It steamed from reheating, but smelled like tar.

Rozella cleaned Danny's face, and then put her coat on a hook by the kitchen door. Holding him, she began to put plates and silverware on the table. Danny squirmed, but didn't want to get down. Feeling self-conscious she began to chatter to John as they arranged the table for supper.

"I brought home some yarn in a bag," she said, "even though I've never knitted anything before, I could try socks, or scarves."

Hannah placed some bowls on the table, and then returned with a plate of bread. "Who are these things for?" she asked, although it seemed she hadn't listened at all. Was she always listening behind that silent withdrawn manner?

"For the poor – actually, the children of the poor," Rozella answered. "Scraps of cloth and unraveled sweaters make smaller things like sweaters, socks, and blouses or shirts for kids. It's pretty hard to make adult clothing out of adult clothing, except to make aprons or socks."

"Or quilts," Hannah replied, " and that's not new."

"They probably still make quilts from the scraps left over," Rozella answered, happy to have some conversation going with Hannah.

"It seems like a lot of wasted time," Hannah volunteered. "There isn't any poor family which couldn't do those things for themselves. Your women don't get that much accomplished in an afternoon."

"They take the materials home, Hannah. It just doesn't end there like a quilting bee."

"This storage of clothes and food sounds more like some kind of cult or communist group. Are you giving things to the Technocrats? Communists, I call 'em." Hannah responded

"Sometimes people are too sick to help themselves, Hannah," John intervened. "A family over in Sumner county was down with food poisoning, I heard, from eating bad canned goods. They were all sick. Nobody in the house to cook or clean, least of all, knit or sew."

"That's true, John, and the women give to fire victims, too," Rozella explained. "Every winter there are several families who lose their belongings in fires."

"It seems to me that God helps them who help themselves," Hannah objected. "Pa always tried to teach us that. Look around you at the people caught in this Depression."

"How's that?" John asked.

"Well, we've always taken care of ourselves. Our taxes are paid. Our animals are fed. The house has heat. The food's on the table. How is it that our needs are met?"

"We have no mortgages," John added.

"And, why?" Hannah asked, "because we all worked, we saved, we paid ahead. We never bought what we couldn't afford."

"Like a tractor?" John couldn't resist asking.

"That – and a lot more," Hannah glared at him. "We could have had a dozen kids running around. What if I had six? Who would be working in the fields with you?"

"A husband, maybe or the kids?" Rozella said, embarrassed after speaking.

"Not if I had to trick one into marrying me, or buy one with promises." Hannah slammed down her cup of coffee and left the room.

There was nothing more to be said. No way even to understand how the conversation had started, or why it had started. Rozella helped Danny down from his high chair noticing he hadn't eaten very much. She cleaned up the high chair and began to clean the table.

The constancy of the activities of the day had left her nothing from the brief lovemaking with Girard. Standing in the dark, she held the key to the cottage tightly closed in her hand until it warmed. In feeling the solidness of the metal, she was trying to reach the reality of the morning. Had it happened? Was it real? That flesh – that warmth – that hunger rising in the coldness of the bedroom once so lonely. It was so bare now of furnishings, but so glowing when your eyes closed and your hands were searching for each other.

Oh, yes, it had been real. It had happened. She felt the swelling of her after-love pressed against the side of the cabinet. Letting go of the key at last, she dropped it into the drawer and went slowly up the stairs in the dark.

Hannah's bedroom door was closed. There was Danny's sweet soft sleeping sound in his room. John was curled up into a half-moon on his side of the bed. He stirred, breathed deeply, and then turned over. He never wore pajamas, but neither did any other man in the county. Men wore their long underwear to bed because they were warm, and bathing was a once a week ritual. Pajamas and foaming baths were only in the magazine ads, and they belonged to imaginary people in the big cities.

Rozella had always washed herself before going to bed, if even just a pan of cold water was all she had. Usually it was easier to use an enameled washbasin in the kitchen when no one else was around. After supper, Hannah and John were in the barn finishing up the chores and Danny was in bed. It was warm beside the kitchen stove, and there was usually still warm water left from dish washing.

She pulled her flannel nightgown off its hook and went quietly back downstairs to wash up, but her bathing this night only served to remind her of her body, as the quietness of the household reminded her of nightly loneliness.

Once in bed, she snuggled against John's back needing his warmth. Sleep came quickly, her dreams wrapping themselves about each other in the darkness, as they searched for Girard.

CHAPTER TWENTY-SIX

In late morning after all the breakfast chores were done, and Danny put down for a nap, she remembered the attic and the boxes stored up there. It would be cold there, she knew, so she put her coat on before going upstairs. The heavy wooden steps were not a permanent part of the house, but like a ladder they were taken down and stored away when not needed. She found them in the back of Danny's closet. Heavy, but sturdy – she thought as she dragged them over to the hallway that had the square hole in the ceiling. She could push open the hinged door well when she got to the top. The steps felt sound when they were braced against the wall he didn't like looking down the attic ladder into the stairwell which was becoming two floors down; it seemed too far to fall, so she tried not to look.

The hinged cover opened backward after sticking briefly. Then, it banged against the attic wall, where it rested. Rozella climbed through the opening, and she was glad that she had worn the coat. It was so cold, even colder than it was outside, it seemed, except there was no wind here.

On the left side of the attic, under the small peaked windows, was wicker doll buggy. It was covered with dust, and instead of holding dolls, there were old leather shoes protruding from it. With one wheel missing, it was listing toward the wall. A pair of Canadian hockey skates lay underneath the buggy. She wondered why they seemed so out of place before she remembered – there was no place to skate around the area. Crenshaw had a river, but there was nothing in the outer farmlands. There was a wooden sled that Danny could use if it, too, wasn't broken. It was leaning against the wall behind the doll buggy. She could ask John to get it down for him.

Between the small attic windows large nails held snow shoes, and cross cut saws. Under the windows were open orange crates and an apple basket. These were filled with empty fruit jars and lids. Grape baskets held glass Kerr lids and rubber sealing rings. Jars and lids were waiting there for canning season. A musty straw mattress lay in the middle of the floor.

Christmas trimmings were lying on top of things, tinsel and ribbons hanging over the edges of boxes, as if hurriedly tossed there. There were a few crocks with blue numbers and letters over their sides telling what they could hold.

The trunks against the north wall were in all sizes, dome tops, tall wooden-slatted, leather suitcases with buckled straps hanging loose. There was what looked like an old shirt spilling out of an unlatched lid. Next to the trunks, leaning against a far wall, was a grandfather clock with one hand missing from its scratched face. A walnut chair with a needlepoint seat, lay on its side, its broken off leg in front of the clock. There was a wicker clothesbasket filled with more old shoes, and overshoes hiding under dusty felt hats. Curtain stretchers lay across the basket of shoes, their ugly steel teeth stretched upward.

Ahead of her on the far wall were stacks of magazines, and wooden shelves crudely nailed two-by-fours held an assortment of dusty books. She took a deep breath of excitement. All these things to read! She would take some downstairs.

But, she had come there for clothes, the coldness reminded her. She opened the dome-topped trunk and began to search the contents: soft kid gloves with buttons, some soiled, some unmatched; a man's three piece suit in heavy black wool, worn edges on the sleeves; old suspenders. stretched beyond use; four pairs of woolen trousers which all looked about the same length, and equally worn; a jar of assorted buttons, many looking like shirt buttons; socks, none of them matched, but thrown together in a random bunch; a flannel nightshirt which was very large, and yellowish-white from storage; two long woolen woman's skirts with ribbon trim around the bottom edges, Victorian style; a ball of old lace that looked as if it had been torn off of discarded clothing, an organdy blouse with holes rotted out under the sleeves, and on the bottom of the trunk were old newspapers stacked up neatly, but yellow and brittle with age, also. She glanced at the dates: 1911, 1913, 1914, and no apparent reason for saving them that she could see at a glance.

A nightshirt she put aside because it could be cut up for Danny. It would make good pajamas, if she could persuade him to wear them. Old sweaters could be unraveled, but with holes in them, what would be left? She tossed them back unto the newspapers in the bottom of the trunk. Then, she looked at each of the pairs of trousers and picked out the lightest weight wool, hoping to make a jumper for Danny. The rest of the contents she tossed back in, leaving them just as she had found them, in wrinkled piles. She began to hurry, as she remembered that she couldn't leave Danny alone downstairs for too long.

The flat-topped trunk was larger. When she opened it, the first thing she noticed was that it contained the cottons. It must have somehow gathered the summer clothes and the women's clothes, perhaps by coincidence. There were a few old aprons. Actually, she could use them herself, as they were long and would cover up her clothes when she was cooking and doing dishes. Why not? They were not completely worn out. She put them aside with the flannel nightshirt and pants from the first trunk. There were silk blouses in here, also, and a couple of women's sweaters, a white one and a dark red cardigan style. Underneath the sweaters were men's underwear, worn and showing bulges where knees and elbows had made their marks through days of use, and gaping openings in the rear, stretched out with age. The drab brown wool of an army uniform was there, too, along with some leather leg wraps, and she was curious about who the uniform had belonged to, since no one had mentioned that John's father had been in the war. John had been too young to serve in the Great War.

There were also some table linens closer to the top, odds and ends of linen napkins, some trimmed with embroidery and handmade edgings. They could be used, she thought, but perhaps they were put away here in order to simplify cleaning and laundry. Old lace curtains lay in a bundle. There was no way to tell if they were still good without holding up each panel to examine them for tears. She noticed the one tablecloth of red checked cotton, which was soft from years of use.

That might make a couple of nice shirts for Danny. It would be just like working with new fabric, a straight, square piece. From the dresses she choose to put aside a white cotton dress. The color seemed out of place now, but if she reworked it for herself by changing the length and shoulder style, she could wear it in the spring, for Easter. Maybe the old lace in the first trunk could be used for trim when she got done restyling the dress.

Getting up from the floor, she put away what she didn't choose to use, and closed the trunk, turning next to the books and magazines on the other wall. How wonderful to find something to read. There were <u>Good Housekeeping</u> and <u>Farm and Home</u> magazines, stacked so carefully according to date and year that the arrangement seemed fanatically exact. In respect to the unacknowledged librarian, she was careful to leave the stacks in order, taking only two copies of each off of the top. The books were not so orderly gathered. There were some business text books, Bookkeeping and Record keeping, Course I; Management, Introduction to...: Animal Husbandry; The Farmer as Veterinarian; German dictionary; 1910 Almanac; Romance of Emily Downs; Married for Love: Chemical Formulas; A Complete Reference Guide; and assorted old school books that must have belonged to Hannah or John, grammar and geography. She would remember these and come back to them later.

Another box nearby held some old records which looked like a list of sales and expenses which was not well kept; deed and land documents bound up in string, some old letters which looked like business letters because they had printed return addresses on the envelopes, receipts, loose and floating around every which way. It's too cold, she said to herself, and shivered closing up the box. Picking up her small collection of items, she went back toward the steps, turning around to go back down the steps, thinking: this attic is a gold mine. What she and her sisters couldn't have done with this?

She dropped the clothing and magazines she was taking downstairs through the opening, then turned around to place her feet upon the first step and reach for the door of the attic to pull it shut behind her. Just as she began to pull the door down, she noticed some framed pictures stacked against the wall. They had been behind the propped up attic door where she hadn't seen them. There was a beauty about them

that attracted her. And she stopped, returning to the attic and pulling
out the pictures. Two of them were framed, the rest stacked behind
the framed pictures were curling with age and neglect and weather.
They were watercolors, lovely and delicate. As Rozella held them in
her hand, she remembered John talking about Hannah's painting. Was
this Hannah? The pictures were so unlike her. The wild flowers and
ferns painted into a shadowed trail through the woods were done with
a light touch, not at all the heavy-handed emanation she would have
expected from Hannah.

It would be so nice to have them hanging in the house where there
was so little color to brighten the walls, but she didn't dare take these. It
would be better to ask John about them. She laid them carefully down
so they couldn't be damaged by the opening attic door, and returned to
the steps leading down from the dusty dormered room.

Rozella didn't bring the things out of her bedroom until after dinner
when John and Hannah were having their coffee. The dishes had been
done, and Danny was in bed. It wasn't easy to interrupt them, but she
had to know if it was all right to take the things she had chosen. "These
are the things I found in the attic. Would you tell me if it's okay to use
them? I thought I could make Danny a jumper out of the pants, and
a shirt or two from the checkered tablecloth. There's this white dress,
too; I'd like to make it over for myself. It would be nice to have for
Easter." She held up the things one at a time. "This sweater would be
good to pull apart so I could knit a new one for Danny. There's a white
one up there, but he'd get that one dirty too fast. This red one would
be good." She made her suggestions.

Hannah looked at her choices. "That's Mama's dress, but it's okay
with me if you use it. Isn't that all right, John? And, I won't wear that
red sweater. I think the only reason I left it there was because it was too
small. We don't use tablecloths anymore than we have to. At least the
lace one in the dining room is enough. Aprons? Well, I don't want to
have to use them."

John said, "I don't care what you use, Rozella. I forgot long ago
what's in the attic, if I ever knew."

"There is a sled that Danny could use, John, if you could get up
there and take it down. And – I took some magazines to read. Did you

know that there were stacks of magazines up there? They have great stories. I promise that I'll put them back. Whoever put them away stacked them up in exact order by date. Imagine that?

And there is an old army uniform up there." she continued with animation. "Who was in the army? I don't remember you ever saying anything about your father being in the army. I wouldn't want to cut that one up."

"That must have belonged to Ma's family. Wasn't that it, Hannah?" John asked. "I don't know what it's good for. Everything ends up there. It's like a museum, as I remember."

"Best of all – I saw some paintings that were beautiful. There are two watercolors that are already framed, and several others that are getting damaged from lying around without frames. They would be lovely to hang so we could enjoy them. They are about this size," She drew an imaginary frame in the air.

Hannah had turned rather white, and her lips drew tightly together. John looked at her, and then turned toward Rozella. "They're Hannah's work, and I agree – they are beautiful. I didn't know there were any of them left."

"Neither did I," said Hannah, "and I wish that there weren't any. I thought they had all been destroyed. I certainly don't want to look at any. That's why they're up there; if I had known they were there, I would have burned them."

"Why" Rozella asked before she knew what she was saying. "They are lovely. You should be proud of doing such work."

"There is absolutely no value to things like that. Sitting around and painting pictures is for fancy ladies who are rich enough not to have to work. I don't know what made me waste my time like that. I was just a kid and didn't know any better, I guess. Don't hang them up; I'll only take them down."

"Oh, Hannah," Rozella found herself hurting for this woman who had been so hateful toward her. She could see that some kind of pain was making her deny her work, and turn away from it as if she could not see her own talent. What kind of soul had been sent out to the barns? Whatever became of the girl who wrote poetry and painted pictures of wild flowers? How had she reached this point of denial?

"They do belong to me. I'll decide what to do with them, and that decision is to destroy them. I don't even want to remember them. In fact, I can't imagine who put them there. I thought that I had burned them."

"Pa probably put them there," John offered, "but I didn't know that he cared about such things. He must have thought they were too nice to throw away."

Hannah left, saying, "I better not see them anywhere around, or I'll rip them in a million pieces and throw then into the fire."

"Hannah," Rozella said before Hannah stomped away toward the stairs, "Think of Danny. Someday when he's all grown up, he will want to hang those on the wall to remember his auntie."

There was no answer, just Hannah's back disappearing up the stairs. She was retreating toward her bedroom, and John and Rozella were left at the kitchen table together. "I'm sorry. Rozella said, "I didn't know this would happen. I thought her art was lovely. She should be proud of it."

"I didn't know there were any left around. The last one disappeared from the walls a long time ago." John answered. "I wonder who put them in the attic. Hannah didn't seem to know they were up there either."

"If she didn't put them there, and you didn't put them there, that leaves only your mother, or father. I hadn't been up there before."

"And my mother was in a wheelchair for years. Even before that, I doubt if she ever went up there," John added. "Pa.. It had to be..."

"It doesn't seem like him. I never saw that he valued anything pretty." Rozella questioned his thinking, playing devil's advocate.

"He valued Hannah. Maybe because they were hers. I thought she did beautiful work, but I was a kid. What do kids know about art?"

"More than you give kids credit for, or yourself," Rozella answered. "There's no limitation for appreciation for beauty. You don't have to be educated to find something is beautiful."

Then, they heard the scraping of the wooden staircase as it was dragged across the hallway floor upstairs. A flashlight gleamed in the darkness on the floor above them. They looked at each other, realizing what the sound meant. "Oh, no," Rozella said, "I wish this wasn't happening."

"Why would she be so upset?" John questioned. They both rushed to the bottom of the staircase to verify what they were thinking. Hannah was pushing the wooden steps to the attic opening. "Hannah, please don't," he cried out as he came up the stairs. "I'll get them for you in the morning when I can see. You might fall. It's too dark to even find them:

John could barely see her in the circle of light provided by the flashlight she held. She was going up the steps slowly. Then, she withdrew the light to put it on the attic door. Rozella was right behind him on the stairway, and she could hear Hannah crying. She had never heard Hannah cry before. It was a heavy and suffocated sound.

CHAPTER TWENTY-SEVEN

What Hannah felt was worse than nakedness; everything was stripped away, her heart plunged into the dark stairway ahead, driving her toward the attic. She needed to destroy the pictures before she could see them again. Fear of what she would see made her breath catch in her throat.

John reached her; she could feel his hands on her ankles. Then she could hear his voice pleading with her to stop as the tears came in great gulping sobs that ripped out of her center like the birthing of a child. He stopped her. She stood at the top of the attic steps, warm tears running down her cheeks, pushing her forehead tightly against the top step, as if to stop her tears, as well as all feelings that threatened her. Her hands were cold and stiff as she relaxed them to let the flashlight drop to the floor with a breaking sound; and then, he was guiding her down, a step at a time through the dark.

She had destroyed the last of the pictures, she thought, that day she took the pictures down from the wall. Before that Pa had taken them from her on the same night he destroyed the poetry. He left only two pieces of work for her to hang; the rest was excess, he said. That was the night he locked her into her bedroom, coming back later in the night to nail her window shut to be sure that she couldn't call out to Nels -- if he appeared.

And, she would never know if he had come. She would remain in her room for a month, a long month that turned into the nightmare of the incarcerated: no clock, only the light and darkness to tell the time of day, no books to read, or no paper to write on. She was depending on Pa for food, water to drink, water to wash with, and a chamber pot to use. She cried off and on for a couple of days, refusing to eat. Then, one morning she had slept out of sheer exhaustion, and she awakened to the sound of his key in the door. Her clothes were smelly from perspiration of the day and night trauma, since she had refused to touch the wash water he had left. She was wrinkled and tear-stained, and she felt like a dog struggling out of the bed where she had lain.

He set a bucket of warm water on the floor, along with the towels and soap. She looked at him as a trapped animal would look, with fear and hatred in her eyes, and brushed her knotted hair out of her eyes to look at the doorway.

"No, you're not going anywhere. Not yet, young lady. We have to break young colts and you're no different, but now that you've stopped your wailing, it's time to clean you up a bit." He poured the water into her washbasin, laid out the towels in an orderly fashion, and reached for her foot. She jerked it away.

"Oh, no, don't do that. You'll only be sorry. You'll feel much better cleaned up." And, he pulled off her shoes, then reached for her dress. "Up now. Stand up. We need to get this off." It was her father, she said in her dream of memory. He pulled it over her head, dropping it to the floor; and then, he pulled her slip off in the same fashion. She was left standing in her panties, garter belt, and stockings.

Did she imagine how he had looked at her sixteen year old breasts? Or was this a memory created by what happened next? He dipped the washcloth in the warm water, put soap on it, and reached for her face. He was washing her face and neck and ears, just like Mama had done when she was a baby. Hannah had stood stock-still and stiff as a rod, the pain inside of her looming up and swelling to fill her whole body. He rinsed the washcloth, dried her face and ears and began to wash her arms. The water was warm and the soap smelt of sweet violets; she would remember the fragrance forever.

She hadn't seen Nels, no matter how many times she had looked out of the nailed-shut window. As Pa finished washing and drying her arms, and his warm washcloth touched her shoulders and moved around to wash her back, she continued to look out the window. Then, his hand returned, he hesitated, rinsed the cloth, and put soap on it again. He had forgotten to dry her off. The washcloth reached upward, and reached her soft tender young breasts, he was washing them slowly and carefully, as if they required his detailed attention. It seemed like he was breathing more deeply and leaning closer to her. The pink nipples of her child-girl body rose like buds. He inhaled sharply, put the washcloth back in to the water, then reached for the panties and garter belt.

She stood still, willing herself into a wooden statue. No words came from either of them. There were not even any thoughts, only feelings left unspoken. It was a meeting of steel wills, hers and, his – willing himself to conquer and to keep. The panties came down, the garter belt, the stockings, and he lifted her feet one at a time to remove the clothes and toss them aside. She could hear him breathe as he began to wash her from the feet upward.

Hannah worked hard to turn herself into stone as he reached around to wash her buttocks. He was saying in a shaking voice, "I never bathed you when you were a baby," but the voice was speaking to himself, not to her. Then, there was warm water on the rinsed-out washcloth, and more violet soap. He was washing the hair of her young womanhood, and reaching backward between her legs. She drew her breath in now, and he looked up at her, as if in surprise that there was really someone there. He dropped the washcloth into the basin, reached down for the soap, and worked up lather in the fragrant soap, looking into her eyes this time, acknowledging her presence. He whispered, "Now we'll find out of you're a virgin," and one hand went between her legs while the other held her buttocks tightly, cupped across the anal area. The large farm worker's hands, adept at birthing cows and horses, encompassed her most private parts, the middle finger plunged into her to probe deeply, the hand in the rear came around to the front where he pushed downward to guide his examination of her.

"It's just as I thought, Hannah," he continued, "There'll be no more secrets between us." The left hand returned to her buttocks, but the fingers remained on her and began to move in a different manner. No longer probing and examining, his hands moved in rhythm with his breathing – deeply and quickly. His thumb was moving over her wet labia. Then, he was pushing her backward against the bed. "Spread 'em, lie back," he was panting now, and she fell backward, off balance, unto the bed.

Her tears were running down her cheeks when he fell upon her, filling her with his gruff male hood, now muttering into her ear, "Little bitch in heat – you don't need to go elsewhere. There's plenty right here..." and he bucked, and came in about three thrusts, filling her young body with unwanted fluid. Everything he had washed had become dirty, and the sickly scent of violets mingled with another smell.

So, he had left her there with the washbasin, and a pile of dirty clothes, not bothering to wipe away her tears, or wash off his sperm. These memories were the pain that filled her, making her sob as if she would die of heartbreak that night as John led her down the attic steps. She didn't need to destroy her paintings in order to keep this out of her mind; everything she tried so hard to deny had returned to her with a vengeance.

Her night was filled with the return of the memories. She didn't need to close her eyes. In the darkness of her bedroom, the scenes played out upon the ceiling.

In the morning before Rozella began to warm up the kitchen and prepare breakfast, John went up the attic steps, which were leaning against the wall from the night before. He hurried, and moved quietly to avoid waking Hannah. Coming down into the kitchen, he had the pictures under one arm, and was carrying the sled with his other arm.

"How do we keep these from her, Rose?" He held out the pictures. "She wants to destroy them, I think, and actually, they belong to her."

"Let's put them away where she can't think of looking for them. If she asks, we must be honest and tell her we don't want her to destroy them, and ask her if she would wait awhile, and see how she feels about it later." Rozella answered, feeling Hannah's pain.

"I never saw her cry like that before, never." John mused. "It was a terrible sound."

"Maybe she'll forget, or not want to mention it. Is that sled okay, John?" She changed the subject.

"Yes. It was mine, Hannah's before that. No reason why Danny can't use it – unless Hannah has had feelings about seeing this, too?"

"Like the pictures, you mean?"

"Yes. That bothered me." Putting the sled down by the door, he turned toward the kitchen stove. "Is the coffee ready? I could sure use some."

"Did you put the attic steps away?" she asked, pouring him a cup of coffee.

"Yes. I didn't want to even remind her of what happened last night. Danny didn't wake up when I put them back into his closet. I tried to be quiet. I guess I was."

"I can't understand what she was so upset about. What's wrong with a picture? It isn't as if they were badly done. They're good. Nothing at all to be ashamed of. Most people would be proud of work like that," Rozella said.

"Danny must be awake now," he looked up, and she was quiet as they listened for sounds.

"I'll go get him," she responded his questioning eyes.

When she returned after dressing Danny, Hannah was sitting at the kitchen table. They were eating their oatmeal and bread, without talking. Rozella put Danny into his chair, and filled his bowl, and his cup. It was a new practice to give him a cup of milk, but add some of the coffee to it. He thought he was drinking coffee, and if you added a spoonful of sugar, he really drank it all.

What can I say? What should I say? She asked herself, and because she didn't know what to do, she remained silent like John and Hannah; she was fearful of starting to talk. Only Danny broke the silence. In his state of innocence, everything remained the same.

After finishing his breakfast, John left for the barn. Rozella could hear the dogs barking in complaint; they were waiting for their breakfast. Hannah scraped the bowls and picked up the hard crusts of bread left behind, putting everything into an old tin pan, which she used to feed the dogs. They'd get their scraps and a bit of warm milk, their reward for guarding the property. Summertime heading cattle back from the barn to grazing pasture was their job.

Rozella could breathe a sign of relief when Hannah left, but the unresolved mystery of the disturbance was lingering. Washing the kitchen floor, planning for coffee time snacks and the noonday meal occupied her. Leftover meat and vegetables put into a large skillet with added tomatoes made a sort of soup. She cooked some macaroni and stirred in some bits of cheese. Bacon bits chopped on top after frying would give it a brisk flavor.

Danny wouldn't nap until after their noontime meal, dinner, as they called it. Hannah napped then, or they supposed that she did when she stayed in her room for a couple of hours.

The things Rozella had brought down from the attic were lying on the floor. She was eager to work on them. When she made the beds, she picked them up, looking at each one, wondering which one she would begin with.

She didn't make up Hannah's bed. Her room was always left shut, so Rozella didn't know what was in there. The room she used had belonged to her parents. Hannah had moved in there when Pa Queist had died. Whatever paper, mementoes, or remains may have been shut up in there couldn't be seen, but since Hannah never went anywhere, she could not have removed them. Everything must still be there.

As they came in to eat dinner, the radio played the *Farm and Home Hour*. John had traded some old tools for the battery-operated radio a few weeks ago, and just the sound of music brightened the house. They could hear news broadcasts now, a luxury they had never had before. It was the most cheerful part of the day.

Danny was playing with his sled in the kitchen, sitting on it and pretending it was going somewhere. John reached down and patted him on the head, "I'll take you for a ride if you eat all of your dinner, How's that?"

Hannah was still silent, not that it was much different than before; she never did say much, except for the nightly conversations with John. After eating, she went up to her room, and they were left alone. John was dressing Danny to go outside, as he had promised, and Rozella was cleaning up the dishes and putting things away. It was the time of day when she looked forward to her time alone. She never thought that she would be happy to be alone, but it had happened.

Now, she would have time to choose which piece of material to work with. Should she rip up the pants, or try to copy a shirt for Danny and use the red, checkered cloth? Maybe she would even have some time to read over the magazines she had found in the attic.

In her mind she could still hear Hannah's weeping, the deep tearing sound which sounded through the darkness of the stairwell. John had never wept with loss of control as Hannah had last night, except when his mother died, she remembered. It was so unusual for either of them to show emotion.

Rozella could remember John crying out the story of how Hannah had cleared off the Sunday dinner table before removing her mother's body. He had sobbed out – they killed her. Did it take so much to make these people cry? So much of them was left hidden that it took a nightmare torn from their souls before a sign of tears could come. But, what were the hideous nightmares? It was so hard to guess. John had never talked about what he had shared with her that day. Even their father's death had brought no heavy sobbing from them. Why? She could understand why no one would grieve for John's father, but children have their own susceptibility; they usually weep for parents, no matter what – as if death forgives all things.

Rozella went to get a shirt of Danny's to use for a pattern. If she cut one a little larger from the red and white tablecloth, it should be about the right size. He was growing. On the way up to get a shirt from his drawer, she passed the door to Hannah's room. Whatever is in that room? She asked herself. Are the records of money in there? She must keep some records. Why doesn't John just go in there, isn't this his house, too?

No, control belongs to Hannah. She could evict us, if we displease her. But, who really knows this? Girard had asked that question one day when they were talking together alone. "Has any one even seen a copy of the will?" He had asked Rose when they talked.

She returned to the kitchen, where she pinned the shirt to the tablecloth, taking care to draw around the sleeves and then the yoke, collar, and front pieces. Using just one half of material, she had left room to cut out a second shirt. She cut the pieces and proceeded to baste them together. Maybe tonight, she promised herself, if she could stay awake, she could start doing some real sewing.

There was something about the pictures that caused Hannah extreme pain, or fear of remembering, Rozella thought. Ah – remembering what? That her father had destroyed the other pictures, her writing? Wouldn't that make her want to save these pictures? No, it was remembering that he made her quit school, quit painting, quit writing. She thought about all the things Hannah gave up after he locked her up. That was after the young man she loved had gone away.

It was as if everything had been taken away from her before she had a chance to experience it. But, now Hannah was free, only Hannah had not freed herself. Rozella could remember how her mother, who had hated everything her father stood for – the drinking, impractical dreaming, non-productiveness, inability to assume responsibility – had romanticized after his death. Even before his death, she had talked about him in pretty word pictures that Rozella and her sisters knew were not true. As children, it was confusing to them.

That February Mama had received a valentine from Papa. It had arrived a week too late, long after the girls had bought home their homemade valentines from the kids at school and shared them with giggles and teasing. Mama's valentine, the only one they had ever seen that belonged to her, hung upon her dresser mirror. It became a permanent ornament; no one was allowed to touch it.

"He didn't send any money," Maggie whispered. "That would have helped more than a letter or a lace-trimmed card. He always writes about what he hopes to get, what he hopes to be...and she believes it, until he comes home."

When he was gone, Mama didn't have to fear pregnancy, she didn't have to get back at him for his drunkenness; she could lie to everyone about him, and lie to herself. It didn't matter that he didn't send any money. As long as he wasn't home, the neighbors couldn't know that he didn't send money. Mama could make them think whatever she wished, by just not talking about it. Instead of talking about money, she talked about the romance of the letters and the valentine. She could create a life for the world that was a lie, and save face while she and the girls made their own living.

She made the payments on their house. They all took pride in "owning" it. After the war, they had remortgaged it and made payments of interest only in order to sustain it. The debt never went down, but Mama could think that she owned it, and remind the children that they owned their own home.

When the women came over for coffee and conversation, Mama would always take them into the bedroom to put their coats and wraps down on the bed. Rather than taking their coats from them, she would somehow get them into the bedroom each time, so she could answer any questions they might have about the valentine, even when it was far the past the season and they had all seen it many times.

"How sweet," they would purr. "Your husband still sends valentines. Maybe I should send mine away. Absence makes the heart grow fonder, they say."

"I'd rather have him here," Mama would answer, lying even to herself. Her mind would trick her into believing that they were great lovers when he was home.

The girls could remember only too well, and their little shoulders tightened up just hearing her words. Rozella could remember the talking in the night, the arguments, and the pregnancies. Did the neighbors, did the women really believe that Mama wanted more babies? Didn't they know, or did they pretend with her?

Owning their own home was their price. Even now when Rozella knew the fiction of their mother's ownership, she still had the old need for security built upon ownership, They would never own this farm, and there was no way they could even know if they would own the house or any part of the farm when and if – Hannah died.

CHAPTER TWENTY-EIGHT

John and Hannah talked very late that night and Rozella didn't know what kept them, if they had discussed Hannah's tears and the pictures, or if they were talking about other things, business perhaps. In the morning, she heard about the plans they made to go into town that day. It was unlike Hannah to go to town for any reason, so this must be something special. Trying very hard not to ask questions, Rozella asked if they would be gone long.

"No, I don't think so," John replied, "But I can't tell, so don't expect us to be home for supper. Go ahead and eat."

"Is there anything you want me to do around here?" she asked.

"No. We'll get the chores done before we leave. And we'll have the cream cans and eggs all loaded up to go. No. I can't think of anything. Is there anything we can get for you?"

"Some white thread, please, and a package of needles. Just regular ones," she answered. She didn't know why she was startled by this trip. Most people go to town every week. John went into town once a week on errands, just as he used to do before they were married. He was doing all the same things, she assumed, selling eggs, cream, and picking up any tools and materials needed for the equipment.

When Hannah came down after breakfast, she was dressed in her Sunday clothes. She didn't look any brighter or younger; she only made it seem like Sunday. The only thing different was the manila envelope she was carrying instead of her Bible. Sundays were the only days she would wear a dress. This must be a special occasion. She still wasn't saying anything about the pictures or her crying episode. Rozella didn't suppose she ever would mention it. Hannah went out the front door, saying over her shoulder, "Tell John that I'll be waiting in the truck."

John came down from upstairs, and he was dressed in his best clothes, too. "You wanted thread and needles?" he asked, "Anything else?"

"No," she answered him, as she lifted Danny down from the table. "You will be home by suppertime, won't you?"

"Oh, yes. I think so. Maybe we won't be gone all day. We'll have a sandwich in town, though, so don't cook for us."

She felt startled, and sad, somehow, like any girl who hasn't been invited to a party. Surely it wasn't a party, but she felt so left out. Why couldn't she have gone along? Danny could have gone with them. It would have been nice to see something different than the four walls of the farmhouse kitchen.

Ashamed of her resentment, she tried to put it out of her mind, and made herself get busy cleaning up the kitchen and pantry and rearranging the shelves. Danny wanted to help, so everything that she put back on the shelf, he took down; and then he laughed gleefully when she said, "No, No." When she finished the shelves of the pantry, she began to wash the kitchen floor. "Danny, help..." he announced crawling around on the floor beside her. He liked it when she did anything that brought her down to his level and size. She grabbed him and hugged him to her. He was such a companion.

She could hear the dogs barking in the stillness of the quiet, cold day. Then there was a knock on the door. Getting up from the floor to answer it, she left Danny playing around with the scrub rag on the floor. "Girard!" she exclaimed in surprise when she opened the door. "How?"

"You mean how did I know you were alone?" he asked. "Well, I saw Hannah and John in town and I knew you were here alone. If you want to ask why – I can't answer it. It was a crazy thing to do, but I couldn't make myself stay away. Right or wrong. You tell me. I haven't had a chance to talk to you, or see you. I needed to talk to you, to be near you. Don't worry, I didn't let anyone see me head out of town, and if they did see me – after all, I live on the same road. They would never know."

"Girard," she said, and there were tears in her eyes. She hadn't known how much she had needed him, or how much she had missed being with him, and talking to him.

"Danny play wash," Danny was talking to himself as he splashed the water. They looked at him, and then at each other, reaching over to kiss one another gently on the lips. The electricity of the kiss served only to remind them of how they felt.

"Could we have some coffee and talk?" he asked. "Maybe there's some coffee left from breakfast?"

"Yes, as a matter of fact, there is." She went to the stove to warm up the coffee in the old enameled pot, while he sat down by the kitchen table.

God, she was beautiful, he thought. Not a touch of makeup, hair flying in wisps around her face, her eyes still dewy from sleep, or did he imagine it? He wanted to touch her. It took all of his self-control to stay in his chair. When she brought the coffee and put it in front of him, she sat across the table from him, he felt better. He could reach out and touch her hand, which he did, then couldn't let go of it. "Tell me, what are they doing in town?" he asked.

"I don't know. I haven't the slightest idea. They just announced it this morning, and they didn't tell me why they were going to town."

"Or, did they ask if you wanted to go along. Of course, you might have wanted to stay home in order to be here with me, but there was no way you could know that I would know you were waiting here."

"That's true. I didn't even think about it because I knew I couldn't tell you to come. If I could have told you, what would I say? It's just too dangerous to be here when they could come home at any minute... and there's Danny." She looked down at him where he was playing.

"I know. We'll just talk. We need to do that. There is seldom any time for us to talk to each other. I need to know how you are, and what you are doing. What's going on with you?" His eyes were shining across the table at her.

"Not much. The same old things. I found some old clothes in the attic and I'm trying to make some clothes for Danny from the things I found in the old trunks."

"What else? You talk. I just love to listen." He was still holding her hand and forgetting the coffee.

"Drink your coffee," she said. "They won't be back for dinner. They said so. Maybe we can have something to eat together."

"Danny goes to bed," he remembered hopefully.

"And we don't dare..." she answered his thought, as she tried to ignore what he was feeling, "Hannah had some sort of a scene when I mentioned some pictures I had found in the attic. I thought they were beautiful and wanted to take them down and hang them on the walls. She became very disturbed about them, and began to cry."

"That's odd." He fingered her wedding ring, turning it around and around, as if he would like to take it off of her finger.

"Yes. She cried so terribly. It was dark upstairs, and that's where she was, trying to get up into the attic, and we couldn't see her. We could only hear her. It was an awful sound, as if her soul was breaking."

"Now, don't get all sentimental over her, Rose. She has never done you any good. All that woman has done is hurt you since you first came here. You tried. She just couldn't find a speck of kindness in her to be understanding. She doesn't need your understanding." He reached out to her across the table. She was sipping her coffee, not really wanting it, but going through the motions. Danny was getting pretty wet, as he played in the pan of scrub water. When Girard touched her, she couldn't even look up at him; but she could feel it, like a shock.

"We can't," she whispered, but his hand was on her breast, fondling it so gently. His fingers had found the nipple, which had become firm under her clothing. She inhaled deeply, as if she couldn't find enough air with which to fill her lungs. Danny looked up at her.

"It's okay, Danny, but we'll need to put the water away." It took all of her strength to pull herself away from Girard's touch and go to Danny to pick him up and dry him off. "Let me go change him," she said.

When she returned Girard had finished his coffee and was waiting at the kitchen table. "I'll feed him first," she said.

"Good. Good," he answered her. "I know that we can't...but we can have a few minutes together. If we stay here, we can recover, perhaps, if anyone should come home early."

"Recover?" she asked.

"I mean, we won't look so guilty. If we go anyplace else in the house, we would look like we were doing things...other than what we should be doing. We need to be careful, for you – Rose."

"Yes. I'm afraid. There's no understanding those two."

"Let me hold Danny while you make his lunch. To me, it will always be 'lunch.' I have trouble with your expressions around here."

"Turn on the radio, if you like, she said, "I won't be long." She got some vegetables out of the pantry and put them on the stove to warm up, along with them, she added an egg in a small frying pan. She scrambled it and buttered a piece of bread. Putting this on a plate, she placed it on the table, and then turned back, "I'll get his milk and be right back."

Girard started to feed him, and Danny pushed the fork away, saying in his child's voice, "No, Danny does it."

She couldn't help but laugh. "You're not used to little kids. They get independent very quickly. Just put him in his high chair and let him do it. It takes awhile, but he eats as much as he wants. Doing it his way makes him feel like he has control."

"I wish I had so much control," Girard looked up at her, after he put Danny in his chair. "Please sit down, so I can touch you."

"Right now...in front of ...everything?"

"Right now. I promise to be decent. Talk. I'm listening. I know you, remember? You haven't had anyone to talk to."

She sat beside him, and they talked as Danny ate and played with his dinner. She could feel his hand first on one breast, then on the other breast, as she leaned over the table, her sweater hiding her breasts from the child. Her body was going crazy and it was hard for her to talk. Talk? About what? She couldn't think.

"I'll talk, then. The mortgage company has an office for deeds alone. Other people talk, you know. I get the impression that Hannah is considering selling all the excess acreage that her father bought under foreclosure."

"To whom?" she asked.

"The federal government. No one else has any money to buy it. You know the federal plan to buy up acreage to prevent crops from being planted in the spring.

"I thought I heard John and Hannah arguing about that. John was very much against it. He wanted to plant the acreage. Hannah didn't want to do it. She would rather have the money."

"I would guess that she got her way."

"She always does. John can't do anything about it. He has no power in regard to this place. It all belongs to her. We just live here, grace of Hannah. Without her, we'd be homeless."

"Is Danny done?" he asked. "He seems to be just playing around now."

"Yes, for someone who isn't a father, you catch on quick. I'll put him down for his nap now. But – that won't change things." She looked at him, blushing.

Carrying Danny upstairs, she wished it would change things. Her breath was coming so deeply and her desires had become painful. How long had it been...how long?

Danny was tired. His floor scrubbing activity had worn him out, and he was especially good. She had given him a warm bottle to be assured that he would fall asleep quickly. When she returned to the kitchen, she wanted to ask questions about the federal land buy-outs. Girard would know, and this might be her only chance to talk to him for a long time.

When he kissed her, she couldn't think. He pulled her down on his lap, and brought her close to him. The kiss was long, and she didn't want it to end. She needed it so much that tears were running down her cheeks. "Rose, sh, Rose," he whispered. "Take off your panties."

"We can't. We can't," she cried.

"Trust me. It's okay. Just take them off and put them in your apron pocket. We can recover, if anything happens. Please." His hands were reaching up to help her, and she stood for a moment, as he helped her, and she stood for a moment, as he helped her take them down and slip them over her feet. When they were in her pocket, she sat down on his lap again.

"You see? You see?" he murmured. "We will only do what we can..." He kissed her again, this time with his hands between her legs where the life of her had begun to flow and she felt the wetness of it against his hand as he caressed her. He opened the front of her dress and pushed her bra aside to release her breast. "We can't...we can't," she whispered.

"But we are...we are..." he answered her. "God, your breasts are the most beautiful things I've ever seen." He was looking at them before he pulled her skirt aside and spread her legs."

"What? What?" She was breathing deeply now, and she felt his mouth upon her as she spread her legs further apart. She could feel herself begin to form a scream of ecstasy. There was Danny, she couldn't make so much noise...She put her hands over her mouth to silence herself...as she began to sob with the release that shook her whole body, once and then – again. And she wondered about Hannah's sobbing, as she felt her own soul tearing itself out of her body. Ecstasy. She had never felt anything like this, and she didn't even know what was happening to her. Her body and feelings were beyond her control.

When he arose at last, he looked down at her, so filled with love for this girl, this country girl with her innocence. She could love this sensuality because she was innocent and didn't know enough to call it bad. She only knew it as his love. He could see the tears that had come to her still rolling down her cheeks. Gently he leaned down a bit to place his loving body against her breasts, such lovely breasts. He needed to feel them; he needed her, but he couldn't offend her. His own restraint was a hard and painful knot in the center of his body.

"I'll fix our dinner now," she said, but she couldn't look at him.

"Come here. You must look at me, or you'll never be able to look at me gain. We must acknowledge love making as part of our love for each other. It's good, darling, It's us. All it is –is our way of talking about our love for each other. Don't be afraid. Don't be ashamed of your feelings." He kissed her lightly on the lips, and raised her chin so she would look at him.

"Yes, It is love. I didn't know about it...didn't know how it could be."

She brought them scrambled eggs and toast, apologizing for not having something more elaborate, but they ate and enjoyed it. Everything tasted perfect. They had a couple of hours together, but didn't dare risk more.

"But, I don't understand, Girard," she asked, "Why didn't John tell me what they had decided to do today?"

"Maybe he doesn't even know, Rose. Maybe she didn't tell him what she wanted to do in town."

"If he didn't know, why was he dressed up? He doesn't usually put on any other clothes than his working clothes in order to do the usual things in town."

"Good question. Why was he dressed up? She must have told him something."

"Does it make a difference, Girard, if she sells the land? It seemed to upset John, since he wanted to plant some more in the spring. Maybe Hannah is right?"

"She might be right. How she got the land, or how her father got the land is not the issue right now. If you are asking what should be done with it – that's a different question. And the answer depends upon who you are, and what Queist's will said."

"What do you mean?"

"Only that it may be unrealistic to even hope that part of the farmland may belong to John. Maybe it never was intended to be his."

"That would make our being here only a matter of survival."

"That's right."

"And if that's right, what's wrong with that?"

"Nothing. Nothing at all, except there is no reason to be obedient to a power that owes you nothing. If neither one of you have anything to gain by staying here other than survival, something to eat, and a place to sleep, you can't pin your hopes here. You must get focused on something else."

CHAPTER TWENTY-NINE

It was nearly four o'clock when Hannah and John returned, and the shortness of the winter day brought darkness early, as the long, gray stretch of the afternoon leaned into night. Girard had left about two o'clock, not daring to stay any later. Every minute gave them added anxiety, so when they could hear Danny begin to stir, he had slipped out quickly before the child could see him. She had heard the dogs barking at him as he got into his truck, and as she lifted Danny from his bed. She had looked out of the window to watch him turn unto the highway.

Hannah still had her manila envelope under her arm when she came in and she took it with her upstairs, not commenting on the trip to town. John handed Rozella a small package; he hadn't forgotten her needles and thread. He brought a small bag of jellybeans for Danny, but she had to take them away before Danny could eat them all. "Tomorrow, tomorrow, save some," she murmured.

There were a couple of other paper bags on the floor. John nodded toward them, as if he recognized her unspoken inquiry. "Just parts for mending the harnesses. Some feed out in the truck. Nothing else," he said.

She must have looked as if she expected more. It wasn't that — it was curiosity, she thought. If you sold something, you got money, a check perhaps. If you didn't believe in banks, the check would be cashed. If Hannah sold the properties, wouldn't she have a check? No, on a federal sale, it would be mailed to her. So many "ifs."

"John, what did you do in town today, other than shop?"

"Hannah had to go to the court house go get some deeds changed, and I went along."

"Does that mean she did sell off the land?"

He seemed embarrassed, and his answers came slowly, as if he had to think about what they would be. "Yes," he said. "I really couldn't see the papers, and don't know what the figure was. I hoped she would tell me, but she sent me on an errand to another part of the building – to the assessor's office."

"You disagreed with the sale, I thought?" Rozella said, as she continued to tidy up the room.

"Well, yes. I had hoped for a piece of this land in my name. Maybe – since there were several pieces, even a place we could have that would be ours." He looked at her.

"A dream you didn't dare share with me, but it would have been wonderful, John. We may be well provided for here, but don't you feel like a hired hand? I know that I feel like a servant, but I supposed all tenant farmers feel that way."

"It's not easy for me either, Rozella. I'd like to make my own decisions. Because Hannah spent so much time working with Pa, she feels that she's a better farmer and manager, and maybe she is. Maybe I am just a dumb Mama's boy, as they both called me, but I'd like to try other things."

"Then, that means we don't have a chance of owning any part of this? Not ever? Did you think we would?" She jammed a chair under the kitchen table.

"I thought we would. I really did. I think we will get this place after Hannah dies; she has no one else to leave it to."

"Not a very pleasant basis on which to build your dreams, or Danny's future. Oh, yes, that's possible; she could leave it to Danny, and name you and I as caretakers. That way we'd spend our lives in the same role we have now. Sorry, I hate myself for thinking that, John. Actually, Hannah's not so old that we should even consider this a property to be inherited."

"I have no way to buy anything of my own, Rose." He shook his head. "Maybe we should move to the city. Maybe there is a job someplace." His voice trailed off as he went upstairs to change his clothes.

Then, this was what Girard meant by "focus," she thought. In a world where plans were made by God, people didn't plan, they expected life to work out according to some greater plan, or by chance; they only hoped chance had a plan. They yearned for there to be a plan in order to escape responsibility. Leaving it to some higher power, they didn't have to take any blame. What was it she had expected of life? Her dreams had not extended further than her goal of teaching, leaving home, and living alone – escape from her family, and the way she felt when she was at home with Mama and the others.

When John had come into her life, she had no dreams about their future together. She had fear – fear that he couldn't return to her, fear that he didn't love her, and fear of even hoping or planning for marriage. All of these fears had blocked her from looking ahead.

She could remember no pattern of planning in her own family. People met, fell in love, married, out of love or necessity, got jobs, lost jobs, all according to chance. You had bad luck, or good luck, were blessed, or cursed. You had an excuse for everything that happened – or after it happened an excuse was waiting for you. The only time she had used the idea of working on what was going to happen to her before it happened was her plan to teach, and to leave home.

If she was to think that way now, where would it take her? Where would it take John? When she sat down to think, it was with a piece of paper, drawing it out like a lesson plan with goals on one side of the paper, and how to achieve them on the other. The side with the answers to how to achieve the goals was nothing more than scribbles when she looked at it. What did John really want? A place of their own – did that mean a farm or could it mean just a place to live, even in a city?

When she thought about it, it wasn't clear to her what John wanted. She had a difficult time even stating it on paper. What did Rozella really want? A place of her own – meaning what? Farm, house, own, or rent? Surprised at herself, she discovered "her own" meant anywhere away from Hannah, even a rented apartment. They had never considered big city living, the cost of rent, travel to get there, or living expenses while John tried to get a job. Women did work, also. Could she teach in a large city? Would they accept her, married and with a child, or would she have to take some other kind of work, if indeed, there was any work? So many people were unemployed in this country. Even if she could work, what about Danny? Who would take care of him?

She didn't like what the piece of paper was making her do. It posed problems never before confronted. When Girard said "focus," she had not realized how frightening it could be. It was not easy to sit and sew during the quiet hours and not think.

Once the questions had awakened her, she could not put them aside. Every stitch put into the small shirts she created for Danny out of the scraps seemed to entail a question left unanswered.

On the next sunny day, she took Danny out on his sled, pulling him up and down the driveway. The exercise and his enjoyment of the sled helped cheer her. For that moment, the questions were stilled.

Joan called her later in the afternoon, and she was almost startled to hear from her. It had been a long time since the four of them had spent an evening together. The Queist house didn't seem comfortable for entertaining. She had hoped their friendship wouldn't change after their move, that they could still get together and play cards on weekend evenings, but John hadn't seemed to be responsive when she had suggested it. Maybe he felt uncomfortable having people over to what he considered to be Hannah's house. Maybe – she entertained her own guilt, another thought she kept hidden as much as possible, she felt the relationship between Girard and her? Was Joan trying to avoid having anything to do with them? Rozella couldn't know, but she did know that John couldn't know. She acknowledged that her fear was only her own. As she talked to Joan, there was fear in her throat, and acknowledgment of what she was doing, she thought, to their marriage.

Joan was inviting them to their house for the evening on Saturday night, offering supper together and an evening of playing cards. They hadn't done this for a long time, Joan said, "I know," Rozella answered her, and in all honesty, continued, "and I have missed talking to you."

"It's my work. I've even been a stranger to Girard the past weeks," Joan answered. "I don't mean to do this. I just become involved in projects I'm working on."

"I'm sure that Girard misses you, too," Rozella replied, even though her own words gave her pain. She found it hard to confront the existence of Girard's feelings for Joan, even though Joan may have a right to Girard's feelings and Rozella did not. Until this moment, she had not really asked herself about what she felt, it had just happened. Girard's attempts to ease her from her fears had only served to put them aside. Now, she could tell, the fears were still there. She did care about Joan. And maybe worst of all, she cared about herself. It made Rozella feel as if she didn't exist, this acknowledgement of her worthlessness to him.

"I'll ask John if we can come over. I'd like to see you very much," and saying that she realized it was true, "But I need to check with him."

Hanging up the phone, she almost laughed at herself. What could they be doing that would interfere with such an evening? They never went anyplace, or did anything. The answer would depend entirely upon John's mood. That was the way things were done, she knew; but for the first time, she wondered why it was this way. Why couldn't she have said simply – Yes, we'd love to...or yes, I'd love to? It wasn't done that way. She shook her head.

Who indeed went anywhere or did anything? People went to church activities, they sang in the choir, they met for financial reports and fund raising activities, they sometimes visited their relatives, especially on birthdays and anniversaries, but never anything else. In fact, when she thought about it, you didn't hear too much about just friends getting together. There seemed to be a social commitment to church and family. And that was the way it had been at home when she was a child, only since Mama had no family other than those she had left behind in Russia, the family consisted of Rozella's brothers and sisters. Papa's family also had been left behind in Russia. He had no one.

She realized that the distance between her sisters and her was a hindrance to visiting them. If they all lived in the same community, they could be celebrating anniversaries and birthdays together. As it was, there was no one to celebrate anything with – except, Hannah, and she didn't acknowledge anything as memorable, it seemed. At least John reflected nothing of this kind. She could remember Tillie talking about birthday parties when she was a kid, but it was another part of their lives that had vanished into the past. Perhaps it had disappeared when John's mother died.

John accepted that the idea of going over to Joan and Girard's' on Saturday evening. He seemed almost eager, as if he wanted to ask Girard questions about the land transactions that Hannah had concluded. Questions may not change a thing, but the answers might help them to understand what was happening. Would John be able to see Girard's point about looking for a life somewhere else, doing something else? Would Girard even dare bring it up? Perhaps she could ask about it again, and get John to thinking.

But – leaving here would mean leaving Girard, and she was reacting to something that she had never thought about before: leaving Girard would be leaving all the joy, love, and excitement of her life behind. With shock, she realized that she didn't want to leave him. The thought of it was extremely painful. Maybe she didn't want John to be awakened, and as a result seek change, if it meant leaving this part of her life behind. How many different ways could you be tied into a pattern of life, she asked herself?

She hadn't thought about what her relationship with Girard meant. So far it had been something that was in the process of developing. It had no identity of its own. Since she hadn't known what it was, she had no way of controlling it, or questioning what it's future would be. It all had sounded easy, and it might have been only an excuse. If she had thought about it as just a friendly exchange that required nothing but her learning about affection and passion, she had no fear. When she took one mental step beyond that to realize she had let a strong need for him build, and she had come to love him deeply, she felt a fear that shook her to the deepest part of her being. How could I leave him? she asked, while the answer was: but you don't really have him, so what would you be leaving? Another woman's husband, was the answer, Joan's husband.

In spite of the questions, she looked forward to seeing them both. This kind of an evening was exciting. It gave her something to look forward to, to plan for. She could plan a dessert, bake a special cake to share, and think about what she would wear. Then, she fell into thinking about Girard, and anticipating seeing him and talking to him. The feelings had become too physical now, and no thought of him was complete anymore without the remembrance of their moments together. The forbidden fruit of it – she accused herself, both fear and desire. And she couldn't be sure what had caused her feelings about him to move in such a strong manner into a different mode. She had changed, that was the truth, but had Girard changed? Did he still believe that their relationship was only a kind and friendly gesture that Joan could accept?

On Thursday of the week, Hannah received a small brown envelope with a federal address printed on the left hand side. Rozella noticed it in the pile of mail she brought in from the mailbox. Of course, that answered a question about the sale of the land. If she had sold it to the federal government, they would pay her by check, and by mail. And, this could be the check. The next question would be – what would she do with the check? Rozella could tell herself that it was none of her business, but she couldn't stop herself from watching the envelope and Hannah's reactions to the contents.

In the evening after supper, when they usually opened the mail Rozella lingered behind in the kitchen, taking more time than the usual amount of time for cleanup and drying the dishes. She could see that Hannah didn't flinch a bit when she opened the envelope. In fact, she was cautious about it, to the extreme of opening the envelope and peering into it from the slot she cut across the top. She didn't even take out the contents. John was busy looking over seed catalogs and didn't even notice either the envelope or Hannah's method of opening it. She put the envelope in the pocket of her sweater, and continued with her conversation with John when she had finished looking through the rest of the mail. "You asked about the south forty, John? What we plant there in the spring depends upon what the government wants us not to plant, doesn't it?"

CHAPTER THIRTY

It was a week before Hannah asked to go into town with John when he made his usual trip. Waiting and watching to see how she would get to the bank (if that really had been a check she had received in the mail), Rozella thought about their shared reliance on John to drive them to town. Joan was the only woman she knew who drove.

Normally, Hannah avoided the trip to town. It was an accepted fact that she didn't go. There was work to be done, and Hannah had always done it. Time was important to a self-sufficient household, and John seemed surprised when Hannah announced her intent to go with him to town, but his recovery was immediate. His perception must have been the same as Rozella's thoughts had been. He recognized that the money from the sale of acreage must have come in the form of a check. The check needed to be cashed, or banked.

"Why do you think that she wants to go to town with you, John?" Rozella asked when Hannah had left to go to her room.

"For the check," he answered, "She will have to cash it or put it into the bank. The government pays in cash, but their cash is in check form. Just the fact that she wants to go to town means that she has been paid."

"I noticed there was an envelope that looked like it was federal. It came more than a week ago."

"I wish you had said something. Not that it would have made any difference, but I didn't notice that she had one. I just wouldn't have been so surprised today, that is."

"What difference does it make, really?" she asked. "There is nothing that you can do about the money, is there? It's hers. She will do whatever she wants to do with it."

"You're right, of course. I just have this idea that if I know what form its in, I can know how I might direct her...or what I can ask for. There might be more logic to what I ask for, or hope to get."

"That's true, but for me there is no logic. The money is hers. She can do anything at all with it. I have no right to anything. Whatever my future needs are, they belong to me."

"Well, to me, the land and the money belonged to my parents, so I feel like I should have some right, regardless of what Hannah thinks that my father wanted. All she has said so far is that he wanted her to guide me, not to cut me off."

He left her to prepare the marketable items for the trip. When Hannah came downstairs, she was dressed for the city, and she gave no indication of why she was going. Neither of them thought to ask if Rozella and Danny would like to go along. The cab of the truck would be crowded, but other farm families were seen traveling to town that way – crowded into a cab with children sitting on laps, and bobbing along happily.

The two of them left by 9AM, long before Danny's naptime. Rozella lingered over the housework. No matter what John's interest in the money from the land might be, the fact that Hannah didn't trust him to take the check into town meant that she had no intention of letting him handle any part of it.

John's dreams of owning a place of his own seemed bleak, as Rozella thought about it. And what of the John she had first known, who seemed to hate everything about farm life. He had felt trapped here until he could get away. Something had changed in John; he had become more involved with the land and his plans for the future were evolving around the land and what it promised for the future

It was a new thought to her. The change in John had not occurred to her. Seeing this for the first time, she was awakened to the thought that she, too, had changed. How? She asked in this quiet time of examination. Much had happened to change her, but how – what had been the result?

She had become a mother. That had changed her. She had left her dreams behind her when she married John, or had exchanged them for dreams of what marriage would make of her life. In her case, her mind had blanked out what she really had hoped for in marriage. It was Girard who had awakened her to thinking about these things, and Joan, too, who had questioned her.

Fear had closed the doors of her anticipation. She had allowed herself to expect nothing of marriage; just the idea of love was a vague, ephemeral idea, lingering just out of reach. Her dreams, if they were that, focused about moving into a larger house, where she could be with Danny all the time, even on Sundays. Now, she took that for granted.

How quickly we take for granted things that once seem so precious and unobtainable? If she dared to ask herself what she wanted now, what would it be? Would she choose to stay here?

No. She would choose to leave. If all the wishes were hers to have, she would not stay here. The house was heavy with Hannah's ways, and the past of Hannah's parents. Whatever strange things had formed both Hannah and John, whatever circumstances had done to create the marriage their parents had shared, and then to create the two of them, she wanted no more part in it.

What she was wanting then was to escape from this house and every memory that it contained. Memories hung like cobwebs from every corner, and seemed to fill every day, if only because they seemed to shape everything that happened. Even now, John was bound by whatever had created the deeds to the land that Hannah had sold, and both sister and brother would continue to be bound by whatever the land could provide.

Rozella had easily been trapped by security; she could acknowledge that now. She could look back into her own life and see that insecurity gave her fear, and fear kept her captive. Every time Joan or Girard had forced her to answer their question "Why? She had answered because there was no place to go. She had dwelt upon her insecurity knowing only that here – there was a place to live and food to eat for she and Danny.

It went back – back into the days of her childhood home where security was the illusion of owning their home, no matter how impoverished they were. They were tied to the home that kept them together – except for Joe, who ran away. He was the only one to run away.

Moments came when she looked out of the windows, hoping to see Girard's truck come down the road, but there was no sound and no sign of him. Their last time together had been a happy accident, she told herself. He had known she would be alone only by chance. He was able to get to her only by chance. She couldn't count on it all the time, she knew, but at the same time she couldn't stop hoping for him to come.

When Hannah and John returned that evening, everything seemed as normal, except for John's agitation. He was withdrawn and involved with his thoughts, and his actions portended more agitation as he prepared to go out to the barns before supper. Hannah had brought no unusual packages with her, just some extra food supplies for the pantry, a sack of flour and five pounds of lard. She hadn't asked Rozella for a list, so she must have looked through the pantry before she left for town.

Supper seemed quieter than usual, perhaps only because Rozella was aware of wanting to know what happened in town and what was going on in the minds of both brother and sister.

"What's going on in town?" she asked, hoping to stir up some conversation.

It was John who answered her. "Not much," he said, while Hannah did not even look up from her plate.

"Did you see anyone we know? Girard, or Joan, or anyone else?"

"No, not a soul. We were in and out of every place as quickly as possible. Did you see anyone at all, Hannah? Other than in the bank?" John turned to Hannah, questioning her.

"No." That was the taciturn answer.

Almost embarrassed by the difficulty of starting a conversation with these two, Rozella gave up the idea and turned to helping Danny and talking to him, as if they weren't there.

Later that night when John came up to the room, she made a point of talking to him about the trip. "I know you wondered why Hannah went into town. Like me, you were sure that she went because she had a check to cash. I felt funny about the conversation at suppertime, but I couldn't go on trying to talk to you."

"But – did you find out what she did, or if there was a check from a sale?

"Yes. There must have been. I can't say for sure. She never lets me near her. There is always some excuse why I must be someplace else other than with her, but she did go to the bank, and yes, I think you are right. I think that she did cash a check. I can only guess that she cashed one, as I don't know. She could have put money into the bank. The only reason I think that she cashed a check is because Pa was that way."

"She might be different."

"I like to hope so, but I really don't believe it. Everything I see of Hannah, especially as she grows older, shows me that she is getting more and more like him."

"Why? I can't see why she couldn't grow more unlike him, if only because he couldn't have treated her very nicely. You said yourself that he locked her up in her room and forced her to quit school. Didn't you tell me that? He probably sent away the only young man she ever cared about, as if he owned her and she was a slave. How could she want to be like him?"

"I don't know why, Rose. I don't seem to know anything. The more time goes on, the more I doubt myself and my own reasoning."

"Do you know what you want, John? I asked myself today while you were gone. You used to want to get away, but things seem different now, like you want most to stay and farm. If that is what you want..."

"I think that I wanted to get away because I felt I had to have something of my own, that I needed money to become a whole person. Getting away, and getting a job in a city seemed to offer me a way of becoming independent. Sure, a rebellion against Pa, and a way of living up to some unstated hope of my mother's – maybe. But now, yes – I'd like to stay if I thought it belonged to me. I don't want to be a hired hand. I want to own my piece of ground, and I don't see why I can't. It's my heritage, not just hers." He was adamant about this, and his voice rose.

"John, I agree that you should have something of your own, but if you can't get Hannah to give you a thing, then there is no way to get anywhere here. You will remain a slave to her, and so will I. Danny will become a slave in his day. You can't force her. I can't see that there is any way that you can do that."

"I'll find out what she did; and then, I'll know what I can ask for," he answered.

"Asking for and getting are two different things, John," she shook her head, ruefully.

"It's only my right!" He pulled the covers up under his chin.

"Don't be angry with me. I'm only trying to point out that just willing it won't make it happen. You may, we may, have to find something else to do, somewhere else to go, if that's our only way to make a life that belongs to us."

"When I find out – then I can decide. Not before. I have to know."

"We're not even sure of how much she owned, or how she got it. All we have to go on is rumor. It's true, most of what Girard knows is fact because he works in the business, but we haven't seen the total of what your father might have purchased. We're still working on rumors, and guesses."

"That's why I have to know. I'll have no peace at all until I know what was done: what was bought by my father, and what was sold by Hannah."

"You can try to find out, but I suspect that the only way will be to search her rooms, and both you and I hate that sort of thing. You'd like it better if you got an answer from her."

"She didn't bring anything large back from town. So, if there was cash, she carried it in her handbag. Maybe she did put it in a checking or saving account, in spite of what she was taught by my father – never trust a bank." He turned away from her, and plumped up his pillow.

"Ask. Just ask. Maybe tell her that you need to know to have peace of mind. Then, ask if she will help you, deed something over to you, if that's what you really want."

His sleep was as restless as his mind, but the only reason Rozella knew was because she couldn't sleep either. Her whole idea of the future, which she had successfully blocked out of her own mind, loomed up large and foreboding. When you ask what you want of life, the answers come back to scare you.

It was the next evening after supper when John, pale-faced and quiet-voiced began his conversation with Hannah. Rozella lingered as long as she felt that she could by taking longer than usual to clean up the kitchen and put away the dishes.

She could hear John's first words, surprisingly demanding for him, as he told Hannah that he wanted a place of his own. "If there is no other way to do it other than take a bare piece of acreage and deed it to me until I can manage to build a small house for Rozella and me – that will do. I'd still be here to help you."

"You wouldn't be much help if you were trying to build your own place, and who would feed you and clothe you and provide all the necessary things to make a living?"

"Only a piece of land, that's all I ask, Hannah."

"Pa said to use my judgment. That's what his will said." She set her coffee cup down.

"Then, show me the will," he demanded, leaning forward.

"You should have asked yesterday when we were in town. There is a copy in the bank vault," Hannah answered him in a tone of voice that said she probably would have found a reason not to show it to him anyway, if he had asked.

"Tell me – why not, Hannah? Why not give me a piece of land?" John was holding his fork in his hand with the tinges straight up, as if he wanted to stab her.

"Because there is none left except this piece, what you see, what you have always seen. There is the cottage, if you want a place to call your own, you can live there, just as you did before."

"You can't call that living. You can't call that a future for a young family. You aren't even suggesting that I own it."

"No. You have no right to it, or anything." was her cold answer, and she turned away.

Rozella was shaking, leaving the room quietly, she went toward the stairs, but hesitated on the bottom step, not able to walk away from what she was hearing.

"No right?" John's voice was rising. She thought that he would break down and cry at any moment.

"I thought you didn't like the land. You were the city boy who couldn't wait to get away and take a white-collar job. You were Mama's little accountant who wouldn't get his hands dirty." She had a brutal smile on her face.

"People can change, Hannah. Look at my hands. They've earned a right to be called farmer's hands. They've earned a right to call a piece of this farm my own. Aren't there any laws against this?"

"No, John, there aren't any laws," she answered. "I have all the law I need to keep you from mismanaging anything."

"What right do you have to take everything? They were my parents, too."

"What right?" Hannah got up, and as she did Rozella moved further up the stairs. "What right?" Hannah repeated. "I earned every bit of this land. I bought it with my body and soul."

Rozella heard the last sentence clearly – *body and soul.* Hard work every day and giving up everything you loved, I guess that could be called soul; and, the work of the hands and body would be paying with your body.

Hannah moved into the dark hallway, and as she did so Rozella went the rest of the way up the stairs and into her bedroom. There were no voices following her, just the sound of Hannah's steps as she moved up the stairs on her way to bed.

Body and soul, Hannah repeated inside of her head. There is no way they could know, or even understand. If she told John, he wouldn't believe it. No matter how much he had hated their father, he wouldn't believe it. There was the old male legacy about women and sexuality.

Pa had returned to her room all those years, until he was at last too old to use his body the way he wanted it. Week after week, she had felt him crawl into her bed after her mother was asleep. She used to lie there, not able to sleep, anticipating that he would come. He didn't talk; he just used her and left her there feeling dirty and alone.

She had become the concubine you always read about, only in this area the concubine did not get the frills and money and attention you heard of in the Orient. You got nothing, except the privilege of not telling because no one would believe you if you did tell. Your father?

Hannah had earned this place. She had earned every acre and every blade of grass, down to every bit of dried up manure. John had not given his body, not even in the toil of planting the fields and harvesting, or cleaning the barns. He had just now begun to work on the place the

way a real man should. Since he had his own family, he had begun to
learn how to work. Until he had a wife and child, he had not made an
effort. He had dreamed his dream about his big city job, and left the
dirty work to her.

But, it wasn't the dirty work that made her feel dirty; it was Pa
and the visits that came after dark. The visits destroyed her memory of
ever being young and pretty. They destroyed her memory of painting
pictures, or reading books. There was no more poetry in her soul; there
was only hate and resentment. Especially of people like Rozella, who
were given the name of wife, the love of a child, and a man to call
husband.

People like Rozella stole their place by getting themselves pregnant.
If Hannah had become pregnant, what would have happened? She
could have created a monster of a child, deformed. Or would her
father even have allowed her to have a child? How would it have been
explained since he had sent away the hired hands that summer; who
could be blamed? He would have had to abort it using the tools they
used on animals, which conceived when not properly bred.

If she had born a child, she thought, she would have killed it
herself with her bare hands because it was born of him and the rutting,
which went on in the night. She remembered trying to keep the bed
springs silent so her mother wouldn't hear, praying to keep herself from
holding any of the sperm, washing herself nightly after Pa had left her
bed, crying into her pillow, and hating him every morning when she
saw him across the breakfast table. She remembered hating John and
his complacency. As though there was no reality other than a magazine
story, John lived as though dreams were real.

Hannah had forgotten what dreams were like. She only knew
nightmares. The pictures – the softness of the colors were colors she
created before she grew up. Growing up was the harshness of her father's
hands on her, the destruction of her love for the beautiful young man
who had promised to take her away. Nels hadn't come; he had left her
to Pa, who repeated and repeated to her what love was "all about."

The pictures she had painted were all a dream. She couldn't
remember how she even saw the flowers that she had created on the
paper with a wash of water and color. When she walked down the
pathway which led to the cottage that John and Rozella had shared,

when she carried Danny to them that day -- she could not see any beauty there that day. She wondered if there had ever been any beauty there, or if she had only dreamed of flowers in the woods. She couldn't remember what it was like. She couldn't remember the kisses of someone young and sweet.

And John thought he deserved any of this farm? He hadn't earned a thing. She had paid for it all, and she couldn't even tell John now she had paid for it. John had been lucky to have been born a male child. He had been left clean. She had been cursed, and she couldn't count all the nights she had wished that she had been born dead.

There had been no running from her life. She had been locked in, and that is the way she would keep John. He could earn every mouthful of food he was given. Rozella could learn to accept working for someone else. After all – what gave her the right to expect any privileges? Who was she? Rozella's education, normal school, didn't make her anything of higher class. She was just low class as far as Hannah was concerned. Hannah's mother – that was different. She had the class and the money; it was the rest of them, who turned the whole household into a disgraceful place. Pa, coming from the lowest of origins, had taught Hannah what breeding was. In his terms, breeding came from animals: From the highest to the lowest – animal level, un-caring, incestuous, and line-bred. Pa had forgotten that animals were bred for a reason, to create more animals, not to just rut around in male pleasure, if he ever had known it, that is. Pa married her mother for one thing only: money. That much Hannah had learned from him, how to get money, and how to keep money.

John had not learned that lesson. He might not ever learn that lesson, and Hannah did not intend to teach him. He had not earned the right the way she had.

CHAPTER THIRTY-ONE

John found no answer to his dilemma. Hannah held unto her rights, and threatened to back them up with legal documents. As far as Rozella could see, John had no way to battle her. If Hannah was offering to show him the will, then it must exist. Control was hers, no matter how John wished to change things. John's hope to stay on the land he grew up with was to yield to Hannah's will that he stay on as her servant as long as she lived.

Could she do this, Rozella asked herself? No matter what John told himself, the reality of what loomed ahead of him was to be confronted. Could Rozella stay on here, a victim of Hannah's will, and let her child become, in his turn, another victim? The answer to that question was a frightening one because when Rozella said no, she had no answer for herself as to how she would escape. Would there be no way out, except without John? And without John, how would it be possible?

John's determination had not changed by the morning, Rozella could see, and maybe it never would change. She was hoping that she could get to see Joan or Girard to talk about things, and to ask questions. Her immersion in the feud between the sister and brother, and her fear of her own developing needs kept her in a state of confusion, and she wanted someone to talk to who had experience she could draw upon.

Later in the week she was to have an opportunity, for the circle meeting came around and she made an excuse to call Joan to see if she could come with her to the meeting. Joan's involvement with her own projects had kept her away from meetings lately, but Rozella hoped that she could be persuaded, especially if she said that she needed her. It hurt a little to ask; she felt the pain of guilt as she asked Joan to try to come. "Please come, Joan," she said, "I need to see you. It's been too long since we have talked to each other."

Hearing her voice, Joan could feel the urgency of her request and listened to the plea, "Of course, you're right. It's been too long. I'll be there, no matter what. In fact, I'll come to pick you up to be sure that you get there. That way, we'll have some time to talk before the meeting on the way into town."

When Rozella climbed into Joan's truck, carrying Danny in one arm and his baby paraphernalia in the other arm, Joan said, "What's up, little one? You sounded like you needed a friend."

"Not much that's different. I just needed someone to talk to. Things keep going around and around in my head."

"What things, for instance?"

Rozella settled Danny down in the middle of the seat between them, propping up his diaper bag on top of him to hold him in place like a giant bolster, his eyes peering out from behind it. "I said not much is different, it just seems like I'm thinking more and more about the same things. Things haven't changed, but what I think about them has changed."

"I have no doubt about that. Girard and I have always wondered how long it would take before this would happen. Now, tell me about what's bothering you because something must be bothering you."

"You can tell me if what I think I'm seeing is true, or if I'm imagining it, that would help."

"Sure. Go ahead."

"Well, I keep thinking that John has changed since I first met him."

"In what way?" Joan shifted the truck once more.

"From what he wanted to be, or what he wanted to become, into what he wants now. It's changed."

"How?" Joan turned away from the wheel to look at her.

"He used to want to be a city person, and said he was only waiting until he could work at what he trained himself to do – accounting or clerical work. Now, he seems to be driven to want part of the farm to call his own."

"You mean the Queist farm, don't you?"

"Yes. He thinks that being a Queist, with a son, he ought to have at least a part of it deeded to him."

"That seems like a logical thing to want."

"It is. My only question is about the change. What he wants now seems to suggest that he has changed from what he was when we first met, I mean, he has changed in what he wants to do." Rozella checked on Danny to see that he wasn't slipping down.

"Okay. I agree. There would be no other reason for him to be interested, unless he would want the land only for what profit it could give, in order to return to the city with you and Danny."

"If there was a profit to give, it might make sense, but these days, there is no profit, so his need to own acreage and build his own house, tells me something else about what he wants."

"Again, I agree. What's wrong with this thinking? You seem to make good sense."

"I just wasn't sure of myself. For some reason, it never occurred to me that people could change so much. I thought John would always remain John, the way I first knew him. When I began to see this in him, then, I was afraid to look at myself. What if what I want has changed?"

"And, why shouldn't it change? If John could change, so could you. And, actually, Rozella, it's not unusual for people to change. Is this new to you?"

"It must be." Rozella was embarrassed by her ignorance, and blushed because she had not realized that she was ignorant before. She reached down to straighten out Danny's bag.

"Don't feel bad. Lots of people go through their whole lives not realizing that they have changed. When you try to live by the same rules you set for yourself at the beginning of adulthood, and you have changed somewhere along the line, you're in for deep trouble."

"I can see that now." Rozella looked at her.

"Or worse, Rose, some people don't change at all their whole life long. Can you imagine having the same outlook as you had at age sixteen until you were ninety?"

Rozella smiled. "Yes, that would be out of place. Especially when you tried to do sixteen year old things."

"Exactly," Joan replied. "It can't work. Change is inevitable. Avoiding it is what becomes difficult. Hiding it from yourself is even more difficult because you have to work very hard at hiding things from yourself."

"You sound like a philosopher, but then, you always did. That's something else about you that I've always loved. Girard..." and she caught herself beginning to share what she and Girard had said they both loved about Joan.

"Yes?" Joan asked her to continue with that one word.

It was even more difficult now, as Rozella remembered just where and when she had that conversation about Joan with Girard. "Girard and I agreed that we both liked the same things about you, that you are a very special person."

"You know – I know. I'm glad that you like me. In fact, I'm glad that you both love me. The feeling is mutual." Joan answered.

"I wish I could be like you." Rozella looked out the window in order to avoid her eyes.

"No. You don't. You would find it's more difficult than it appears to be. I only make it seem easy. It's not." Joan looked serious as she offered that about herself.

Rozella reached out to touch her on the shoulder.

"Yeh, we needed to talk. We've been apart too long, and too much has happened to both of us," Joan continued. " Maybe we should 'ash can' this woman party and just spend some time together. If we go – we won't have any time to talk except on the way to and from."

"Where would we go; what would we do?" Rozella asked, surprised by the idea.

"What would be easier – to my house, of course? Girard is at work and won't be home until late. Danny will be comfortable there, probably more comfortable than he would be at the meeting with all their young nursemaids. He won't enjoy teen-age girls until much later in his life."

"Well, sure. I didn't think about it at all when I called you. I only thought about the meeting, and how long it's been since we had a chance to talk to each other. We haven't seen anything much of you and Girard on the weekends either."

"I know. This idea just came to me, too, at the moment, but it seems like a good one."

"Then, let's do it," Rozella agreed.

Joan pulled down the road, which turned into their farm and slowed to a stop in front of the kitchen door. It did seem like a relief to Rozella. The group of woman was interesting, and often the only social life to be had, but this was a retreat, a quiet place, which held pleasant memories of happy times together. They got out of the truck, taking Danny and all of his belongings with them. The kitchen was still warm from the morning fire, and Joan added some fuel to the glowing embers in the wood stove to make the stove heat up.

"The breakfast coffee is still warm, believe it or not," she said, pulling the pot over the stove to the part, which was heating up. "By the time we get settled and comfortable, it will be time for lunch. Is there anything you need for Danny?"

"No. He's fine. I'll just take off these outside clothes, and spread out his blanket on the floor in the living room. There's a rug and he won't be so cold on the floor in there."

"Let me start a fire in the heater in there, too. It will be warmer for him, and we'll enjoy it too. We can sit in there where the soft chairs are and visit, and he can play until he gets tired."

"It's a nice room. I'd like that," Rozella answered.

Joan dug around in the firebox beside the heater, taking out some old newspapers, crumpling them up, and putting a few pieces of kindling on top of them. As soon as the fire started, she added some larger pieces, and then some coal. The chill was leaving the house. The kitchen had been still warm from the morning fires, but the living room hadn't been heated since the evening before. Now, it was responding to the fire in the heater.

"We can have our coffee in there," Joan called out from the kitchen, "That way we can watch Danny and relax."

"Sounds good." Rozella brought out some toys for Danny and sat down on the couch to watch him.

In a few minutes, Joan returned with two cups of coffee and found a chair to slouch down into. Handing a cup to Rozella, she rubbed her forehead, saying "Now, where were we...?"

"I'm not sure," Rozella wasn't any help.

"Oh, yes, you were saying that John had changed, and that you just now realized it. And, I was saying that change was inevitable. That sounds very general in scope." She laughed at herself for saying it.

"Yes, that's right. I just now understood, or thought that I understood that John had changed. It was such a surprise, that I needed someone to talk to about it. I'm not sure that John would realize how he has changed."

"Did you talk to him about it?"

"Yes, but it didn't seem important to him. What he wants right now is important to him, but the idea that he has changed doesn't appear to matter."

"Why does it matter to you, do you think?"

"Because...because it brings up a lot of questions. If he isn't the same person that I thought he was, then do I still want the same things he wants? In fact, if he has changed, maybe I have changed. And, what does that mean? That's whole lot in one mouthful, I know." She shook her head in confusion.

Joan took a sip of coffee from her cup, and looked up at her slowly. Her eyes were soft and warm, but slightly tearful. "You are still like a little girl, Rose. There's that naive quality in you that makes life a constant discovery for you."

"I remember that you and Girard told me that before. Is that still true of me? What does that mean to you? That word?"

"It means that you are innocent, and it's as if you always will be innocent. Maybe because you have no bad intentions, no matter what you do. As long as you stay that way, you will be naive. Innocence... that's what you have. A native innocence."

"Is that bad, or good?" she asked.

"I think it's good, but it will keep you unaware of many things. Sometimes it will restrict your learning and slow you down. At times you won't notice certain things because of this innocence."

"You mean that I'm missing something at home, about John, or Hannah?"

"Maybe. But, you are sure missing something here, and only because you are not able to see it, or understand it, and that may be because of a sort of blindness called naiveté."

"I don't understand..."

" I know you don't," Joan answered her, "and I shouldn't play around with words. Rozella...don't you know that I know about you and Girard? He did tell you. I know him. He doesn't lie to me."

"I...I..." Rozella gasped.

"You heard him, but didn't want to hear him. Yes? He told you it was okay. You had my blessing. I didn't know that you would learn to love him, and I should have guessed that. After all, I love him – why not you? It was a mistake for us, Girard and me, I mean, to think that we could be so frivolous with our marriage."

Rozella was horrified, and her face was pained as tears started to run down her cheeks. "I didn't mean...I didn't want to hurt you."

"I know. I really know that. It's true for both of you. You haven't really hurt me. I think the only pain I have is one you are too confused to acknowledge yet, the same pain you struggled with today in asking questions of the universe: people change. Even Girard and I have changed, and you – Rozella, have changed the most of all."

"I'm so ashamed."

"You don't need to be ashamed. There are many things you don't know. There are many changes we can go through. When we are most sure of ourselves, and think we know exactly who we are, we are most likely in for our biggest surprise."

"How is that?" Rozella asked.

"The worst part of dealing with such changes is finding out what they are; once you know what the changes are, it's easier to do something about them. Sometimes you don't need to do anything at all. Life is strange. For instance, the one thing I never expected to discover about myself, and the last thing that Girard ever expected would happen to me has happened while you and Girard were falling in love with each other."

"What is that?

"If I didn't know better, I'd think you were being sarcastic. But, I know you – you wouldn't know how to think that way."

"What are you trying to say?" Rozella was twisting her handkerchief in her hands.

"I might have known I'd have to spell it out:" Joan sighed. "Women who love women.""

"Does that mean you don't love Girard anymore?" Rozella asked.

"No, Rozella, and that is some more of your innocence. I still love Girard; I always have; I always will. But, the change in my life is that I now know what kind of love it is. I also know why my crazy idea of letting him go to you to teach you how to love had some basis, unknown to even me, in my own need."

"How can that be?"

"Because I found this out about myself, I no longer can live in such a small community. I have been busy working with other women, trying to work out groups that share understanding of some of the problems, but I know that I must move on. Go back to the larger cities where my ideas and life style can exist. Possibly back to Europe."

"Does that mean leaving Girard?"

"A natural thing for you to ask," Joan went on. "Sorry, Rose. That **was** sarcastic. I didn't mean to be that way. No, I don't know. People like Girard and me have lived together for whole lifetimes knowing what you and I know now. In some societies it doesn't matter. Loving each other holds people together, no matter what."

"Now, I'm really confused. You said that John has changed, you have changed, and Girard has changed, but I have changed the most. In what way have I changed?" she asked Joan.

"You're the person who should know best of all." Joan just shook her head. "If I told you, I could be wrong. That's not good, you know, Rose, to let other people decide for you. The decisions about your life should be yours alone." Joan got up to tend the fire in the heater.

Danny crawled around on his blanket. The heater was getting warmer as the fire grew, and it felt cozy and warm close to the big black heater. Rozella looked around the room as if she were seeing it for the first time. She felt as if someone had hit her hard in the stomach. Looking out the window at the snow covered countryside, seeing the outer buildings of a scene that was familiar to her; she caught her breath, and wondered silently what changes had come to her.

"It's okay," Joan whispered, "It's really fine. We all still love each other. We're just defining it in a different way. If you are trying to discover just how you have changed you just began by making a list of things that are different about you. Go ahead. We've got all day."

"I don't want to stay here, on the Queist farm, that is."

"You just now discovered that?" Joan asked.

"Yes. I hate living there. It isn't the house. It isn't even the farm, or the work on a farm."

"I know. It's Hannah, and what it does to John. Right?"

"I think so. I said that John has changed, but when I look at myself and say that I can't stand how he has changed, that means that I have changed because I can't stand it anymore, but that sounds insane."

"Ah-ha, that's where you are wrong. That's the sanest thing possible. Not a thing wrong with what you just said. The truth is – you never could stand it, but you are just now allowing yourself to react to it."

"Maybe. I didn't know..." Rozella looked away, hesitantly.

"Let's go back and look at what you just today said to me: John has changed, and he wants to stay on the farm. You have changed and you can't stand it there anymore. What does that pose for you?"

"Two people going in two different directions. How is that possible?"

"It isn't," Joan offered, "and I don't say that to hurt you or try to make you change your mind about anything. What I am, and what I must do with my life has nothing to do with your life, no matter how much your guilt about Girard makes you think that we are answerable to each other."

"I hadn't thought about that," Rozella stammered.

"I know you hadn't. That's why I love you still. Your innocence. You never have thought about anything like taking him away for yourself, any more than he has thought about leaving me to make a home for you...and God knows, the two of you would be happier together than you and John will every be."

"No, I love him, and..."

"And you never had such good sex," Joan finished. "I know about that, too. I can say that because I'm not jealous. Isn't that interesting?"

"Interesting? If I didn't know you, I'd say that was impossible, or that I didn't believe you."

"The question you have to resolve, Rose, is not what Girard and I will do about our life together, but what will you and John do with yours?"

"John doesn't have any idea of what I'm thinking about and trying to reason my way through."

"Good. Then, you have plenty of time to think things through. What do you want to do about your life: The question is -- what do you want, Rose? And don't say: Girard, because you can't have him. What do you want for yourself?"

"I want...a place to call my own. A home for Danny and me. Work that I get paid for. I want to get away from here...oh God, I didn't know that. It just came out."

"What just comes out like that is usually very true. Well done. Now that you've surprised yourself, go over it again and see what you can do about those things. What can you do to make them come true?"

"What can I do? I can ask John to leave the farm, to take Danny and me away."

"Yes?"

"And he'll say he can't. He has no money, and even the truck belongs to Hannah."

"Then, what will you say?"

"I could say – ask Hannah for money, but he would say –she will refuse."

"All that means is: if John cannot think of a way out and gives in, what then? It would be up to you to do something. What would you do? Mind you, we're only talking now; you're safe to work your way through. We're only using words."

"To leave I must have money, too. To get money I must borrow from my sisters, or try to get a job in Crenshaw."

"Which will it be? And why?" Joan put her hands under her chin, propping her head upon her knees.

"Which would I do? Do I have to know?" Rozella asked.

"Be brave. This is like a game. You don't have to do it. Pretend."

"I'd choose to try to get a job." Rozella was surprised by her own words.

"Why?"

"I think...I think because I'd have more time to see how things would work out."

"Time for John to change his mind? Time for Hannah to change her mind, or time to find out more about you and Girard?"

Rozella was crying now and couldn't talk.

"I didn't mean to make you cry. I'm so sorry," Joan went on, "Those were very real things, but it was too much, too fast."

"What if I try one way, wait to see how it works, then try another way if it doesn't work?" she asked Joan through her tears.

"That's sensible really, and most often that's what people end up doing; they just don't plan it out ahead of time."

"What will you do, Joan?" Rozella asked, after wiping her nose. "You said you would have to leave here."

Girard and I have talked, so it's no secret to him, Rozella. He hasn't told you either because he hasn't seen you, or because he felt it was our worry alone. We'll take things one thing at a time, as you would choose to do. You can't just leave a job; jobs are hard to get. You can't just leave a farm, unless you want to give up your equity."

"What will you do first?"

"I have letters out, resumes for jobs in New York City, so does Girard."

"Does that mean you'll stay married?" Rozella asked in a half-cry.

"We couldn't think of why not – for now. You and John are married." She looked up at her. "I have no commitment to anyone other than Girard. I – I did fall in love with a young person. A woman, but she was far too young. In a way, it was a blessing; it made it senseless to do anything about it. It was easier to confront it, myself, that is, then – let it go."

"You mean you made love?" Rozella stammered.

"Yes," Joan whispered, "the way you and Girard made love. It was then that I knew about myself."

"How could you?"

"You mean how is it physically possible? If you think about it, Rose, think about the way you and Girard made love, and what happened. Then, you'll understand the physical part of it."

"It's hard for me to understand."

"I know, honey. I know. God love you; you may never understand."

"How can you say you love Girard and still love another person – a woman?"

"Loving him has nothing to do with sex anymore; it has to do with respect and concern." Joan got up and went into the kitchen, "How about some lunch. Maybe that will give us a better perspective."

"I hope so. And of course, Danny won't mind, if the food suits him." Rozella followed her into the kitchen to try to help with lunch. Danny was a shadow behind her, moving between pieces of furniture, and making small sounds mimicking words. "The impossible dream," Rozella added, "I've asked the impossible—to find a job. And if I do, who will take care of Danny?"

"Take one thing at a time, Rose," Joan answered her. "Just one thing at a time. That's what I keep telling myself."

CHAPTER THIRTY-TWO

The idea of taking one thing at a time included finding out how to get to town, Rozella realized. There was no simple way. Knowing this and finding a way could not stop her, if she planned to change things at all. She would have to get to town in order to apply for a job, or to interview; and after that, she would have to get into town each day in order to work.

Before she could confront the problem of transportation, she would have to say something to Hannah and John. She would have to go to town with John, or with Joan, or Girard. She would have to arrange to leave Danny with someone, as she could hardly find a job with him under her arm.

She didn't feel happy with what she and Joan had discussed. It was more than the difficulty of facing Joan's knowledge of her relationship with her husband. It was seeing no way out except the hard way, no way out unless she was to do it alone.

Taking all of the responsibility for both she and Danny was frightening. Rozella could understand why most women stayed in their places. They kept their own counsel and didn't complain. There was a reason for the ultimatum: *until death do you part*. You had no choices offered, no alternatives to fulfilling that promise, even though you may have made the promise not knowing what difficulties it would create in the future.

Rozella and Ola were tagging along with Maggie that early summer afternoon when Maggie and her friend Elvira went to town shopping. They were in Maggie's care as they always were when school was out. Elvira looked back at the two of them with distaste. When they were along, she always had to be careful of what she said. Confidences were difficult.

...divorced? Rozella heard her say to Maggie. She didn't know what the word meant, or what had gone before it. Then, she heard Elvira repeat the question —"Are your parents divorced? Your father is never here."

"No," Maggie had answered. "They aren't. My father has to work up north because of his asthma."

Hearing that, Rozella could relax. It was a part of the story she had always heard, but that evening long after they had returned from shopping, she heard the word again.

This time it came from Maggie, and Maggie was confronting Mama. "Why do you stay married? You don't get any support. You don't get any help. You do it all yourself, using all of us to help. How long will this go on—for all of our lives? Will we always be helping you to earn a living?"

"Now, Maggie, that's not fair," Mama tried to interject. "Your father will be home. He'll send money when he can. He must make more money in order to have some left to send to us."

"That's what you've said for years, now. What kind of a foolish thing is this? What is marriage all about? Does it give all the privileges to the man?"

"We marry for better or worse, until death do us part," Mama answered slowly, enunciating every word with care. "Nobody knows what that will be."

"Why not?" Maggie shouted. "Why don't you know what it will be like before you marry? Why can't you change your mind if it doesn't work out?"

"You just don't, not Christian people," Mama answered, big-eyed with a painful look. "And, Maggie — what would it change? I'd still have all of you children to care for, and myself." Rozella as small as she was could see that Mama was about to cry.

"You wouldn't have all of us if you had divorced him years ago. You had plenty of reasons: drunkenness, non-support, irresponsibility..." These were words that made no sense to Rozella as she listened. Mama's answers were simple; those were clear to her as she listened.

"You would want to be an only child, Maggie?" her mother had asked.

"Why not? It would be easier on both of us. You could have stopped it long ago. You could, you know. Now, it's too late to stop the children from being born into this hopeless place, and you could get some money for us to live on, if you tried. What are you afraid of?" Maggie demanded.

It was silent for several seconds, and then Mama said, "People treat divorced women like harlots. Maybe because most of them act that way, Maggie. Married, I still have some pride, and people still accept me. Without marriage, I'd be all alone. No friends, and no church."

"No church?"

"Yes, even that. So, tell me, daughter, what would I gain?"

"Nothing, I guess, Mama. From nothing to nothing. I'm sorry, Mama," Maggie answered, and Rozella could hear Maggie crying.

Just looking for a job was not the same as getting a divorce, Rozella consoled herself, but the thought of asking about being allowed to go into town, and the thought of leaving Danny with someone else, was frightening. Rozella just knew it would be a shock for both Hannah and John. Beginning that conversation that evening was the hardest thing she had ever done.

She decided there was no place to begin other than at the supper table even if Danny was there. With both of them there, she may as well open up the subject. "John...and Hannah...I would like to go into town with John this week, please."

John was the first to look up from his plate. "Why?" was his question. So far, Hannah was not listening, as if it was of so little importance that she couldn't be bothered.

"Because I want to try to find a job."

"A job?" John asked. And this time, she had Hannah's attention. "Doing what?" he continued.

"Doing any kind of work I can get. I can't teach, but I must be able to get something else. I'm willing to do anything that needs doing, no matter what."

"What for?" Hannah joined in. "You have everything you need, and you can stay home with Danny. Who would take care of him if you went to work?"

"And what do you hope to gain by this, even if you do get a job?" John added before she could answer.

"I hope to get enough money so you and I can get a place of our own. If nothing else, it would get enough money together so we could move to the city, if you still want to do that."

"I don't want to. I told you that," he said, looking at Hannah to see what she was thinking. "I want to stay on the farm. My interests are here. It may take a long time to get anything to pay much, but time will bring it together."

Hannah looked up from her plate. "I agree, and he is needed here. How could I take care of this without him?"

"Exactly." Rozella answered her directly. "He is needed, but a man needs a place to call his own, and this one will never be his." That was a direct assault upon everything that Hannah didn't want to talk about, but she braved making it just the same.

"It will be, someday." was Hannah's answer.

"You can't leave Danny," John insisted. "If you did find a job, you'd have to pay someone to take care of Danny, and that will take all of your earnings. Where do you get such wild ideas, anyway?"

"Probably from Joan," Hannah suggested, "I saw her come here to pick them up yesterday. Apparently, it doesn't take much to get Rozella to listen to her way of thinking. Don't you have any influence, John?" she said, as if Rozella was not there at all.

"I don't know yet who will take care of Danny. I don't know even if I stand a chance of getting any king of work, but I do know that I have to try. The problem of Danny's care can be solved when and if I actually get a job."

"If you do," and now Hannah was speaking directly to her, "it won't be the same as your teaching job. You won't make as much money... and you might have to get your hands dirty doing things that you don't like to do."

"Hannah, what makes you think that I don't do things I don't like to do now?" Rozella looked at her hands, and remembered washing out the pots that were shoved under the beds at night. "What makes you think that I don't get my hands dirty?"

"Go ahead, John." Hannah addressed him, "Take her to town. She'll find out that she can't find a job. Let her worry about who is going to take care of Danny. If you don't take care of him, and I don't take care of him – who can she turn to?"

"Fair enough. Rozella, go ahead and try. I'm not convinced that you can work this out at all. And beyond that, I don't see that anything you do will change things for us. You are needed here more than anywhere else."

"Yes. I'm needed here, but I don't get paid here. In fact, neither of us gets paid." She looked at Hannah directly. "If we did, maybe this wouldn't be necessary, but someone has to take a step forward toward the future, or there won't be any future for us. It can't happen unless we try to make it happen, John. Can't you see? Nobody can live on dreams alone."

She left them there, looking at each other across the kitchen table. It wasn't until long after she went upstairs to the bedroom, and she had put Danny to bed for the night, that she remembered that she had not done the dishes. She had left them behind for someone else to do.

Later in the week, when John began to get ready to go into town, she was ready. She wouldn't let the opportunity pass, for if she did, they would both ignore what had been said and pretend that if they ignored it, it would go away. She had suffered from a whim and it would pass. John looked at her, as she put her coat on and dressed Danny for the trip to town. "What do you plan to do with him?" he asked, as if posing this challenge would make her reconsider.

"Take him with me," she looked at him, realizing that at the moment she hated him. So this was to be their approach. If they would refuse to give her any support, or help, at all, they could make her change her mind.

John had not spoken to her about her plans since the evening of her request. He had dug down into his pillow every night, avoiding any kind of conversation. So, now she found herself playing her part in this game that had been created. They had not answered her request to go to town, and she had responded by not taking no for an answer. She would go with him; and, she knew that she would be lucky if he didn't go off and leave her stranded in town with Danny and no money, or any way to get home.

That wasn't going to stop her. She had packed as much food as possible for the two of them into her purse and into Danny's diaper bag. And, she had called Joan in the afternoon the day before telling her what she expected might happen. Joan had provided an address where there was a children's daycare center, and promised she would check on Rozella and Danny. She had told Rozella there was an employment office in the courthouse, and it would be convenient to start her search right there.

She wasn't so afraid as they expected she would be. Hannah and John thought, she assumed, that she would back off and not go, or that she had forgotten the whole idea. It would be so much easier for her to go backward, and accept their way of doing things. *Their way* — yes, she was noticing; things were becoming apparent.

John had moved a long way in his thinking; his acceptance of the barriers Hannah had put up for him had changed his approach; in fact, it had even changed what he wanted. But, he didn't even realize what was happening to him.

"Why are you so dressed up?" he asked, as if he didn't know.

"Staying so skinny makes it possible for me to still wear my teaching clothes, and I told you... I wanted to try to find work. The only way I can make applications is to start in town."

"You may have to stay all day. What will you do with Danny?" he asked, looking at Danny and noticing, but not admitting, that Danny, too, was dressed up for the trip.

"There is a child care center, Joan says. She gave me the address. I can leave him there as long as I like, just as long as I pick him up by 6 PM."

"Don't they charge for that?" John asked, as Hannah looked on smugly.

"Yes, they do, but there is a federally funded program that allows you to fill out a form stating that you are seeking work. They don't collect until you get a job and get paid," she answered them both, the silent one and the one who had to do the vocalizing, John.

"How is this possible?" Hannah asked, "I've never heard of such a thing. She was so surprised, that she hadn't been able to keep out of the conversation.

"I've never heard of it," John added, "and how do you know it's a safe place for Danny? Do you know who runs it?"

"Joan works with the ladies who run it. She knows them well. And, it is a very new program, so not many people have even heard of it. The people who run it – they are local women, just like me. Some of them donate their time in order to help others get started working. Women like me. Perhaps I will donate my time after I get some applications put in, if I have to wait for work, that is."

"That's crazy. If there aren't any jobs, what's all this for? It's a great waste of money," John objected.

"There isn't any money involved. Everything is donated, including the time; the women who run it collect toys, materials, even food and diapers in order to make this work," Rose answered. "I just hadn't talked to Joan about what she was working on, so I didn't know about it before. It is one of many projects for women that Joan works on."

"Putting a bunch of kids together in one big room where they get little care, catch each other's germs, and give the mothers too much time to stay away from home is not my idea of a good thing. It's not good for the children. It can't be," Hannah entered her objection, as she put on her working boots.

"It's not really any different than the church school nursery centers that they organize for church meeting, ladies' aid meetings, and everything else. Basically, it's the same women. Think about it, now, it has to be. This is a small community. Those women who give time for church childcare are the same women who make time to help with this."

"What will happen here...?" Hannah began to ask, and then stopped in mid-sentence. She realized no one would be at home to help with housework. She could see that she would have to make her own dinner, or warm up a few leftovers when she came in from the barn.

Rozella was in the truck before John got it loaded for town. Danny squirmed restlessly as he waited. Rozella felt exhausted from all the preparation and didn't dare allow herself to think about how this would be every day of the week – if she was lucky enough to get any work.

John slammed and banged the milk cans around in the truck bed, banged the door after he got into the truck. She felt sad since she had never seen him act like this before. He had left her alone so much, spending most of this time with Hannah and his father, he had turned aside at night when she needed his closeness, but he had never shown anger this way. Perhaps, he had never shown it because he had never before had reason. Yes, she had never crossed him before. This was open defiance of the right of the husband's control. But who controlled the husband? she asked herself, because it made her feel so depressed. Was this going to be worth it? She wasn't even sure of how she had put herself in this position. It would have been so much easier to let things go on just the way they were.

In town, he begrudgingly asked her where she would like to be dropped off. "At the Lutheran church, Norwegian Lutheran, that is." she answered, looking at him to see if the use of a church for a working women's child care center would surprise him. He and Hannah had acted like this women's center was some sort of criminal activity.

"For job applications?" he asked sarcastically.

"No. It's where the day care center is. I'll walk from there to the courthouse, or any other place I need to go. You won't be bothered after dropping me off, because Joan said she would come and get me later, and take me home t his afternoon when she is off work."

"Okay," he said, as if speaking to a disobedient child. "If you must try this, Rozella, then you'll find out for yourself – that there are no jobs. When you do, don't expect me to pay for the child care that you don't have the money to pay for."

"I understand," she answered, thinking to herself, *Yes, I understand much more than I used to understand.*

He dropped her off at the Lutheran church, fidgeting while she gathered up Danny's things, and Danny. He drummed on the steering wheel as if his business was so urgent that he couldn't wait for anything. John was trying to making a point that his business was so much more important that he couldn't take time to help her get from the truck into the Sunday school rooms.

She had a sick feeling as she went toward the doorway. Along with the sick feeling was the knowledge that she had never asked John for anything before, and this experience was showing her the response she would get. She felt very alone, and very unmarried, but as she entered she saw other women who came in who also looked alone. Maybe they weren't married, she told herself, but she knew better.

She had to admit they were all in like circumstances, when she saw women she knew, coming in alone, as she did. She could see now, that their husbands reacted like John, resentful of the women leaving the homes to try to find work. Why? A sense of pride in providing had been violated. The public could now see their weaknesses. Just the fact of the presence of the women in the working force, embarrassed the men. In their embarrassment, they acted hatefully and cruelly. So she assumed, because that seemed to be John's attitude. She would ask Joan later on if what she was thinking was true. It had come as a shock to her.

A pleasant young woman greeted her, asking her name. "Oh, yes," she said when Rozella responded. "Joan said you would be here today. And this is Danny. We're happy to have him. We hear good things about him."

"He's never been left anywhere except with the sitters at the church meetings." Rozella made excuses for his behavior because she was so full of fear that he would be afraid to be left here.

"He's a good humored child, we hear, and they have no problems with adjusting to different surroundings. Besides, there will probably be women here during the day who recognize him."

"Here are his things," Rozella handed her his bag, " and I put some snack foods in there, in case you didn't have anything like that."

"That is the one thing the government does provide, excess food. We get the throw aways, and there is usually someone in the kitchen who can think of something creative to make with them. But, your own things will help until he gets adjusted to us," the woman answered her.

Rozella hesitated, not knowing quite what to do. She needed to leave, but didn't want to leave. Danny was put down on the floor with a couple of other youngsters who were surrounded by some wooden blocks. A pregnant woman was sitting on the floor beside them, helping them build houses, and pile up blocks one on top of the other. She was involved with the children and paid no attention to Rozella, just looking up as Danny joined their play circle. "Go on, now, the first woman advised Rozella "It's sometimes best to just leave without a word and let us explain if he asks questions. Especially if you have talked to him about this trip, and you probably have, because he is so calm. You can pick him up anytime before 6PM. After that – well, we just raffle off the leftovers!" she laughed at Rozella's dismay. "Kidding, of course. You won't forget to pick him up, I know."

Going out in the street alone, Rozella felt almost as bad as she had when she had confronted Hannah and John about going into town to look for work. Just talking about something was different than doing it. Her heart was divided against itself. She wanted to get a job, and didn't want to get a job. She would enjoy working with the babies, and older children, like the women in the childcare center, but she had to have some money. She would rather be at home with Danny, yet couldn't stay there if she ever wanted to have a home of her own, where she could make decisions which were not dictated by Hannah, and now, she could add – John. She hadn't known him to be dictatorial before, but now he had become quite different in his attitude toward her. What would this mean to their future?

The streets were still quiet. A few cars stirred, the bread trucks, and delivery wagons, mostly milk trucks this early. People were walking to work. Many of them lived close to the center of town and could easily walk to their jobs. A couple of coffee shops and restaurants were open, and people inside were drinking their morning coffee and reading the newspaper, some with cigarette smoke making its cloud above their heads. The smell of bacon and sausage being fried on the commercial grills made her hungry, but she hurried on past the inviting doors toward the county court house, telling herself that she would wait for lunch. She had a peanut butter sandwich stuffed into her purse, because there was no money to be had at home, and John had not offered to give her any. Actually, she excused him; he most likely didn't have any to give. That was why she was here. Living in the world without money was a difficult thing.

The old red brick courthouse was blackened with the charcoal smoke from years of winter furnace smoke. Inside, the floors smelled of oil polish on the hardwood floors; and, tobacco spittle was left in the brass spittoons along side each stairwell. The stairs were worn from so many years of footsteps, that they had softened curves in front of each step. You could see where the traffic had stepped each day. The perimeter of each step was unworn, still varnished, and level.

She climbed the stairs to the second floor, and wandered down the hallway looking for the room where she could make an application for employment. The Department of Employment, County of Beltranson, appeared on a frosted glass door. Room 220. She and John had been in this building when they were married, but it had been in the basement, she remembered. That seemed like a long time ago.

A bald-headed man with a white starched shirt, and rubber bands holding up his sleeves asked her if he could help her when she entered the room. "Applications?" She asked him, wanting to know where they were. She could see there were slanted green-topped tables like the kind in the post office. These must be to write on when standing up; there were pens and inkwells at the top of each.

"Right here," he said handing her one. "We don't leave them out, because it wastes too many. People scribble all over them, make mistakes, and throw them away. If they don't think they can get more than one, they tend to be more careful filling them out."

"Oh?" she said, taking the offered form.

"Are you on any kind of government aid plan?" he asked her.

"No. I'm just trying to get some kind of work."

"Well, there may not be anything, but federal work, you know. WPA programs, and so on," he said, as if she knew all about everything.

"Sure," she voiced a simple reply, not wanting to let him know that she didn't know anything at all about t his sort of thing. She had not planned on working. It was something that didn't occur to a woman with a child, and usually it didn't occur to a woman who was married. You thought that your husband...but her father had been different, and her mother, too, had lived differently. It was for that reason she and the sisters had tried to create different sorts of dreams for themselves. They had told themselves that they would not live like Mama had lived...

Other people had fathers. When there was a school play, when there was a church supper, when houses needed painting, when the toilets needed fixing, they had a father to be there, or to repair things around the house. Not them. Mostly things were left without repair. The house needed paint so bad that you couldn't tell what color it had been. It was peeled down to the gray of weathered wood. When you asked, Mama would say -- when Papa gets home. But, Papa never came home.

Rozella told herself marriage should never be like this, she and her sisters talked about how it would be when they got married. Mostly they never said, we won't have a husband who is gone all the time, we won't do everything ourselves, or leave it undone, but they did paint their verbal dreams with the things they would dream of having a husband and father do. Things were always painted in their dreams. Fathers were always there to pick up fallen children when they ran and fell and bumped their knees. Fathers would never, never take a drink and mothers would never holler at them. Even in their play times, when they made pretend families with their dolls, their little voices were never raised to the fictional fathers of dolls. The fathers in their worlds were revered, but so was their behavior, as the fathers asked what their adored wives would like them to get for them, or do for them. They were children dreaming of how they would like things to be.

Mothers never went to work in other households, scrubbing floors, washing clothes. They waited at home with the doll babies, in their proper "homes" all dressed in fine silks and setting the endless fancy dinners that they made believe by putting a dishtowel across an apple box, arranging the doll babies around the box.

They had believed their own dreams...that had been their mistake. They had blamed Mama, as if her choice to have them had some how been a mistake, or as if it was her fault she had not chosen a better father, one who would behave as they perceived other fathers behaved...

Name, the form said. Sex. Married. Address. Telephone number. Children, it asked. Education. Where have you worked? She filled it out carefully, remembering that you weren't supposed to ask for another form. Two men came in and the bald little man handed them each a form. They took places at the next "desk." She looked up, feeling strange to be the only woman in the room. There were three women in the room behind the counter, doing clerical work, but the man seemed to dominate the office. She tried not to look at the women, in fear that they would notice her.

When it was completed, she returned it to the man at the counter. He scanned it, and looking up at her said, "Former teacher? There isn't anything in teaching this time of year. And usually we never hear of the openings. They are filled by the school board chairman and his committees."

"I wasn't expecting to get anything teaching. We aren't allowed to teach when we are married, and have children."

"Oh, yes. That's true. At least, I've heard it's true. What did you think you could do?" He looked down over the form, as if checking to see anything of interest, any reason to lay claim to a right to have a job.

"I could do a lot of things. Like clerical work isn't too different from keeping school records and giving grades."

"You weren't trained to do bookkeeping when you went to normal school. That's quite a different thing. I don't think you could get that kind of a job."

"Wouldn't someone try? Wouldn't someone take me on and teach me?" Even when she said it, she knew it wasn't true.

"They don't have to do that," he shuffled the papers. "There are plenty of trained bookkeepers without jobs, all waiting for work."

"That's true," she said, remembering that she had married one. She had forgotten for a minute, just because John had become so immersed in farming.

"I could do most anything, like cooking, washing dishes in a restaurant, sewing...I could do sewing..."

"Do you know how to operate a sewing machine?" he asked.

"Yes." She was getting excited about that possibility.

"Put it down on the paper then. That's the only way people can know that you can sew," he pointed to a place on the second sheet of the application. She hastily added that information and handed the paper back to him.

"But, there isn't anything listed right now," he repeated.

Her hopes had gone up over his interest in her ability to operate a sewing machine. Now, they fell as fast as they had risen.

"We call you if anything comes up. And – you have to check in with us every week, or we take your name off the list. We don't like to have people on the availability list who don't want to work. Usually women change their minds." His mouth drooped in a crooked fashion.

"Oh, I'll come back. Does it have to be on Tuesday?" she asked.

"Yes, on or before, or your name gets scratched, and we throw your application away."

"That's not so easy. I live in the country, about five miles out."

"That's your problem, isn't it? You would have to get to work every day. If you can't get to the employment office, how could you get to work?" He frowned.

"True," she answered, subdued. "Thank you." At the last minute she remembered her manners. The man hadn't made her feel like remembering them.

When she left the two men were still filling out their forms, and three women had come in and were lined up to get a form from the cranky little man. She closed the heavy oak door and walked back down the oiled wooden corridor, wishing she hadn't come. It was easier not to know. As she had remembered her childhood when she and her sisters had pretended that they had their own homes and husbands and marriages, it was easier not to know what reality would be like for them. They had been able to fashion their own dreams, to make up make believe lives You could always make up jobs and money, until you faced the fact that you couldn't get any.

That was what had happened to John. He couldn't stand to face the negative reality, so he wouldn't try any more. It had become his escape, this avoidance.

When she left the building, she noticed that the clock in the main hallway showed it was only ten o'clock. She had two more hours before she would meet Joan for lunch, and she could feel the peanut butter sandwich in her handbag. She opened the bag, and she could smell it. The smell made her hungry, and she stopped on the step outside, taking out half of the sandwich to eat it. Half now, half later, she told herself. Her stomach was growling with hunger, and she worried about Danny. What if he was crying? What if he was scared?

Eating the sandwich made her feel better, and she turned toward the business section of town, walking down the street, telling herself that she could walk up one side and down the other, just to see if anyone had a sign out for help wanted.

CHAPTER THIRTY-THREE

There were ghosts here that she had never met before. Walking down the main street, she passed the mortgage company where Girard worked. Her heart gave a jump and her pulse soared when she saw his truck parked in back of the office. She wanted to see him, yet couldn't bring herself to enter into the place where he worked. It would embarrass him, she thought. She kept walking without slowing down, and then crossed the street to the Woolworth store where a girl stood in the display windows washing the glass and dusting the window contents.

The theater had a sign up for help wanted, but it was for night work and that would be impossible for her. The childcare center was only open until 6 PM in the afternoon. She would have no place to leave Danny, and there was no way she could leave him with Hannah or John. The argument that she couldn't drive would have no debate. John would not offer to teach her to drive, or to loan her the truck, which really belonged to Hannah. Hannah would be in control again, and now with John's support.

There were men loading trucks along side of the Land O'North Creamery. Large silver cream cans were going into the creamery and crates of butter and cheese moving out into other trucks. She stopped by the office door; and, even though she saw no sign for help wanted, she opened the door. A middle-aged woman in glasses looked up from her filing, and asked, "May I help you?"

"Do you have any openings?" Rozella asked.

"We haven't had any job openings for ages," the woman answered. "Usually we fill them from the applications we already have on file. We just call the one on top of the pile. But, if you want to fill one out, I guess we don't mind." She smiled. Getting up from the floor where she was working in the bottom drawer of a large file cabinet, she went into the closet and came back with an application form. "Do you have a pen?" she asked.

"No," Rozella blushed because she hadn't thought to bring anything to write with; and, she had to depend upon everyone to give her both form and pen or pencil.

The woman handed her a pen. It was an old Parker badly in need of new insides, and it leaked ink, staining her fingers as soon as she took the top of the pen off to get at the point. Rozella wiped her fingers the best she could on a piece of scrap paper she found in the wastebasket, and began to fill out the form. When she got to the part about what kinds of experience she had, she didn't know what to say. She didn't even know what people did who worked for a creamery. They wouldn't let her unload trucks of milk cans.

What could she do? She thought she could do clerical work, but had run into that before. John had not been able to get bookkeeping jobs, and he had an education. What good would she be to them, if they could have people like John? But, she filled it all out anyway. When she had finished it, the woman took it from her, looked it over, and said, "You didn't say what kind of work you wanted."

"Any kind. Rozella responded. "I'm willing to do anything or learn anything."

"Even if it means washing milk bottles, or scrubbing the creamery floors, or tubs where the cheese is made?"

"Work is work. I wash floors at home, and wash bottles, too. In fact, I fill cream cans, since we work on the farm."

"Is it your farm?" the woman asked with curiosity.

"Not really. We're just tenant farmers." She didn't want to get into talking about their arrangement with Hannah.

"Well, as I said before, don't count on anything. I'll add it to our list of applications. If someone leaves town and leaves an application behind, sometimes you get moved up a bit in the stack of waiting applications."

"Thank you. I appreciate your help anyway." Rozella said, and picked up her purse, returning the leaky fountain pen to the kindly woman.

Further down the same street she saw a help wanted sign in a dry cleaning and laundry establishment. But, when she went in to ask about it, the owner hastened over to the window to take down the sign. "Sorry. We forgot this. Our nephew came into town last week and we put him to work. No, we don't have an opening any more."

By the time she returned to the courthouse where she had begun her walk, Rozella had filled out only two applications, just the one in the creamery and the one for the unemployment office in the courthouse. People who had jobs stayed with them, feeling themselves lucky to have work. People, who could not get work, left town. People who had businesses, which survived, sometimes had jobs to offer. However, they gave the jobs to relatives who came in from other communities, or farms, which had been foreclosed. Competition was tough. That was what John had faced, and he had given up the effort.

Joan drove up at noon, as she had promised, to pick up Rozella, and together they went to the trucker's restaurant on the outer edge of town. They both ordered a hamburger sandwich, which was served hot with gravy on top of the sandwich and a heap of mashed potatoes. Fried onions adorned the top of the gravy, spooned off of the grill with a spatula; they were browned from the heat, and fragrant.

Joan looked over at Rose, and reminded her that she would pay for the lunch, as she knew that Rozella had no money, and guessed Hannah would see to it that Rose didn't get any money at all to take to town. If John worked with Hannah, she thought, there won't be any money for her to use in order to find work.

Joan had seen this before. Perhaps other women didn't have any sister-in-law named Hannah, but they had husbands and mothers-in-law who resented their leaving their babies and their unpaid housekeeping in order to earn enough money to survive. Other women had come to the center hungry, and without money to find their way out of the trap built for them by society and family. She knew how it was for Rozella.

"I love these onions," Joan smiled, "As I said before, they are the heart of the farmland."

"The only heart, maybe," Rozella looked down at them, and scraped them off of her sandwich. Whatever they reminded her of, it was something she didn't want to think about, and she hoped to avoid it by getting rid of them.

"What did you find?" Joan asked.

"The child care center was just what you promised. They were helpful. They knew who I was and what I needed. I felt good about it, even if Danny had not been left anyplace like that before. He didn't even cry, at least, not before I left."

"He'll be fine. He's a good kid, not the fussy type any day of the week. Did you find the unemployment office in the courthouse okay?" Joan reached for her coffee.

"Oh, yes. The man there took my application, but didn't seem to be very encouraging. There were some other people there, but they came in after I arrived, so I must have been pretty early."

"Anything else? Joan continued.

"I stopped in the creamery and filled out an application. They didn't have any openings, but the women did let me fill out a form."

"That's good. They usually don't do that. They have so many, that they get real cranky over being bothered normally." Joan smiled again.

"She was nice. She said I shouldn't expect anything, but she was pleasant anyway, even though her pen leaked all over me," Rozella added, looking down at her fingers, as if to check the reality of the incident.

"It won't happen in a day, or even a week, Rose. But you have to keep at it, and not give up right away." Joan summarized. "Do you have any other places to go during the afternoon?"

"I don't have anything special. In fact, I don't have the slightest idea of what to do, or where to go," she admitted.

"Look, borrow the phone book from behind the cash register – the girl working there will let you use it. We'll go through it for ideas for places to check."

Together they made a list using a pencil that Joan had in her pocket, and a paper napkin for notes. Even if she only put in applications at two out of three places, it would serve to organize her efforts. You couldn't depend upon the employment services to do anything with the application forms that they received. There were so many, and so many were very old, that they had become blasé and unconcerned about their work in placing people. They were like John, and had given up. When they left the restaurant, Joan said she would be back there about 3:30 PM to pick her up. "Don't go over to pick up Danny. I'll be here in plenty of time; we'll go over there together. Besides, I have business there."

"Oh," Joan added, "by the way, if I can't make it, I'll send Girard, so you won't be stranded. Someone will be here to take you home. As I recall, John never stays in town much past noon."

At that Rozella became nervous. Since Joan left so quickly, she didn't have time to say anything, but having Girard pick her up frightened her, if only because the two of them were so much aware of each other, with Danny in between them, and the knowledge that Joan knew about it. It made her shiver. She couldn't trust herself, and yet she knew that she cared about what happened to Joan and Girard as a couple.

I wish I could understand what is going on with those two, she thought, and forced herself to go on with the job-hunting without thinking about whether Joan or Girard would be there in the afternoon to take her home.

She visited a drug store, a dry goods store, and a meat packing plant, which was just now getting into frozen food lockers, a printing office, and the farm machinery store before she was allowed to put in an application. The drug store hired only high school girls, they said. Probably this was because high school girls attracted boys, who spent money on ice cream, candy bars and cokes. The farm machinery place didn't hire anyone anymore they said because sales had been down to nothing and they ran the place themselves without any outside help – family only, now. The frozen food locker plant did take an application because they would be hiring in the spring. It was a new operation, and they didn't know if they would need any help, other than meat cutters, but at least, they let her fill out a form. The printing shop was running on all family help, and didn't know when they might hire anyone. No one was advertising, and no one was doing much printing of envelopes or billing forms. By the time she had visited each place on the list, and filled out the one form, it was time to make her way back to the courthouse and wait for Joan to pick her up.

It was Joan who came to get her, and Rozella sighed a breath of relief that it wasn't Girard, not that she didn't yearn to be with him, but she just didn't know how to handle it this particular day. She couldn't trust herself to decide what to do. Joan and she drove across town to the childcare center, and stopped in the parking lot in front of the church.

"Where has the time gone?" Rozella asked of no one in particular. "It seems that I just dropped him off, and the whole day has flown by."

"That's the way it will be every day when you start working," Joan answered her, tugging on the truck door to close it.

"You sound as though you have hope that I'll get a job," Rozella answered.

"You will. I just know it. Maybe it's instinct, but I think that things are beginning to change, just beginning; but, some change is better than no change at all."

The door opened and Rozella could see into the large room where the children were playing. Her eyes were scanning the perimeter of the room searching for Danny. There –in the far corner, he was crawling around on the floor. He could walk better than that, there must be something he was pushing around the floor, she told herself. And, of course, there was—a big red fire engine toy truck. He was envied by another little boy standing over him trying to reach for it. "No, Danny does it." She could hear him saying, as if he had everything under control, and he did. She laughed at him.

When he heard her laugh, he left the fire engine to the delight of the other boy, and came running to her. She gathered him up in her arms, hugging him and almost crying over him, while Joan just watched, smiling at the two of them.

Someone from the office called out to Joan, and she left to go to the office. There were records of applicants for care to go over. Part of the work that had kept her so busy the past months was the creation of this daycare center, finding the women to run it, and getting the message out had kept her busy days, nights and weekends. Now, it was functioning, but the woman coming there to work were volunteers and often without any clerical experience. They changed so often that they required constant supervision. Never a day went by that Joan didn't stop in before going home to other things. But she had built this model system out of her own dreams, even though her dreams were the dreams of a childless woman. Her love for other women and her caring about what happened to them in a time of trial and deprivation had driven her. She had always seen how much they worried about their children, and how little help they ever got from husbands or families. They were the slaves, literally household slaves, and Joan saw herself as trying to free them.

When the three of them left together, the woman in the office waved at her, called her by name. "Come back, Rozella. When you get your job, we'll still be here. Danny was a joy to take care of, he doesn't cause a bit of trouble."

Driving home, Rozella was quiet because Joan was quiet. Joan was involved in her own preoccupation with the duties she had given herself in creating programs for women.

In this quiet, Rozella became filled with fear, the fear of what would happen when she got home. What would John say? What would Hannah say, and do? She felt threatened. And she had no job she could hold up to them as a measure of success. Would they ever let her go again?

She held Danny close to her, and he slept in the warmth of her arms until she woke him up when Joan drove into their yard. The dogs were barking at the truck. There was a light in the kitchen window, as well as the barn. She gathered Danny's bag of toys and clothes, put her purse under her arm, and said goodbye to Joan, who promised she would check on her progress with job hunting. She walked up the steps to the kitchen door, dreading what she would find.

CHAPTER THIRTY-FOUR

Danny needed to be changed before she could begin to make supper. No one was in the kitchen, and that was a relief in itself, so Rose hurried up the stairs with Danny and his belongings. She changed his clothes and her own before she returned to the kitchen. Putting him down with a toy truck and his teddy bear, she started to peel leftover boiled potatoes into some heated grease. They would have fried potatoes and some canned tomatoes mixed with pieces of bread and onion into what could be called escalloped tomatoes. Bread and butter with applesauce, and milk. Coffee for Hannah and John. She felt hurried, as if they could fire her if she didn't maintain her regular routine. Going into town would be no excuse.

John came in from the barn, saying, "You're home?" as if he was surprised.

"Yes," she answered, "I promised you I would be home by supper time."

"I know, but I wasn't sure if Joan or Girard would be home by the time we have supper." He was pouting verbally.

Hannah was coming down from her bedroom upstairs where she had stayed hidden while Rozella had changed herself and Danny. Not a sound had come from her bedroom. She didn't act surprised, because to show any interest would be an acknowledgment of feeling, Rozella supposed. Setting the table was left to Rozella, as well as cooking the meal. She rushed around the stove and table, trying to put all the dishes on the table in the right places without burning the potatoes, or tripping over Danny. She didn't remember ever feeling angry over making supper before, but tonight she was becoming angry, and everything was falling, and spilling, and not going well at all. She had never felt so rushed before, and it made her clumsy.

They sat themselves at the table, waiting for her to bring the filled dishes to the table, and to pour the coffee. It was a ritual, and Rozella was surprised to find herself becoming aware of what had seemed no trouble at all in previous evenings. Danny cried, which he had never done at the table. He was too tired from the day in the childcare center. He had played for too many hours, and even after sleeping on the drive home, he was still tired.

John was the one who opened the subject of her trip to town, as Hannah didn't want to talk about anything, and that was normal for her. "Where did you apply?" he asked, "or, did you get a chance to put an application in anywhere?"

"Yes. I made an application in the unemployment office, and the creamery took an application from me," she answered.

"You took all day to do that?" Hannah spoke at last.

"It didn't take all day for just those two things; I stopped to inquire at several places, that involved talking to people. I had lunch with Joan."

"How did you pay for that?" Hannah asked, angrily, as if someone had stolen from her.

"Joan paid for it," Rozella answered, feeling like crying, or throwing something.

"We told you to bring a sandwich for you and Danny," John added, as he reached for another slice of bread.

"I did, but it was a long day for me, and I got hungry early. I used half of the sandwich for breakfast, because I didn't have time for breakfast."

"You see? That's what would happen every day, if you went to work. And the child center...was Danny all right there; did he cry when you left him?" John was asking questions.

"No, Danny didn't cry. He was fine. He seemed to enjoy it there. He's tired tonight because he didn't sleep as he usually does." Rozella moved her plate back, not wanting to eat.

Hannah was thinking that Rozella was really crazy. How could she leave this house, where she had a husband to sleep with and to provide for her, to struggle in the world for a small bit of money? Most of her earnings would be spent in childcare, lunch money, and clothes to wear to work. She hated Rozella for wanting to leave this behind.

No babies, no man. No anything, but Pa, thought Hannah. Pa never did make up for what she had lost. Nothing could make up for the lost kisses of youth, or the gentle touch of a loved one when it all turned into animal behavior, like the breeding barnyard scenes. All the pastel beauty of life, the spring colors she had painted once, all the hope, turned hard and sour, like fruit left too long on the branches of the trees, and abandoned.

"You have it all!" Hannah was saying, and Rozella didn't know why her voice was so gruff, but she thought she understood Hannah.

John evidently did understand her, because he said, "I agree. If you try to leave to work, you will lose what you have. You have an easy time here. You can nap with Danny, sew in your leisure time, visit with the women of the church at your circle meetings...all this will be lost. Not to mention what will happen to Danny in a care center."

"You could take care of him here, if you wish," Rozella answered him, knowing that she was being sarcastic now, because he couldn't take care of Danny and do the work on the farm, and Hannah wouldn't go back to doing the housework. Even though she had done it before Rozella came to live there.

"One thing Pa taught me..." Hannah began, "is the woman's place is in the home."

Rozella looked at John, remembering how they had talked about Pa Queist's locking Hannah up in her room because she had fallen in love with a field hand. Her look was questioning. Didn't John remember their conversation? Was that the way you learned that a woman's place was in the home?

Rozella didn't care to be locked up, although she was feeling "locked up" in a different way. It was the feeling of not being allowed to have any future, but one that Hannah would allow her to have. She and John would always have to live as Hannah chose to have them live, if they continued this way. Something had to change, even if the change would not be easy.

Hannah would hate her for leaving this baby that she adored; and, Hannah could see that Danny was too tired from his day in the childcare center. His eyes were red-rimmed and tired looking. She had taken her place in the fields as Pa had trained her to do. Rozella could take care of Danny and the house, was her view, and she would maintain that view.

Couldn't she see that Hannah had lost what she wanted most to have? The first days of Danny's life, it had been Hannah who held him and changed him, the Hannah who held him closely while walking with him. That was before Rozella persuaded John to take Danny home to her, and now –Rozella was rejecting her own baby, Hannah thought. I knew she wouldn't do right by Danny. I knew he wasn't safe with his mother. If I had been able to keep him, he wouldn't have to leave his home. I'd be here for him. She looked over at him again, still not revealing that she wanted more than anything just to hold him once more.

Just one trip to town had stirred such emotion, and such resentment, Rozella noticed, looking around the table. John's resentment, Hannah's anger and jealousy, and even Danny, as much as he seemed to like the day care center, looked at her with eyes that seemed to accuse her of abandonment. What would every day bring?

John looked back at her, angry with her for doing what he couldn't bring himself to do – trying to escape. He had given it up, tried to forget it, given in to staying here with Hannah, and making it into his own dream. He was recreating the farm, acknowledging that it was his only way, in the hope that he would become part owner of the land and the buildings, by default. By not leaving, he might be able to take possession.

Rozella is going through the same circles that I went through, he told himself. You can't leave without money; you can't get any money unless you leave. Eventually, she'll give in.

There will be one trip to town one day, when Hannah will be tired and will say, "You take the money to the bank, John. You do it. Take over, John. Men will listen to you better than they will listen to me." When that day came, the place would belong to him.

Meanwhile, his family was safe from hunger, safe from finding a place to live, and safe from looking for outside work, as others were—the whole country over. Waiting was what he had decided to do.

Why couldn't Rozella see what he was trying to do? Everything she was doing with this crazy search for work was destroying his plan. Hannah couldn't live forever. She couldn't even control them forever. All they had to do was be patient, and be glad to have what they now had. They were safe here, not exposed to hardship, as others knew it. Why did Rozella want to force such risk?

And Rozella thought, this is what it will be like: One tired day after another, with these three looking at me over the supper table with accusation in their eyes.

Meanwhile, at the Girard farm, Joan and Girard were talking about Rozella's day also. "She did well," Joan was saying. "She wasn't shy about asking for work."

"She was a teacher; she shouldn't have been shy," Girard countered her surprise.

"That's true, but she had always seemed so naive about what goes on in the world, and even in her own home with John and Hannah, that I think of her as shy. In some ways, she is," Joan said, thoughtfully.

"I think of her that way, too, but it isn't the same sort of thing. Personal things, and business things are different for most of us. And, I can't blame her for wanting something different."

"No. We do, too We are planning to leave, and we once thought this was the one thing in the world that we wanted most to do...live on a farm, and become self-sustaining." Joan added.

"Farmers. I've had enough of them to last a lifetime," Girard was emphatic. "To think that I wanted to become one."

"That's a radical change from a couple of years ago," Joan noted. "Things in your business have changed your views somewhat, I see." She put her hand on his shoulder.

"Just watching how they act reminds me of Menken's essay on farmers. I think it was called 'Husbandman.' He hated farmers, and called them frauds, hypocrites and a few other distasteful things. He said they were self-seeking. Some things he said I agree with, watching them grow an excess of produce, and then, in order to make money, destroying it. Watching them steal from each other. The only thing they understand is profit, and they talk about big business. There is nothing out there more selfish than the American farmer in spite of all the mythological ideas of what they represent."

"I haven't had the same experiences that you have had in business, but you know how much I struggle to overcome the backwoods ideals that keep women down in these parts. Some of that is the same thing you are expressing. In order to make a greater profit, the farmer turns his wife into an unpaid slave. Is that what your writer meant by 'husbandman'?"

"I don't think so; it probably was a term meaning those who breed animals."

"The farmers I meet, men that is, are sure breeders, I notice. The more children, the better. And, they are raising farm animals in the purest sense of the word. Their kids turn into beasts of burden, and locked into the land."

"As they were before them," Girard added, "and as John is locked in with Hannah."

"That's an unnatural arrangement, as the whole Queist family has been. All of the truth has not yet been revealed," Joan said. holding his hand.

"You're probably right, but who are we to judge? Our own life style would be called unnatural by everyone who lives around here."

"True, if they could manage to speak after the shock of knowing about us hit them. You and your innocent Rozella. And, I don't mean that sarcastically. She really is innocent, if only because she doesn't have a cruel bone in her body. If she wasn't..."

"Thank God, we can be honest with each other." He put his arm around her. "What you're saying is that if she wasn't heterosexual, you would be attracted to her yourself," Girard added on her behalf.

"Yes," she whispered, "I think so. She's beautiful and so fragile looking, like fine china."

"That's the way I find her, only..."

"It's okay, in your privacy, I imagine she turns quite different, but one would never guess it. That's why I say the townspeople would die of shock, not at the threat of your love affair with Rozella – which they could understand. What would bother them the most is our marriage."

"Our open marriage, and our acceptance of each other as we really are, staying together in spite of everything." Girard got up to walk about the room restlessly.

"We hope. I'm not too sure about you and Rozella. Our love is strong enough to last because it's not based on sex – any more, but your relationship with Rose, sometimes it threatens me."

"I promised you, Joan. And, I have loved you always, and I admire and respect you. It's all the good things we have shared, all the changes we have seen in each other. These things –weathered, that is what makes this thing work."

"It may not carry us past the passion you and she share. That may cause a fire we can't control, no matter what our minds tell us is wise," Joan shook her head, sadly." For instance, what will happen when Rozella finally realizes that when she chooses to leave John and Hannah and the farm in order to escape her entrapment, she will also have to leave you? What do you think will happen?"

"I don't think she has any dreams about a future with me. We haven't talked about one," he answered, thoughtfully.

"But that is not normal for the traditional woman, Girard, And to all appearances, Rozella is very traditional. She is only learning how to mature in a more sophisticated way. It will be a long time before she will give up hoping for the great Cinderella dream that most women pine for, a prince to carry her away, and take care of all her troubles."

"I didn't think she was like that." He was looking puzzled.

"And that makes you just as traditionally narrow minded as all the rest of the men who just 'don't realize.' You're always hoping that women don't expect anything of you, and surprised and shocked whenever they do!" she answered him.

"Oh, dear, I wouldn't want to hurt her," he said.

"Don't worry, you won't have to – she'll do it herself," Joan said, going into the next room and ending the conversation.

John's thoughts carried him through the rest of the evening meal, and into the coffee he shared with Hannah each night. Long after Rozella had taken Danny up to put him to bed, he was still engrossed in his own worries. He pretended to look at a seed catalog, but his mind wandered. His coffee cooled in his cup, as he sat at the table absentmindedly stirring the sugar he dropped into the cup. Hannah had gone upstairs also, presumably to get the record keeping manuals for the farm, in which she noted down each sale, and each expense as it was made. Every evening, it was her habit to record any pieces of paper that were created during the day, or record any bit of money received. But, that was what bothered John, the money. He had become more and more convinced that there was a lot of it somewhere around. Her last trip into town with him had been to visit the bank, and she hadn't said anything about what she did there.

As usual, she had found reason to send him off on an errand before he had a chance to enter the bank with her. He had dressed up to be presentable, as a business man, in order to talk with her to the bank manager, but had been left, like a child, at the heavy front doors of the First National. Then, she instructed him to go to the feed store, three blocks down the street, and ask the manager there for a copy of their monthly bill. As if they couldn't mail it to them, he thought in disgust.

When she returned to the truck, he could see no sign of money, but with her big black handbag, she could be carrying a lot of it. Or –she could have put it into a bank account. Which had it been? This was what bothered John this night. What would it take to get her to reveal the amount of the family holdings? Before he could lay claim to it, he had to know how much here was. He couldn't believe that there had been nothing but a break-even operation going on here all these years. When you don't spend anything but the bare minimum, there must be some profit held back. Knowing Hannah, they didn't sell things at a loss. He knew prices better than that. Why did she think she could fool him? He wasn't a fool, and that was what he wanted Rozella to understand – he wasn't a fool!

Hannah, too, was surprised to confront things she had never considered. For instance, she had never thought that John would think of demanding a share of the farm or the family holdings. She had taken for granted that he knew his status; that when he had returned from a fruitless search for the job in the field he had educated himself for, he would be grateful for what was offered to him. She had felt the payment extracted by her father was so heavy a burden on her that she owned every part and parcel, much the same as a wife who had endured years of unhappiness in order to inherit. How many had outlived the head of the household? And then were subdued by the eldest male in the house, or lost to their own son who took over the stance of the father.

She hadn't considered that Rozella would even try to find work. Even with John's failure a matter of record, Rozella had not been daunted in her search. Now that she had tried, perhaps she would forget about it and fall back into the routine that Hannah felt secure in maintaining.

They were working together, as she and Pa had worked, creating a place for themselves. Pa had his insecurity, his doubts about himself, as the past revealed. His marriage to a woman of higher class kept him on alert for any possibility of loss. Even Hannah could see that, when she heard the tales told by the gossips of the town. It had taken her years to overcome the agony of her youth, and the dark and terrifying nights when he came to her.

She could never feel clean again, but she could understand his fear of loss. He needed every dollar he had hidden away in order to be sure that he would never again be dependant upon another person's generosity. Her mother's parents had made sure of that. Pa had never talked about it to Hannah, but she could remember bits of the past.

John couldn't leave, not now when she had taken Rozella and the child into the house. Danny had always been a part of them, he was her own dream of a baby, but Rozella was the intruder, the woman with education, as her mother had been. Hannah was reminded of her own mother, as she watched her. Rozella was a woman who could look down on Hannah's soiled overalls, and her shoes covered with cakes of sticky manure from working in the barns.

Without Rozella, she would have had no threat to John's future; she could have counted on him to be there forever, even if forever was only until she died. Things would stay in their hands, and someday, when she was gone, he could live out his years in the security that she was seeking.

Mother – had kept herself away from Pa, closing her bedroom doors upon him, locking up her sex as if it was too good for him, and he had come to Hannah in her soft and tender years, stretching reality into a nightmare-thing that her soul couldn't contain. The way he had forced himself upon her, she blamed upon her mother, who thought she was too good for him. Hannah wasn't too good for him, but she had been forced to give in to him because of his greater force. She had done the work her mother should have done, in every way.

Would Rozella do the same to John? If so, where would he turn? He should let her go, and keep Danny there for the two of them to share. Danny could grow up and one day have the farm to himself. That was what life was all about. It wasn't made of beautiful dreams that were painted of fictional places, it was building things with land, and money, and hard work. With the extra land Pa had acquired in auction, there could be a comfortable future.

Hannah had not been able to tell John about the acreage, or what she had sold it for. That had been her secret, one she had shared with Pa. Pa had bought the land, and told her about the deeds. She had kept it secret because the land once had belonged to her neighbors.

Now, with Pa gone, here was no longer reason to hold unto it. He would have chosen to keep it. Land was more important to him than money, but her choice had been to sell, even when she felt she was not heeding his wishes. Money, put away, not in a bank, was safe. It wouldn't go down in value, the way the land might go down. Right now the government was paying a fair price. What if they changed their minds? That could happen at any time. Politicians changed their minds more often than they changed their hats. Keep the money. If she could, she would have put it into gold pieces.

Instead, she put it in the bottom of the old trunk in the attic. The part in the bottom of the largest trunk, that Mama had shown her years ago when she was a little girl, a hidden compartment, where travelers had put their valuables when they took ocean liners to the continent. Mama had known. She was of the class which was able to take trips for pleasure. Pa hadn't known anything like that. He had been born to the soil, and the peasants of the earth. There had been no pleasures in his life.

Hannah had put the money she brought back from the bank in the bottom of the old trunk, and replaced it in the exact same spot where it had stood these many years. The compartment underneath was not visible. They would never know. Now, with John no longer to be depended upon, he could not be told either. He was becoming so demanding that he might try to take money, since she had refused to give him a deed to any of the land.

She had paid, oh, how she had paid for this money and this land. Rozella knew nothing of hardship. She just thought that she knew. Her friends had told her things; it was their advice that spoiled her, Hannah thought. Maybe if they hadn't come to take her to town, if they had left her there alone with she and John, they would have been able to keep her sheltered long enough to teach her their ways.

What had spoiled it?...the Girards and their peculiar ways...and, John who was too good to Rozella. He left her alone with Girard, who was capable of who knows what? Any couple who had lived where they had lived...and lived as they lived...

Danny, he was the dearest child, warm and soft, his laughter sounding through the evening and morning hours. She looked forward to seeing him every noon when she came in for the noontime meal. She looked forward to seeing him play before he went upstairs at night at bedtime. Every time she looked at him she was reminded of holding him those first weeks of his life, when she had pretended that he was her own child.

If Rozella would only go, just go away and leave she and John and Danny with the land that was their own. Rozella belonged somewhere else, back in the city she came from with her own family: the father who drank himself to death, and the many sisters who all lived in poverty.

What had she known of work, as Hannah had known it? What had she known of providing for a man? There are things a woman must do, even when she hates doing it. There had been...she remembered. That was how it had been with she and Pa. The Bible might say that Adam and Eve were fashioned like God had made them, in the image of God, but she could see as she walked through the farm yard, that man was related to animals. Even pigs rutted shamelessly, and there was no way to stop them. Females endured, that's all. Endured.

She would watch, and she would wait to see what Rozella would do next.

CHAPTER THIRTY-FIVE

The morning after the day in town, things reverted back to their normal pattern. It was as if nothing had happened. Hannah and John went about their work. Rozella prepared their breakfast for them. Nothing was said. Later, over the breakfast dishes, Rozella had the strangest feeling that her day had been erased. They did not acknowledge her attempt at change, perhaps. It felt like a dream, something she had only imagined. There was no point in trying to call Joan, as Joan would be busy working and there was no way she could get back into town again. John wouldn't leave until next week, and even if he did – where else could she apply for work? All she could do now would be wait, and try again next week, that is, if he would take her with him again.

Danny was trying to take all the kettles out of the cupboard in the pantry. Rozella could hear them falling and scraping against the doors of the cupboard as he dropped them on the floor. She didn't worry about him because he had done this so often that the arrangement was made mostly for him. The least breakable things had been left on the bottom shelves for a long time now. When she needed some time to clean up the kitchen or to cook, she could ignore his playing in the pantry while she worked. Eventually he would tire of playing with the kettles and come out into the kitchen to find something different to play with. Next time in the pantry, she would put everything away. It was for she and Danny to know, Hannah and John didn't need to know that she allowed him to play this way.

Joan had said that she had sent out resumes across the country. That meant that the two of them would be moving, if she found a job. Would it be that easy for Girard to find a job? Would it be easy for either of them to find work? Even so, they would have their farm to sell, or lease out. What would happen to their life as they had planned it? Who could buy a farm these days? Except Hannah, maybe. Hannah would have the money to put the down payment on one.

February's days marked time in tedious gray steps toward March, that unpredictable part of the year, torn between raging storms, and cold endurance. The grimmest time of the year, it was the introduction to the longest month of the year, nothing ahead but waiting for April and spring.

Every day when the mail came, John looked it over where it lay upon the sideboard awaiting the time of day when Hannah and he opened the mail and took care of the finances. It would appear that he helped her take care of them, but it was only slight of hand. He watched her, but never was asked an opinion, or given any piece of paper to work with. Occasionally she would ask him a question after reading over a bill received. She would even write out the checks needed to pay bills and sign them. John was allowed to put stamps on the envelopes and put them in the mailbox for the rural carrier to pick up the next day.

John would always look over at Rozella whenever he glanced through the envelopes waiting for Hannah's perusal, his look meant to say, she was sure, that he was aware there had been no response to her applications for work in town. He needed that assurance because of his own failure. He wanted to rationalize his entrapment into a life with Hannah on this homestead shared by the three of them. He had tried; and, he had failed. Rozella was bound to fail. In that way, both he and Hannah could forget about the disturbance created by Rozella's desire to change.

Hannah didn't ask to return to town with John. Whatever her business had been, it had been concluded, they assumed. But, Rozella recovered from the excitement and fatigue of the day in town to ask if she could try once more. When John's day in town came around the next week, she was ready and waiting right after breakfast, just as she had been the week before.

John was angry, too, as he had been before, when they repeated their trip. He grumbled at her all the way into town by using Danny as a whipping tool, "I don't like to see you put him into a day care center. You also remember how he came home last time. I have some rights about this, Rozella. You also have some responsibility to your child."

"My child?" she asked, "When did he become just my child?"

"Our child, then," he responded pointedly. His words had been designed to make her feel guilty, she was sure.

"Since he's our child, and not just mine, maybe you could take care of him during the day while I work?" Rozella was specific.

"That's impossible, and you know it," he spoke into the frosted windshield as if she wasn't there.

"Why? I always thought that farmers didn't have as much to do in the wintertime. That's what people told me. Some of them even move away in the winter, go south, as a matter of fact."

"That's all storybook crap, like the junk you read in women's magazines. It's not real. I don't know anyone who can quit working in the winter and just do nothing. Never have."

"Actually, watching Danny wouldn't be so bad as you think. Danny takes a nap in the afternoon. So does Hannah. They could nap in the same room."

"What about the rest of the time?"

"There are plenty of times when you could take him with you. When you're working in the barn, for instance. Why can't he dress warmly, and play out there? You're milking cows, and shoveling up cow piles. He can watch, or just play. Make a play room for him, use one of the empty stalls..."

"Who ever heard of a man baby sitting out in the barn? That's a ridiculous idea."

"It's not ridiculous, it just hasn't been done before, as far as we know."

"Meaning what?" He pounded on the steering wheel.

"Meaning that someone else may have done it and just not talked about it around the neighborhood."

The argument went on all the way to town, where he dropped her off in front of the Lutheran church day center. "You'll get a ride home with Joan?" he asked as she opened the door.

"Yes," she answered, picking up Danny, who whimpered this time; as if to make his father feel justified in saying that leaving him there would be a form of abuse.

When John left, she turned away in relief, as if a nagging fly had flown away in the wind. Breathing a sign, she opened the door of the church school building to a warm and cheery interior. People were happy here, she thought. Even the babies seemed content. There was no pressure, and no animosity in this room. She found a place to put Danny's things. Even though he wasn't there regularly, there was a place to put his things: a large box with a blank tag tacked on it. She filled in his name on the blank tag. These "lockers" without doors had been fashioned by some creative woman from orange crates, by using bright enamel colors and scraps of fabric glued into the interiors of the boxes. It was a great idea. You could make kitchen cupboards out of these, Rozella thought.

One of the younger girls took Danny from her, carrying him over to a play area where there were four other children. Rozella, feeling somewhat rejected because he didn't cry when taken away, turned toward the door, experiencing another reminder of what it would be like to work all the time.

Not exactly knowing what to do after dropping Danny off, she decided to call on each place she had left her paperwork. The man at the courthouse said, "No, there haven't been any openings in the past week." He sounded irritated to be bothered by her. "You're on a list," he snapped.

She retraced her steps through the town, even passing Girard's office and noticing his truck once more. It was early for his day to begin; he must have started early to allow time for fieldwork in the afternoon.

The creamery was open when she returned to the office where she had left her application. The woman looked sorry to say that she didn't have a thing, but "Stop back," she suggested, "late this afternoon before you go home. I shouldn't tell you this, but we have an employee who can't decide whether or not to stay. Even if she does leave, they may not replace her. Don't get your hopes up – but do come back."

It was the first encouragement she had received, so she left there with high hopes in spite of the woman's caution. She didn't even ask what kind of work it would be.

People hadn't even begun to take their morning coffee breaks; it was still so early, but it was a good time to catch them in their offices. She planned to go up and down the streets, asking every storeowner or shopkeeper she could find.

Leaving a note for Joan at the day care center, she had asked her to pick her up before she went home. If she returned there to pick Danny up, and just waited for Joan, it ought to work out for them both.

As she passed the post office, she recalled that people were hired there for clerical work, and she went in to find the postmaster. After waiting ten minutes for him to appear, all she got for her trouble was information about civil service exams. The process itself would take a year.

The dime store lady said they always hired high school girls. More than likely they hired high school dropouts, Rozella thought, or their own daughters. It was a 'family affair' like the drug store lunch counter.

At the Ford garage, they laughed at her when she asked for work. "What kind of work could you do here?" the shop foreman chided.

"Clean up your windows, for one thing," she suggested.

"Hell," he answered her, "who needs clean windows? We don't want the men to start looking out the windows," and he stared at her legs, running his eyes up and down them as if searching for a way to get under her skirt.

The coffee shop would be another place to try, she thought, glad to escape the embarrassment of the garage. It was now coping with the influx of coffee break people from surrounding businesses and offices. The coffee break was a ritual, not really based on hunger or thirst; it was more like a kind of medication you took in order to make it through the day. As she entered, she surveyed the doors, seeking a clue about which one could point to the manager, a place, or a person to apply to. "Rose, Rose?" she heard a soft voice call, and turned to find Girard at her elbow.

"I didn't know you'd be in town today," he was saying. "Come. Sit down. Have coffee with me."

"Thank you, but I was looking for a manager."

"That's okay. Just have some coffee," he gestured to a waitress, "Bring her a cup with cream please. I'll introduce you to the manager before I leave," he promised her.

She sat down, removing her coat, folding it to lay it on top of her purse. "I've been here for hours. You know how early John comes to town." She said to him.

"Will you be counting on Joan to take you home?"

"Yes. I left a message for her at the day care center."

"That's fine. No problem. It's just that I'm leaving early today for field trips, visiting farmers who are filling out papers for refinancing, arranging appraisals. I could take you home earlier, if you don't mind."

"What about Joan?"

"Oh, she calls me during the day, and we do share the truck, so I'll tell her when she calls."

"Danny is in the day care center," she said hesitantly. He must guess what she's thinking, even if they would be alone, they would not be alone without Danny.

"I know," he said, his hand reaching for her, as if he couldn't help himself. People here knew him; he must be careful. She must be careful not to reveal too much. She looked around the room.

"We'll have some time to talk, anyway, Rose."

"Tell me what time to meet you, and I'll be sure to be there, then," she answered him. "At the day care center? And, you're sure that Joan won't mind?"

"It's just part of our day. We juggle hours and transportation every day." The waitress set the coffee cup down for Rozella, looking her over, as if she was competition before a race.

"Anything else?" the waitress asked.

"Yes. Give her a jelly donut. She looks too thin to me." That pleased the waitress who flounced off to fill his order.

"What's new?" he asked Rozella.

"Nothing, except the creamery lady said to come back before I leave town."

"Great. That sounds hopeful. What kind of work?" He picked up his coffee cup.

"I didn't even ask, because I didn't think it sounded hopeful. It had something to do with someone who was quitting."

Looking at him across the table, she could feel a surge of desire. She managed to keep it hidden from herself during all the times apart, but times like this, when she saw him – it hit her. It was undeniable: orgasm made a relationship bonding. It became an instrument of immediate recall.

"I won't have long this morning because I'm busy preparing my paper work for this afternoon." The waitress returned with the jelly donut and a bill for Girard. "But, eat this, Rose. Do you have lunch money?" he asked, knowing how things were at the Queists.

"I have a sandwich in my bag," she answered, glancing over at it as she spoke.

"Maybe so," he acknowledged, "But I don't like you to be going around without money for telephone calls, coffee, or something to eat. If you need to get out of the cold – it costs something to buy coffee." He was pushing a couple of dollar bills toward her from the change the waitress had left from a five-dollar bill.

To Rozella, it looked like a lot of money, and no man had ever given her money before, not even John. Her sisters had loaned her money, but no one, no one had ever given her money before. She felt frozen by it, not knowing how to respond. In Mama's terms, taking it would be...

"A housewife can be a whore, too," Mama was responding to a story about Mrs. Lull's daughter, Evelina who was mistress to the furniture storeowner. Women talked about Evelina's furs and jewels and refused to speak to her when they went past her on the street.

"How do you mean?" asked the shocked housewife, who couldn't understand this response.

Wasn't Mama one of them? Rozella had asked herself, she too, confused.

"All life long they get paid. Their husbands buy their clothes, pay their rent, they never go to work outside the home," Mama pointed out. "That's getting paid for services, isn't it?"

The uncomfortable gossip stammered. "But marriage, that's what marriage is for. You, too, are married," she ventured to add.

"Yes, but I provide for myself. I'm not just a taker, a user, I work hard."

And why aren't you given the things that other women have, Rozella listening in from where she stood over the kitchen sink, thought in anger. Why do you have to work so hard, when other women don't work at all, except at home?

"You work because you like to Dorthea?" The woman asked, her tone a mixture of sarcasm and surprise.

I like having my own money. I like making my own decisions." Mama was emphatically sure of herself. It was true, Rozella could agree, but the truth was – Mama had no choice. Pretending to choose must be a matter of pride, and Mama couldn't see the pain in herself that her daughter watched daily. She couldn't even see the anger in her that tore at Papa when he was home.

A woman could grow to hate another woman, and only over the pain of not getting help from a spouse...

Reaching out to take the two dollars, Rozella was again aware that John had never given her even a dollar. She had excused him because Hannah kept him penniless, but now with another man, one she loved, she was beginning to see how it felt to be cared for. It was more than words, and it touched her. No, it did not offend her; it made her want to cry, as if someone had put value on her, yet the value itself was more than a monetary thing.

"Thank you," she said," "I don't know when I'll be able to pay you back. Maybe I won't need to spend it."

"Rose, don't be silly. I want to help, it's part of what we are – to each other," he answered as he got up to leave. "Wait a minute, I almost forgot—I promised to introduce you to the manager if you'd sit down and have coffee with me. You see the office door over there? Please be brave before you leave, and knock on that door. Just say that I sent you to apply for work. His name is Bjerke.

I'll see you at the day care center, about 2PM. Okay? Gotta hurry. I've been away too long now." He continued.

"Yes, I'll be there," she answered him, and he was gone. She watched him cross the street, then turned to see the waitress watching her watch him. Deciding to wait until later to knock on the manager's door, she put the money into her purse and go up to leave.

Every open door along the way was a place to stop and ask for work. Most often people avoided her by saying the owner made the decisions and she questioned their honesty. Weren't they the owners? Why couldn't they answer her?

She stopped at the county library to get warm. It was a quiet place to rest, even though small, and there were books and magazines to read. Smelly, and dusty from unused books, and oily polished floors, it still was a good smell; it smelled like the schoolroom, and books and papers were he most comfortable surroundings.

By one o'clock she had exhausted her possibilities, so in order to eat lunch without spending money, she went to the railroad station. There she could eat a sandwich without being asked to buy a drink, or a ticket. The musty old stationmaster never looked out into the waiting room. She tried to eat slowly in order to pass the time, but at 1:30 she could find no more excuses to linger on. Stopping by the ticket office, she got the man's attention by shuffling train schedules loudly. "Excuse me, where can I put in an application for work?" she asked him.

"Not here," he glared at her for disturbing him. "All help is hired out of St. Paul." He walked away.

I haven't heard of anyone moving here from St. Paul, ever, she thought, as she left.

On the way back to the day care center, she stopped by the creamery to see the kind lady who had asked her to return. "I'm glad you came back," she said. "The woman did leave. It was a family problem. They haven't decided whether or not to fill her job with another person, but they may have to have part time help."

"What kind of work?" Rozella remembered to ask.

"Cleaning, just scrubbing out the vats daily. I thought you wouldn't mind what kind of work...any work is so hard to find."

"Oh,no. I'd be happy for anything at all. May I call you, and find out for sure?"

"Yes, I'm Tulla, but it's okay. I answer the phone, so you'll get me whenever you call. Here's the number." She wrote the phone number down on a piece of paper. The number would be indelible for Rozella.

She would never forget it. Just the thought of finding work would etch it into her memory.

Danny squealed with delight when he saw her and came running across the floor, even as his teacher cried, "Don't run." She picked him up, kissing and hugging him, then looking up at the clock. Girard would be here at 2PM. It was almost that time. The young woman from the office came over to say, "Joan was here for a minute or two. She said her husband would be by to pick you up, and that she'd see you later, or call you, this week."

"Thanks," Rozella answered, looking for Danny's clothes, and his bag, as she prepared to dress him for his trip home. He tried to talk as she pulled on his snowsuit and boots. He was at the stage of making up words when he couldn't think of any, so his conversations at times were disjointed and became nonsense.

"Your timing is perfect, Rose," Girard said, as she lifted Danny to his feet. "I didn't know how scheduled you were, or I would have left the truck running," he smiled. "Let's go!"

Leaving with him, they piled into the truck cab, as if they had always traveled together.

It was still early afternoon, people were working; children were in school. Hannah was napping at home, and Rozella didn't know what John did at this hour. Danny usually slept so he nodded, and then fell sound asleep leaning against her. She and Girard fell silent, so terribly self-conscious with each other that neither could manage the words for the many things they wanted to say.

"We could – " he started. "We could go to the cottage, but it would be more comfortable at my house."

"I didn't bring the key to the cottage. I didn't know I would see you," she answered.

"The house is heated, and Joan won't be back home until I pick her up. I don't have too much time because I really do have calls to make, but we'd have some time together alone, before I take you home."

"What about Danny?" was all she could say, and she remembered the two dollars. It didn't make her feel better about herself. Earlier, it made her feel as if he cared – now, it made her uncomfortable.

"We'll have time, Rose, and Danny will be there with us. We won't do anything to shame him – or you. Whatever happens, happens."

And she felt better again about herself, and about Girard. It was her own desire that was driving her to these thoughts; she could acknowledge it, at last. She wanted him, so much!

CHAPTER THIRTY-SIX

She waited for Hannah and John to leave the house the next morning before trying to call the creamery. It would be easier to call without any listeners. As it was, she had not told them there was any possibility of a job for her. Telling them would only complicate matters; if she didn't get a job from this call, it would easier if they didn't know about it. They would be upset and angry if they knew. Now, they had been irritated when she left for town with John, but she saw that they recovered the next day, seeming relieved that the trip was over for the week, and she had found nothing. Their anticipations had been met.

Her own fears kept her busy with unnecessary things, putting off what she expected would be a disappointment. She took care of Danny, and finished cleaning up the kitchen, and then went upstairs to make the beds. Even using the phone was a difficult thing to do; she had heard too often from Hannah that each call was expensive. It was not to be used except for emergencies or business. With that instruction given, neither she nor John had ever used it. It was very rare to have anyone call them, so it hung there, an instrument to be dusted every week. Its black receiver perched on the wooden box mounted on the kitchen wall.

When the operator answered, she gave her the number from the piece of paper. It was ringing. She waited, thinking that it was too early for any business; after all, with the kitchen and household chores done, it was still only 7:30. After three rings, someone did answer. It was a woman, and Rozella remembered that Tulla said she would be the one to answer the phone.

"This is Rozella Queist," she spoke to the mouthpiece, standing on her toes to reach it, as the phone had been mounted too high for her.

"Good. I'm glad you called so early. There's no excuse for them to contact the employment office, then. Yes, they did agree to let you have a chance at the job, but it will only be part time. Is that okay?"

"Yes...yes." She was so excited that she could hardly talk, "It's fine. When?"

"Be sure, now, because it doesn't look good if you take something and it doesn't work out. It means your references aren't so good. That's what happened to the woman who left. She was cut from full time to part time and couldn't handle the cut in pay. It's only four hours in the morning every day...and you start early."

"It's fine. I can do that, as long as it doesn't start before the day care center at the Lutheran church opens. Danny will stay there while I work."

"No. It will work. The day care center opens at 6AM. Pretty early, but there are women in town who start work early. They had to have help with their children. I know someone who helps out there, so I'm sure of the time. You can start here at 6:30, and work until 11:00, that gives you a half hour for a sort of delayed breakfast, or long coffee break, whatever you choose to call it."

"When? When should I be there? What should I do next?" Rozella asked, not knowing where to begin.

"First of all, come in tomorrow. Come into the office as you have before. I have your application for work, and I'll have you fill out the employment papers before you see your boss. He doesn't like to see anyone before the trucks are loaded and out on the road. That usually takes until 7:30. We'll talk while you are waiting for him."

"Yes. I'll be there, for sure."

"And, wear comfortable clothes. You'll be doing cleaning, so don't dress up. You need to wear flat shoes, with rubber soles if you have them. And wear pants of some kind because you'll be crawling around in steel tanks. A handkerchief to put over your head would help, too, even though you'll be inside. It keeps the muck out of your hair, and your hair out of the tanks."

"I'll do that. Tomorrow, then. At 6:30 or before. I'll be there." breathlessly, she hung up the receiver.

How would she tell John, and Hannah? If she told them when they came in to eat their dinner, it would be very soon. She went about setting the table for the meal, even though it was too early. Then, she went upstairs to look for the right kind of clothes. Old blue jeans, that was easy. She had a pair left over from the days when she had the cottage, and painted it herself. Rubber soled shoes would be difficult, if not impossible. She might have to wear old rubber overshoes over her shoes, unless there were some in the attic. She had several cotton handkerchiefs, which were large enough to put over her hair. Tie it back, she assumed, knot it behind the head in the back, like a cook would, or a washerwoman. In fact, that was what she would be: a washerwoman, of sorts. She found her clothes and laid them out on a chair beside their bed. In Danny's room she worked to find enough extra clothes for him, and these she packed into a bag to take to he day care center.

Returning to the kitchen, she put the noon meal on the stove and finished setting the table by bringing out the bread and slicing it into heavy thick slices, which would wait beside the small crock of butter. Much different than the white margarine they used to eat, she remembered. The stuff that looked like lard, which she used to find in the 'baskets.'

By the time they came in to wash up, she had everything finished, and Danny was sitting in his chair waiting for something to eat. She didn't want to eat, her stomach was filled with fear and she felt sick. Telling them would bring on a tirade of complaints. John and Hannah banded together. She would never have thought John could move so much toward his sister's thinking. It hadn't been that long since they lived in the cottage, since Danny was born. Those days isolated and away from this house, they had felt closer, or she had felt closer.

But, she reminded herself. John had always gone to the Queist house, taking Danny. She could remember now. Clearly, she hadn't wanted to face it before, John had always been tied to this place. She was the one who didn't want to see what was always there. She had only heard him mouth the words which denied it by saying that he wanted to get away – and couldn't.

Before dinner, or after? She asked herself. After, if I can catch them long enough to listen to me. That way, we'll at least get to eat in peace. It seemed that the meal stretched on endlessly, as she waited. Danny was restless and didn't want to eat the salmon and potatoes that she had made into a casserole. He spit out the salmon. Hannah looked at him fiercely. "He had to learn that he can't have whatever he wants," she pointed out.

"I don't know what he wants." Rozella made excuses, "I only know what he doesn't want." She stopped herself before she said too much.

"He can't live on peanut butter sandwiches," John added.

"Maybe they aren't so bad, Actually, I like peanut butter better than salmon." Rozella answered. "But, now I have some news that I need to share with you," she ventured into the conversation that she feared. "I have a job."

Both of them dropped their forks to their plates and looked at her with interest. The first time, they had noticed her instead of the food she served at noon, she thought.

"Where?" John was the first to speak.

"At the creamery," she answered with some pride.

""Doing what?" Hannah wanted to know, as if she needed a reason or even a space in time with which to attack the idea of losing Rozella to a paid job.

"Cleaning vats and containers. It's only part time," she added the last in order to depreciate the job before they attacked. Maybe if they were defused, and thought she was not important enough to notice, or that the job wouldn't last long, they would be easier on her.

"That's a foul job, for a low-born uneducated woman," Hannah interjected.

"These days, you can't be choosey, besides, they won't let me teach. People made the laws that states a married woman can't teach." She wanted to add – people like you made the laws, but she didn't dare.

"You won't make any money there," John grumbled, jealous that she had found something which gave her value, even such lowly value.

"It will all be relative," Rozella argues, "if I work part time, the day care center will only charge for the hours that I work. It won't cost me so much to care for Danny, and I will be home with him for half a day…and here to do the housework as usual." She had found the argument that they couldn't refute. She would still be here to do the job, which she now did for them in half of the time, for nothing.

"How will you get back and forth?" John asked angrily. "I'm sure not going to take the time, or spend the gasoline money to drive you back and forth."

"I haven't asked yet, but if I can ride with Joan and Girard into town, perhaps I can get a ride home with the mail carrier who comes out this way, or even a creamery driver who is picking up milk cans along this road. I haven't worked it out yet. I just now found out."

It was a problem, she acknowledged to herself as well as to them, she hadn't thought it out yet. With full time work, she could have ridden both ways with Girard and Joan. A part time job meant that she had to create a way to get home at noon each day. She refused to let it stop her; there must a way, and she would find one. Anything short of walking would do.

"Tomorrow, then. I'll go to town. You may have to make your own dinner at noon, unless you can wait for me to get home. I should be here by noon if I get a ride. If not, it may take me the rest of the afternoon. You can't expect that everything will work out the first day. But—I must go to work tomorrow in order to keep this job."

"I've cooked before," Hannah stumbled away from the table. "I can do it again. It's just that I thought you were happy to be working here for your board and room."

There was no way to answer her, for she had left the room abruptly, not allowing time for an answer. Rozella felt more acutely why she needed to get away from this. It was clearly visible what her role was here. Couldn't John see what Hannah was doing to them both? As it was, he just sat there, speechless for the couple of minutes it took him to finish his coffee, then he, too got up and left, going outside without a word of further comment. It wasn't the end of this conversation, Rozella felt. There would be more to follow, as soon as they had thought it over, and gathered their arguments into a consolidated force.

She picked up the dishes, stacked them in the dishpan, picked up Danny and carried him upstairs for his nap. Undressing him, she felt glad to be escaping this if even for just a half day. All of the quiet hours, she had not noticed much about her life; she had not realized that she had been employed as a servant. Now, she could see more clearly. It wasn't a pleasant thing to confront. Reality could be frightening, when you could see what it would take to get through the illusion of your life and strike out to find reality for yourself.

Hannah was closed up in her room, John out in the barns, or wherever he went after his dinner, Danny asleep, and she was at last alone in the kitchen again.

Her clothes were laid out, Danny's clothes were packed into a bag, and she was determined. If she called Joan, now, or Girard, she could ask them to pick her up in the morning. She searched the phone book for the number of Girard's office, not finding it. Maybe she was so nervous that she couldn't see well, or the phone book was too old. She lifted the receiver once more, this time to ask the operator to ring the savings and loan office where Girard worked. She felt guilty that she wasn't trying to call Joan by trying to put a message through the day care center, but she waited for the call to go through just the same, recognizing her need to call him for help. When the girl at his office answered, she asked for him.

"Girard, here," he answered his phone.

"I got a job!" she announced to him, proud of herself at the moment.

"Wonderful. I knew you would do it. You were determined to change things, and this is the beginning. What kind of a job? Did you get a job at the restaurant where I told you to speak to the manager – where we had coffee?" he was running his sentences all together.

"No. I mean, I never did get to speak to the manager of that place, but the creamery had an opening. It's only a part time job, but it's a start. I'm so excited. Not many people even get a chance at anything these days."

"They'll be glad to have you, I know," Girard assured her, "Now, how do you get back and forth?"

"That's what I need help with...I need to have a ride into town in the mornings, Monday through Saturday, I think. Would I work on Sunday?" she wondered out loud.

"No, Rose, even the creamery closes on Sunday. But, yes, you can ride with us in the mornings. I'll pick you up tomorrow. What time?"

"Early. I hope not too early. What time do you go to town?"

"We usually leave about 6:30 because I like to start early, in order to get out in the field by afternoon. Joan works all kinds of crazy hours with no special schedule she has to follow."

"Oh, I have to be there earlier than that. I start at 6:30." Rozella said with fear in her voice. What if she couldn't get to town in time for her job?

"Then, I'll make it earlier. It's just a half an hour. I can handle that. But, we will have to work on how you will get home. Part time you said? What time do you get off work?" he asked.

"I should get off at 11:00 AM. That's what Tulla said, and that will let me get home by noon, in time to make dinner for John and Hannah, and do my work around here."

"In time to keep up your household chores?" he questioned. "I bet that helped pave the way for your leaving the house."

"Maybe. It's not over yet." She hesitated, because of Hannah's caution about using the phone. The phone was there for some reason, but it wasn't to be used if it cost money. "I must hang up. I'll be out in front in the morning. Is that okay?"

"You bet," he answered her. "Rose? I'm proud of you. Whatever you do, you do it well."

Rozella cried when she hung up. No one had ever told her they were proud of her, not once in her entire life.

John couldn't understand why Rozella persisted in looking for work. She had plenty to do around the house, and taking care of Danny. There was no way in a thousand years she could save enough from her meager earnings, no matter what they would amount to, that could begin to buy even a part of the land and homestead where she lived. Hannah was right; Rozella must be crazy to throw it all away and that is what she could do if she persisted in going against Hannah's wishes. The threat was there. Earning the Queist place was what they were doing – if they continued to work there, and didn't disturb their status on the land

He put his fork down along side of him in the haymow where he was working that afternoon. It was little enough to do; his was the hardest work, out in the fields with Hannah constantly beside him and never a moment's peace. Every idea he ever had was pushed aside, every question evaded. No matter how he tried to meet her standards, she pushed them higher. There was never a thank you, or a word of appreciation or acknowledgment. He could understand Rozella's frustration living here, but he couldn't see there was any way out of it; pitching it all away, any chance of ownership of even part of this estate was sheer craziness. All she would ever earn would never amount to anything except enough to pay for the shoes she might wear out, or the clothes that a job like that must require. The whole thing was pointless. It proved nothing, only making the point that it was possible to get work. Work without much dignity. When had a Queist ever worked at such demeaning labor – cleaning out creamery vats?

Hannah, shut up in her room, was thinking about the unexpected announcement Rozella had made. In a world where jobs were impossible to find, how had this woman managed to charm her way into any kind of a job? Had she talked to the manager or owner? Hannah felt sure that she had used her youth and appearance to wile her way into a job. There'll be no tips on this job, she muttered to herself. It won't be like a waitress who flirts with every man who leans over the lunch counter to get a better look down the front of her dress. If there are tips there, they'll be given in the back room, where no one will see. You can't trust anyone who will give that girl a job. They could end up like John, a slave to her support for the rest of his life.

Hannah wouldn't mind leaving the place to John, but he would have to stay put in order to earn it. There was no way, she would consider letting him go away to some far away city where he couldn't be reached when she needed him, and let him expect to inherit this. There was all the land surrounding the buildings. She hadn't sold it all. Pa had acquired acreage before the farms around him had started foreclosing. These pieces she had kept. The foreclosures, she had sold, only those. John didn't know this. It wouldn't pay to let him know. He still didn't know what Rozella was really like. Hannah could try to show him, but he still believed Rozella to be innocent. Innocent! That was a joke. Hannah had always known about her. Once they have used sex to get a man under control, women never stop. The pattern continues their whole life through.

She would work her to death. Just let her try to keep a job and try to keep things going here. There was no way Hannah would let her cut corners and make short shrift of things. Rozella would toe the line. This job idea had been her choice. It was great that she only got a part time job; now there was no evading her responsibilities here. Danny needed someone. Hannah would see that he got someone to care for him. He had always been her darling...pretty baby. If she couldn't have him, she would see that he was taken care of no matter how hard it was to drive this woman.

Rozella had come from worthless roots, and John could never be made to see that, not even when Pa had tried to point it out to him. He had insisted in marrying her. The only good thing that came out of the marriage was Danny, and he had Queist blood, her blood. He deserved to own this place, and Hannah had no intention of letting John get sidetracked by this harlot of a woman. There was always something just beneath the surface that Hannah could never quite put her finger on. She had a sense about such things.

There had been a time of innocence for Hannah, but it had been long ago – before Nels had left – before Pa's visits had begun. Before those days, Hannah had been innocent about men and women. Not any more. You got what you paid for, and you paid with your body. She looked down at her own body now: hard, brown, and calloused from work, turned her hands over, looking at the palms of them, at the scarred up fingers, and broken nails. There had been a time when she was soft and young, when her hair spun fine and shining down on her shoulders, when she smelled of something violet and sweet, and not of Lifeboy soap. Her overalls dropped upon the floor, she kicked off her shoes, and lay back on the bed. There was no way she would let Rozella take Danny off the land. He would stay here; if necessary he would stay here with she and John. Let Rozella go, but she would go alone, if that's what the young bitch wanted.

While they were occupied with their thoughts Rozella was busy in the kitchen. She was trying to cook ahead of time in order to make time for the hours she would be at work. Planning every meal ahead, she organized the foods so she could quickly get the noontime meal served as soon as she got home from work. That is, if she found a way to get home at all. Without a ride home from work each day, she wouldn't be able to take the job, but she couldn't let herself think of that. The clothes would be all right. This was the week that she didn't wash clothes. Next week she would have to worry about that. She made another peanut butter sandwich for her mid- morning snack and wrapped it in waxed paper. Even with Girard's two dollar bills in her purse, she didn't feel secure.(It wasn't good to spend them it unless it was a real emergency.) She checked her purse to see that she had everything she would need -- make up, a comb, and a handkerchief. Perhaps a net to put over her hair would be helpful. If they were concerned about her hair falling out into the vats she was working on, wouldn't a hair net help?

Tonight, the conversation over supper could become dreadful. She would try especially hard to please them, and maybe they wouldn't be so critical. Make a bread pudding, she thought. They both liked bread pudding. Treat the leftover stew to the glory of a hot biscuit topping. Biscuits and bread in the pudding, she asked out loud, as if someone was listening to her thoughts. But they like that, she answered. Oh, dear, it had begun – answering her own arguments the way old people did. It would be good to get away from here. Maybe there would be someone to talk to where she worked.

The supper hour lived up to her expectations. Both Hannah and John had been able to arrange their thoughts into neatly piled up objections, arguments designed to make her afraid, designed to keep her at home where they could keep control. She could see that, but it didn't make it easier for her. When she heard them speak, she reacted as if a jolt went through her, a reaction much like a jailed person would have to the adding of more bars to the windows.

John reminded her once more, "If you don't get a ride home, you won't be able to call me to come and get you. Don't plan on it. It would be better not to go then to get stranded in town."

"I won't be stranded in town, no matter what happens," she answered him. "Even if I have to wait until 4 o'clock or later when Girard and Joan drive home, I'll still get home. It may be late, but I'll still get here."

"It's that I'll be too busy. I just can't start this business of picking you up and dropping you off. It's much too expensive to warrant the small salary you will earn. And—you don't even know what they'll pay you," John excused his refusal.

"If you spend all of your time in town waiting for a ride home, you won't be able to keep up with the work around here," Hannah suggested. "That might make it necessary to hire someone from outside to do the cooking and cleaning. I don't like that at all."

"You don't need to worry about that. It will work out. I just know it will. Please wait and see before you decide how it will be," Rozella asked.

"If I have to hire someone to do the work, then I'll have to charge you board and room," Hannah smiled. It wasn't a nice smile. Even John looked horrified, hearing what she had said. The thought had never occurred to him. What? Hannah charge them board and room? That would be frightening. He was sure she couldn't mean that; it must have been just a threat to Rozella to keep her thinking about what working outside would mean.

"You won't, Hannah, you won't have to hire someone," Rozella promised. "I'll get it all done, no matter what. Please, let's not talk about it. If it doesn't work, I'll quit. How's that? That's what you want to hear, isn't it?"

"Not really," John said, lying. "We just want you to know what you're getting into."

Danny looked from one to the other as they talked, sensing somehow the tone of their voices was different than usual. He played in his food with his fork, mashing it into little piles, and then pushing them off of his plate. It wasn't what Rozella needed to be coping with at that moment. She cleaned off his high chair tray quickly, hoping that they wouldn't notice what he was doing. But, she wasn't lucky enough to have it go unnoticed. Hannah pointed at him, saying, "See. Even Danny knows there is something wrong going on here. I don't like to see him disturbed."

As if you care, thought Rozella.

John knew though, that this was not the case. Hannah had tried to keep Danny when he was first born. She hadn't wanted John to take him back to his mother. Taking him back to Rozella was against her wishes. It didn't sound like her to care, but that was only because she didn't talk about it. She didn't show any emotion. John had been the only one to see what she really felt for Danny. Sometimes the little touch on the head, done so quickly and without any notice, revealed what she felt about him. That was all that could be seen. The first weeks she had him, before Rozella even had held him, Hannah couldn't be separated from him. He had been like her own child, and, without a doubt, the only child she would ever have. She had held him for hours without ceasing. John thought she might have stayed up most of the night just so she could hold him. Yes, Hannah did care more for Danny than she ever revealed, he was sure of that.

There was little more to be said, Rozella had her ride to town in the morning. She promised them that she would be home by noon to prepare the noon meal. If not – she didn't know what to say. Maybe she would have to pay room and board. That would be the end of everything she had hoped to gain. Was that the method they would use? How? They couldn't stop her from finding a ride home before noon. There would be no way they could do that.

She cleaned up the kitchen without allowing herself to be drawn into more conversation, and cleaned up Danny's high chair, mopping around the floor beside his chair to get the stray bits of food up. After finishing with that, she took him up to bed, leaving the dishes stacked so she could get them done later.

"Will you be able to get the dishes done later?" she could hear Hannah asking, as she was walking up the stairs with Danny.

"Yes, I'll be down soon. Don't worry," she answered Hannah, feeling like screaming an answer to that question. She had never waited with dishes before; it was just this one night. She couldn't stand listening to them, no matter what they were going to talk about, she didn't want to be involved. The dishes could wait until she put Danny down for the night. The table was cleared for Hannah and John and their nightly coffee. That was enough. There was no way she could allow herself to become the centerpiece of hat table.

She finished the dishes later, as promised, trying not to hear what Hannah and John discussed. She didn't care. Her anger was filling her to the point where it was hard to keep quiet about anything. All she could hope for would be to get out of the kitchen and up the stairs before either of them could say a word to her. Trying to be quiet and not noticeable was her aim. The sooner to bed, the better, she thought. And she made it through those tense minutes, and into bed long before John came up the stairs.

Before dawn she was up and down to the kitchen making coffee, and taking time to dress herself, putting on the clothing Tulla had suggested. Danny was left in bed as long as he was quiet and not restless. This early he was apt to just lie there dozing while he sucked on his fingers. John was there close by if Danny called out. With breakfast laid out, she went up to get Danny and picked up the bag of his clothing to bring with as she brought him down for his breakfast. It was 5AM, and still dark out.

Hannah and John soon followed. Rozella didn't feel like eating anything at all, her stomach was feeling shaky. Queasy. She drank a little coffee, trying to clean up every dish as it was emptied. Would she ever get out of this kitchen? She thought. She could see the clock on the sideboard; it was almost six o'clock. "I have to be out in front at six," she said, as if anyone really wanted to hear it. Picking up Danny, she put his snowsuit on, as he fussed about being dressed so soon. She then gathered up the bag she had prepared for him, after putting on her own coat. They looked up at her from the table, as if horrified hat she would go off and leave them with their coffee cups.

In answer to the question in John's eyes, she said, "Just leave your cups when you're through. I'll get to them when I return. It will be before noon, you know. I'll have plenty of time to finish any cleaning up."

"You think you'll be home before noon?" was John's response.

When she closed the door with Danny under one arm and her bags under the other, she was relieved to be out of there. Thank God. The tension was stifling.

CHAPTER THIRTY-SEVEN

Hannah watched Rozella leave before she put on her mackinaw jacket and went out into the cold. No woman had ever left this place to go to a job. Her mother had never left at all; the days and years gradually establishing her confinement to the house; and, her body keeping her from moving about, as if a conspirator in keeping her from involvement in the affairs of the farm, her husband and family.

The days Pa had kept Hannah locked up in her room in order to break her spirit and redirect her thinking, as he called it, only made her more aware of Rozella's breaking away. Rozella owed a debt to this place, if she owed nothing to John or to Hannah, she owed it to the land that supported her, Hannah thought, and she owed it to the old house, which kept her sheltered. No one other than Hannah would have provided for her, even her own mother would not have kept her through a pregnancy, and then – made a place for the child. She owed Hannah. She owed John.

It would be better that Rozella came to understand that there was no way out, and the sooner, the better, Hannah thought.

Hannah could remember when she was still going to school, and the way her dreams had been then. There had been both dreams of the night, and dreams of the day. They came from reading, she supposed. When she read the books and magazines that were in the school, when she listened to the teacher talk about far away places, she had begun to think that she would go to those places, and that she would do those things. She had heard about artists in Paris, and she daydreamed about going there. Part of her dream was going to art school; and, the part of the dream that kept her sheltered from her surroundings was in the paints and paper that her mother had obtained for her. It had been Mama, too, who had encouraged her to paint.

For so long, she had hated Mama for letting her father use her and prohibit her from going away. She had blamed her for what Pa had done. She had blamed her for keeping her from running away with Nels. Now, she could see that leaving with Nels would only have meant leaving for another kind of trap. Hannah would have been trapped with Nels, and still not free to become a real artist.

These had all been dreams. She was sure of that, now. Everything was a dream, everything except what she could see and touch and be sure of as concrete reality. Reality was what is, she said to herself. It isn't far off lands. What if the things she had read were all fiction, and there were no far off lands? For all that she knew, these things didn't really exist. And that, too, was Rozella's problem, she decided. Rozella, too, had read too much.

Look at John. He had been victimized by his mother, too. He had been led to think that he could do most anything that he desired. He had been given schooling, and money to use in order to get his education. He had been given his mother's support, and loving attention, yet – he had returned with nothing.

In the end, there was only the land, and what you got from your parents. Everything else was part of an unreality created by a fiction of words.

What would it take to change Rozella? What would it take to make her realize that she was trying to do the impossible? If she would give up now, she would realize what she was doing was hopeless, and that the circle of her behavior would lead back to the same place. On the other hand, if she was allowed to continue, she would drift away, leaving them behind, but taking Danny.

That was another story. Taking Danny meant that Rozella would be taking away the part of the family who belonged the most to the land, their heir apparent. In the distant future, Hannah could see Danny taking over the farm when she became too old and ill, and John --? John would never be able to cope with management. He couldn't even cope with his own affairs. Pa had taught her that. He had pointed out to her along the way that Hannah must learn because John would never be able to learn. It had not been hard to believe. Everything that John did, or didn't do, had only served to prove Pa's point.

Danny, she would be able to direct and teach. She could form him as she had not been able to form John. John had been dominated by his mother.

After Hannah had been locked up "for her own protection," as Pa had called it, she was no longer able to talk with John. When she held everything about herself within, she held it from John, no longer enjoying the confidence of brother and sister. She couldn't do anything about his direction, or his understanding. There was only distance between them. It was as if they were separated by their association with the parents; each one on a side of an invisible barrier. They seemed lined up to do battle. Even now, it still remained that way when neither parent was there to create the barrier.

Only Danny represented the family no longer divided against itself.

John, too, watched Rozella leave. His thoughts were a confusion of misunderstanding. He waved at the Girards as they waved at him. He saw her take Danny, but with the certainty that it was the right thing to do – make her take him with her and become responsible for his care. It was her job. She inherited that when she gave birth to him. It was not a father's job to see to the child while the mother worked outside the home. Everyone knew that.

Rozella's determination to make a change, to work toward their independence, frightened him. He was surprised that she had found a job He was even embarrassed that she had found work when he had not been able to get a thing when he returned from Business College.

The money she would earn would not be enough to even begin to help them get a place of their own. That was a point that she didn't see. What would the money provide? It would only be a small amount that they could spend without asking Hannah for permission. It was a kind of freedom., but very small.

And, the money would be Rozella's, not his. It hadn't even been earned yet; still he was aware of it. Did he have a right to control the money she earned? Yes. He did have that right as head of his own household. Women had only earned the right to vote; they had not learned anything about business matters, or how to protect themselves in the world. Every man alive agreed with that. Most women couldn't even talk about what the issues were in local politics. And, they didn't understand anything about what was going on in Washington.

Yes, he had the right to control her money. All husbands had that right. When Pa married his mother, he took control of all the property and money that she inherited, as she inherited it. It was understood, and not something that he had devised. Even John's grandparents knew that when he married John's mother.

Sometimes Mama had talked about it, how her parents evaluated his father's position. In their world, it was better to have a working farmer without the benefit of good breeding, but one who would work the land, and appreciate it. And there had been Mama's age, too. She had been too old, an old maid in those days. She had no alternatives. If she had not married him, she would have been left on the farm alone when her parents died with no man to protect her, and no one to work the land. She had not been trained to do it; she needed someone.

Looking backward, John was seeking answers. Looking forward, he tried to see what the future would bring. If Rozella could only be patient, if she could only see that all they had to do was wait, and work. They would be rewarded. That was Hannah's promise.

Hannah, too, had no other way. She wouldn't marry, that was obvious. Through their hands the land would go to Danny. If there were no other children born to them, the land would be his alone. And whatever John and Hannah could create and salvage from the work of their combined lifetimes, would be his.

The question was now, how to get Rozella back into the house where she belonged, or how to use the money to complement their work around the farm. If he could get her to save it, put it away and accumulate it, later on, he could use it to buy farm equipment. The equipment that Hannah refused to buy might still be owned by John and Rozella. If – he couldn't get her to stay home, he might be able to get her to save the earnings and invest in the farm. That farm, he intended to hang unto, no matter what. He wasn't going to be forced into giving it up because of some woman's whim.

Women and their emotions were just too hard to deal with. He would be sorry that he had ever become involved with her, if it hadn't been for Danny. Danny was the future, and his reason to build, he told himself, picking up his tools in the barn and starting to repair the one wall that was rotted away in the grain storage bin.

With great hammering movements, he threw his weight into the sledgehammer he used to break out the old boards. The boards were so rotten that he didn't need all that effort, but at the moment, it made him feel good to be smashing things. The efforts eased as his mind eased, and the smashing turned into the building up process, when he sawed replacement boards and began to hammer them back in place. There were solutions, but being forced to confront them made him weary. He didn't need any additional problems. He didn't need problems created by a woman who didn't have any business meddling in a man's affairs.

As Rozella rode to work safely squeezed in between Girard and Joan, she was quiet. At that time of morning, when all was quiet, it seemed natural to turn inward, to think, to dream, to yawn. Danny was sleepy, lulled by the truck, he too, was quiet. He wouldn't be aroused until they got to town and he took off his warm clothes, and was able to move about with the other children.

At this point, she couldn't even guess what her earnings would be, and it wasn't important. The most important things on her mind were the ride home – how would she and Danny get home in the afternoon – and how to please the people she would work for.

"Do you have any ideas about how I can get home in the afternoon?" she asked, throwing herself on the mercy of Joan and Girard and their ideas once more. She hesitated because she felt guilty about how much they had done for her. Asking again for help, was painful, and embarrassing, too.

"I was thinking, ever since I heard that you would be working only mornings," Joan answered thoughtfully, "that we could work something out to help you, but let's try to find someone in town who goes your way every day at noon. Let me check on it today. I will have time to use the phone at work, and Girard – you might help, too."

"That's a county road that goes our way," he answered. "I'll almost always be able to take you home, if you have no other way to get home. Joan and I can work it out somehow. But there should be a regular route for someone going that way, and that would save us juggling the truck around and driving back and forth twice instead of once during the day."

"Oh, yes," Rozella acknowledged. "I wouldn't want to disturb your working hours, and the cost of gasoline – I would be glad to pay when I get some money for working. You couldn't pay for that much gas, running us back and forth. I could pay someone who has a route that way, and that would give him extra money, too."

"Actually, you might be sitting on your ride home," Girard smiled.

"What do you mean, for heaven's sake!" Joan commented, now fully awake.

"Not what you think Joan. Calm down. What I meant was – she may find a ride home with one of the creamery trucks," he laughed.

"I didn't think of that. Yes. That should be an easy one." Joan responded, and she was smiling, too, now.

"The only thing is, from what I saw, they load up in the earliest part of the morning. And probably all have left town long before I get off of work." Rozella offered. "It is a good idea. I'll ask Tulla today about it."

"You won't know until you ask," Girard said to her. "We'll phone around today, both of us. Don't you worry about it, just worry about your job, and asking at the creamery if anyone goes out at noon. Today, one of us will take you home, or if we can't, you'll just have to wait around until I get off, later in the afternoon. I'll get a message to you, or drop by. You get off at eleven?"

"Yes," she answered.

"Okay," he said, "I'll call you or be out in front with my truck to talk with you at 11:15. Just wait for the phone, or look out the window in front of the office there. One way or another, I'll get a message to you."

They approached the day care center, and he was slowing down to drop her off. The truck slid to a stop on the iced snow in front of the double doors, and Joan got out to let Rozella and Danny off. Before Rozella knew what happened, they were gone and she was alone in front of the doors, holding Danny and his belongings, preparing to drop him off before her first day at work.

When she reached the creamery, there was a sense of anxiety in the air, but it was a healthy anxiety, the involvement in getting a job done, on time and right. Everything done depended upon the time element as well as the product. People hurried from room to room, and truckers moved quickly across the loading docks. Tulla even seemed more hurried than usual, as she introduced Rozella to the foreman, and to the bookkeeper who would take down her records for the payroll. Tulla had to leave her with Grundy and his record keeping while she returned to the office to answer phone calls. The hurried sense of things made Rozella nervous, and she didn't know why. There was no reason for her to hurry, as she didn't even know what she was to be doing there. Her one worry was how to get home that noon, and even that worry was soon pushed out of her mind.

In her department, she was given the cleaning equipment, shown where the supply stores were kept, and left to work without much instruction. "Get them cleaned before the afternoon batch is brought in." With those words, she was left alone. Her bucket in one hand, and her towel scraps were in the other. The floor was wet already, so it must not matter if she spilled water and soap on the floor. She leaned into the first steel vat and began to scrub the sides. It appeared to be pretty clean. Once cleaned, however, there was the need for rinsing, and she could see that thorough rinsing would be important or the cheese would taste of soap.

Trucks left the loading docks, leaving the outside of the building quiet and empty. Activity on the inside became noisier, and movement increased. She could smell milk products, sour smelling, strong enough at times to make her stomach churn. The strong soap made her hands sore; when she wiped them off they were red already. The soles of her shoes were wet, and her socks up to her ankles were wet, too, from slopping water over the side of the giant mixing vats when rinsing. Her hair was plastered down tightly against her forehead, and it was wet, too, but that was from sweat. No wonder they asked you to wear something over your hair. Your sweat could run down your cheeks and fall into the cheese. She used to like cheese, but as the time went on during the morning, she wondered if she would ever eat it again .The smell of sour milk lingered in the air.

In mid-morning a bell sounded and workers stopped the machines, and stopped their moving about the building. It was their practice to have coffee all at one time evidently. The sudden quiet spell was like permission given for her to stop and rest. She wiped her forehead with the back of her hand, and leaned on the closest pillar, which stretched into the high white ceilings, which glowed with a high gloss that made them shine almost as if lit up. This was a clean place. And of course, that was why she had been hired – to keep it clean.

Tulla came by to find her and suggest that she take her time off to find the restroom because she wouldn't have another chance to get there. She also suggested that Rozella might want to have a cup of coffee and a donut, or cookie, because it would be a long time between the time they started in the morning, and the time she would get off. "You won't notice it at first because everything is so new to you, but you will get hungry. And you need your strength to work like that. At home, it's different; we don't burn up so much, in spite of what we may say about how hard we work at home. Eat something. Tomorrow, you bring yourself a little "lunch" for a morning snack." She offered Rozella a piece of yellow cake that she had brought from her home, and a cup of coffee.

"Thanks. Are you sure this isn't taking away your lunch?" Rozella asked.

"No. I brought extra for you. No one thinks about food when they start working here. It's after the first week that you begin to notice what your body needs. It takes that long to understand what you're trying to do. After that—it's different. You're an old hand then." Tulla smiled at her. "Take it."

She hadn't noticed she was hungry until she put the cake into her mouth, and then, it tasted like something made in heaven. Working made you hungry, she could agree. Rozella had no idea of how hungry she had become until she started to eat.

As the rest of the morning hours passed, she didn't even think about what she could do about a ride home after work. There was a sort of whistle sound at 11, which must have invited the whole crew to break for lunch. Would there be another whistle at 12 to put them all back to work, she wondered. It did help her to remember to quit. Her day was ended with that whistle.

Stopping by Tulla's office on her way to find her coat and prepare to leave before she kept Girard waiting outside, she found people going over papers that lay on Tulla's desk. She had to wait in order to talk to her.

"Do you know of anyone who goes up county road #6 after 11, Tulla? I'm trying to find a way home each day. I thought that if a creamery truck went that way, it might be possible to ride home."

"You don't have a ride home?" Tulla asked, and for a moment, her face reflected her worry that Rozella might not stay on the job without a ride home.

"I have friends who will help me out by taking me home when I finish work, but I don't think I should ask them to do that all the time. It's too expensive, and too inconvenient for them. They suggested there might be a driver going out that way."

"Tell you what, I'll try to find out, but I can't get to it right away. I'll let you know tomorrow. You have a ride today?"

"Yes. I'm pretty sure, but I haven't looked out the window. No one has called for me?" Rozella answered.

"No, no calls, but there is a truck waiting at the curb, and since it's one I've not seen here before—it might be your ride."

Rozella looked out the window of the office, "You're right. That's my ride." The sight of Girard waiting patiently in the truck, gave her joy. His face, his caring enough to be there...that made the day turn suddenly beautiful.

She finished putting on her coat and smiled at Tulla as he left, saying – "I'll see you in the morning. I sure hope that I did a good enough job today."

Tulla waved at her as the door closed.

Together they went to pick up Danny, and began the ride home. "I'm sorry, Rose, I won't have much time today. I'll just be able to drop you off, then return to work."

"That's okay. I didn't expect you to do this much. The morning passed so quickly today that I didn't get a chance to ask about who drives out our way until just now. I'm sorry, Girard."

"It's not that, you should know that, Rose. I want to do everything I can to help. I – just wanted you to know that I wanted more than a quick drive home and dumping you off."

Danny looked up at him, as if understanding what he meant by that. "It can't...we can't...every time. I know, Girard," she answered, knowing then what he had meant. She felt very self-conscious; as if he thought that all she wanted was the physical contact he could give her. "I'm happy just to be with you. To have you do this for me is more than enough. Tomorrow, I promise that I'll get someone else to give me a ride home."

"That's not a problem, Rose. We want to help you get started. You can't expect that it will all work out the very first day. Give yourself time. At least a week. Let me do this all week and then we'll talk about it again. You need a chance to at least get to know people, and the business."

"Tomorrow," she found herself promising again, as he dropped her off.

"We'll see you in the morning, if not before," he answered her. "Please," he reached for her hand, "take it easy." he squeezed her fingers, then patted Danny on the head, as she lifted him out of the truck.

The morning was over then, and it was only 11:45. The old kitchen clock was pointing to the nine as she and Danny entered the door. She had put in her day's work, and it was still before noon. "I can do it," she said aloud to no one in particular. It was a point of exhilaration, seeing there was still time to get dinner on the table before 12.

Hurriedly, she hung up her coat, took off Danny's outside clothes, and checked to see that his diaper was still dry. It wouldn't be long until she could try to toilet training him. She was lucky the day care center would take him since he was still in diapers. She put him in his high chair, and began to put dinner things on the table before John and Hannah would come in to eat. Sliced cold meats, bread, jam and coffee. The coffee pot was soon making sizzling noises as it began to reach boiling. She searched through the pantry for something to add to the cold sandwiches. Left over vegetables, and some tomato sauce, canned last summer. Put that together into a pot and add some rice. Home made soup. Wouldn't that make a good hot meal? There were some sugar cookies left in the cupboard. Put those on a place, and it would be dessert, along with some canned fruit.

She was going to make it, she told herself, as she rushed from pantry to table, and back to the stove, getting everything ready on time. Just on time, for the door opened for Hannah, and John was close behind her. A little late, and that helped. Why did they linger today until after 12? Was it because they didn't expect her to get the job done? They were hoping that they wouldn't have to get their own meal put together, that's all.

After washing up in the kitchen sink, they seated themselves, looking about the table to see that there was plenty to eat, before even talking to Danny. Exchanging looks with John, Hannah asked about the job first. "How as the new job?"

Rozella was both surprised and pleased that she asked. "Good, I guess. The morning went so fast that I didn't have time to think. I was home before I knew what happened."

"How did you get home?" John asked.

"Girard."

"You mean you have to ask him to take you home every day?"

""Well, it isn't what I wanted to have happen, but there hasn't been enough time to get myself a ride. Something will turn up. I only got around to asking this noon."

"Humph..." was more of a noise coming from Hannah than a comment.

Was dinner any different today, Rozella asked herself, looking around the table and trying to remember what they usually ate at noon? The radio was now playing softly in the corner, a voice giving the price quotations from the marketplace. John had turned it on when he came in. The table looked as it did on other days.

It was mainly her own feelings that created the difference; she was feeling that she hadn't done justice by the meal. John was looking at it as if she hadn't prepared a thing. He turned over his spoon in his bowl of soup, pushed his bread around on his plate, and Danny was watching him. It wasn't more than a couple minutes and Danny was pushing his bowl away and laying his spoon down. What's wrong with it? Rozella questioned. She tasted it. It needed salt, that's all. "Here's the salt shaker," she offered it to John. "It needs a little more salt, that's all."

Hannah smiled, but didn't say anything.

Mama never could cook, Hannah was remembering. Pa used to push his plate away from him whenever she tried to cook. He could hire a cook, he said, no reason to tolerate such dull food. Hannah had never learned how to cook much better than her mother, but she was aware of what Pa liked to eat, and in that way usually pleased him, by catering to him.

What women never seemed to learn, she thought, was the way to please a man is to give him what he wants, not what you think he ought to eat. Women, who have husbands, never seem to understand that. "Humph..." she made that noise in her throat again.

John asked, "When are we going to have a full meal again, Rozella? We used to have roast beef and mashed potatoes once in awhile. This is cold food, leftovers made into soup; it's not what we're used to having. And, besides, we need more than that after a hard morning of physical labor. My father always used to say, you have to feed the farm hands, or they can't work. They need strength. He wouldn't listen to Mama's ideas. In her mind, all you needed was some kind of food to stop the hunger. She didn't know what hard work was, so she couldn't judge what was needed. Is that the problem, Rozella?"

"No," she answered, "I thought we had eaten this kind of food before. It didn't seem so unusual."

"Maybe you ought to work like we do, then you'd know more about it? Huh?" he asked.

"I worked pretty hard this morning." she argued that point.

"I'll bet. Was anyone around to check up on you? How could you know? If you don't do the job, you'll end up fired. That's probably what happened to whoever had that job before you had it. Are you sure they didn't have all day to do the job? Sometimes, that is what they try to do these days...cut the time for a job in half."

"That's why it works out best if you work for yourself," Hannah added to his commentary on jobs.

By this time, Danny was whimpering and refusing to eat at all. Rozella took him down and washed his face and hands. "I'll take him up to his room," she said, "too tired to eat, maybe."

"I don't doubt that," Hannah agreed with this, "He hasn't had the kind of a morning he was used to – here at home."

Hannah left her dishes on the able, as she always had done before. Only this time -- Rozella noticed it. With the whole day to wait of them, and take care of the household duties, she had not really paid any attention to the habit of John and Hannah to let her wait on them. Today, it was irritating her. John, too, left his mess behind with the unspoken statement of the uneaten food spread all around his plate. There was Danny's untouched bowl, John's barely touched plate and bowl, and Hannah's bowl, in which no soup at all had been ladled up. Messages.

What would they say if they had to make their own noon meal? Rozella was asking herself. Maybe she ought to give them a try. No, that would be a dangerous display of temperament. It was hard enough to get started working outside this family, least of all challenge them to take care of themselves. Not now. Keep your self-control. She walked over to the radio which John had left playing when he went out, and turned it off. Why must she listen to his choice of programs? Who made these rules?

But, it was Hannah who heard a voice shouting in her head: **I make the rules**. I make the rules. That was what Pa had shouted at her. The question now would be: how would Hannah enforce her rules, and the rules were hers now. Neither John nor Rozella had a right to make rules. They had no right at all. If Pa could only talk. If they could hear what he really said. Then, they would know.

She had learned from his hardness. The first weeks were a nightmare. The discovery that Nels was gone, and the cottage was empty hurt her in ways she wanted to forget forever. There never would be another man in her life, so what difference did anything make from then on? Pa could do what he wanted with her. Never again would she allow herself to hurt that much. And she didn't, she prided herself, remembering. She could hold herself tight, wound up inside like a steel rod. When Mama died, she showed nothing because she had allowed herself to show no feelings. Feelings were for fools. Whenever you gave in to your feelings people turned on you and hurt you.

Death for people was no more than an animal's death. An animal could turn away, walk away, without tears, and go on with living until the last minute, when it would drop without

thinking or caring. That was the way it should be. Mama died and it made no difference. Pa died and he lived on in her head, telling her what to do, directing everything on the farm whenever she chose to listen. It was his will that shaped things.

His will – would never give in to John's will. Rozella's actions would never be forgiven. Pa would have shown Rozella where she was intended to be. She was lucky that she had been allowed to marry John. Everything was against it. Even John had not been eager to marry her, Hannah was sure of that. He only got caught up in the ethics of the day. Ethics and animal husbandry did not mix. Male animals had no allegiance to offspring or mates, except for the transference of the control the male held.

That would be Danny...from John to Danny. And Danny's birth was an accident like any animal mating in the woods. Hannah would have to guarantee Danny his rights. He would need her to do that because John was weak. Pa always said that John was weak, and because of his weakness, John couldn't be trusted.

Night would come. She would talk to John, but in all of her talking she would never reveal to him what he wanted most to know: what happened to the money? He always hinted about money, wanting to know what the sale of the properties had gained and what she had done with the money. That money, she kept hidden for Danny. When he was grown and ready, she would give it to him. For now, it was safe from John, and Rozella. She could talk circles around John, whose intelligence was limited by his experience. What John didn't know was that inside of her lived Pa's cunning and experience. Whenever she had need of it, it was there to be drawn upon and used like a sharp weapon.

Thinking about how to control John, and to make the best of Rozella's big mistake – leaving the farm in order to work in town—she drifted off into her afternoon nap. Across her bed, staring up at the ceiling, her mind had been making patterns against the ceiling tiles, made of pressed metal which had been painted with ivory enamel, she floated, feeling sure of herself.

Sleepily, she drew the old coverlet in a bunch and rested her cheek against it. Breathing deeply, she could smell Pa on the coverlet where he had laid like an animal of the land, talking about the land and the people and the stupidity of the farmers around him.

He was a successful farmer, but he hated farmers. His was a mind that reached for more than the land; he was a manipulator of both money and people. He only read what he needed to read in order to see which way to bet upon the future. One thing you can count on, he always had told her, is man's greed. If that's the only stable emotion man has, then stay on the side of greed, develop your own so you may be greedier and steal from you friends, neighbors, and family. If you don't – they will steal from you. She slept, hearing his voice, smelling his smell on the old coverlet they had often shared over the years.

Downstairs, Rose busied herself cleaning up the kitchen, and preparing something for the evening meal. Laundry had been done. She was glad that she never let it collect, but finished the ironing as soon as the washing was done. She had changed her clothes, not because she needed something else for her kitchen work, but because she smelled like sour milk, and soap and stale water from her morning's work. Washing herself, and changing into clean pants and shirt, she felt better. Now, what could she make for supper that they wouldn't sneer at? Dinner had been such a bad experience.

Danny slept longer than he usually did, but because he had played harder at the day center, she was sure. That part was a good part. The energy he expelled there was good energy, and he would learn to play with other children, too.

She wiped down their pantry shelves, washed the floor, which seemed to have collected more footprints than usual. Was it possible that they had deliberately brought dirty feet into the kitchen in the same way they had turned up their noses at the meal she had prepared for them at noon?

She would not give in, was her thought. In time, they would adjust. Even she and Danny would be making adjustments. If she could only not let herself get upset, if she could only stay calm, and keep going. The first problem at hand was the ride home. Tomorrow, she would know more. There had to be a way. When she heard the kitchen door close, she looked up in surprise from her knees where she was wiping up the floor. John had come in early. He never quit his work in the barns this early. Normally it would be dark before she would see him. Hannah and Danny would sleep upstairs while she got her housework done downstairs. Danny would get up and she would dress him. Then, a little later, Hannah would come down and expect to find a fresh pot of coffee made and waiting for her. Afternoon coffee. Then, Hannah would go out to the chicken coop and finish up her day's work there, cleaning up and feeding the hens, and checking for any eggs which she would bring in when she came in for supper.

This was early for John. Her face registered her surprise. What was on his mind?

"Is there any coffee?" he asked.

"Not this early. I usually don't make it until Danny gets up from his nap, but I'll put some one, if you wish." She got up from the floor, picking up her pail of scrub water, as she had finished the wiping up she was doing when he entered.

"Just set that by the door, and I'll empty it when I go back down to the barn," he said.

First time you've thought of that, she was thinking as she went to get the coffee out, setting the pail down beside the door. How many days and weeks and months had she carried out her own slop water because the buckets used to collect the small bits of wash water, or water used to clean vegetables filled too soon.

There was a cream pitcher left on the sideboard along side the sugar bowl, and she put that in the center of the table, along with some cups and saucers and spoons. The coffee pot was filled and on the stove, before she returned to the kitchen table, thinking that this was unusual for him. What did it mean? Her hands were red from morning scrubbing compounded by afternoon scrubbing. What difference did it make where you cleaned? The only difference was you could get paid for doing it. That was what her mother had done – cleaned in many places. Because they had lived in town instead of the country, she could walk to work at any home, which employed her, and she often got jobs, which weren't cleaning. Dorothea Ehalt's jobs as temporary maid for some families consisted of just setting tables and waiting on guests, handling beautiful silver and linens, making the glass sparkle, and often cooking sumptuous meals. No. Mama had not always scrubbed floors

How times had changed, Rozella laughed at herself silently. She used to think that kind of work was too good for her, and that she would never do it. What would her sisters think if they could see her now, scrubbing both at home and at work? They would never believe it. She had turned into the scrub woman and washer woman that her mother had been There were parallels to be drawn here that she had never seen before: Rozella was enslaved to a husband who couldn't break away from his family, and Mama had been enslaved by a husband who couldn't stop drinking.

Mama had children to provide for. Rozella had a child to provide for. Her husband's family intended to care for the child and his needs, but this protection had exacted a price from her, and it extended the control of the family to the child. In exchange for home and clothing and food, the child would belong to them. It had started in the beginning with Danny's birth. She had fooled herself into thinking that being with him had protected him, and kept him safe in her love. It had been a facade. Danny would belong to the Queists as long as she stayed in this house.

The coffee boiled and Rozella brought out a small plate of cookies for their late afternoon coffee. Her mind wasn't on this and she felt his presence to be an intrusion. She wanted to think about what to do with the coming day.

"What's for supper?" John asked, and it was the first time he had ever asked that question. The coffee simmering down and the grounds dropping left it ready for drinking. She poured them each a cup.

CHAPTER THIRTY-EIGHT

By the end of the week the combined efforts of Joan and Girard, and Rozella had been rewarded. They had found Rozella a ride home at noon. There was a mail truck, not the regular carrier, who went that way; the idea about the regular carrier had proved fruitless as all the route carriers left very early in the morning. All regular carriers were traveling back into town by noon. The mail truck that left at 11:30 in the morning was contracting to haul a load of mail for a small community further north. This truck didn't leave until later in the day because of the incoming mail on the train, which didn't arrive until after 9:30 in the morning.

This driver had hesitated because it really wasn't legal for him to have passengers, and even though he owned his truck, he was bound by the laws regulating the hauling of mail. Girard had talked to him, asking him to please help Rozella out until she could find some other way to get home. "Always be sure to be on time," Calvin, the truck driver cautioned Rozella, "If you are late it will attract too much attention. I'll pick you up every day at the corner one block down from the Lutheran church, but I won't be able to wait."

"I'll be there," she had promised, wondering afterward if she should have offered money.

"You can't," Girard answered her question about money. "Maybe later you can do something for him. Give him a gift, or give him a thank you card with some money in it. As it is, money would only make his position worse. Be glad of it. You can't afford to pay anyone."

It worked out very well. She was able to get to Danny, and get to her corner every morning. By noon, she was home and busy in the kitchen. She was only a half hour later than she had been when Girard had driven her home the first week, but John acted like it was a great inconvenience. "How do we know when to come in for dinner?" he asked, as if they were children.

"All you have to do is look. The truck stops at the mail box out by the road. Besides, the driver travels on a time schedule that's so important that he hardly can slow down. It always will arrive here at the same time. His truck runs like a railroad car. In fact, that's the reason for the trip. There is no railroad that runs out to Roseville."

Destroying John's reasons for complaint was beginning to be a regular task. On top of his objections, which were regularly voiced, she had Hannah's strange commentary running through every evening meal. It seemed like Hannah had time in her room each afternoon to think about what to say at night; and it was at night that she voiced her ideas. At least, Rozella thought, I have until evening to be free of her; with John, it's all day long. The only time I'm free of his commentary is when I'm at work.

Working hours passed so quickly that she hadn't found time to become acquainted with the other people there. During her coffee break in mid-morning, she had begun to exchange a few words with the women, but by the time they gathered together and got their coffee poured, it was time to go back to work. Fifteen minutes didn't seem long when you used part of it to for the rest rooms. There wasn't any other time for the women to use the facilities. They couldn't take extra time for that because they had a definite time frame in which to finish the job. Saddled by a time frame, it didn't take a strong arm to supervise them. Doing the job was the most important thing. To keep a job, they must complete what was expected. Coffee breaks, and probably lunch hours for others, went by with barely a nod between bites.

It was healthy activity, but she did have time to think about her life and what went on at home. When she was teaching, there was no time to think of other things. Her mind had been occupied every moment. In this type of work, her body was busy, but her mind had time to work on its own. Scrubbing didn't take thought, and once the task was learned, her mind never stopped working – on other things.

Hannah's evening comments had become stranger. Last night she had asked, without any introduction to the topic, "How many men are working at the creamery?"

Rozella had told her that she didn't know. But Hannah had smiled in reply, saying, "I'll bet." Every night she had a different way of asking about Rozella's work, and every night the direction of the question had a certain pattern.

John would watch and listen, as if taking notes on Rozella's answers. Even if he didn't think up the questions, he seemed to be very interested in her answers. Rozella felt constantly surprised that they could wonder about the social implications of her job, when the time went by so fast that she hardly had time to go to the toilet during the morning. On the way home, she was holding Danny on her lap, so she surely couldn't have an affair with the truck driver. John had never guessed about her relationship with Girard, but now Hannah asked questions that were designed to accuse her, or to make John question her behavior.

Hannah had a specific direction of thought, obviously. It became like a tennis match, trying to answer the questions parried. Days went on into the first weeks of work, and a month was completed before she knew what had happened. She had her first pay check, and that became difficult to deal with because she had to cash the check, and then pay the day care center before she could get any idea of what she had earned during the first month. Again, she had to depend upon the Girards; she had no way of getting back into town to cash a check, and the driver couldn't wait for her to get to a bank.

Girard came over when she called, took her check to his own finance company, cashed it and brought it back. There had been no other solution, except to give it to John to cash, and if she had done that – she was afraid that she would never see it again. In fact, she wasn't sure that he would even give her enough to pay the day care center. Her thinking almost frightened her, but what was happening at home made her become paranoid about the money she had earned. If nothing else, she wanted to put it aside for Danny, and for her own security. She couldn't know what to expect of life.

Looking down at the cash Girard had left her with after the first check was cashed, she felt suddenly rich. She knew better, but teaching had paid her $50.00 a month, and it was full time. This was only scrubbing, she was a cleaning lady, that's all, and the work was only part time. The forty dollars in her hand was more than she had expected. She would be able to pay the day care center, and have quite a bit left over. Now, the task would be – how to hide it from John.

Money was an issue with the Queists, and maybe it was with her, too, she acknowledged. After all, she had gone to work in spite of all the obstacles to earn it.

The hardest, coldest days passed. Rozella's ride home could be depended upon regardless of the weather, because as the old saying went – the mail must go through. The snow became thinner; the snow banks along the road were shrinking imperceptibly each day as the sun became warmer.

In late March, Joan and Girard spent a Saturday evening with them, and that day chose to tell them that Joan had found a job in a federal agency in Washington, D.C. All that was left was a place for Girard in that area. They felt it wouldn't be difficult. If they could sell their farm, they could move right away because that would free him to look for work without worrying about income for a while. If the farm didn't sell, and buyers were few these days, Joan would have to go on ahead and wait for him to join her.

The feelings Rozella responded to as she heard the news that night were very painful. Girard had told her, tried to forewarn her of what was coming, but hearing it put so lightly, she then realized that it meant the loss of two of her friends: Joan, who had been her closest friend, and Girard whose love had kept her alive through the months of emptiness and confusion. He had helped her focus on her future, but now he was leaving her – alone, in order to create his own future.

She hadn't looked far enough, hadn't dared to hope about any kind of a relationship with him. Somehow her eyes had closed to that, in fear perhaps, but she had avoided thinking about it. Closing her eyes to it had not prepared her for facing life without him. Where would the joy be? What would give her something to hope for from day to day? Danny? The job? That would be all that was left. She could feel tears forming in her eyes, and didn't know what to do with them. It was no time to cry.

Joan looked at her and saw the tears before Rozella could try to wipe them away. "I'll miss you, too," she said softly. "But we will promise to see you. If you can't come to us, then we'll come to you."

"You mean you would come back here to see us?" Rozella asked. After all, her own family never came to see her. No one had ever come to see them. Since she took Danny back home to see her mother that one time, no one in her family had come to see them. Danny had not even met her sisters. John had never seen them, for he had never gone with her on the two trips home. Travel was for rich people; it wasn't for the poor.

"We would, definitely," Girard answered for her, his own eyes soft. He must have thought about it, Rozella, internalized. If I could only talk to him, right now.

John was quiet, as if this friendship was hers and something he was not really involved with. But that was his way, the Queist way; they were never involved with anyone. They walked away, stood alone, removed from the rest of the world, protecting their privacy.

Confused by feelings she couldn't turn away, Rozella endured the rest of the evening without joy in their company. She dreaded going home, yet felt every moment to be pain filled. At night when they were alone in bed and it was dark all around her, she would have to face the thought of being totally alone, not just for a day, a week, or a month, but for always, and that was frightening.

As the weeks followed, things didn't improve around the Queist house. Hannah's commentary in the evening was sporadic, and if Rozella listened closely, it didn't always make sense. John chose not to listen to it, and when Rozella questioned him about it, he shrugged off her inquiry, as if irritated. The patterns of Hannah's daily living changed also. It would not have seemed so strange if she had not been so rooted into time schedules of her own creation at all times in the past. Now there were times when she wandered out into the farm buildings right after eating her noon meal, then came back into the house at 3:30, about the time Danny was getting up from his nap. John didn't pay attention to the variance because it didn't affect his activities.

It did affect Rozella, because Hannah would ask for things when Rose least expected it. Sometimes she would want to see supper on the table at 4PM in the afternoon. After supper, she and John usually stayed at the kitchen table to discuss financial matters, or he listened to her and watched her pay the bills. Later she would to up to her room and shut the door, not appearing again until the next morning. John didn't care, as he didn't miss their sessions. It did upset him because he couldn't make any impression on her with his questions or answers. It was easier this way, if she turned away from him.

"But does she still get everything done? Attended to, I mean?" Rozella asked. "Are the bills getting paid?"

"I can't imagine her not paying the bills, and she still expects me to go into town on my regular schedule. She never forgets to ask me for any money that I get from sales of chickens or eggs, or milk and cream."

"True, Hannah's mind is always sharp when it comes to money." Rozella could agree with that, it was her actions that confused her. Even though she was very tired by the time she finished the supper dishes, she did not miss Hannah's words, which now seemed to be directed to an unseen person over her shoulder, and not to Rozella. It would be a comment on the state of the world around them, or a moral debate in which she took both sides. It would be mumbled at times, and difficult to hear.

John said that they had no right to judge Hannah just because she had changed her routine. The fact that they were surprised by changes meant that they were the ones who couldn't change. Who was it that had become stuck in a rut, as he put it?

But, he did take time to look through the mail, and tried to find the records that she no longer showed to him. He must have been more concerned about what Hannah was doing, or not doing, than he wanted to reveal to Rozella.

In her own mind Rozella was trying to face the departure of the Girards. Before this had become a definite eventuality, she had not thought about her relationship with Girard with any reality. It was as if the two of them had lived in a dream world, and anytime she was confronted with how she felt, she would put it aside, and not choose to deal with it. She could avoid thinking about it, and isolate her feelings by containing them, just as if she could close the doors of the world about them in thought, as carefully as in deed. Even the parting with Joan was painful, and she had not thought of that either.

Strangely enough, the one person who was closest to her, who could most understand her, was the one who shared her life in the strangest fashion. No one else in the community was close to her emotionally. Tillie had been a good friend to her, but Rozella had kept her personal feelings to herself.

Without them, what would there be? Who would be close to her? The world loomed empty and fearful when she thought of her loss. Ending the relationship with Girard meant ending the happiest moments of her life, and without having any idea of when this kind of happiness could possibly come her way again. It was like saying goodbye and closing the door to the future at the same time. She wanted to think that Girard really loved her, but she couldn't allow herself to think that because of what she felt about Joan.

Even remembering the strange comments that Joan had shared with her, the talk of her changing sexuality seemed unreal. Rozella couldn't believe it, recalling Joan's discussion of her relationship with Girard. There was no way two people could go on living together and accept a relationship other than "normal." Was there?

It must have been Joan's feelings for Rozella; maybe she felt it was a way to shield her from hurt, all the while knowing that the two of them would be moving away and rebuilding their life, far away where they would be safe from women like Rozella. What do I mean *"like Rozella,"* she asked herself when that thought went through her head?

These thoughts dogged her working moments. Scrubbing out the huge cold vats, her mind was never still. Lying in bed at night, remembering how it had been with Girard and her...she came back to these thoughts. The thoughts were painful enough to keep her from eating properly, and again, as when she was pregnant and going without food because of poverty, she could not eat. This time it was an emotional refusal of food. As days passed, she lost weight, but told herself it was because of her work.

Mornings she rode to work with Joan and Girard, and she couldn't ask how their plans were going. She waited, with fear in her heart, for them to tell her – when they were going away. When they dropped her off in front of the day care center, it was with pain that she watched them go.

It was into the second month she had been working when Joan told her that she would be going on ahead of Girard. She said this so casually that she could hardly be heard. They were together on the way to work when she said this. Girard's hands were still upon the steering wheel of the truck and he kept his face turned toward the road. There was a moment of silence, which made it seem as if nothing could be said.

Words shaping themselves wouldn't come to Rozella. She had spent no time alone with Girard, so they hadn't time to talk to each other about anything. Everything was jumbled up in her head. It meant that Joan would leave before Girard. It meant that Girard would be there alone. For how long? There was no way of knowing. Joan reached up and touched her shoulder. "I'll be sorry to leave you, Rose, but it won't be forever. Maybe we could spend a Saturday night together, just as we have done so many times before – sometime before I leave?"

"Yes. Oh, yes, please." Rozella shook herself. "I'm sorry to be so thoughtless. You caught me by surprise. You know how Hannah is... can we bring some dinner over to your house? I can plan something... cook it there?"

"Sure." Joan answered for both of them. "And, how is Hannah these days? Last time we talked, you were worried about the way she was acting."

"Maybe it was all in my head. I just thought she was different. John doesn't agree with me."

"We can talk Saturday night, if that's the best night for you to come over. I'll leave next week, so any time after that you'll have Girard to entertain – and we hope he won't be here for long."

"Yes. Yes. I'll ask John, but we don't do anything else, so Saturday night should be a good time. See you then." Rozella got out with Danny, dropping one of his blankets on the ground. She had to bend over while holding him and pick it up, feeling very awkward and nervous because she was keeping them waiting for her recovery.

Leaving? So soon. It would leave Girard and her alone, but this would be only for a while. So much, and so little, a contrast in living that would be hard to handle. To have so much of him, only to lose him would only hurt more. She put Danny down on the floor where his teacher was involved with babies, looking to be sure that the floor had a warm rug for him to sit on. Smiling vaguely at the young woman there with the children, she hurried away to the door,

and toward her job.

From now on she would be counting the moments until she and Girard could be together alone. In the meantime, she would plan what to make for their little party before Joan would leave them.

CHAPTER THIRTY-NINE

Hannah didn't like to sleep anymore. The afternoon naps that had kept her from thinking, and were her escape from the daily routine, had left her. It didn't work anymore. Instead of thinking, she would lay there staring at the ceiling, until the time went by. She made up stories and let them appear on her ceiling. Like marionettes, her created people walked across the blank stage of her mind, they turned and talked, usually saying things she wanted to hear.

But there were times when they went other ways now, and began to say things that she had never imagined, or allowed them to think when she was controlling this pageant of daydreams. It had started out like counting sheep; it was a way to fall asleep, and sleep was a pleasant escape from thoughts.

No longer. The puppets had become like bad children. They were misbehaving. Today, she willed them to be silent. She tried to make her mind turn the ceiling black, and it refused. The ceiling stayed white, just as it always had been. Maybe this time, they would not appear. If she had not summoned them, they should stay away, she told herself, keeping her eyes closed, and then opening them slowly with the smallest bit of light showing through her eyelashes. She was hoping there would be no one there.

It was blank. She breathed deeply, sighed, and turned over to put her face into her pillow. Maybe she would sleep today. With her eyes closed, colors swept into the screen before her eyes, swatches of color, like stripes, washing across a sheet of paper or a canvas – green, gold, and pale yellow.

There used to be a tangle of green in the spring, the spring green of the grass, weaving itself together against the moss and small flowers bursting from the new weeds under the trees. Both lucid and fluid, colors drifted like new clouds after a rain, becoming like opening blossoms caressing themselves in the breeze. There was a silent seduction there with the sun shining through flowers. In her dreams, the flowers were fading now, as if trying to become invisible, and then they turned suddenly into heavy and opaque things and the things became loud noises screaming through her head. How could the world not see pain when it becomes invisible? She could. She had always seen pain like this.

At first she had not known it was pain. It had only seemed strange to have it happen to her whenever she closed her eyes. Sometimes the scenes before her closed eyes could have a tenderness, like the washing away of warmth, like it had happened to her flesh when she had been young and in love. She could hardly remember it; and then, the pictures that appeared would remind her of how her flesh had been when her flesh had abandoned hope. In the coolness of memory, afraid and alone, feeling cold, and wanting, she hid herself in a memory.

Instead, she found grief and no submersion in which to hide. She had wanted to drown, the way she had drowned when she had loved... that one time...the other side of the waving transference...that golden moment. There were tears of another essence at times, but they could not feed her starving being. The memories could only whimper the song that she yearned to hear. Deep in the center of her anguish, there was the loneliness of a love-cry that found no answer.

The colors, which faded and arose like geometric patterns painted upon her eyelids, recreated themselves before they shattered and fell away into the brown and colorless backwash she allowed to happen. She closed her eyelids more tightly, as if to hold the colors in, not allowing them to fade away or to shatter. Shadows collected themselves in triangular shapes against the luminous screen of her closed eyes. Clouds telescoped into grays and whites, fighting her memory.

I'm afraid, I'm afraid, she whimpered; don't bring me any more shadows. I can walk through this house and see the wind, which tears away at falling dust. I see it falling across the empty rooms where Pa used to walk, and Ma used to sit. It is a sifting shade, weaving the ragged floorboards into patterns and reflections from the windows. I can't say anything. I can't tell John or Rozella what I see when I walk through this house.

The branches of the trees outside the living room window are knitted together, then hung there in the pale sky. The dogs howl louder when I see these knitted branches. The branches are hung upon the sky, but there is nothing there to hang them. I can't tell how we came to be trapped in this place of barren things that hang upon nothing. Rusted wire builds up around the yard; higher and higher it must go in order to keep back the coarse yellow weeds. It builds a tangled web, as the poets used to say: when first we practice to deceive. Rozella deceives... She deceived John.

Spring green came back again, spinning and silver next to the spring green where the spider wove patterns between the stalks of new grass. Can no one see the wind? I can see more than the rain; I can see the wind, but it hurts me. She whimpered and pushed her head deeper into her pillow.

There once was a wagon wheel in the front yard. I used to play upon it, skipping over the spokes. That was before John was born. I was an only child. Daddy's little girl. Long before the gossiping whispers dirtied my petticoat. Pa hoarded have-not-ed-ness. He didn't want any reminders; he only acted the way he acted because of it. Escaping him was a trap, a joke upon the living. One false choice and the old hatred was written out upon the walls in large black letters.

You couldn't write on the winds, you could only write on walls, and these were the only walls they had. Outside they would find hummocks of mud, puddles rimmed with reflections of what they had known, she and Nels. Together they had played the game of children, the touching of children, innocence, wondering, and promises that couldn't be filled. She had run down the path of fear, seeking him, after Pa had let her out of her room. The same old path to the cottage, which had once been so light with hope and beauty, had turned dark and fearful. It had never found light again.

Even when she had walked there with John, holding Danny, it had been dark as a cavern, not like the sparkling lights that she could not paint anymore; there were now only dark pines, and the eyes of the silent woods. She could always hear the dogs howling into the wind...

When the pictures faded totally, she slept. It was when she couldn't sleep that the terror arose in her making her walk around the room until exhausted. She only hoped they couldn't hear her downstairs as she walked. She walked in bare feet so Rozella and John couldn't hear.

Downstairs Rozella couldn't hear the walking; she only thought that Hannah was having her usual afternoon nap. It was when Hannah didn't stay up there that she became concerned. Today Rozella was studying the shelves in the pantry and trying to make up her mind what she could make for their Saturday farewell party. When they went out like this, she left a supper made ahead for Hannah, or they waited until later and had their meal at home. This would be the last supper, an ominous sound, she thought. She must keep it simple or Hannah would complain, and John wouldn't stop her from nagging. No wonder. He had heard it from his father, and Hannah's carrying it forward didn't sound a bit different to John. He was used to the refrain.

These were differences that Rozella had never experienced. She and her sisters had never gone elsewhere to cook somewhere else. They had not been married and living at home. In fact, every one of them had left home before they married. This kind of problem had not come up. She took some jars of vegetables down, choosing one, she put it aside, and along with it measured out some flour and baking soda so she could whip up some biscuits. She remembered that Girard enjoyed them one time before when they had cooked together. Gravy and biscuits. Canned corn mixed with peas from last summer's garden. Everything had a memory, a past, even vegetables!

These nights John sometimes sat alone when Hannah went upstairs earlier than usual. He looked through the mail, if Hannah left it there, and then continued his search for record keeping books. How could you lose control of something you never controlled, he asked himself as he dug through the bookcases in the living room? "Why don't you ask her?" Rozella inquired, "Just knock on the door and ask her for the records."

"It feels like I've been asking her for a million years – all the years before I went away to school, and every day since I came back."

"And what happens?"

"She either lectures me, or ignores me. It's always the same. I get nowhere."

"One of you will have to get somewhere, or the paperwork won't get taken care of. You won't even know if you've been paid for the product you deliver to town."

"In a way, I do know that, because I carry the money home."

"But that doesn't account for everything produced by this farm. That only accounts for what happens daily or weekly. What about the summer harvest? The wheat, the barley...the corn?"

"Don't worry too much about the corn." He was sarcastic. "That's a total loss. No, she's not senile. She's too young for that. She's just distracted and her mind wanders. It's your job, your going out to work that upsets her; she can't cope with your going out to work."

"Are you sure that's not you, John--that you aren't the one who can't stand that?" Rozella asked him.

"It doesn't make any difference. We agree on that. We both told you what we thought about it. It makes things too difficult for us. Just this – what is happening to her, is enough to prove how upsetting it is," he answered, sticking up for Hannah in a protective manner that he hadn't used before.

CHAPTER FORTY

When spring came an abundance of water flooded the small river, running over flowers cascading over banks, running through the woods and along the roads. The work Rozella had taken had hardened her muscles, her thighs growing firmer from the constant bending over vats, and her arms developing muscled cords from stretching to scrub. The routine was an ordinary one for her now, and the only frustrating moments were those when she had trouble with time, reaching the end of the work before she ran out of time. Her paycheck remained stable and she tried to put most of it away after she had paid for Danny's care.

Saving the money that she earned became more difficult as Hannah chose not to pay for things that she had allowed them to have in the months before Rozella went to work. Whenever Danny or John needed clothing, Hannah would now refuse to pay for it, saying that they had their own money. This would place the burden on Rozella because John was still given no money at all, and Hannah's explanation of why remained the same as before.

You couldn't save, Rozella told herself, when the demands upon the money you earned kept growing larger. Instead of becoming more independent her fears exaggerated her dependence.

Danny thrived in the day car center care in spite of John's objections. It was good for him to have someone to play with every day. He had stayed well except for one day, when the women had asked Rozella to keep him home, and John had refused to take care of him. To Rozella's surprise, Hannah had stayed in with Danny, waiting until Rozella came home, and giving up her afternoon nap; she then went out to take care of her chickens and turkeys – the birds, as she called them. It was unusual for Hannah to do anything that would help Rozella. In the past it always seemed like she wanted to put obstacles in front of her, and she still did when it came to finances. With Danny, it was different.

The last night they had spent with Joan and Girard before Joan left for Washington had been both bitter and sweet. Their evening meal together had been like a celebration meal, much as Christmas had been. Danny had gone to bed early, and they were left to be together for the last time. Conversation had turned to Joan's new position with the government, and the status of Girard's job was not mentioned. It had been so long since Rozella had been alone with Girard that she found it hard to look at him over the table that evening.

When she was setting the table he had come up behind her, putting his hand on her waist, and she jumped with the warmth of the touch. All she could do now would be to wait for him to get in touch with her. Next week, she would be driving into town with him, just she and Danny, in the early morning.

Late in the evening, long past midnight, she gathered up her dishes, and put Danny's things into a bag, as she prepared for them to go home. They had walked over, but Girard insisted on driving them home. "You're all too tired," he had said. Leaving Joan wasn't easy for her, the women held each other closely, tears running down their cheeks.

"I promise that I'll see you soon," Joan whispered to her.

"Please," Rozella answered, and not able to speak anymore, she thought, and I mean that. I really mean that. She's my best friend, and may be the best friend I'll ever have. If I had to choose between the two of them, it would be hard to make a choice. Joan had not made her choose. Maybe this parting was designed to see what would happen to all of them.

"I'll write," Joan said, and they went out to the cold, dark truck and the ride home. Rozella didn't even look back to see if Joan was watching them drive down the road. She couldn't bear to see if she was there at the window, looking out.

Girard said nothing except to tell John that he would be seeing them after Joan had left. "I'll be by," he promised. "You'll keep seeing me until I get some work on my transfer. When I do, I'll let you know."

It was late, and they were all tired, so going to bed they slept without thinking more about what the loss of a friendship would mean to them.

Monday came, and things hadn't changed, except that Girard came by alone to pick her up. Nervously, she got into the truck and placed Danny in the middle, pulling him up behind his bags and diapers, to pad him against any unexpected bumps. She couldn't think of what to say, except to ask, "Did Joan get away okay?"

"Yes," he answered her. "And, I thought that I might take you home myself starting later this week. If you could tell Calvin that you won't need him, at least until I leave for the east coast, then he won't have to worry about why you aren't there at noon."

"Won't that be too difficult for you? It means that you will have to bring me home, and then go back into town."

"Right now it won't make any difference. Joan and I have always done a lot of running around because of our different jobs, and there's also the fact that I've applied for another transfer. I don't expect to be here long. If I schedule my afternoons in the field every day, it can't have much effect on my job. I just need to get it done, in whatever way possible."

"I'll still have..." and she looked down at Danny.

"I know, but we'll talk about that later. You might have days when you could leave him in day care a bit longer."

"For us? Yes, but I still will have problems at home." She was thinking about what John and Hannah would say if she was to come home at two in the afternoon instead of before noon.

"Think about it, please, Rose. We can't have much time left for us. When the transfer comes through, I'll have to leave."

"I know, and it scares me."

She did think about it, and the next day when he picked her up, she told him that it was all arranged. Calvin understood that she wouldn't be riding with him until further notice. She could call him when she needed him to pick her up again. He had given her his phone number at home. That day, Girard could begin by taking her home at noon.

"Good. We can plan, then," he answered her.

He was there waiting for her at ll:30 and a couple of women from the creamery who were eating their lunch could see him there at the curb as she left. They would ask her about it the next day, she was sure. Girard and Rozella picked up Danny next, and on the drive home, Girard asked. "Can you plan to be a couple of hours late tomorrow?"

"Tomorrow," she repeated, like a parrot.

"Yes, It's been a long time since we've had a chance to be together alone. Can you tell John that you have to work late? Couldn't Hannah make something for them to eat at noon?"

"She could, but so could I. I mean, I could prepare something ahead of time, and all they would have to do is put it on the table." She answered.

"If that's what you do in order to make yourself feel good, that's okay with me. I just think that they ought to be able to take care of themselves. Its just another way of tying you down, Rose. Face it."

"Either way, I'll make something work," she was afraid, knowing that anything was an excuse for verbal abuse when it came to her work.

But, she would do it, in order to be with him the few times they would have left together. After he left, what then?

That night, she prepared sandwiches and wrapped them after the supper was cooked. Trying to tell them about it was more difficult by far than making the sandwiches. She tried to begin her explanation several times during supper. Finally, she got it out, the fact that she would be late getting home the next day. Hannah looked at her over her glasses as if examining her for flaws.

John said, "What?" and followed it by "Why?"

"Because I need to work some extra time. There isn't enough time during the morning to get everything done."

"Why not?" Hannah demanded, adding to John's questions.

"Sometimes the other women are out sick, and things get behind with not enough workers. It adds up, and we can't get everything done. There are times when I race through the morning, and I get home aching all over from forcing it."

It was true, even though phrased into a lie for the next day.

Hannah responded with, "I could have guessed that this would happen. It's only a matter of time until you find a way to put off coming home. And what about us, who will get our dinner made?"

"I'm making sandwiches for you, after supper. You'll only have to put on a pot of coffee, and fill some bowls of canned fruit. I can fill the bowls for you, if you don't mind having them set here overnight." Rozella offered.

"Certainly, you can do that," John's angry tone surfaced. "That's the least you can do."

"I work, too, and –" she began, and then thinking better of continuing, she stopped mid-sentence.

"It was your choice," Hannah emphasized, "You didn't have to work. You wanted to work. There's a difference."

"I'll leave things out for you. Sorry," she said, "It's the best I can do tomorrow. It won't be that way every day."

"It better not be that way every day," John's level tone seemed to bounce off the kitchen walls.

Danny stirring was stirring his milk with his fork, mixing in vegetables, and he looked up at them. The words were strange, harsh sounds, and he was puzzled. His small forehead was wrinkling up, in question. He was making soup, Rozella could see; any mother knew what their baby thought he was doing. Children and mothers communicated.

True to her promise, she made their dinner for the next day, leaving it in the pantry, everything lined up with military precision. In the dark, she tossed around the bed most of the night, waking in the morning, with a taste in her mouth like a sickness, and her body weary as if she really had been washing six more vats than usual. This did not pave the way for lovemaking. Starting out with fatigue left you trying to get yourself prepared to enjoy life, when you were too tired to appreciate it.

Yet, she wanted to kiss him when she saw him; the sweet and tender lips that she loved had been withheld from her for so long. When her regular workday was over, she hurried to find her coat and looked up to see two women who had nothing to do while eating their lunch looking at her again. The handsome man in the truck was waiting at the curb. She had promised to tell them who that was when they had first seen him and tell them why he was there to pick her up. But, there had not been enough time; so she had to leave them with their curiosity aroused. As Girard pulled away from the curb, she could see them, still looking out of the window as they left.

"Everything all right?" he asked, smiling.

"Yes, I hope so, at least I did the best I could. Those two, watching us, are curious as can be, and I haven't had time to explain anything to them." she gestured at the women.

"Make time tomorrow, or they'll make your life miserable." Girard answered. "You did remember – we're going to pick up Danny later, in a couple of hours?"

"Where are we going now?" she asked, wondering about the cottage, since she didn't have the key and it would be a long drive home.

"To my house."

"That's a long drive."

"I know, but we'll have a place that's private and all ours for a time. It hasn't been ours to use before," he reminded her. "We can pretend, for a time."

"That's right, pretend," she answered, but the sadness tore at her. Pretend meant it would never happen.

Pretend, said Val. Pretend, said Tonie. Rozella didn't like to play at pretend. Pretend things never happened, she said. Whenever they started these games, she rebelled. Why not? They asked. Everybody plays pretend because there are no pretends, she had answered them. What do you mean? They asked. Mama pretends that Papa will come home. She pretends that he cares about us. It's a lie. Not so, they shouted at her. Tonie reached out to push her. But she knew that Papa never came home, no matter how Mama pretended. They all waited all year long, watching while Mama pretended that he was coming. On every holiday she pretended. Rozella was getting older now, and she could listen to Maggie and hear about the real things in the world of grownups. Maybe Maggie never had played the game of pretend. Sometimes she wore a dress, which Mama had made out of her own best dress, and Maggie was told to pretend that it was new. She would look down at it, and turn away. Rozella could see that Maggie could not pretend it was new, no matter what.

Real things had to be there where you could see them, touch them; they couldn't be made of hope, and dream-stuff. Rozella wouldn't pretend, she told herself, and her sisters. Never.

He could pretend, she said to herself, as they drove into the yard. The Girard's house where they had spent happy hours together, the four of them, now opened quiet and inviting to them. He had left a fire in the kitchen stove, and soft warmth enclosed the room. She could see that he had prepared a sort of lunch for them, and it was laid out on the table, covered with waxed paper so it wouldn't dry out.

He took her coat in his hands, gently pulling it off of her shoulders. Dropping it unto a chair, he pulled her into his arms. She felt him so firm, so warm and close against her, and her insides cried out with all the need kept inside of her for so long while waiting. There was nothing that could be said now. The two hours would not be enough. There would never be enough of this. Time had become an enemy.

Later, when he brought her home, she felt the red in her cheeks; her hands held up told her what they looked like. Her cheeks were warm. She had no need of a mirror. What would they say, if they saw her come in? She hurried up the porch steps, holding Danny against her. Put him in bed for his nap, she thought. Don't think about it. Maybe you'll be lucky, and they'll both be outside and not see you.

She was lucky. John was out attending to his usual chores, and Hannah was in her room. She could take him upstairs and put him into bed before hurrying downstairs to clean up the mess they had left from their dinner. The radio had been left on, music drifting through the room. She turned it off. The last thing Hannah usually wanted was any kind of cost. Why didn't she think of the batteries? No, John had left it on. Why hadn't they cleaned up the mess? It was their objection, she could see. They would do this. She had been lucky that they hadn't been there to see her reddened cheeks, and accuse her.

What could she say if they accused her? Her body was alive and vibrant with the memories held in check, and she wanted to keep it that way. She hoped that no one would speak to her at all before bedtime. Please leave me alone, she said under her breath. Please...

Cleaning up the kitchen, the quietness began to calm her, and she slowed down as the cleaning tasks were eliminated, one by one. At the end, she sat down and drank a cold cup of coffee, looking over her coffee cup into space.

She had needed him so much. How would she ever endure parting with him? He had told her that day that Girard's farm would be up for sale, or for lease, he didn't know which. Whichever came first. He suggested that she and John talk about it. If there was any way that Hannah could be persuaded to loan them the money for a down payment, maybe they could buy it. If not, maybe they could lease it, but even leasing it would require some money to bind the lease. There was no way that he and Joan could let them have it without some cash. Without cash, they couldn't live in the east. They had to have some to use for rent and food until their jobs began to provide for them.

"I'll ask," she promised, thinking fearfully that no matter how wonderful it might be to have a place to call their own, it would mean that she would be parted from Girard forever. How could she hope for something like that? It made her feel sick inside. The contrast between having and losing. The realist that he was, he couldn't see how much the thought was hurting her. He only wanted her to have something better than what she had; he didn't know what losing him would mean to her.

Her fears had eased as time slipped from late afternoon into suppertime. Her breathing eased, and she fell back into her regular routine, hoping that John or Hannah wouldn't say anything about her delayed return home. Sometime during the meal, she brought up the subject of the pending sale of Girard's place.

Hannah looked up with interest. "For sale, or lease, you say?" she asked.

"Either one," Rozella answered. "Girard said it would be a good place for John and me."

"What?" Hannah stood up. "What kind of ridiculous kind of idea is that?"

"Why is that so ridiculous?" John replied to her outburst.

"Why? You shouldn't have to ask. There's enough for you both to do here. You can't have that place, and earn it, too. It just isn't possible. Nothing for nothing. You can't do that," she said.

In confusion, Rozella tried to understand what Hannah was saying. "You mean that we have to work here in order to earn a right to part of this, and also earn a right to that place?" Her face was tied up in a wrinkled perusal.

John was listening." I think that's right, what she means, that is. But, Hannah why couldn't we work to earn our right to the Girard place, and forget this place?"

"Because you have to stay here. I can't farm this place alone, and it is your home. You can't forget that, John. This is your home, too."

"Many times I don't feel that way," he answered, more truthfully than he usually was, Rozella noticed.

"If we could get that place now..." Rozella added, wanting to help him.

"Don't get in too much of a hurry. You haven't earned a right to anything. There isn't enough money to buy Girard's place." Hannah stood up.

"Only a down payment would do," John suggested. "Maybe if we could only lease it, we could earn enough from working it during the next couple of years to put a down payment on it...that and Rozella's earnings together?"

"It would take all of Rozella's earnings to feed you. You're a fool, John. That's what Pa always said, and it hasn't changed," Hannah was pointedly rude in response. "No. No. And No. No matter how many times I have to say it. You can't have what you haven't earned." With that, she turned away from the table and left the room. Not unusual for her to leave abruptly these days, but this departure seemed like the end of an argument rather than a normal retreat.

"Maybe she's right," John hung his head, and then put his hands up over his eyes. "I wouldn't have the money to order seed, or to feed the cattle, and I wouldn't have any cattle. All of these things belong to Hannah," he gestured, sweeping his hand to include the whole of the farm.

It was true. All of it belonged to Hannah. If they took nothing along, they would have to buy every animal on the Girard farm, and that alone would make the price rise far above what they could afford. There was no way out. No way to make such a change.

"Tenant farmers?" he looked to Rozella, as if hoping that she had some such answer from Girard.

"They have to have some money from the farm, John. They have to pay rent and eat, too. They just can't give the place to us, even if they are our friends." It was true. It couldn't be done, and Hannah had made her point once more.

This was all there was and all there would be, John said to himself as he looked around him the next morning. It was beginning to fit together. In all of his years he had never understood Pa. His mother had not understood him either. If you had only one chance in a lifetime and you recognized that one chance, then you would cling to it with every bit of strength you had. You could become defensive, hard, ruthless, and terrorizing.

Pa had nothing when he came to work on the Queist farm, and he had married the daughter who would inherit the place. It had been his only chance, and he defended the right to own the farm and all it contained with a vigor that bordered on madness. What seemed cruel to John in his childhood had become clear. That was why Pa had called him soft.

Hannah was hard because she mimicked Pa. She had always had it all. She had been taught and had not been given reasons. That was clear. If his father had not given John reasons, then Hannah had not been given reasons either. Whatever the anger and bitterness was that drove her, it was a different kind. John knew now what it was to have the one chance held out in front of him. He knew that if he turned away or lost his hold on it, he never would have another chance to own anything.

John would do whatever he had to do to succeed, just the way Pa had done before him. If he couldn't get control of Hannah, he would bide his time, until she couldn't hang on anymore. He couldn't allow Rozella to cause the loss of his one chance to become a landowner. She would have to be controlled, but it was easier to control her than to control Hannah. Rozella had reason behind her feminine emotions; Hannah had lost reason if she ever had any. His future was here, and

Rozella would have to work with him no matter what her ideas were. She was his wife, and she had no choice.

John took his jacket off of the hook in the kitchen and left for the barn. Rozella had already left for work with Girard, and the room was quiet as death. Hannah was outside attending to her chores. He couldn't remember that there had been any particular way of choosing who would do what, other than it had always been done that way, or some chores were "women's work."

Hannah brought in the pails of milk after they were separated into cream and milk. She wiped the milk cans clean after placing the covers on them tightly. Too bad that Rozella didn't work other hours. The creamery drivers picked up their cans every morning except Sunday. He put them out by the mailbox for their pick up. The check arrived in the mail addressed to Hannah. Becoming more aware of the matters of ownership and money, he realized that the checks, which came in the mail, must go back in the bank. He had carried envelopes each week that contained papers dropping them off at the bank. Since Hannah had never made a habit of going into town this must be the transmittal. He had been delivering a bank deposit himself. Next time he would force open the envelope and see what it contained.

He had been blind to her devices too long. This land would be his, and he would find out how and when it would be his.

CHAPTER FORTY-ONE

In late May, Girard finally got his transfer to another farm mortgage company in the east, close to Washington D.C. It would be Maryland where he and Joan would live. Joan had found a small place on the outskirts of a rural community where they could at least have a dog and cat, and maybe a few chickens. It wouldn't be the same as what their farm had been, but life had proved to them that the idea of full-scale farming was not meant for them. It had been a dream that hadn't worked out.

What were their new dreams? Rozella wondered. Over the weeks, she had come to see that what she had with Girard had been only a game of pretend, and "pretend" was something that she couldn't accept. There was nowhere for it to go, no matter what she might have seen as possible. She couldn't tell herself that Girard would be better off with her, nor could she tell herself that the arrangement made between Girard and Joan was better than what her life had become. In her own confusion about what a disappointment her marriage had become, she had no right to tell others what they should do. There was a world somewhere where people got divorced, she read, but it wasn't this world. Girard and Joan were part of the continental world at one time, that was a world of divorces, if you weren't Catholic, but in this farmland – it wasn't done.

There was not one divorced person in the small town of Crenshaw. You would have to travel to the larger cities before you could even find a case. It had been true years before. When the women of the town wondered between themselves why Mama had waited for her father to come home from Canada, and had asked each other why she kept of up the pretense of marriage, they guessed: he didn't support her at all. Mama's answer was that a person married until death do us part. The old quotation.

If, indeed, all marriages were made that way, then the solution arrived at by Girard and Joan was just as logical as the answer her mother had found by working all of her life, and waiting to hear of better things from her husband. That the children had to work, too, and the message of better days never came – made no difference. What alternatives could her mother have had?

There wasn't one that Rozella could see, now that she could look back on it. It was the way things were done; the way life was lived, just then. Maybe it would always come down to that – *it was the way.* John's father had said. that was the way things were done. Maybe someone made up all those silly stories for women to dream over.

The tension of Girard's leaving had pained her for so long, that the day he left, she could feel relief. Waiting for it to happen had been worse than the reality, at least the first day. The following days, she would take one at a time, and there would be days she could foretell, that she would grieve for him, and the loss of touching him and talking to him would wound her beyond anything she now could now bear to think about. But it had to come. The fear of the day had been wearing her down. Now, alone, she could face what she would do next with her life.

It had become "her" life, and that was different. Before she had not allowed herself to have any concept of what was hers and what was John's. John had controlled her life, what Hannah wanted had controlled John's life. And Danny -- his control didn't extend further than the small tantrums that he had developed lately.

There would be a day when Danny's control would develop in the fashion of Hannah and John. If not genetic, it would be learned from his observance. He mimicked everything. He would learn quickly.

She and Girard had talked of this, and he had cautioned her against falling back into the trance of following the easiest path again, reminding her that the only way out was the way she would create herself. He promised that he would write to her, and Joan would write to her, and that they both would always be there for her, in spirit and reality. If she needed to come, they would make a place for her until she could find a place for herself and Danny in the city.

The last days, they spent as many hours together as possible, making John and Hannah nervous and irritated by her absence when they thought she should be at home and attending to her duties there. During these days, she no longer cared what they thought. She didn't even care about the women who watched her leave every day with Girard at noon. When they continued to ask questions, she didn't care enough to bother giving them answers to appease their curiosity. Answer them, Girard had cautioned. If you don't, they will make up things.

"They will make up things, anyway," she had answered him. "It's all they have to do except work."

The last minutes of the last day she counted out like deep breaths before dying, and time refused to be held back. The word goodbye choked her until she couldn't speak. Only Girard could speak, and he said, "It's not goodbye, you know."

"I wish I could believe that," she whispered.

"You will, in time," he kissed her on the forehead. "You'll see. Please don't hurt so much. Trust me."

And Girard was going. His truck was leaving the Queist place that early Sunday morning when she and John and Danny stood there watching him check the trailer hitch connecting the truck to the trailer with wooden slats on the sides he had put behind it. It contained all of the belongings that he could pack into the trailer, and into the truck bed. Cheaper than shipping it, he would drive carefully all the way across the Midwest to the east coast, and travel up the coastline to Maryland.

"Go?" Danny pointed at the truck as it went out the drive toward the county road."

"Yes, go." She answered him, choking on her tears. "I can't believe that they won't be there anymore." she said to John. But, John had already turned away. He had his own thoughts and hadn't noticed how hard it was for her to say goodbye to Girard.

The days that followed didn't become easier for her. Without Girard, she needed a way to work in the morning, and that was harder to find. Everyone who traveled on that road was going to the farms, not into town. Those cars and trucks going into town were the occasional trips, not regular. John would make one trip each week, and she could count on that, and she had a ride home every day with Calvin on his mail truck, but she didn't know how to get a ride in the mornings. The fact that Girard and Joan had driven into town for work was unusual, most farmers stayed on the farms, trying to make their living there. And there had been no jobs available for them, even when they were in need.

Asking Hannah to let John drive her into town every day caused a quarrel with repercussions that lasted most of the night. Hannah couldn't justify the cost of gasoline, and refused to pay for it. Since John had no money, except what Rozella had, and he seemed to feel some claim over that, she had no choice but to offer to pay Hannah for the trips daily. This paying would be costly, since her earnings were small enough after paying the day care center for Danny. Hannah could drive a hard bargain, just as her father before her, and Rozella was reminded of the day she had rented the cottage from him. Hannah had been well taught.

She had no choice, but to pay Hannah. She wasn't even allowed to give the money to John, but it had to pass directly to Hannah.

"Hannah, just having John make the trip every day would give you a chance to bring whatever you wish into town also. You'd gain. He could deliver our milk cans to the creamery when he drops me off. He could take whatever papers you have to the bank. Pick up supplies? Don't you see? It could help all of us." Rozella argued, trying to make Hannah see it could work.

"Yes," John agreed with her, perking up when he thought about it. "I could do all that every day, not just once a week. Don't you see that sometimes we forget things? Bank deposits could go..."

Hannah interrupted, "Bank?" What do you think, that I have money going to the bank? There isn't any money these days. We all live from hand to mouth. You dream about money, that's all. It isn't real. The only real thing around here is the mud," she looked out at the roads, wet with the melting snow of spring, "and the cow shit."

They both looked up at her with shock; Hannah had never used such language in her whole life. Rozella hadn't even expected that she knew such a word. In her childhood, her brother introduced her to the language of the men, and her father, when he was drunk could use words that were strong, but oddly enough he seemed to always put them into German or Russian so the children couldn't hear them. Danny looked up from his supper, too, his eyes a reflection of his parent's surprise, even though he didn't have any idea of why they were startled.

In the end, after the argument Rozella talked with her boss at the plant, as she called, it and he agreed to have her work longer hours. That would give her, as Tulla had suggested, the extra amount for Hannah. John would drive her to work, and she would give Hannah the extra money she earned.

John didn't talk about the amount, but Rozella had learned about the finances of living the past months, and she could see that Hannah would be making a profit from letting John drive the truck into town, ostensibly as a favor to Rozella. So much for family business, she thought.

The melting months of spring passed and with them she could feel her heart melting from the loss of Girard, and Joan, too. Letters came from both of them. They wrote separately and sometimes they wrote together. The letters were interesting and bright, but never made any reference to the personal conversations they had both shared with Rozella. Little Rose, the letter would begin, and her tears would come if she was alone. They couldn't say anything personal to her, as Hannah and John both could get to the letters at any time.

As John searched for records and money whenever Hannah was not around, Rozella could see that no piece of paper or letter would be safe from him. She put her letters in the top of her dresser drawer in their bedroom, as if to say – you won't have to look for them. They were right there. It was true, but that was different than having your best friends right there.

Weeks passed, turning into the months of summer. John worked longer hours in the fields, sometimes he didn't eat his evening meal until after Hannah and Rozella had eaten. It made two meals to be prepared, or the second one became a warmed up version of the first, and she had to wait until he had eaten before she could finish up the dishes. By that time she was too tired to keep her head up, and would sit dozing by the kitchen table after she had put Danny down for the night. Twilight stretched long into the night, the horizon looming broadly, and stars barely visible. It wouldn't be until the middle of the night that she would be able to see the stars shining at their brightest.

Walking about restlessly some nights, Rozella would look out at the night sky, wondering what time it was in Maryland and what Girard was doing. Was he asleep? Did he ever look out at the sky and think of her? Or was she totally alone? The letters tried to make her feel less alone, she knew that, but they couldn't say anything very personal. How long would this life go on? She asked herself on nights like those. There would be no answer because she couldn't let herself think about what was ahead, except survival. Had her choice been so much better than John's choice? The small store of money she had saved up grew so slowly, and as it grew, so did John's determination to stay right there – on the Queist farm that he chose to call his own. But he could only call it his own when Hannah was out of sight and couldn't hear him.

There are many types of addiction, Rozella thought. Her father couldn't leave alcohol alone, and John couldn't leave this farm. Obsessions were related, she observed. It didn't matter what the object of the passion. It didn't have to be a person; it could be a thing. Love affairs were not always between men and women; they could be between men and objects. She felt old now; the time of romance had passed forever out of her life.

John felt more in control now as he carried things to town every day. He held his head higher, it seemed to Rozella, as if he took pride in having business to take care of in town every day. Not every farmer could drive to town daily. His pretense of importance kept him happy, but she knew, and didn't speak of the fact that she paid for the gasoline, and the trips to town had nothing to do with the business at hand for the Queists. It was only pretense, a sham. At the end of every pay period, she paid out the money for gas, counting it out to Hannah in the evening.

At least with the longer working hours, she was in town during the day, and had a proper lunch hour. During that time she could go to the bank and cash her check, keeping the amount to herself. After paying the day care center, and Hannah, she still kept back a small hoard toward some kind of freedom.

What that would be, she didn't yet know. Leaving for the city? There wasn't enough there to even think about train tickets, or bus fare. And, there was no way to deter John from trying to hold unto the land. Whatever it would be used for was not apparent to her – yet.

Late in summer, Hannah and John hired a couple of men, transients passing through, to work in the fields with them, harvesting the crops. They were given the cottage for their housing, and Rozella worked there in the weekend, cleaning it up for them, washing sheets, making beds, and making sure there were enough pots and pans for them.

The home she had once known was dust covered and musty smelling from all the abandoned days and weeks since she and John had left there. The empty square place where the phone had once been left two holes for screws so rudely yanked out of the wall. She hesitated going into the bedroom where she and Girard had spent those cold winter days making love. She found it hard to look at the bed, and when she did, she wanted to touch it, and run her hands over it, as if caressing a friend. It had been so long ago. Was she so old already? Danny would turn two in the fall. August was there with its lightening storms and the threat of frost. Northern lights flicked across the skied at night to remind them of cold places. It wouldn't be long before winter would come again, and was still there, working and saving and not getting any further than John. Could John be right, and there was no escape? She put her bucket of water down on the floor, bending over to scrub the floors of the place that used to be her home.

After washing around the table and chairs, washing the kitchen floor, wiping it with old shirts, torn into rags, she changed the water in the pail because it became too dirty. Adding more soap to the fresh scrub water, she moved into the bedroom, back toward the bed that reminded her of a part of her life that seemed like youth lost to her now. Not yet twenty five years old, and that part of life gone? She washed around the bed, reaching under it to get the space clean, then getting up to push and move the bed and properly wash under it. You couldn't get it really clean unless you moved it.

Down under the old dresser was a piece of black paper, and she bent over to pull it out from under a dresser leg...a piece of the old photo album, just a torn black bit of paper, but left behind it, under the leg, was another piece of paper. She lifted the empty dresser to get it out. It was a round piece of photo, the cut out piece from the old album that had caused her so much curiosity when she first came to this cottage. She could see a round, flat nosed face, blonde hair, black cap sitting back on his head like a Greek seaman's cap...it must be Nels. Hannah had wanted to destroy his pictures. Why? He was so young, so clean looking.

What damage could this young man have intended? Yet, what had he left behind him? Did he ever wonder, wherever he was? Hannah's life had ended when he left her behind. She had become hostage to the Queist acres, and her father's "insurance plan." Rozella put the small piece of a picture in the pocket of her jeans and went on with the cleaning.

When she left the cottage that day, she didn't want to return. The memories it stirred up were too hard to bear. Danny had been born there. The lonely hours she had spent waiting for her family to come home from the Queist house hovered there; and, the deaths mourned there lingered. The hunger. The death of love. Lovemaking with a beloved that didn't belong to her. She closed the door firmly, as if never intending to open it again.

Hannah, too, resented the cottage and the occupants. She hated hiring the working hands, not wanting to even look at them. Without John to talk to them, she would have worked day and night without stop to avoid hiring help. Rozella and John thought it was the money that she resented paying it, but it wasn't. Even Rozella could understand one day when she cleaned out her pockets to put her jeans into the wash machine, and she pulled out the small piece of photo, and the black bit of album paper. Looking at the small piece of photo, cut so neatly round, and the soft blonde youth, she understood why Hannah didn't want to hire anyone. She couldn't bear to remember, any more than Rozella could bear to remember – about the cottage and people who had been there. Shadows of the past were clinging to the cottage for both Rozella and Hannah.

Hannah worked to hand-bale hay until her hands were raw and blistered, and her back ached from too many hours. Rozella, now confident in her job, felt lucky to escape to town where work was not easier than what John and Hannah were going through. She had to cook extra in order to provide for the field hands, who needed their morning coffee breaks, and dinners at noon. Leaving with the extra food prepared and covered in the kitchen became part of her chores. At least, there was food now, and no sign of the scarcity that had been so hard to bear in the first year of their marriage, when she and John had lived in the cottage. Cooking wasn't bad when there was enough to cook. It didn't take more time; it just took more food. She didn't mind.

In the evenings they ate alone, the family: John, Hannah, she and Danny. The field hands went to the cottage where they made their own evening meal, after washing themselves – however they managed. She supposed they used the granite washbasins and plenty of water. Hot days, flying straw and dust. Sweat. Working like that made a man a mess. Looking at John in the afternoon told her what it was like. His hands, too, were blistered and red. His face sunburned, and his forehead a streak of white where his cap had sheltered it from the sun.

Neither of them talked, except to exchange questions about the work at hand. John still drove her to town in the mornings, but sometimes he wanted to leave earlier than she needed, and she would end up waiting for the door of the creamery to open. She could sit there on the cool, shaded concrete steps and wait for Tulla. It could be worse, she thought, and learned to bring not only her lunch, but also a magazine from the old collection she had found in the attic. It was a good time to read, and the stories were never old, although they did seem to be fairy tales about women Rozella had never known. No woman she had ever known had lived as these fancy dressed city women had lived. Were the stories truth, or fiction, without any relationship to life at all?" She asked Tulla one day.

"Seems to me," she had answered, "that some of it must be true. Or everything they write is based on what they see in the movies. I like to think that there are real people who have nice things, other than the Vanderbilts and the Roosevelts."

"Me, too, "Rozella said, "Even though I don't expect to have clothes or furniture like the rich have, it's nice to think that it does exist. We lose too many dreams as we grow older."

"Old woman!" Tulla had laughed at her.

And Rozella couldn't understand why.

John slept deeply at night, snoring at times, his nose filled with the straw dust of harvesting. Hannah went up to bed right after eating, looking more tired than ever before. Rozella expected that she was sleeping as soundly as John, due to the physical fatigue of working in the fields. But there were sounds at night, scraping sounds, and walking sounds. She could lie there in the dark and listen to the sounds.

On the other side of the house, Hannah couldn't sleep, her arms and back ached with the pain of daily physical labor meant usually for a man. She wouldn't give up. Pa had taught her to take work in her stride. She was as good as any man. John had asked her if hiring two men wasn't enough. With the two of them and John, they could do the fieldwork, and she could stay in the house to prepare the meals, he had said. In fact, she could take care of Danny and cook. Rozella could pay her what the day care center would receive.

But Hannah was not a housewife; she refused to ever become a housewife. She wasn't anybody's wife. She was the head of this household, and so she would stay. Letting John take control was the last thing she would allow.

Drifting sometimes into a pain filled sleep, she would cry, cold from the air, her eyes sticking shut with the dirt left from the fieldwork of the day...you can't climb walls. She cried into her pillow, excuses... excuses...the winds are filled with doubts...the ferns are crying...under the trees. Her hands crushed the sheet to her chin, then pulled it up to her ears, as if to shut out the sound of the cries...inside, her own hurt cried, and fluttered with the wings of a dirge's song. She wanted to pull her hair, but in her sleep, her hands wouldn't move. Only in her mind's eye would her hands move from where they held the sheet up to her chin. Pictures of bleeding eyes washed across the screen of her sleeping mind, nightmares without words, mysteries made into distortions, a charade without words.

In her sleep, her mouth opened, and no words came out. Her breasts shivered, and her skin felt like tissue paper. There were lines now on the screen of her mind, and they were strung with old pieces of laundry, bleached white, and some with holes, like old worn out sheets. They were frozen stiff with frozen rain. She shivered again in her dreams. In the dreams, she reached into the basket setting on the snow to pick up weathered wooden pins, and put them on the line, as if the frozen sheets would blow away. Looking up, trying to find the sun, she wrapped herself in her hair, and children of the air floated above her, just circles of opalized lights. Gossamer breaths brushed her hair, and she listened carefully to hear what they might be saying. Waiting for him...waiting for him. Would she never see him again? Together they could have gone...anywhere...In her dream, she ran down the path to the cottage...the door stands empty...where...where...birds cry, and memories fall to the ground where the pink mushrooms lay, where thick brown pine needles and tender new blades of grass form... she couldn't bear to remember...close the swinging door...force it to close, kick it...a dulcimer string sounds: love too soon forgotten...and she walks, naked feet across the floor, dragging her quilt, sometimes dragging a chair, not knowing what she is holding, just trying to look through the screen of dreams...down below her bedroom window she sees a silver strand of loneliness, and then darkness, and earth grown cold...she shivers again, and sleep still holds her prisoner to her own erosion.

Across the hall, Rozella who lies awake too much, only hears garbled sounds, a voice speaking in solitude, and then scraping sounds and a voice again, crying out as if in a ritual.

CHAPTER FORTY-TWO

It was the second time that Danny had a cold and because he had a cold, he had a temperature. Rozella had asked Hannah once before if she would care for him, and she had stayed with him, asking John to take care of her chores. The difficulty of asking John to do the work was in reminding him that he could have done it every day. Hannah's work was a sham now that John was living with her, and that's why losing him frightened her so much.

He pursued her day after day about the money she had left from selling the land. He never stopped asking about the bills, had she paid them, where were they? Every night, Hannah avoided him as much as possible, learning now to retreat to her room early and leave him with Rozella. Afternoons when she stayed in her room, she planned ways to hide the paperwork of the farm, stuffing papers into her mattress, and under clothes in the drawers. She would do anything to keep them away from him. If she gave him control of the money, she would be at rest, but as long as he thought he was in love with Rozella, he would want the money in order to escape.

Danny was quiet that day. He really did have a temperature high enough to make him listless. Laying down most of the day, he half-dozed, going back to sucking his fingers, little noises emerging from his throat. After they had left in the morning, Hannah felt free to stand and watch him, literally hanging over his bed and watching him breathe. The money had always been the key to keeping John on the land.

Back when Pa was still alive, and John went off to school, Pa had repeated over and over that if they didn't keep money away from John, they would lose him to the city. Losing John would mean losing Danny. For two years she had watched him, his smile, big toothy grin and sparkling brown eyes making the morning bright with the life within him. He had no prejudices, no fears. The world was his. He trusted everything and everybody.

Today, after his nap she would take him up to the attic and they would find some old toys that he would like. She could look through the old things that she hadn't seen for so many years, and she could move the money in her mattress to her secret hiding place before John could find it.

Every time she went outdoors to work now she feared that John would go through her room and find the last week's cash. She watched him carefully from where she worked each day in the yard. When he went toward the house, she found a reason to go into the house also.

Sometimes this happened when Rozella was there in the afternoons, but sometimes it was in the morning before she came home. Each time so far she had not found that he was into her things, but there was no real way she could lock him out of her room. Turning the key in the door was not enough. His key turned all of the doors in the house, and she didn't know any way to put a new lock on her door. She had heard of a kind of a lock that would be mounted unto the door above the regular doorknob and keyhole, but she couldn't put it on the door even if she could get John to buy her one. He might do that, but he would keep a matching key. She was sure of it.

She didn't want to leave Danny to go out into the yard and feed the chickens. There was no way he could be safe unless she took him with her, and today he was too sick to go along to the chicken coops. The wind was whipping around the corners, seeping through the woolen shirt that she wore for outside work. It would be soon snowing again

When she felt him waking, she changed his diapers. He still was wearing diapers when he slept, and Hannah did not want to risk having him wear little underpants which would get cold and awful if he should wet himself during this sickness. Feeling his forehead, she worried that he might have more than just a cold. His nose was running, and his forehead hot. She opened his shirt to look at his chest, assuring herself that he didn't have any pink spots that pointed to measles or chicken pox. Small pox would be the worst thing, but she found his skin was clear, and she wiped his face with a cool cloth.

"We'll go now to the play room in the attic," she said to him, taking his hand and waiting while he made his wobbling steps across the hallway with her to her room. She put him down on the far side of the bed giving him her ring of keys to play with so he wouldn't be noticing how she was reaching under the sheet on her bed. He was such a mimic that she couldn't risk letting him see her lift the sheet, and reach into a finely sliced opening in the side of her mattress. From that hole she pulled a handful of bills and hurriedly stuffed them into her sweater pocket. And, she picked up some paperwork from under the bed. She could feel something else in her sweater pocket, and curious she took that out of the pocket to find out what it would be. Matches left from the morning fire. She put them back; surprised with herself for not laying them back on the shelf at the top of the kitchen range. She would need them later in the morning.

Danny waited and watched quietly while she pulled the attic steps out of his closet and put them against the wall. He was docile today, and not as active as usual. That was good. It would make it easier. "Now," she said to him. "Take one step at a time. I'm right here behind you, holding you up, lifting you. One, two. Rest. Wait." She took two steps herself. "Again, One, two, and rest." she repeated. "One, two and rest." There were twelve steps before he was at the top of the attic steps where she had pushed the door open and the opening stretched before them, the opening a little lighter than the hallway where there were no lights and no windows. "Stand there. Just a minute now, while I get up there with you." He stood there, looking down at her as she reached upward with her feet, trying to hold unto him and keep her balance. Her papers were getting in the way, and she had to let go of his hand in order to shift them into her other arm, and out of the way so she wouldn't trip. "Just a minute," she repeated, but he pulled his hand away from her, and darted toward the side of the room. Why? He had been so quiet this morning. It must be the old toys stacked on the other side of the attic room, she guessed. "Danny, come back here this minute," she called to him, hearing the little feet scurrying across the rough boards. "Danny, come." he was talking to her in his language.

He had an old wooden spool clutched in his hand as he came back to her. How he could move so quickly with that wad of diapers filling out his baby sized overalls? His interest in his surroundings had taken away the lethargy of his fever and he darted toward her as he heard her. "Here, here…"

He was holding out the spool, when he tripped. He fell past her, just as she lifted herself into a standing position from the last step on the portable stairs. There was a scream of fear, and a half-muffled thud as he hit the railing to the stairs between the attic floor and the bedroom level, and another thud as he hit the hallway floor. It happened so fast that her mouth was open with an unspoken cry. "My God," she half fell down the stairs that she had just climbed up. She picked him up, holding him to her closely. He can't be hurt. There is no blood. She searched all over his body. There was no blood. She held her hand to his forehead, which was still hot. It had a small red mark just above the left eye. "It will be all right," she whispered. "You'll be all right," she said to him, and began to climb the stairs again." He doesn't have any blood on him. He will come around in a minute," she was talking to herself. "I'll just hold him close to me an keep him warm."

Once back in the attic, she saw the old mattress laying next to the trunks and remembered how bright and white it had been when it was new, in its ticking of blue and white stripes. How long ago had that been? She brushed some papers off of the mattress and lay Danny down. He was not awake yet, but still breathing. She could see his little chest moving slightly. It was cold. There were old clothes in the trunks, too, she remembered. Some were strewn around on the floor, but they weren't clean. Not clean enough for Danny. She felt his forehead again. "Danny." She called, "Wake up, now. Don't sleep. I'll get you something to keep you warm, but you can't take another nap. You already had your nap."

She began to pull clothes out of the trunk. Noticing a childish short-waisted organdy dress, she began to remove her own clothes, as if confused. When she had taken her clothes off, tossing them to the floor to lay with the other abandoned clothes, she pulled the dress over her head, and smoothed out the ruffles. Her breath was a mist-like cloud in the cold air. "Danny, Danny, wake up," she whispered to the child, but he lay still, not answering. The bare skin of her legs became pimpled and blue with cold. She shivered, clutching her arms about her, and looking down at the child, as if wondering how to care for him." There's no blood," she whispered, as if someone was questioning her.

She gathered up her abandoned clothes and laid them one piece at a time over the child lying on the mattress. His face was white, and a small red mark was turning into a bruise, red-rimmed, which was rising upon his forehead. It went across his cheek, too, she noticed. She touched his cheek, but his eyes remained closed, his long dark lashes resting on the pale cheeks. Her gray sweater still covered him. "You can't run that way, Danny. It's dangerous. You might fall." She looked about her, as if thinking of a way to keep him safe. After untying the laces on his high-topped shoes, she left him for a moment and went over to a heavy oak Morse chair, which she dragged across the rough wooden attic floor to place it next to the mattress. He still lay quietly. Next, she carefully tied the shoelaces to the bottom rungs of the chair, and then breathed a sigh, as if assured that he couldn't move now. "He will be safe from danger now," she said aloud.

Once this was done, she began to sing under her breath, as she started to dig through an old chest as if searching for blankets to cover him. She took things from the drawers, carelessly flinging them about the room—clothes, newspapers, parts of books, and bits of materials. When she turned again, she turned toward the dome-topped trunk, and tipping it over, she suddenly had a look of recognition and began to pry at the bottom with an old screwdriver she found on the chest of drawers. When she found the hinged secret compartment with the leather thong, she pulled it to open it. Bundles of paper from inside the false bottom fell out.

"Danny," she called the child, moving to stroke his hair and feel his forehead." Mommy will be home soon, please...you must wake up. You're cold. Auntie Hannah is cold. We don't have enough clothes on to keep warm. Warm." and she reached into the pocket of the gray sweater she covered him with. Old newspapers that she had thrown about on the floor were close to her, and she reached out to take them into her hands, to crumple them up into little wads of paper, all the time whispering about dresses, and how pretty they are, but not warm enough..."We are so cold,

aren't we?" she almost sang to him, as she stacked the bundles of paper in neat piles, making a pyre-like pile mound.

The voices were closing in around her now, silver strands of sound that scratched upon the dirty attic windows. She pulled him closer to her to protect him.

"Pretty baby...pretty baby," she sang to him, before she lit the matches and waited for the fire to warm the room. She held him in the curve of her arms, just the way she had held him when he was first born, " pretty baby..."

Epilogue:

Rozella and John moved back into the cottage after the fire. They returned to where they had been when they first met, only this time there was a past to share: their grieving was shared. Putting Hannah and Danny down together was an event neither of them had foreseen.

John's determination to keep what was his never wavered. Even when Rozella told him it would be possible to lease the farm and leave, he would not listen. Holding it was having it, and he would never feel safe in leaving it behind. For her, it was a nightmare that she had lived with too long, and in spite of all her fears of what might come to pass, she told him that she was leaving – he could choose to leave with her, or not. Her plans were made, and she purchased her ticket to be sure that she wouldn't change her mind.

"Where will you go?" John had asked her. "To Denver to be with Val. She said I could come to her and try to find work again." Rozella had answered him, knowing that it made no difference where she would go; only that she must get away. She couldn't bear to live on here without Danny. The ghost of him would fill every minute of the rest of her life.

Surviving the fire, and the funeral had been difficult without her closest friends. Joan and Girard had written and had called, but it wasn't the same. They weren't there to reach out to, or to hold her when she grieved. John tried, but he had his own pain to deal with. There was nothing left of the love they had once shared, so he had nothing left to give. Long ago their paths had separated. They shared a child, but nothing else. Now—he had paid with their child for the land he was determined to hold.

The morning she left, John drove her to the train station. With just one bag packed to its fullest, she walked toward his truck for one last trip to town. He looked up at her, and the sky and stumbled over his words "I feel so bad, that I..."

"You couldn't help it. The choice you made was your own to make. Nobody could decide differently for you and make things turn out for the better. We'll never stop missing him. There'll never be another..."

"If you ever decide you want to come back, Rozella..."

"It's over," she shook her head. "I won't be back, but I will write to you some day...when I get settled."

"Val – say hello to Val," he said, getting in the truck.

But, you don't know her, Rozella thought -- anymore than you know me. And, she picked up her bag to put it into his truck, knowing that all the old pictures would only be in her mind. Nothing more could fall out of empty drawers, or slip out from under weathered seats. It was over.

Printed in the United States
138606LV00001B/98/P

9 780595 529292